NEPTUNE'S MARTYRS

J.E. Park

Neptune's Martyrs
By J.E. Park

Book 3 of the Tequila Vikings Series

Mailing List Sign Up for Newsletter and New Release Info: https://jeparkbooks.com/

Follow me on Facebook at https://www.facebook.com/JE-Park-100409961692113

Twitter handle: @JEPark94519501

Email at: jeparkauthor@gmail.com

ISBN: 978-1-7350940-4-5 (ebk)
ISBN: 978-1-7350940-5-2 (pbk)

Table of Contents

PROLOGUE

Staff Sergeant Emilio Payan laughed at the Pampanga Aeta when they fled their homes that April. Payan always considered the *negritos* a funny people. They were short, very dark, and the hair on their heads was coarse and kinky. They looked and lived more like African pygmies than Filipinos. They dressed in rags and lived in bamboo huts without the benefit of electricity or running water. The Aeta also prayed to the spirits of nature, which Payan considered an affront to the tradition of Philippine Catholicism.

Their animistic religions, along with their ways as hunters and gatherers, made the Aeta seem primitive. Emilio Payan was far from the only Filipino to regard them as unsophisticated and prone to superstition. It was why the sergeant ridiculed them when they abandoned their homes on the slopes of Pinatubo. All it took was a few minor earthquakes around the mountain's summit, and the runts went running for the lowlands.

On June 15th, 1991, ten weeks after the start of the Aeta exodus, Sergeant Payan realized that the *negritos* had been on to something. He started wishing that he had fled with them because, from where he stood, it looked like the entire world was about to end.

Pinatubo erupted on June twelfth, spewing a column of ash more than twelve miles into the heavens. Payan saw it happen firsthand from the Cesar Basa Air Base. Standing on the front porch of his barracks, it looked as if he were right in the middle of it. A massive ash cloud blotted out the sky and when the sun set that night, it would not rise again for two days.

Like everywhere else within a hundred miles of Pinatubo, the base descended into chaos. The facility had received no warning about an impending eruption. Because of that, they never got its squadron of F-8 Crusaders off of the ground. Most of Basa's airmen had to be dispatched to the hangars to save the jets. The commander of the base sent others to secure the food and water supplies. Some rushed to maintain communications and coordinate the base's response to the disaster. Payan ended up on a detail ordered to secure the armory on the other side of the facility. This gave the sergeant pause. The armory was that much closer to the source of all the commotion.

The airbase's arsenal was housed in a square cinderblock building. It had a flat roof perfectly designed to capture all the ash spewed by an erupting volcano and hold it in place until it collapsed under the weight. When Payan stepped inside, the rafters were already creaking in protest. They were not going to hold up for long. Within thirty seconds of their arrival, half of the detail was urgently ordered to find shovels to clear the roof. The other half was sent scrounging for materials to shore it up.

The shovel squad was first to find success, ransacking a nearby groundskeeping shack. It does not snow much in the Philippines, so the scavenged shovels were not quite the right tool for the job. Still, they were better than nothing. Upon their return, Payan's men tied bandanas around their mouths to keep ash out of their lungs. They then climbed atop the building and started shoveling feverishly to save it.

Despite their obstacles, the frantic digging of the Philippine airmen gave the roof a fighting chance. None of Payan's troops had construction experience, so the scaffolding they built was worthless. The sergeant eventually ended up sending the rest of his people outside to scavenge for shovels also. Trying to reinforce the roof at that point was an exercise in futility.

Digging was an exhausting effort. The airmen were working in a blizzard of ash that was accumulating quicker than Yukon snow. Still, the troops' efforts were paying off, and they were able to get ahead of the crisis. Eventually, they even earned brief periods of rest after the girders stopped groaning.

Then the rain started.

June is the beginning of the monsoon season in the Philippines, and torrential rainfall at that time was the norm. Any moisture added to the volcano's ash would have been devastating to the troops trying to save the armory. What the airmen had to deal with the day Pinatubo blew defied comprehension, though. While at the peak of a historic volcanic eruption, the island of Luzon had to contend with the added catastrophe of getting slammed by Typhoon Yunya as well.

The moment the rain started to fall, Payan realized that the battle for the armory was lost. The sergeant ordered his men down off of the roof. "Airman Zubiri!" he screamed, trying to get the attention of a mechanic in the motor pool.

"Yes, Sergeant!" Sonny Zubiri answered.

"Do you know how to hotwire a truck?"

Sonny grinned. He was from Olongapo. He knew how to hotwire a car long before the Philippine Air Force trained him to be a mechanic. "Of course I do, Sergeant!"

"Good," Payan said, placing his hand on the young man's shoulder. "I need you to go out on base and steal me every truck you can! Bring them back here. We need to move these weapons before we lose them."

"Where are you going to move them to?" the airman asked.

Payan shook his head. "I don't know! One problem at a time! Go get me my trucks!"

Another airman, Ronaldo Dela Rosa, approached the sergeant once Zubiri left. "There's an Aglipayan Church a few kilometers from here. It's been empty a while, but the building is still good. It has a pointed roof, so the ash should fall off instead of building up like it is here. The weapons should be safer there." A blast of wind shook the armory and started the roof supports creaking again. After hearing that, Dela Rosa added, “And so will we.”

Payan nodded in agreement. He looked at his watch and then out the door, shaking his head in disbelief. It was one in the afternoon, yet dark as midnight outside. The wind was screaming, it was raining concrete, and the volcano was making the ground shake. Turning to the airman, Sergeant Payan sighed. “Yes, I would feel much better sheltered in a house built by God than one built by a crony of Ferdinand Marcos. Even if it’s not Catholic.”

Emilio Payan tried to radio his plans back to the command center, but there was no answer. When Airman Zubiri returned with the first transport, a Kia-built M35, he tried again with the truck’s CB. Still, he came up with nothing. “I think the main base is out of power,” the airman said. “The road to it is cut off, and I couldn’t see any lights at all ahead of me.”

“You can’t see anything in this shit,” Payan answered. “Not even the sun.”

Zubiri turned a dial on the console, and the men heard a local news announcer come over the truck’s speakers. “At least the regular radio is working.”

“What have they been saying?” Payan asked.

Zubiri looked at the sergeant. “They’re saying it’s bad out there. Very bad. Bridges are washed out, and landslides are happening all over Pampanga and Zambales. There are reports that a couple of villages were completely swept away.”

That concerned Sergeant Payan. The base was close to the Gumain River, which originated somewhere up on Pinatubo’s slopes. He feared that the ash could form dams in some of the highland streams. If that happened, they could burst and send lahars, towering waves of mud, barreling down the sides of the volcano to bury them all alive. “We need to get these weapons the hell out of here.”

“Fuck the weapons, Sergeant,” Airman Zubiri said. “We need to get the hell out of here ourselves.”

The sergeant shook his head. “This base is going to take some severe damage. It’s going to be very compromised when this is all over. You know as well as I do that the New People's Army is all over these mountains. If we don't secure this armory, the communists are going to march right in here and take…"

It was 13:42 military time, almost a quarter to two in the afternoon according to the civilians. Mount Pinatubo roared in what was recorded as the second most powerful volcanic explosion of the twentieth century. It was bested only by Alaska's Novarupta in 1912. The shockwave rocked the truck Payan and Zubiri were sheltering in and blasted them from the M35's cockpit and into the mud.

Nine hundred feet of mountain top was blown into the sky, some of it landing as far away as the South China Sea, twenty-five miles away. Much more of it poured into where Payan and his men were struggling to hold their ground. Besides the wind, the ash, and the water, Payan's detail now had to contend with volcanic rocks raining down upon them like mortar fire.

"GO GET ME MORE TRUCKS!" the sergeant screamed as they both dove back into the deuce-and-a-half for cover. Zubiri could not hear him, however. Temporarily deafened by the explosion, the only thing the airman registered was the ringing in his ears. Still, he was able to read Payan's lips beneath the vehicle's dome light. Leaving the truck, Zubiri scrambled to carry out his orders. He figured that the faster they completed their mission, the faster they could get the hell out of there.

The next truck Airman Zubiri got to the armory broke down as soon as it arrived. The other vehicle was already gone, delivering its first load of weaponry to the church. The mechanic discovered that the ash had plugged up the air filters and, starved of oxygen, the engine stalled. It was not a difficult situation to remedy in a closed garage, but trying to fix it amid a concrete tempest was something else entirely. It took far more time to get the second truck running than it should have. The church was not that far away, so Zubiri expected the first M35 to return before he finished. When it did not, the airman worried that it could have stalled too. Instead of looking for another vehicle, Zubiri decided to accompany the men on the second gun run to see what happened to the first.

As the airman suspected, the first team broke down on the way back to base in Pabanlag, shy of the bridge to Apalit. Zubiri disembarked to get their transport running again while the crew doubled up to unload back at the church. They at least were able to pick up the mechanic on the return trip before breaking down again.

Staff Sergeant Payan decided that that was the best they could do. They would run two trucks back and forth while keeping Zubiri on the road to get them running again when they broke down. In three hours, the sergeant's men made five trips. They dropped a considerable amount of arms on hallowed ground but barely made a dent in the cache still left in the armory.

*****

Airman Zubiri was finishing up the exercise's seventh repair when a loud crash went off behind him. He was in Apalit, about a half kilometer from the bridge. Judging by the sound, Zubiri suspected that the span over the Gumain River had just been obliterated. At first, he wanted to run up the road to confirm his suspicions, but the racket was loud enough to be heard over the ringing that still filled his ears. That alone was plenty to convince him to ride in the opposite direction as fast as possible.

Sonny cursed. If the men were stranded, it would be better to be at the church where the roof was less likely to collapse. The armory was a death trap. Zubiri already knew that they were cut off from the rest of the base, so there was no option to retreat to the command center. "What the hell are we going to do?" the airman asked himself as he raced back to Sergeant Payan to give him the news. *Stay in those flimsy houses outside the perimeter? They can't survive this any better than the armory. Nothing can.*

As the airman approached the base's fence, he sensed things were beginning to lighten up. He could see the headlights of the other truck from the far side of the guard post. Zubiri was using them to guide himself to the armory when he heard another roar rising in front of him. Then the lights went out. The trucks, along with the buildings, weapons, and men, were swept away by a massive lahar that swallowed them from the west. They vanished right before Zubiri's eyes. Instinctively, Sonny threw the M35 into reverse and stomped on the gas, but it was a pointless effort. He did not make it twenty-five yards before the wall of mud took him too.

The M35 weighed more than two tons, but it was thrown to its side as if it were a toy. The lahar pushed the vehicle off the road and into a field, relentlessly forcing it forward until it slammed into a row of trees. The impact snapped the palms like toothpicks and blew the truck's side windows out. The Kia then flipped onto its roof, allowing the mud to pour in with no way for Zubiri to escape.

"SERGEANT PAYAN!" the airman screamed. He knew no one could answer his cries, but it was all that he could do. The mud was rising fast inside the cab, and Zubiri could see that drowning in it seemed all but inevitable. Near tears, the airman cried out again. "SERGEANT PAYAN! PLEASE!" When the sergeant failed to answer, Zubiri appealed to someone higher up the chain of command. "JESUS CHRIST! HELP ME! JESUS, SAVE ME!"

Nothing. The mud crept up the cab, engulfing Sonny to his waist. At that point, he gave up trying to call on his sergeant and his savior. He started crying for his mother instead.

Of all the names the airman invoked to save his life, only Imelda Zubiri proved powerful enough to intervene. As if guided by her divine hand, the overturned truck struck something solid enough to flip it over onto its side. The mud within the cab lurched up and slammed Zubiri into the dashboard hard enough to force all the air out of his lungs, then it buried him. But only for a moment. When the airman fought his way to the surface, he not only caught a breath of precious oxygen, he found a path of escape through the window of the passenger door as well. Sonny was able to climb up the seat and pull himself from the M35.

Once out of the truck, Zubiri discovered that he was much higher off the ground than he realized. The Kia was riding atop a lahar that was at least twenty feet high. It stopped moving with the wave of mud only after becoming entangled within a clutch of trees a kilometer from where the airman started. Sonny was among the upper limbs, balancing upon a massive vehicle being sucked into the muck. From the cab, Zubiri raced along the side of the transport until he could reach branches thick enough to support his weight. The airman then scrambled as high up into the canopy as he dared. As Sonny held on for dear life against the wind, he watched the mud engulf his truck beneath him until it completely disappeared.

The eruptions of Mount Pinatubo ceased at about 10:30 that evening. Typhoon Yunya, by then a tropical depression, ended a short time later, pushing out into the South China Sea. Airman Zubiri remained stuck in the trees, wet and freezing, while the winds lashed at him through the night. Morning brought little relief. When the sun finally rose for the first time in thirty-six hours, it baked him without mercy. There was no cover. The leaves had been ripped off the trees by wind shear that often exceeded ninety miles an hour.

By the time he was discovered by an American helicopter surveying the damage to Clark Air Base nearby, Zubiri was delirious. Driven mad with thirst and ravaged by both hypo- and hyperthermia, he was hallucinating and hysterical. The airman had stripped down to his underwear and was shrieking for his mother to save him once more. When a rescue chopper from the Philippine Air Force finally plucked Sonny from his perch, he collapsed from exhaustion. He passed out the moment the medics placed him on a stretcher and did not wake up for more than three days.

*****

A week later, Zubiri was in a hospital on the outskirts of Manila. Lieutenant Carlos Enverga from the Basa Air Base told him that he was the only survivor of the twelve-man detail sent to secure the armory. The search and rescue teams located two bodies, but hopes were not high that they would find any more. There was little left of that part of the base. The only thing that remained of the armory was the foundation, and even that sat beneath fifteen feet of hardening sludge.

"What about the weapons?" Zubiri asked.

The lieutenant shrugged. "Lost. We found a few that were salvageable, but most of what we recovered was ruined."

Since the officer did not mention anything about what they had stashed at the church, Zubiri did not, either. "Payan was worried about the NPA getting hold of them."

Enverga laughed. "Good luck to them. It's like trying to find pencils in quicksand. We can't even locate the truck you said you were swept away in. I don't see how they would ever come across the odd rifle in that stuff."

Sonny nodded. "What a waste. Eleven men gone, and we lost the armory anyway. It hardly seems worth it."

"It wasn't." Lieutenant Enverga thought for a moment, then asked, "You don't blame yourself for this at all, do you? For not getting to them with the truck in time to evacuate?"

Zubiri flinched as a realization struck him. *The lieutenant thinks the truck was for the men, not the weapons. He has no idea what we were doing.* Airman Zubiri shrugged, running with the lieutenant's assumption. "I failed. How can I not?"

"Stop it. You men were up against the fury of God that night. Your opinion of yourself must be very high to think you had any chance of holding back that kind of power. Is there anything I can do for you, airman? Have you heard from your family?"

Zubiri shook his head. "They're all displaced, too. Phones are down. I don't know where they're at."

"You know anyone else we can get in touch with who may be able to track them down?"

Sonny thought for a moment. "I have a cousin in the Philippine National Police. It might help if you somehow got in touch with him."

The lieutenant pulled a small notebook and a pencil out of his shirt pocket. "Do you have a name?"

Zubiri nodded. "Sergeant Tejada. Rico Tejada. He works in Olongapo." *He'll know what to do with the weapons we saved.*

*****

"...and now TJ's sitting on truckloads of M-16s, hand grenades, MP5s, 9mm pistols, and a bunch of ammo." Master Chief Darrow stubbed out his cigarette as he finished the story. Leaning back in his chair and putting his feet up on his desk, he added, "As far as the Philippine government is concerned, it's gone. It's buried beneath a couple dozen feet of volcanic concrete. The only people he can sell it to in PI are drug runners, communists, mutineers, or Moro separatists. The kind of people most likely to use the weapons against him. He's willing to unload the cache at a bargain to someone who can get it out of the country."

"And he thinks we can find someone like that in Japan?" I asked.

Darrow shrugged. "I do too. The *yakuza* are a pretty sophisticated group with international contacts. They could unload them to the Burmese or someone else in the Golden Triangle. Or even the Chinese triads. The trick is going to be finding someone to talk to."

"And you think I can do that?"

My master chief shrugged. "You speak a little Japanese. You're pretty knowledgeable about the culture. You'd be better doing it than I would. That also happens to be the least risky part of this, too. The way I see it is we split the operation to keep our exposure down. I'll handle the merchandise, the samples, and never be seen with our contacts. You manage the connections so that you'll never be seen with the merchandise. If I get pinched, I'm fucked, but I can't give up our *yakuza* guys. If you get pinched, they can't tie you to the guns."

I had to trust Darrow on the operational side of what he was proposing. It was too far out of my area of expertise. "What's our cut on this?" I asked him.

"Ten percent."

"Of what?"

Darrow grinned. "TJ thinks he's sitting on roughly eight million bucks of product. He might be overestimating a bit, though."

My jaw dropped as I did the calculation in my head. "That'd be $400,000 apiece."

"It would," my master chief agreed. "Not bad for simply arranging a meeting, is it?"

*****

CHAPTER 1

February 1993 was a bloodbath.

William Jefferson Clinton was inaugurated as President of the United States on January 20th. Captain Richard Darcy relieved Stephen Fleming as the commanding officer of the *USS Belleau Wood* nine days later. Clinton campaigned on a promise to allow homosexuals to serve openly in the US military. Letting business go on as usual aboard a vessel where a radioman was murdered after coming out of the closet would have set a bad precedent. Having his ship dubbed a "floating Animal House" by the national press did not help Captain Fleming's cause, either. Nor ours.

Darcy came aboard with the intent of showing the crew that he meant business. During the first week of his command, seven men were brought to captain's mast for gun-decking. They were accused of signing off that they completed preventative maintenance work that they had not actually done. Six of them were reduced in rank and sentenced to sixty days of restriction. The scuttlebutt was that the charges were bogus. The new skipper demanded sacrificial lambs, so the officers offered him their lowest performers. The seventh man was caught red-handed. The captain threw that poor bastard right out of the Navy.

The carnage did not stop there. Darcy kicked two other men out of the service for sleeping on watch. He took a chevron from three more who had not sobered up enough before morning roll call. The skipper then eliminated a watch section so that we had to serve duty every four days instead of every five. He threatened to remove another if the ship was not cleaned up to his standards before the Team Spirit exercise in Korea the following month.

The entire Ops Department lost liberty for two weeks after failing a zone inspection. A pair of Operations Specialists earned three days in the brig on bread and water for complaining about it. The captain considered voicing displeasure a form of blatant insubordination. After that, the crew started calling our new skipper "Reaper Dick."

In the modern Navy, bread and water rations had fallen out of vogue as a disciplinary tactic even before I enlisted. The fact that Darcy was resurrecting the practice had my division officer almost giddy with the prospect of sending me for my third stay in the ship's brig. He even thought he could make his charges stick for once. "Does bread and water sound like a feast to you, Petty Officer Murphy?" Krause snarled at me in the EMO one evening.

I forced myself to keep my eyes from rolling. "Sir, you are aware that bread and water sentences can only be handed out to those ranked E-3 and below, right?" LTJG Krause was a prior-enlisted man and had more than two decades of service in the Navy. It defied comprehension that he did not already know that.

The color rushed into the lieutenant's face. "I am NOT going to be lectured on Navy regs by a second-class petty officer on his first enlistment! But if that's the way you want it, I have no problem getting you busted down to E-3 before recommending that you cool your heels in the stockade! Now, explain this situation on the SPN-43 radar to me one more time!"

The grievances our lieutenant had against my men and me were typically petty and frivolous. They held no weight when escalated up the chain of command. Krause had a credibility problem with our department head, who also happened to consider my shop amongst the department's best. LCDR Winston knew our division officer was out to get me and was not about to allow the lieutenant to sabotage his department's efficiency rating to further a personal grudge. Krause could threaten me all he wanted, but as long as I was right, my department head had my back.

As long as I was right. Unfortunately, this time the lieutenant had a legitimate gripe. The SPN-43 was due for annual gearbox maintenance. This was a complicated activity requiring extensive disassembly high upon the aft mast. That was never a problem in San Diego, where it rarely rained. During the middle of winter in Japan, however, it was cold, windy, and wet. I was concerned that my technician was not accustomed to doing such a complex job under those conditions. Palazzo could cause more damage than he would prevent. That was what I was trying to tell Krause.

"Why the hell didn't you guys do this job while we were in the Philippines then? You had perfect weather there!"

And *that* was another legitimate point. The truthful answer was that Palazzo was too preoccupied with getting drunk and laid in Subic Bay to get ahead of the maintenance schedule. On the flip side, I was too busy doing the same thing to call him out for it. Most of us were. We were goofing off and only did what we had to. We figured we would get to the big jobs when we got back to our homeport, a locale with far less exciting environs.

Of course, I could not say that to Krause. Instead, I told the lieutenant, "We did not want to do a job that difficult on a base where the technical support facilities were being dismantled. If something went wrong, we wanted to be on a base capable of rendering heavy assistance. We assumed it'd be safer to do it here. Having never been to Japan before, we didn't take the winter weather into account."

"Winter weather?!?" Krause scoffed. "You're from Detroit, aren't you? You should be used to far worse than this! It's in the forties out there!"

"It's not about comfort, sir. It's about coverage. The colder it is, the more solid the grease gets. It doesn't flow as it would normally. We can't be sure it's getting to all the places it needs to be. It might, but then again, it might not."

"Does the PMS card have anything in it about not being able to do the maintenance if the temperature falls below a certain threshold?"

I shook my head. "No. It does not."

"What about the tech manual?" the lieutenant snapped.

For once, Krause's train of thought was entirely on track. He was making sense and pursuing a logical argument. It was pretty out of character for him. "No."

"Then what on earth are you basing your conclusion on that this check needs to be delayed?"

I sighed. "Experience, sir. Right now, we have a very good radar that is working exactly the way it should. We're getting ready to go on a major exercise with the Koreans. If we leave this radar alone, it'll work fine until we return at the end of March. If we start tinkering with it under conditions that we're not yet accustomed to working in, we're adding a significant amount of risk to the device."

"You telling me that you don't trust your technician?"

"I didn't say that." I sure thought it, though. Besides being a porn addict and a serial masturbator, Palazzo was by far my weakest technician.

Krause stepped forward into my personal space. "Then get your man off his butt and up the mast to get this job done! And tell him, from me, that if he messes it up, I'm going to have him in front of the captain so fast his boondockers will be leaving skid marks down the passageways!"

"Aye aye, sir," I answered as Krause stormed out of the EMO. *That's not the only place that boy will be leaving skid marks.*

*****

As much as ET2 Palazzo had detested Captain Fleming's "work hard, play harder" style of command, he was positively wilting under the new regime. One of the men Reaper Dick threw out of the service for sleeping on watch was a lifer. He was a man cut from the same cloth as Palazzo was, but without the pornography obsession. Like John, the guy was a regular Joe Navy. He kept his uniform sharp, his shoes spit-shined, and followed orders with a degree of fanaticism that was rare to find outside the Sunni Triangle. Unlike Palazzo, he was also very good at his job. As much of a pain in the ass as this kid was, none of us doubted that he would go far in the Navy. I thought he would finish his career in the officer corps after thirty-odd years at sea. Nobody imagined that he would be crawling home in disgrace before his second anniversary in the fleet.

Word around the sewing circle was that SN Chris Egan did not fall asleep on watch. He passed out. Seaman Egan had the flu, and the ship's doctor pumped him full of a depressive cough suppressant to help him rest. At the same time, the medical officer also refused to write him a chit to excuse him from duty. Sick as hell, unable to sleep, and dosed with a medication that made him drowsy, the seaman never had a chance. If Reaper Dick could ice a man like that, Palazzo knew that his career could come to a screeching halt just as easily.

At first, John was looking forward to having someone in charge who would bring an acceptable modicum of discipline on board. After seeing Egan hung from the yardarm, though, he had a rapid change of heart. Already an outsider, Palazzo knew that the only person inclined to stick up for him in a jam was ET3 Kent. Kent, the most junior man in our shop, would also be the least able to help him.

Palazzo thrived in his last command. He used his military bearing to mask his technical deficiencies. You can do that when you are in charge and can make others do your work. The problem Palazzo had on the *USS Belleau Wood* was that he was *not* in charge. I was. That made his weaknesses much harder to conceal. Knowing this, he did whatever he could to keep his profile low, like spending most of the day hiding out of sight in the fan room, for instance.

To a civilian, this often sounds weirder than it was. There is very little privacy on a Navy ship, so sailors will carve out a refuge of their own wherever they can. I was fortunate enough to have my SPN-35 radar dome, my own little apartment at sea. Palazzo claimed the Radar One fan room, which was also used as an unauthorized storage space for personal gear. It was far enough out of the way that no one casually stumbled into it. It was big enough that Palazzo had enough room inside to do whatever it was that Palazzo did in there. Since the main thing he did was pornography, we all learned to knock before entering. There was a reason we called him "Spanky."

"The lieutenant chewed my ass about the request to delay the SPN-43 gearbox maintenance," I said as I stepped into Palazzo's lair. I was relieved to find him reading a book about Star Trek and not having caught him in some stage of undress.

"And?"

I shrugged. "And, we're the same rank, John. Technically, you're even a senior E-5 than I am. You should be able to face Krause on this shit instead of hiding behind me."

Palazzo did not have a whole lot of pride. My insinuation that he needed to develop a backbone rolled right off of him. "What did he say about the gearbox maintenance?"

"What do you think? He said to get it done before we start Team Spirit. That means today."

John looked at me in disbelief. "Are you serious, Doyle? Did you tell him how the grease changes when it's colder? Or..."

"Hey," I interrupted. "I told him every reason I knew to delay this maintenance. You don't get to question my questions. If you don't think I was persuasive enough, you can get up and march your ass down to the EMO office to press your own case."

"Should we get Chief Ramirez or the master chief involved?"

I shook my head. "No, we shouldn't. Look, John, my trepidation about this has far more to do with your technical abilities than the grease. You've got a job to do. I did my best to try to have you do it in optimal conditions, but it didn't work out. You're on duty today. Get it done."

"Can you help?" Palazzo begged. "Please?"

I let out a long sigh. I had assisted Palazzo before. Helping him meant that I did the actual work while he read the directions. The job in question was not challenging. It was just long and laborious. It was dirty work, the kind that Palazzo did not like to do. It was well past time for him to start pulling his weight, especially on his own equipment. "No, John," I told him. "When was the last time you helped me with one of my radars? Or anybody else with theirs? I've got my own work that I need to get done today, and I'm not sacrificing my off-time to do yours."

"But…"

"But nothing. Put your party away and get your ass to work. Now." Getting frustrated with the man, I looked around the clutter in the fan room. "You know, we need to get this place straightened out too. If the captain walks in here and sees all this shit, he's going to have a conniption. Besides, we've got maintenance on the fan filters coming up soon, and I can't even get to them through all this stuff."

"Okay. I'll have Kent come in here and…"

"Kent doesn't hang out in here. You do. If you want to keep hanging out in here, lead the effort to get everyone to move their shit somewhere else."

Palazzo flashed me a look that he had not turned on me since we were still in San Diego. Contempt.

"Look, John, I'm not interested in harassing you for the sake of it. Your radar is your responsibility. You need to fix it. This fan room is used by you far more than anyone else. If you want to keep it, you need to take care of it. The other guys…"

"Fine!" Palazzo snapped as he got up. There was not much space in the fan room, so he practically pushed me out of the way to get past. I felt the hackles on my neck rise up, and my instincts were compelling me to reach out and wring his fat little neck. But I didn't. It would not have been worth it.

You see, I heard the rumors about Reaper Dick demanding the names of his officers' lowest performers. He wanted a pool of men from whom examples could be made. If Captain Darcy turned his eye upon the CSE Division and demanded a sacrifice, I wanted to be sure I had one to give him.

I could not give up ET3 Rick Hammond. He was an electronics genius and the primary reason our shop had the highest efficiency rating in the department. Dixie and Metaire were both excellent technicians, as well. They were also close friends of mine, men that had my back. I depended on them. There was no way I would ever let them go either. That left Steve Kent and Gianni Palazzo. Kent was at least a competent technician. Palazzo was not.

That made Spanky the sacrificial lamb I needed to keep in my back pocket. I had to keep my hands off of him until the captain demanded a pound of flesh from Radar Repair.

*****

I was crossing Nimitz Park on my way into town when I spotted a familiar figure sitting on one of the benches. He was staring at the restroom where David Miller had been beaten to death four months before. Tentatively, I approached him and asked, "Sir?"

Captain Fleming turned his head toward me and smiled. It had been a couple of weeks since he was relieved of command, and I was surprised that he was still in the area. "Doyle Murphy! I'm glad to see you! How are you?"

I shrugged. "Been better. Truth be told, we're all already missing you, sir."

"Yeah, well, it's going to get worse before it gets better, I'm afraid. It will get better, though, Murphy. It always does. You want to take a seat?"

I always had a high opinion of Captain Fleming, so I leapt at his offer, sitting down beside my former commanding officer. Nodding my head toward the direction of the restroom, I asked, "Meditating on what went down here with Miller, sir?"

Fleming nodded. "Yeah, how did you know?"

"I've sat here and done the same thing a few times myself."

"You know, I keep forgetting you were one of the guys who found him. Jesus, it has to be tough on you to have seen that."

"I don't know, sir. As far as I know, my career was not affected by what those assholes did like yours was."

Fleming shrugged. "I'm going to be fine, Murphy. Trust me. The worst-case scenario is that I'll be forced into retirement with my full pension. It hardly seems fair, does it? My punishment for letting one of my men get killed will be to comfortably live out the rest of my days in financial security. Meanwhile, David Miller got the death penalty for being gay."

"You didn't let anyone murder Miller, sir."

"Deliberately? No, of course, I didn't," Fleming assured me. "As the captain of the *USS Belleau Wood*, though, I was responsible for the welfare of my crew. Every. Single. Man. I failed that responsibility. As a military officer, I need to figure out what went wrong and develop ways of doing things differently. I don't want any woman in the world to go through what David Miller's mother is right now if it's within my power to stop it."

"Do you honestly think that there was anything you could have done to prevent what happened?"

"Of course there was," the captain said. "I just didn't know how to at the time." Fleming wagged his index finger at me. "For starters, I should have made an example out of you for what you did to Randy Green."

"What?" I asked, swallowing hard.

The captain grinned. "Relax. I'm not blaming you for Miller's murder. I'm faulting myself for sending mixed messages to my men. Randy Green was a piece of garbage. He abused his stepson and it looked like he was going to get away with it. If there was ever a man who deserved to be beaten to within an inch of his life, it was him. When the NCIS ruled that you acted in self-defense, I was only too happy to drop the matter and move on to better things.

"The problem is that that sent a message that certain people are so horrible that it's okay to deal with them outside of official channels. I was giving the green light to junior enlisted men to take some matters into their own hands. The recipient of their abuse just had to be sufficiently heinous."

"Sir," I said. "I don't think that being gay quite reaches the same threshold as snapping a five-year-old's arm to lure your wife out of a locked bathroom."

"To you or me?" Fleming asked. "No, it doesn't. To Pruitt, though, it sure did. You know, I saw that guy as soon as he got out of the hospital after being arrested. While getting processed back on base, Pruitt acted like he was some sort of hero for what he did. He legitimately believed that we would take his side in this thing like we took yours after Randy Green got hurt. It was shocking for him to realize that we considered Miller the victim. In Pruitt's head, the severity of what Randy Green did and what David Miller was doing was one and the same."

Captain Fleming shook his head in dismay. "Pruitt was raised in Oklahoma. He came up in an environment where homosexuals are viewed as Satan's work. Even though Pruitt himself was not particularly religious, he grew up in a world where everything is black and white or right and wrong. There are few degrees, few shades of gray. You're either virtuous, or you're evil. To him, gay people were the same as Nazis, Communists, serial killers, child molesters, or the Old Testament demons of Hell."

"That explains why he seemed to be having so much fun beating Miller," I mused.

"Yeah, I heard he was singing while he killed that kid."

I nodded. "Yes, sir. Army cadences. *I wanna be an airborne ranger. I wanna live a life of danger...*"

"My god. What a nightmare." Fleming let out a long sigh and then stood up to take his leave. "Murphy, it's time for me to get going. I'm flying back stateside tonight. Look, son, I've told you before about getting your junk together and keeping it that way. I've also warned you about letting yourself be overly influenced by Master Chief Darrow. You never seemed to take it to heart before, but you need to now. I'm telling you, Murphy, I know Captain

Darcy. That man is no joke. If you step a little bit out of line, he will ruin you. And I mean *ruin* you."

The captain offered me his hand, which I stood up to shake. "Sir, I am honored to have had the privilege of serving under your command. Thank you for everything that you've done for me."

"Yeah, Murphy, you owe me," Fleming said. "You can repay me by heeding my advice for once. Take care of yourself. Put some distance between you and Darrow, and keep yourself in line."

"Aye aye, sir." Though we were both in civilian clothes, I saluted Fleming anyway. He answered it with a single nod of his head before walking away. I stood fast as I watched the captain stroll toward the base until he passed out of sight. I then sighed and marched off in the opposite direction. I had to quicken my pace to make my appointment with Master Chief Darrow. We were plotting the first step in a plan that proved me incapable of heeding Fleming's advice to "keep myself in line."

*****

"That's them?" Darrow asked as I slurped down a mouthful of *yakisoba* noodles.

I looked out the window and saw two men emerge from the *pachinko* parlor. Most Japanese men wore their hair styled and either parted down the middle or at the side. The men Darrow spotted had hair cropped close to the scalp. It looked cut with clippers equipped with a short attachment. One wore a deep burgundy suit, the other a suit of dark green. Everyone else that passed by wore suits of gray or blue. The men we saw also wore patterned ties. They had rings on their fingers and thin designer sunglasses on their faces. It was all in stark contrast to conventional fashion norms in Japan. They stood out. Just like they wanted to. "That's them," I said.

Darrow looked at me as if he did not quite understand. "I don't get it. It's almost as if they want people to know who they are. It doesn't seem very smart. You sure these aren't some posers who're trying to look like they belong to the *yakuza*?"

"Check out their hands," I told him while reaching for my bottle of Asahi.

"Ouch," my master chief said after seeing the men were missing the tips of their pinkie fingers. They had been cut off at the first knuckle. "Yeah, that's a little extreme for someone trying to make a fashion statement."

"Japan doesn't have much in the way of RICO laws," I explained. "It's not illegal to belong to the mob. Believe it or not, I heard from a friend of mine that they even advertise. Another wild thing is that if there's an earthquake or some other natural disaster, these guys are usually the first on the scene to help. There are even festivals here where they'll come and show off all their tattoos. On the one hand, these guys are outcasts and shunned by Japanese society. On the other, they're semi-legitimate businessmen. It's like the Japanese don't want these people, but realize everyone needs a place somewhere, so they tolerate the *yakuza's* existence."

"Like I said, I don't get it." Darrow took his *hashi* and used them to throw a whole *gyoza* dumpling into his mouth.

"I don't either. But I'm not Japanese."

"What're they doing with the *pachinko* parlor?"

I grinned. "Gambling's illegal in Japan. Even though *pachinko* looks like some variant of a slot machine, it doesn't pay you any money. You win small prizes, like stuffed animals or something. You then have to take the toys to a different business nearby that'll buy them for exorbitant prices. If you win fifty bucks, they'll give you a little turtle. If you win a thousand, they'll give you a teddy bear. You then walk around the corner to another shop where they'll buy your trinket for whatever you won. That shop then sells back the prize to the *pachinko* parlor for a minimal profit like a buck or two. It's a loophole that's exploited by the mob to make the whole thing quasi-legal. These parlors are all over the place here, and the Japanese are as nuts about *pachinko* as they are about *karaoke*. It's all run by the *yakuza*. If you want to find a mobster, all you have to do is play *pachinko*."

"Interesting." That was the master chief's way of ending the conversation. We were in a noodle shop across the path from a mob-run *pachinko* parlor. If the Japanese cops wanted to keep tabs on the local malcontents, they would be there, too. The noodle shop offered a perfect vantage point. If anyone around understood what we were talking about, all they would pick up was that we were fascinated by the local flavor of organized crime.

We finished our bowls of *yakisoba* and changed subjects to our upcoming trip to Korea. We then had a couple of drinks at Shooter's Bar before returning to the *Belleau Wood.* Someone could have followed us all day until we stepped across the quarterdeck and it would have looked like nothing more than a typical night out.

Ideally, Master Chief Darrow and I would have met in the SPN-35 radar dome for the most privacy. While the dome had the best air conditioner on the ship, it had no heat at all. It was not a very comfortable option for a lengthy discussion. The radar repair shop was empty, so we went there to pick up the conversation we had cut short at the noodle shop.

"So those are the guys you're thinking about making a run at?" Darrow asked.

"Unless you've got a better idea."

My master chief shook his head. "I'm not sure about the strategy of running in cold like that. These guys don't know you. It seems risky. What if they suspect a trap?"

"Master Chief, I don't travel in the same circles that these guys do. I don't know anybody who could make that kind of introduction. It's not even like I could track down where these guys like to party and get to know them there. As a foreigner, I can't even get into most of the bars here that these guys would frequent."

"What about a nightclub? I would assume that the younger guys like to party. Could you find some in Fukuoka or something?"

I shook my head. "I doubt it. Like I told you, these people are outcasts and misfits. They keep to their own and don't mingle with polite society much."

Darrow groaned. "I don't like it."

"I don't think we have much of a choice."

My master chief thought for a moment, then cursed. "I guess we don't. Okay, look, we're going to do most of this by dead drop. I've already brought in a few samples of what Tejada is trying to sell and stashed them around the area. I've got maps drawn out showing where they are. If they take you seriously, pass them one. Once they find the product, they'll know you're legit. Remember, all we're doing is setting up the meeting between them and Tejada. Play as dumb as you can. If you can get away with it, pretend that you don't even know what it is that you're selling."

I nodded. "You know, the way Japanese laws are set up, I'm not sure that arranging a meeting between the *yakuza* and a Philippine cop with an opportunity is even illegal."

"Doyle, it's fucking illegal. I smuggled some serious hardware into Japan on this ship to get this done. If we get caught, we're going to be in a whole shit ton of trouble. Do you understand? You can NOT fuck this up. When do you think you're going to try this thing?"

Reaching for my cigarettes, I shrugged. "I'm thinking as soon as we get back from Korea."

Darrow looked nervous. "Okay. You do realize that after we make contact, there's no going back, right?"

I nodded my head.

My master chief let out a long breath. "Alright. Let's do it."

I discovered that deciding to carry out a crime was a lot like contemplating suicide. There's a lot of tension and stress while you are working yourself up to it. Once you finally commit, though, it's almost a relief. Everything is suddenly in the hands of fate, and either it is going to work or it isn't. It's out of your hands at that point, so you just accept the outcome as inevitable.

It was odd how effortlessly the conversation pivoted from the illicit arms trade to the more mundane intricacies of running my shop. "Did Palazzo get that gearbox job done?" Darrow asked, now that we had said everything there was to say about the Tejada deal.

I craned my neck to look at the PMS board. "He marked it off with a 'C,' so I guess he did." I got up and walked over to the garbage can. Lifting the lid, I looked inside and counted seven expended grease gun cartridges. I knew that was how many it took to complete the job, so I nodded my head in approval. I did not approve of the trash not being taken out when they called evening sweepers, however. I made a mental note to bring that up with the duty section the following morning.

Something else that caught my eye was Palazzo leaving the rags he used for the job bundled up in a bag on the workbench. They should have been in the garbage. Slightly more irritated with the man, I picked them up to throw them away, only to notice that they were a lot heavier than they should have been. When I opened the plastic sack to see why, I found that the rags were all saturated with gearbox lubricant. Shaking my head, I muttered, "What an idiot. Judging by the amount of grease on these things, he put more of the shit outside of the gearbox than he did into it."

Had I possessed a crystal ball, I would have weighed that bag and found out just how much grease was actually on those rags. Instead, I discarded them and thought nothing more of it. I had no clue how much impact they would eventually have on my life.

There was no way that I could have known it, but Spanky figuratively pulled the pin from a grenade that day. Considering what we would eventually do to him, it was almost a shame that he would not be around to see the carnage it would wreak when it went off.

Until it detonated, none of us knew that a trap had been set. We spent months in blissful ignorance. We went on with our lives, completely unaware of the seconds ticking down until Palazzo's time bomb went off. Tick. Tock. Tick.

Tock.

Tic…

*****

CHAPTER 2

We were on our way to Okinawa to pick up the Marines when I came face-to-face with Reaper Dick for the first time. I was in the Nixie Room performing maintenance on the winch when I heard someone clear their voice from just inside the hatch. Turning my head, I caught sight of Captain Darcy right behind me and dropped my tools, snapping to the position of attention. I would have called out "Attention on Deck!" but I was the only one there.

Captain Fleming always put you "at ease" immediately after his presence was recognized. I discovered right away that our new skipper did not have that habit. Darcy relished the power to keep you standing ramrod straight whenever he was within view. He savored all the privileges of his authority. Reaper Dick did not even acknowledge that I was there at first. He just strolled into the space and began looking around. The captain ran his hands along the angle irons to check for rust or dust. He inspected the Nixie fish for salt residue. That was a sign of improper cleaning and something he could chastise me for.

"What's your name, sailor?" Darcy asked after he had finished looking over the room.

"ET2 Doyle Murphy, sir!"

I could see from the look on the captain's face that he had heard of me. "You're Petty Officer Murphy? The guy that nearly beat a man to death on my ship?. That must have been here, in this room, wasn't it?"

"It was, sir."

"You want to tell me what happened?" It was not a question. It was an order.

"Sir, Petty Officer Green attacked me as we entered this space to clean it. The assault was caught on the camera mounted outside, above the well deck. During the fight, Green came at me with a spanner wrench. He left me no option but to defend myself. I had to beat him until he stopped moving."

"Why did this young man assault you, petty officer?"

I resisted the urge to shrug while at the position of attention. "My best guess is that he assumed we were going to rough him up for abusing his wife and stepson, sir. He recently got away with breaking a five-year-old's arm to get the mother to come out of the bathroom so he could batter her some more. He must have thought he needed to hit me before I hit him."

"Were you going to beat that man up for what he did to the kid?"

"No, sir," I lied.

Darcy quickly walked over and stood directly in front of me. "Look me in the eye and tell me that."

My gaze was focused straight ahead when I answered the captain the first time. That was what we were taught to do in basic training. I locked eyes with Reaper Dick the second time I lied to him, but I was no less convincing. I grew up forced to tell my father whatever he wanted to hear to keep myself from getting throttled. Lying to people that I considered a threat came naturally. I did not want to fall into a staring contest with the skipper that he could interpret as a challenge, though. The moment I gave him my answer, I broke off eye contact and went back to staring out in space.

The corner of Darcy's mouth curled into a grin. "Did he have any reason to believe you would do him harm?"

"Not that I'm aware of, sir."

"Okay," the captain laughed, conveying that he was not sure if he believed me. "I got word that you had a reputation for that kind of thing. I heard that the Green incident was not your first rodeo."

"Sir, in boot camp, I heard that they put saltpeter in the food to prevent us from getting erections during basic training. I've heard twice in the past two months that we would be going to Australia before April. I also heard that David Miller was beaten to death by a dozen sailors and not just Pruitt and Decker. Because I heard all of that stuff doesn't make any of it true."

"You know, Murphy," the captain scowled at me. It looked like he was trying to figure out if my answer had questioned his judgment or not. He must have decided that I had not committed any unforgivable breach of etiquette because he went on without excoriating me for it. "I read that thing about Miller in a newspaper before I left for Japan. How are you so sure that Miller was only killed by two men? I saw the autopsy report. I find it hard to believe that the kind of damage inflicted upon that boy was done by a couple of drunks."

"Sir, it wasn't even done by both of them. Airman Pruitt did most of it himself."

"Oh? Really?" the captain asked. "I take it you were involved in the NCIS investigation?"

"No, sir," I answered. "I was there. I was on Shore Patrol that night and was one of the men that carried Miller to the other side of the Albuquerque Bridge."

Upon that revelation, Reaper Dick stood there staring at me for a long moment, sizing me up. "You know, Murphy, I've heard things about you, things that are inconsistent with what I've read in your service file. On paper, you're a model sailor. Based upon the rumblings that have reached my ears, though, you're a common thug, an irrepressible libertine, and a dangerous man. I'm not sure which to believe right now."

I had little doubt that it was Lieutenant Krause who had bent the captain's ear about me. "Sir, I have every confidence that you'll reach a fair and accurate opinion in due time. Whatever you heard that's given you concern, well, all I ask is that you consider the reliability of the source of that information."

The captain laughed. Darcy may have been something of a sadist, but he was no idiot. He understood that I was questioning both my division officer's intelligence and integrity. I was just doing it in a way that could not be construed as disrespecting the EMO's authority. The tone of Darcy's laughter suggested that he may have had his suspicions about Krause as well. "Okay, petty officer. Rest assured that I will be keeping an eye on you until I figure it out. You seem like a smart guy, Murphy, so I probably don't need to say this, but I will anyway. Keep your hands to yourself. Understand?"

"Yes, sir."

Darcy gave me a nod. "Good."

Looking over the Nixie Winch Room one last time, the captain turned his back on me and started walking towards the hatch. "The space is clean but looks due for a fresh coat of paint. Get that done soon."

"Aye aye, sir!"

"Carry on," Reaper Dick told me as he stepped out of the winch room. My body, once finally relaxed from the position of attention, sought out something to lean upon. I let one of the winch drums take my weight.

I reached into my pocket and pulled out my cigarettes, hoping to soothe my nerves. The man had read my service record, meaning that I was already on his radar. That had me gravely concerned.

On the other hand, I doubted that he would have mentioned that had I been under an active investigation for anything. I could take solace in the fact that my dealings with Darrow and Tejada had not landed me under any NCIS scrutiny.

Yet.

*****

When a technician has worked on a piece of equipment long enough, he begins to get a feel for the quirks of his gear. For my SPN-35 radar, a high voltage capacitor in the transmitter unit tended to go bad about every ten months or so. Since I showed my radar a lot of TLC, she showed me a lot of love right back and gave me plenty of warning before she blew. She would start by showing phantom returns on the indicators. Then she would exhibit random spikes on the crystal current meters. Once she started showing signs of arcing around the capacitor's base, I knew she was going down within weeks.

"There. Did you see that?" AC2 Cory Boggess asked as I was checking out his indicator. "It just started."

I nodded my head at the air traffic controller. He was talking about the three-hundred-foot tall target that would irregularly show up on the radar screen. "Yeah, I caught it. It's a phantom return. One of the high voltage capacitors is getting ready to go. Either that or Godzilla is emerging from the ocean behind us."

Major Pete Kowalski, the ship's air boss, nodded. "Well, we're in the right neighborhood for that kind of thing. If it turns out that it isn't some radioactive sea monster, though, do you think you can fix it?"

"Actually," AC1 Darren Turner asked, "Didn't this just happen?"

"It did," I told him. "About eight months ago, when we were still back in San Diego. I had to swap it out with the one in the spare R/T unit."

"So, we have a replacement part on board?" the major asked.

I shrugged. "I hope so. The EMO postponed my last requisition until the new fiscal year. That's past, but I can't say for sure whether they put it back in stock."

"It better have been replenished," Turner said. "That's our primary air traffic control radar. This is an amphibious assault ship. That equipment is mission-critical."

"Roger that," I agreed. "Those are almost the exact words I used when I told Lieutenant Krause that we needed to make sure it got ordered as soon as we had the funds."

The Marine officer rolled his eyes. "If the part didn't get ordered, what are our options?"

"Well, the good news is that the radar's perfectly usable; it's just giving you a bit of noise. If we did nothing and let this thing run its course, I wouldn't expect it to suffer a hard failure for a couple of months still. We've got plenty of time to get a replacement on board."

Major Kowalski nodded. "Alright, Murphy. Do you need me to do anything to help? Like, talk to Krause? If you do, you let me know."

"Thank you, sir. Like you said, this is a mission-critical piece of gear. I don't expect too much push-back on getting this thing ordered."

Boy, was I wrong about that.

When I handed Lieutenant Krause the requisition chit for the replacement capacitor, he lost his mind. That was when I realized that the stress Reaper Dick was putting on the officers was even worse than what he was heaping upon the enlisted men. "What is this?" the lieutenant asked when I handed him my request. Then, once he saw the price tag on it, his hands started to shake. "$1500?!? FOR A LITTLE CAPACITOR?!?"

"This isn't something that you pull out of a transistor radio, sir. It's roughly the size and shape of a flashlight."

"AND YOU WANT TWO OF THEM?!?"

"Sir, we never replaced the last one that went bad, and we need…"

"Do you have any idea what I went through with the captain about the budget? Do you?!? We can't afford this right now!"

"Sir, that's what you told me the last time I tried to order…"

"WHY ARE THESE THINGS GOING BAD?!?"

Krause appeared to be pivoting from severe anxiety to his default state of anger. It sounded like he was implying that these bad capacitors were somehow my fault. That caused Master Chief Darrow to step in. "Lieutenant, we went through this months ago. We swapped out the R/T units and it had no effect. There could be a manufacturing defect in the caps causing them to go bad or…"

"Well, if there's a manufacturing defect, whoever made these things should be paying for them! Not the *USS Belleau Wood*!" Turning back to me, Krause bellowed, "Get them on the phone, Murphy! Get *them* to send us these capacitors!"

Master Chief Darrow was sitting at the desk beside the lieutenant. Chief Ramirez and Moore were further aft in the office. The Repair Parts Petty Officer, DS2 Kyle Brennen, was seated across the aisle from them, near the coffee pot. Krause was melting down in front of an audience this time.

"Sir," I told the EMO. "This capacitor is made by a multinational defense contractor that pays millions of dollars to lobbyists. They buy senators to protect their ability to sell us stuff like this for 10,000 times what it's worth. A cold call from a second class petty officer half a world away will not get through the first firewall of requisition clerks. I won't even go into their army of lawyers. Not to mention we're bobbing around the Sea of Japan right now where it's kind of hard to come across a working payphone."

"I just turned in my revised budget! With a fifteen percent reduction! I can't go back now and revise it again!"

"Sir, I requested these parts back in October. Were they not included in the budget then?" The lieutenant would not answer. I grabbed the requisition chit from Krause's desk and handed it to the RPPO. "Kyle, can you check to see if this was on the requisition list we filed before we went to the Philippines?"

"What on earth do you think you're doing?" Krause asked me as he stood up from his desk. He started marching towards us, tripping over the corner of the filing cabinet on the way. Had he not been wearing sunglasses indoors, he might have actually seen it.

"Checking to see if..."

"Checking to see if I did my job?" the lieutenant snapped at me. "Who the hell do you think you are?!? Do you think that I report to you or something?"

"Sir, this ship's main function is to launch helicopters and Harrier jump jets off this flight deck and..."

"I KNOW WHAT THE *BELLEAU WOOD*'S JOB IS AND..."

"...the SPN-35 radar is mission-critical, so..."

"...AND I KNOW WHAT THE 35 RADAR DOES!"

"Then, you understand the importance of having a functioning..."

"THEY'RE ALL IMPORTANT, MURPHY! MY JOB IS TO KEEP THEM ALL RUNNING, NOT JUST YOUR GODDAMN RADAR!"

We had liftoff. Krause screamed as he had never screamed before. I shut up and gave him the floor. There was never any chance of reasoning with the lieutenant under normal circumstances. Trying to do so after he had gone nuclear was a waste of energy. DS2 Brennen's jaw dropped wide open as the EMO exploded, and our RPPO looked like he was contemplating hiding under the desk. The two chiefs, Moore and Ramirez, stared at the lieutenant in disbelief. They both looked unable to comprehend that this spectacle was over a $1,500 repair part. Military electronic systems are notoriously expensive. Nothing significant ever got fixed for less than three grand.

Master Chief Darrow was the only person in the EMO who did not look shocked. He was more entertained than anything else. Darrow knew what he was looking at: a man cracking under pressure. He was enjoying the show. Krause was not thinking logically, nor was he making much sense. The master chief was hanging on the lieutenant's every word, studying him, and committing his rampage to memory. Darrow was identifying what Krause's triggers were so that he could set the man off again, at the exact right place, and at exactly the right moment.

Krause ranted at top volume for five minutes, coming down from it only when his voice began to give. Panting, he asked me, "Do you understand, petty officer?"

I actually did not. I had checked out about thirty seconds into the EMO's outburst and was not paying attention. "I'm sorry sir, can you repeat the part about whether we're going to order the high voltage capacitor or not?"

"YOU'RE NOT GETTING YOUR FUCKIN' CAPACITOR!!!" Krause bellowed.

Before he could go any further, ETC Ben Ramirez, forever the voice of reason, chimed in. He was the one man capable of talking the lieutenant down from the worst of his instincts. "Sir, we can't just let this radar break and not have the repair part on hand to fix it. That..."

"I know what I'm doing, chief," Krause snapped, even though he clearly did not. If there was a time that I wished I could penetrate the lieutenant's sunglasses and look at what was going on in that man's eyes, it was then. The lieutenant was out of breath and twitching his arms as if they were being rocked by muscle spasms. I imagined his eyes must have been going batshit crazy at that point.

"Lieutenant Junior Grade Krause," my master chief started, getting out of his chair. Saying the EMO's rank in full form was a mouthful. It was not done often. It was usually shortened to "lieutenant." Saying the whole thing when addressing your division officer was something akin to having your mother call you by your middle name. It let you know how bad you were messing up. "We cannot sit back and let a mission-critical piece of equipment fail. If you are refusing to order these capacitors, I have to inform Lieutenant Commander Winston of this decision so that..."

Krause spun around and stuck his finger out at the master chief. "You will not! YOU! WILL! NOT! THAT IS A DIRECT ORDER! DOES EVERYBODY IN HERE UNDERSTAND THAT? I WILL NOT HAVE YOU SABOTAGING MY BUDGET TO GET ME INTO TROUBLE WITH THE

CAPTAIN! YOU WILL NOT GO OVER MY HEAD ON THIS! BRENNEN!"

The RPPO stood up from his seat. "Yes, sir!"

"You will not order that capacitor behind my back and you're going to keep your mouth shut about it!"

Brennen shot a very uncomfortable look toward the master chief, who nodded his head in approval. "Yes, sir."

"CHIEF MOORE! CHIEF RAMIREZ!"

Moore looked tempted to tell the lieutenant anything he wanted to hear. Ben Ramirez stood his ground. "Sir, you've got me to the point where I need to…"

Darrow cut the chief off. "Ben isn't going to say anything, lieutenant. Have it your way."

Chief Ramirez looked at the master chief like he had lost his mind, and Darrow glowered at him in return. He was psychically willing the chief to keep his mouth shut. Turning back to the lieutenant, the master chief then said, "I'm going to make it perfectly clear to you, though. When that capacitor goes, and make no mistake, lieutenant, it will go, and there is no replacement on board, it is NOT going to be Petty Officer Murphy's fault. It's not going to be Petty Officer Brennen's fault. It's not going to be Ben's fault, and it's not going to be Chief Moore's. It is going to be your fault. You're going to own this."

"Okay," Krause said, his voice now heavy with uncertainty.

"Okay, what?" Darrow asked. "'Okay,' you accept full responsibility for what's going to happen or 'okay' order the part?"

"Just okay!" the lieutenant snapped. "Okay means okay! OKAY! Okayokayokayokay! What do you think okay means? It means okay! This conversation's pointless, and it's over! I've got a meeting with…with…I got a meeting in…I gotta go!" Flustered and agitated, the lieutenant threw his hands up into the air and stormed out of the office.

All eyes in the EMO followed Krause as he left. "What the…?" I stopped myself before I finished my thought. No matter how incompetent or insane our division officer was, saying my sentiments out loud would not have been helpful. We all saw what had happened. There was nothing to be gained from reinforcing it.

It was Kyle that broke our silence. Holding up the requisition chit, he asked, "So what do I do with this? Order the damned part or not?"

Darrow grabbed the chit out of Kyle's hand. "The lieutenant was very specific, Brennen. Did he not give you a direct order? I suggest you follow it."

"But…"

"Shush," the master chief told him. "What was the last thing you think the lieutenant told you to do?"

"Not to order the part…"

"Good. Carry out the order the way you understood it. Now, go get me one hundred yards of gig line." A gig line was formed when the seam of a sailor's shirt lined up with the edge of his belt buckle and zipper. It was how you judged whether the uniform was being properly worn for inspection purposes. Gig lines did not exist in any physical form, so green sea hands were often sent to requisition some as pranks. By asking Brennen to get some gig line, the master chief was telling him to go get lost for a while.

When the RPPO was gone, Darrow turned to the two chiefs. "Ben, Scott, what did you understand the EMO's direction to be as far as that capacitor is concerned?"

"I have no fucking clue," DSC Moore said. Ben Ramirez was similarly uncertain.

"Good," Darrow said. "Why don't the two of you go chase down the RPPO and make sure he gets the right gig line, then."

Master Chief Darrow did not ask me how I interpreted Krause's directions after the chiefs had left the room. He told me what my opinion was. "The way that you and me understood it was that 'okay' meant 'order the part.' You got that?"

"You sure that's a good idea?" I asked.

"If the SPN-35 goes down," Darrow started to ask. "How is it really going to affect air operations?"

I shrugged. "It won't. The air traffic controllers will just switch to the SPN-43 to guide the planes. They can patch into one of the fire control radars for altitude. We've got redundant systems. To cripple the AC tower, we'd have to lose the 35, the 43, and the 40. Even then, the choppers and Harriers could land by sight."

"Exactly. Krause has plenty of time to come to his senses on this, right?"

"I'm guessing eight weeks, at least."

Darrow smirked. "If he can't get his shit together by then, we let the 35 go down. I will personally explain to the Combat Systems Officer why we do not have any replacement high-voltage capacitors onboard. You and me understood that Krause told the Brennen to order them, so we had no reason to escalate this to the CSO. Brennen understood his orders were NOT to order them. Ramirez and Moore had no idea what the fuck the division officer expected us to do. There is more than enough ambiguity here for the confusion to be legit, allowing those capacitors not to get ordered."

"And when the radar does go down?" I asked.

Master Chief Darrow showed me the requisition chit he took from Brennen. "We have this chit, dated and signed by you, me, Chief Ramirez, and the RPPO. The only person who hasn't signed it is Krause. Now, Krause can claim that we never gave the chit to him. He probably will. We've got five witnesses here who will *not* forget an epic meltdown like this and will be more than happy to state that Krause *was* handed this requisition chit. He just never signed it. That covers the RPPO's ass if Krause implies that Brennen didn't do his job."

Smiling, Darrow walked over to the RPPO's filing cabinet. Opening it up, he tucked the chit away in the file for unapproved requisition chits so that we would know where to find it. "Malicious obedience," he said.

I nodded in agreement. "Malicious obedience."

*****

Lying in my rack that night, I could not help but marvel at how brilliant Master Chief Darrow was. I could not have thought of a plan like that to neutralize Krause if I had an entire week to think about it. Darrow assessed the lieutenant's meltdown, identified an opportunity, and acted on it in real-time. The only variable to the situation was whether or not Krause came to his senses. If history was any judge, it was probable that he would not.

Thinking about what happened with the EMO made me feel much more comfortable about what we were trying to do with Sergeant Tejada. Darrow seemed to know what he was doing and had built a career out of thinking several steps ahead. He was correct that the riskiest step seemed to be making that initial contact with the Japanese underworld. Once we survived that, we would be clear.

I found myself unable to wait to get that over with. I wanted to get back to Sasebo and see how I could approach the *yakuza*. Once we got that deal done, we would be home free. Hell, once we got that meeting set up and collected our commission, I could not care less if Krause figured out a way to throw me out of the Navy. It would get me back to the Philippines that much sooner. It would get me back to Mari.

And Tala. I closed my eyes and dreamed about the rustic surf resort Darrow, Tejada, and I were going to build. I fantasized about sleeping on the beach within a little bamboo hut with a palm roof, making love to Tala as Mari slept in the other room. Smiling, I wondered what it would be like watching Mari grow up. I wondered if she could come to think of me as her father one day despite us not sharing any real blood.

I remembered that last night in Olongapo, lying in that little bed back in my apartment, Tala on one arm and Mari on the other. I had never been happier than I was that night in my apartment.

That apartment. The one near the alley where I shot that boy, the one hired by Rafaela Green to kill me in revenge for what I did to her husband. I shot him in the head, watched his skull open up, and saw his brains blow right out the top of it.

Brains. I felt them in my hands—David Miller's brains. I was trying to hold them in his head as we ran him out of that bathroom to the other side of the Albuquerque Bridge. He died anyway, murdered by Marty Pruitt.

I noticed the sweat, the shortness of breath, and the noises sounding like I was hearing them from underwater. I knew what was coming. It was one of my episodes. I rolled out of my rack, pulling my dungarees on. "Doyle," I heard Dixie groggily call out from his bed. "You okay?"

"Yeah, Kevin, I'm fine," I said.

Dixie knew better. He could hear what was going on in my voice. Kevin let me have a head start; let me get to the SPN-35 dome and get the chance to really get deep into my episode. Eventually, he would follow me up there and make sure I got through everything safe. He was getting pretty good at it, but he was no replacement for Tala. When I was with her in the Philippines, my episodes never seemed to occur in the first place.

*****

CHAPTER 3

We had been calling Lieutenant Junior Grade Krause a lunatic from the moment he came on board. Before the Team Spirit exercise with Korea, we said it as a joke. After Team Spirit, we meant it as a medical diagnosis.

I suspected that there was something amiss with the man for quite some time. After the outburst over the capacitors, I thought that he was dealing with some sort of psychotic break. Considering my own issues, I felt I had a pretty good feel for that sort of thing.

Three thousand dollars was not very much when it came to military systems. It was not the budget-buster the lieutenant made it out to be. I doubted that the department head would have batted an eye at the expense. If Winston questioned it at all, it would only be to glean more information on the failure's nature. He would have far more pressing questions for the lieutenant if we could not get the SPN-35 fixed. There was no real choice to make in that situation. The correct course of action was clear, yet Krause managed to make the wrong call anyway. Then he went paranoid.

Our desire to escalate the capacitor situation to the Combat Systems Officer was akin to mutiny in the lieutenant's eyes. To him, it was a unified effort to usurp his authority. That rattled Krause. Deep within some recess of his mind, he must have known how insane he was acting. He was making a non-issue into a major one, something that could be fatal to a man's career under the regime of Reaper Dick.

The lieutenant had to have known this. Hell, Master Chief Darrow said what was going to happen. He told Krause that this would blow up in his face and that we were going to burn him for it when it did. It would not be a surprise flank attack by Krause's underlings. It would be a full-on frontal assault with plenty of warning. Darrow even told him how to thwart it. All the lieutenant had to do was order the parts. Doing that would defuse the situation. It would leave no evidence of the EMO's incompetence. He had all the power to put the pin back in the grenade, but he could not bring himself to do it for some inexplicable reason.

My best guess was that Krause was terrified of being seen as incompetent. He was compelled to project the image of an all-knowing and omnipotent leader. The lieutenant was far from that, though, so the more he pushed to show his expertise on things he knew nothing about, the more inept he appeared. Intellectually incapable of introspection, my division officer could never come to terms with any of his shortcomings. Not when it was easier to blame me for them.

In his view, Krause had fallen into a trap that I had personally sprung on him. He knew that the SPN-35 was sure to fail and did not see any way to escape it without conceding that I was right. When the shit hit the fan, it was going to be his word against that of five enlisted men who enjoyed the complete confidence of the CSO. That was going to hurt him.

Krause reached a conclusion that only Krause could reach. Instead of making the problem go away by ordering the parts we needed, he seemed to think that he could cast doubt upon my technical abilities if things went sour.

It was a flawed plan born of desperation. It could not work when people knew the radar was in the process of breaking down. The lieutenant must have thought that since the witnesses in the

EMO worked for him, he could somehow coerce them all to keep quiet about knowing that the equipment was in peril.

If that was indeed the lieutenant's plan, I accidentally foiled it before Krause even knew there was a problem. I did not even know what I had done until the lieutenant kicked open our door as we were pulling into Pohang. My men were used to the lieutenant's habits. They all got up to leave before Krause had the chance to order them out. "I gave you an order not to try to mess up my budget by going above my head on those SPN-35 parts," the EMO snarled.

"You did," I answered. "And I didn't."

"BULLSHIT!" Krause roared, slamming his fist down on my desk. Despite claiming to be a devout Christian, I noticed that the lieutenant was coming around on the subject of vulgarity. It appeared that he finally discovered the therapeutic value of cussing.

I let out a little sigh before I lifted myself out of my chair. "Sir, as far as I'm concerned, going over your head on this would be doing you a favor. It's too much effort protecting you from yourself, so I'm committed to following your orders to the letter. Whatever happens, happens."

Sticking his index finger in my face, he snapped, "You lie!"

"Yeah," I admitted. "When it can get me out of trouble or into a woman's panties, I'll stretch the truth into whatever shape I need it to be. In this case, though, I'm the envy of Honest Abe Lincoln."

"You told the air boss about those capacitors!"

I scoffed. "Major Kowalski knew about those capacitors before you did."

"What the hell are you doing reporting to Major Kowalski for?!? He's not in your chain of command!"

"Sir, the control indicators for the air traffic radars are in the Air Traffic Control Center. Major Kowalski, the *air boss*, runs it. I was in *his* house, fixing *his* equipment. If a major in the United States Marine Corps asks me a question, I'm going to answer it. Hell, if Airman Atkins asks about the equipment he uses every day, I'm going to answer him, too."

"You need to be more discreet!"

As hard as I was trying to keep a poker face, I am sure my expression betrayed my disbelief in what Krause was telling me. "These aren't the nation's nuclear secrets I'm dealing with, lieutenant," I said. "But sure, I'll tell the major that from now on, if he needs to know what's going on with his air traffic control equipment, you'll brief him. I'm sure he'd be as entertained by watching you wing your way through highly technical situation reports as I would be."

Krause inhaled as if he were gearing up to unleash a verbal barrage upon me of biblical proportions. For once, though, he realized that he had nothing to say *before* he started saying it. He let it all out in a pathetically long sigh.

"Sir, what did Major Kowalski say to you?" I asked.

"He asked me if we had the part on board ready to go if the SPN-35 went down."

"And what did you tell him?"

Krause started stammering. "We...we...we're l-l-l-looking into it."

I shook my head. "Sir, Kowalski did you a favor. If that radar goes down and we all know it's going to…"

"That radar is not going down."

My jaw dropped open. "You're kidding me, right? The Navy sent me to school to learn that radar. I'm on my third year of working on it. I've seen this happen before and even discussed it with the contractor who installed it. What makes you so sure that…"

"I'm an officer. I've been in the Navy twenty-two years, eighteen of them as an enlisted man. I know how enlisted men think, how devious you can be in undermining an officer's reputation."

"Sir, your reputation is going to be damaged far more when the SPN-35 fails and..."

"You think you've won here, haven't you? You think that because the air boss got involved and is making me give you your capacitors that you've won?"

"Trust me, sir. If anyone has won here, it's you."

Krause shook his head. "Oh, no. You may have won this battle, but rest assured, mister. This little victory of yours has cost you the war! I can't seem to get to you. Everyone seems to think you're some sort of golden boy around here. You get away with everything. Your men are not so high profile, though."

I paused for a moment to process what the lieutenant said. I wanted to be sure I understood that Krause was threatening my men because he could not get to me. "Sir, do you not realize that the more successful this shop is, the more successful you are? How will messing with my men help you? These guys are your best technicians! They work hard and they're really good at what they do. If you do anything that compromises the combined experience of this shop, you're shooting yourself in the foot."

"I'll be showing the people that hold you up on a pedestal that without your men, you're nothing!" the lieutenant spat.

I could not believe Krause's incomprehensible ignorance of the concept of leadership. "I'll save you the trouble, lieutenant. I'll admit to you right here that my success as the work center supervisor of Radar Repair is completely dependent upon my subordinates. Without their intelligence, work ethic, dedication, and expertise, I'd be completely ineffective. Without the support of my men, I'd be nothing."

I took a step towards my lieutenant to make sure that he was getting my point. "I'd be *you*."

Krause was set to explode. His jaw clenched so hard that I heard his teeth grind. Even behind his sunglasses, I could see his face twist into a series of tortured expressions. To be clear, I had crossed a line, and any other officer would have made me pay for it. Krause had a credibility problem, though, and he knew it would not get past the CSO if he escalated the issue.

If the lieutenant reported me, LCDR Winston would sink his teeth into my backside and see to it I paid for my sins. Krause knew that whatever punishment I received would fall far short of putting me in front of Reaper Dick, though. I would also expose the lieutenant's idiocy on the capacitor issue. With me backed by five credible witnesses, Krause would suffer far more damage than I would.

The EMO grimaced, trembled in rage for a moment, then finally turned his back on me and stormed out of my shop. He was not conceding defeat. Far from it, in fact. The lieutenant wanted to make me pay for that insult. He just did not know how at the moment. He withdrew only to regroup. Krause wanted to figure out how he could hurt me in a way from which I would not recover.

The funny thing was that, after everything we said, the moron still forgot to tell Brennen to order my capacitors.

*****

I do not think ET2 John Palazzo had a problem with the methods of Lieutenant Krause. He just had a difficult time coping with them when they were inflicted upon him.

When Palazzo was in charge, he was all about canceling liberty and assigning pointless work just because he could. He kept his subordinates running circles around the equipment while he sat at his desk, doing next to nothing. He did things like ordering us to clear our personal gear from the shop and then filling up the empty spaces with his comprehensive pornography collection. That was what got him fired.

After his demotion, Palazzo was not a happy man. He was furious with Captain Fleming for his role in getting him canned as our supervisor. Everyone else thought the skipper was pretty generous. Spanky could have lost a chevron for not following the captain's orders. Palazzo also blamed Master Chief Darrow for not sticking up for him. He hated me for taking over his old job despite being a junior petty officer.

Palazzo never said as much, but he was happy to see Fleming go. He hoped that someone would enforce discipline the way he believed discipline should be enforced. He probably also harbored fantasies about getting his old job back under a new regime. His hopes for that got dashed once Krause realized that Palazzo was the infamous porn hoarder and not me. Though the two men showed similar sadistic tendencies and had common adversaries, the lieutenant was a Bible thumper. He was as repulsed by Spanky Palazzo as he was by the master chief and me.

That became obvious when Palazzo's gear went down on our way into Pohang. The IFF was a touchy piece of equipment. It was a glitch in the IFF system that was blamed for downing an Iranian passenger plane over the Strait of Hormuz in 1988. Two hundred and ninety people died in that tragedy, so when the IFF went offline, it got a LOT of attention. Reaper Dick immediately lost his composure and reamed out Lieutenant Krause for it. In return, our division officer went off on Palazzo in a way that Spanky was not equipped to handle.

I could endure the worst of Krause's verbal abuse because I knew that I was shielded from any real consequences of the EMO's lunacy by my master chief and our department head. If Krause tried to write me up for something asinine, it would never get past LCDR Winston. Even if it did and I ended up in front of Reaper Dick, I was not a career man. As long as I was still eligible for an honorable discharge, it would have little effect on my post-Navy life.

Palazzo did not enjoy the protection that I did, and he had every intention of staying in the Navy for life. No one thought very highly of him, so if Krause wrote him up, there was little to keep it from going all the way to the captain. That could cause significant damage to Spanky's career. For that reason, Krause's threats resonated with the man and he was terrified of what the lieutenant could do to him.

At first, I had fun watching Palazzo get a taste of his own medicine. After Krause's third go at the guy, however, it was getting ridiculous. Spanky got the point that the IFF was a high-profile failure. He was also painfully aware of his technological shortcomings. Krause's constant interruptions were not helping him get his equipment fixed any quicker. After ensuring my men got off the ship on liberty before the EMO found a reason to cancel it, I returned to help Palazzo work on his gear.

"No offense," Spanky told me after I returned. "But, I'd rather have Hammond here."

"Well, Rick's been going non-stop since we left Japan. He's troubleshot every failure that Radar Repair's had and assisted the guys in Comm Repair with their problems as well. The crypto techs even had to borrow him a few times, and last night he got called in to fix the television in the officer's wardroom. That boy has earned himself a break."

"Is he going out in town?" Spanky asked. Rick was our shop's only married man. After Bill Kramer in Comm Repair falsely implied to his wife that Hammond might have been screwing around on Melissa in Olongapo, Rick tended to stay close to the ship.

"No," I answered. "He's going to bed to sleep for a few days."

Spanky looked a little cross. It was as if he thought Hammond should be helping us before hitting the rack if he was not carousing about Pohang. "You know anything about IFF?" he asked me.

"Nope," I answered. "Not a thing."

"Then what do you expect to do here?"

"Keep Krause off your back so you can do your job," I told him.

Palazzo paused to think about my offer, then nodded. "I'll take it."

Krause arrived a couple of hours after I did. I intercepted him at the door to the Radar Room as he walked in. "What are you doing here?" he barked at me.

"Assisting Petty Officer Palazzo in getting the IFF back up and running."

"Well, tell him to get over here! I need a report!"

I opened the door and led the lieutenant back out into the passageway. It was quieter out there. "I'm working shoulder to shoulder with him, sir. I know what's going on and can report."

"I don't want you! I want Palazzo!" the lieutenant yelled.

"Sir, right now, he's got his hands in a piece of energized equipment. At this point, interrupting him would be a safety issue." Using the word "safety" was an effective way to expel an annoying officer from a situation that he added no value to. It was like screaming, "The power of Christ compels you!" during an exorcism. It got the demons out.

"Well, go ahead, then!" Krause snapped. "Tell me what's going on in there!"

"We've developed a short in one of the PCBs that has bypassed the thermal protection circuitry. That caused a cascading sequence of failures…" Because of Krause's sunglasses, I could not see the lieutenant's eyes glaze over, but I knew that he did not understand a word that I was saying. I went on for fifteen minutes, explaining the situation in the most complicated jargon I knew. I even made up a few words to see if he could call me out on it, but he didn't. When I finished, I asked, "Do you have any questions, sir?"

Thoroughly lost, our division officer did not even know where to begin. He stuttered a couple of times, then said, "No, it's pretty clear. I expect an update every hour! Do you understand?"

"Aye aye, sir."

Krause left and I returned to helping Palazzo. We got the scorched components replaced on the PCB and were about to test it when Krause walked into the radar room again. For the second time, I stood up and rushed over to block him from rattling Spanky's nerves any further. "What are you doing here?" he barked at me.

I stopped in my tracks and looked at my watch. Forty minutes before, the lieutenant walked in and asked me that same question.

"I'm, uh, helping Petty Officer Palazzo fix his IFF gear, just like the last time you were in here."

From what I could tell without actually seeing his eyes, it looked as if the lieutenant was just standing there staring at me. He was swaying ever so slightly, as if he was having a little difficulty maintaining his balance. Krause swore that he did not drink, but I leaned in towards him to see if I could smell booze on his breath. Unable to detect anything, I asked, "Sir, are you all right?"

"I-I'm fine," the lieutenant answered. He seemed confused for a moment, then got fidgety. It was as if he now remembered having talked to me before but was embarrassed by having forgotten. He tried to play it off like he was only there for an update. I drastically dumbed down the geek-speak for him, but it was evident that he still was not following me. He seemed unable to concentrate.

The more I watched the lieutenant, the more I suspected he had been drinking. Vodka could be hard to smell, explaining why I was not picking it up, but something was off about him. He was either a closet drunk or dealing with a premature case of Alzheimer's. Either would explain a lot.

Sensing that I was evaluating him as I spoke, Krause cut me off. "Save it, Murphy! How long do you think it will be before the two of you fix the SPN-43?"

"You mean the IFF, sir?"

"No! The SPN-43! The gearbox maintenance!"

Our conversation was getting weirder. "Sir, that was done last week. The IFF is what we're working on now."

"Huh?" From what I heard, Reaper Dick ravaged LTJG Krause when the IFF went down. There was no way he forgot that that was what we were working on.

"The IFF, sir. We're not working on the..."

"Yeah! The IFF! How long before you fix the IFF?"

"Before we leave Korea." That was four days away.

Usually, that would have set the lieutenant screaming that it was too long. He would want it fixed within a couple of hours. Now, he seemed as impatient to end our conversation as I was. He ordered me to get it done and then stormed off.

As I watched him leave, I knew he had to have been drunk. I began to suspect that Krause's teetotaling had more to do with alcoholism than religion. Now that Reaper Dick was piling on the pressure, the lieutenant was falling off the wagon. Normally, I would not consider someone's relapse a reason to celebrate. In this case, though, I went back to Palazzo with a renewed sense of hope.

If Krause was smuggling alcohol aboard the ship, he risked getting into serious trouble. It meant that he was desperate, and his need to satiate his craving was more powerful than his desire to salvage his career. The man was falling apart.

At that point, I knew for sure that the lieutenant's days were numbered, especially if Master Chief Darrow could figure out where the lieutenant hid his bottle.

*****

It took two days for Palazzo and me to fix the IFF. The problem ended up being a little metal shaving that found its way into one of the slot plugs. That shorted out the connection. Even when we figured out where to look, the shaving was virtually invisible and took us forever to find.

Happy that the IFF was running, Darrow wanted to show his appreciation for the hours we put into getting the job done. He and Tony Bard decided to treat both of us to Korean *bulgogi.* I had already tried it in a Sasebo restaurant, but there was a big difference when you had it in Korea. There, it came with *kimchi.* The Japanese were somewhat averse to any strong odor, so I understood why this staple of Korean cuisine was missing there. If nothing else, *kimchi* was pretty damned aromatic.

Kimchi is a Korean side dish consisting of pickled cabbage, heavily dosed with garlic, fermented seafood, and chili peppers. It smells like terminal crotch rot. After our experience with food poisoning in the Philippines, no one was particularly anxious to dive right in and graze on it.

I have a little rule, however. I have to try whatever is put in front of me at least once, so I forced myself to take a bite of the stuff and found that it was insanely delicious. I devoured my portion and then went on to steal everyone else's before ordering more.

After a few beers and filling our bellies, Master Chief Darrow led us a little deeper into town to another Asian staple – a hostess bar. This was right up Palazzo's alley.

Japan had hostess bars too. They were places where you could sit across from a pretty girl who would laugh at your crappy jokes, pour your beer, and flirt with you as long as you were buying her drinks at double the usual price. They would lead you on all night, but you went home by yourself when closing time arrived. There was never a happy ending involved. The girls working hostess bars in Japan were not prostitutes. Even if they were, Japanese call girls were far too expensive for a man on Palazzo's salary.

In Korea, hostess bars were different. On the surface, they looked like their Japanese equivalent. They were clean, chic, and staffed by girls who were every bit as flirtatious as in Japan. The difference was that some of them were receptive to the idea of having sex at a price that Spanky could afford.

As we walked towards the place Darrow had found, Palazzo's excitement was palpable. "John," I asked after we had fallen back enough for Darrow and Bard not to be privy to the conversation. "Have you ever tried to have sex with a woman without paying her?"

Palazzo did not say as much, but I could tell by the look on his face that he had not. "You know, I could try to help you build up some conversation skills and…"

Spanky shook his head. "I've got no use for a girlfriend, Doyle. I prefer whores. Unlike all the other cunts, they don't think they're better than me." He said that with a startling amount of venom in his voice.

I was rarely shocked by what Palazzo said or did, but that one threw me for a loop. Spanky was a little overweight but not morbidly obese. His face was symmetrical, he was well-groomed, and he lacked disfiguring acne. He was not what I would consider horribly unattractive, just mildly so. Had he put some effort into it, he could have found himself a girlfriend somewhere. Palazzo's problem was that he was just weird. He was fidgety and ended his sentences with an odd nervous laugh. He also gave off creepy vibes that women picked up on and were very wary of.

My former fiancé, Hannah Baxter, met Palazzo very briefly once. Their interaction was limited to a handshake and a "Nice to meet you." Still, he made an impression on her. She later told me that Spanky made her very uncomfortable, ogling her like a piece of meat.

The fact that Palazzo had issues with women was evident. What caught me off-guard was how deep his animosity toward them went. Unless they were prostitutes. I had seen him with working girls in Tijuana and the Philippines. There he seemed entirely at ease.

We were not the only guys that Darrow had brought to his Pohang haunt. When we walked in, we discovered that several CSE men were already there, including Dixie and Claude Metaire. Palazzo went one way when we entered the bar while Tony and I went another. We joined Metaire at a table in the back where he was chatting up a pretty young lady from Daegu. Within an hour, Darrow and Dixie disappeared with their hostesses, and Metaire suggested to his girl from Daegu that they do the same.

Smiling at him coyly, the girl declined. She suggested he speak with another woman sitting in a group of hostesses near the other end of the bar. As the other woman was even cuter, Claude left to take her advice.

"You don't like black guys?" Tony asked her after Metaire had left. Bard had been out with Claude several times in Japan and got to see firsthand how unwelcome our friend could be. That stuff rolled right off of Metaire, but Bard was getting sick of it.

"No, I like everybody," the Daegu girl said. "But I just hostess. I no go to bed with boys at work."

I looked around. "Wait, not all of you are working girls? How can you tell which ones are and which ones aren't?"

Our hostess smiled. "You can't. You find out when you make offer."

*****

John Palazzo had a lot of pressure to let off after all the grief he took from Krause over the IFF. He spent most of the evening talking to a fetching hostess directly across from us. John was buying her plenty of drinks and irritating her with that nervous laugh of his. She was as gracious a hostess as any of the other girls and did what she could to keep him entertained, even as he got himself sloppily drunk.

All was going well until Spanky asked her how much it cost to sleep with her and she let him know that she was not a prostitute. Like with Metaire, she offered to introduce him to someone who would be more receptive to that kind of proposition, but Spanky wanted none of that.

John took her rebuff as a rejection, a rejection by a whore nonetheless. “But, I’ve been blowing my money buying you drinks all night!” he exclaimed, much louder than he should have in a place like that.

The aggression in Palazzo’s voice turned a few heads, so I decided to intervene. I threw a handful of *won* bills on the table to cover my drinks and stood up to get to Spanky before the bouncers did. Patting my man on the shoulder, I said, “Hey John, it’s different here than in the Philippines. Not all these girls do what you’re looking for. Let’s get you to one that will…”

“Bullshit!” Palazzo yelled. “I don’t want some other chick! I want this bitch here!”

I winced. The line had been crossed. It was no good trying to get Spanky to another woman. I needed to get him home. “Okay, John, it’s time for us to go. Get up.”

Palazzo looked surprised. “What? No! Hey, everything’s cool here. We’re all right.” Turning to his hostess, John asked, “You’re okay, right? Hey! We’re doing okay!”

The hostess kept smiling, but she was backing away. Palazzo saw this and reached out, grabbing her by the wrist. “Hey! Where’re you going? Hey! I’m trying to work out a deal here! What’re you…?”

I grabbed hold of Palazzo’s shirt by the shoulder. “What the hell do you think you’re doing, John? Let go of her! You’re going to get your ass kicked in here! Let go! Now!”

It did not appear that Palazzo had heard a word that I had said. “Hey! Look, bitch! We’re talking here! Why are you…”

“Goddammit, John! Let go of her!”

“Hey!" Palazzo shouted. "Listen to me! I…”

I grabbed an empty beer bottle and rapped Palazzo across the knuckles with it hard enough to make him release his grip. As soon as he let go, the hostess scurried away. I pulled him out of his chair and manhandled him towards the door. "You need help?" I heard Tony call out.

"Nope! I got him. I'll see you all in the morning."

"Hey! Doyle! C'mon man, I was only talking to that chick…I wasn't doing anything…"

Two severe-looking men came through a door in the back of the establishment and started walking our way. Fortunately, they seemed content to hang back and let me take care of the situation as long as it looked like I had it under control. I nodded to thank them for not kicking my ass. They nodded back, appearing appreciative that I was saving them the trouble.

"Doyle! Goddammit! Get your fucking hands off of me! I'll…"

I pitched Palazzo out of the front door and into the cold night air. Once outside, he started screaming obscenities at the sky. When he settled down, I faced off across from him. "What the hell's the matter with you? What did you think you were doing in there? Dude, that looked less like a proposition and more like the larval stages of date rape! You want to go to jail?"

"Rape? Fuck you, Doyle! They're whores!"

"It doesn't matter who they are! If you get rough with a woman in a place like that, you're going to get your ass kicked. If not by them, then by me! You can't force her to fuck you, asshole."

"Doyle! She was ripping me off! In fact, I'm going back in there to show that bitch…"

I turned my back on him and started walking away. "Fine. Do whatever you want to do. Those goons are going to break your kneecaps before you get a dozen steps into that place."

Palazzo looked at the door leading to the bar and then back my way. Knowing that I would not cover him if he went inside, he jogged to catch up with me. After what I had just witnessed, I would have preferred to walk back alone. Up until then, I had always considered Spanky harmless. He was more of an embarrassment than a danger. What he displayed in that bar smacked of something ominous, though. It was more than an overactive libido and an inherent difficulty in getting it relieved.

I always thought Palazzo too much of a pansy to ever resort to violence, but after that night, I didn't know. He was under a lot of stress, and I wondered if that could have triggered some latent aggression. I was going to keep an eye on him.

It would have been a long cold walk back to the ship, but we were lucky enough to be intercepted by a Shore Patrol van. I recognized the petty officer behind the wheel but did not know his name. "You guys from the *Belleau Wood*?" he asked as he pulled up alongside us.

"Yeah," I answered.

"Jump in. Liberty's secured."

"No shit?" I asked as I walked around to the side door. Once Palazzo and I were inside, I asked, "What happened?"

"A couple of Marines were in a bar and ordered a bottle of champagne. When they popped the cork, it hit one of the girls in the back of the head. She got pissed, picked up a beer bottle, and broke it across the face of some poor jarhead that had nothing to do with it. It sliced him up pretty bad. The poor bastard almost died. The captain called off liberty within thirty minutes. Reaper Dick doesn't fuck around."

"No," I agreed. "He certainly doesn't."

*****

CHAPTER 4

All told, I saw about five hours of Korea. I would have liked to have seen more. I could also have used more time away from Krause and Reaper Dick, but securing our liberty was probably the right call.

The crew of the *USS Belleau Wood* was under a lot of strain. Between the tempo of Team Spirit and our new captain's constant harassment, the men were ready to blow. Feeding us alcohol and turning us loose on Pohang was not going to result in anything positive. Forcing the men to sober up and get some rest would have been a good idea.

That is not what happened, though. Reaper Dick canceled our port call and then upped the ante. We got two days of back-to-back fire drills, security drills, and any other drill the captain could come up with. And they happened at all hours. By the time we left Pohang, we were more worn out than when we pulled in.

As exhausted as I was leaving Korea, my star technician was in even worse shape. As luck would have it, Rick Hammond had duty the day before we put out to sea. His section had a fire drill at 19:00 that the captain was entirely dissatisfied with. Darcy ordered another at 21:00. From the captain's perspective, that one was even worse, so he initiated another at 22:00 and then another at midnight. Hammond had the Petty Officer of the Watch from 04:00 to 08:00. He had to wake up at 03:00 to make it on time, and he was so afraid of being late that he never slept at all.

After getting off watch, Rick had to man the mooring lines as we cast off from the pier. By the time he made it up to the shop, he looked like the walking dead. He estimated that he had slept no more than ninety minutes in thirty hours. Hammond's first chance to catch some shut-eye was at lunch, but he got a trouble call on the SPS-40 just as chow was announced. That kept him from his bunk even longer.

The SPS-40 call turned out to be nothing. The only thing wrong was that the new OS using it did not know how to turn it on. OSC Wallace did not want to cop to his men being under-trained, though, so he escalated the issue. It took a full-blown argument between Wallace, ETC Ben Ramirez, and myself to get it resolved. By then, Rick barely had a chance to eat. Catching a nap was out of the question.

From the time lunch was secured until the end of the workday, I kept everyone busy cleaning the spaces. Even though I told Hammond to disappear somewhere and sneak in some rest, that was not the way he worked. He toiled alongside everyone else, trying to power through the day until he could go to bed.

Once the 1MC heralded the end of the workday, the SPS-40 went down for real. That vindicated Chief Wallace's assertion that the radar had been broken all along, despite having seen his new OS improperly energize it. That caused another CIC dust-up between the OSs and the ETs. Reaper Dick called both department heads upon the carpet and let them have it. Shit rolls downhill, so it was not long before Lieutenant Krause jumped into the fray to make everything worse.

As I gathered up the test equipment Hammond needed to troubleshoot his radar, Krause burst into the Radar Room. He gave Hammond the same treatment he had given Palazzo a couple of days before. Rick was a cooler character than Spanky, however. He was able to tune the lieutenant out while analyzing his gear.

When I got back to the radar room, I did what I could to distract our division officer and get him out of Hammond's way. While Krause screamed at me in the passageway, Rick figured out what was wrong, fixed it, and buttoned everything back up.

That was not good enough for the lieutenant. Not content with screaming just at me, he had both Hammond and me follow him to the EMO office. There, he yelled at us more, accusing us of gun-decking and incompetence. We were cut loose just in time to catch dinner, and then both of us tried to hit our racks for a little rest.

We did not even sleep an hour. The ship went to General Quarters to drill for a submarine attack, and my team had to deploy the Nixie. The Nixie was my baby. It was a miniature torpedo-looking device that hooked to a cable strung out behind the ship's stern. It emitted an acoustic/electromagnetic signal that made it look more attractive to an enemy torpedo than the ship itself. If it worked right, the torpedo would hit it instead of us.

The entire Radar Repair shop had a role to play in the Nixie deployment, as did a couple of other people. Kent and Metaire were in charge of activating the fish and attaching them to the cables. I was in control of the winch that let the fish out from the stern and drew them back in. Palazzo maintained communications with the bridge. Dixie and Hammond worked the electronics generating the signal. Darrow was on site to supervise; ET2 Cleveland and ET3 Willis were on standby if anything went wrong. Of course, it did.

Letting out the fish went fine. The retrieval did not. While bringing in the decoy, we heard a loud "POP," and then the starboard spool started freewheeling back out to sea. Darrow immediately ordered everyone out of the space on the double. If the cable reached the end of the spool and broke off, it would kill everybody in front of it if they were lucky. If they were not, they would just end up maimed and mutilated. As the winch operator, I was behind the freewheeling drum, but only by about eighteen inches. I was not taking much comfort in that, but I took enough to try to turn the brake wheels to manually stop it.

I cranked the brakes as fast as I could. When they reached the point where they started to engage the drum, all they did was bounce off it. I never got enough leverage on the winch to stop it completely, but I did slow it down. When the cable reached the end of the spool, it did not break off. Nothing got destroyed, and no one got injured. I thought I had saved the day, but Master Chief Darrow had an entirely different perspective. He chewed my ass even worse than Krause for not evacuating the space when he ordered me to.

The starboard spool was toast. There was major damage to the transmission, and the clutch would not engage to pull the fish back in. We could not leave it out there, so the decoy had to be pulled in by hand. Reaper Dick was pissed. Once again, he clobbered our department head over our malfunctioning equipment. Once again, our department head clobbered Lieutenant Krause in return. Time better used to get people down to help retrieve our decoys ended up being wasted by another of our division officers' tirades.

When Darrow finally got Krause out of our way, we had to muster the entire division in the Nixie room to pull the decoy back on board. That was like having twenty-two people playing tug-of-war with King Neptune himself. We measured victory in inches, and it took hours of back-breaking effort to get our decoy back. It was murder, and when it was over, we were all exhausted and sore. We were still far from done, though.

We had to get the saltwater off the cable to keep it from corroding. We had to fix the winch enough so that we could spin the drum by hand. Then we had to re-spool the cable. It was 01:30 when we finished. That was just in time for ET3 Hammond to stand a two-hour watch in aft steering. By now, Rick was approaching his fortieth hour of being awake. “Go to bed,” I told him. “I’m qualified. I’ll take your watch.”

“You’ve got the EMO watch at four, though, don’t you?” Hammond countered.

I shrugged. "Yeah, so it's not like I'm going to get any sleep anyway. Go get some rest."

You could not get any deeper into the bowels of the ship than the aft steering room. It was at the very bottom and the very back of the vessel, just the other side of the bulkhead from where the rudders were. This space was manned underway so that if the bridge got destroyed, we could still steer the ship from below. It was not a pleasant place to spend two hours. Depending upon the temperature of the ocean, it was always extremely hot or cold down there. You were also positioned directly above the bilge, and the smell was so offensive that you could taste it. Aft-steering was also insanely loud. You needed both foam earplugs and insulated headphones to bring the noise down to a manageable level.

One would think that enough was going on in that horrible space to keep a man awake. Oddly enough though, the muffled noise became a source of tedium. With no other stimuli to keep your mind occupied, it tended to lull sailors to sleep. I was on station fifteen minutes before I caught myself dozing off the first time. After an hour on watch, I groggily stood up and did jumping jacks to get some adrenaline flowing. That was what I was doing when Lieutenant Krause threw open the hatch.

Seeing something he was not quite expecting when he walked into the space, he screamed, "What do you think you're doing?!?"

"Staying awake!" I yelled back, struggling to be heard over the rudder's pneumatics.

"No! What are you doing on watch down here? You're an E-5! This watch is for E-4s and below!"

"Petty Officer Hammond has not been to bed in two days! I'm covering for him so that he can get a little sleep!"

Consistent with his character, Krause feigned outrage. "Did you run a request chit through me?"

I could not stop myself from shaking my head. "No, sir!"

"Why not?!?"

"There was no time! We just got done…"

The color rushed into the lieutenant's face. "That is no excuse! There are procedures in place for this kind of thing, and you're actively circumventing them! What time do you get relieved from this watch!"

"Zero four hundred!"

"And what time does your watch start in the EMO office tonight?"

"Zero four hundred!"

Krause looked like he was about to have a stroke. "SEE?!? YOU'RE GOING TO BE LATE! THIS IS UNACCEPTABLE! IT'S…"

It was too late for another Krause meltdown, so I let him rant. I tuned him out the best I could but still picked out that he was pulling Hammond out of his rack. Krause wanted him to assume what was left of his aft steering watch and wanted me to report to the EMO as soon as I was relieved.

It took Rick about twenty minutes to assume his station. The poor guy looked like hell. His hair was disheveled, his eyes were puffy and glazed, and he could barely stand on his feet. He staggered around like the village drunkard. "Rick!" I shouted to make sure I had his attention.

"What?"

"You've got a little more than a half-hour left on this watch! Do NOT sit down! Do you understand me? Stay standing!"

"Why?" Hammond asked.

"You'll never make it! You'll fall asleep! Stay on your feet!"

"Okay!"

If I could have, I would have stayed with Hammond to keep him occupied, but Krause ordered me to report back to the EMO. I left Rick and climbed a vertical ladder four decks from the bottom of the ship, then hiked up six more flights of stairs to the Electronic Materials Office. When I arrived, Darrow was waiting for me, rolling his bloodshot eyes in frustration. ET2 Cleveland was on the EMO watch, but since I was his relief, the master chief let Darius go early.

"You know, the lieutenant wants you written up again," Darrow told me.

I was hardly surprised. "For what this time?"

"He suspects that the SPS-40 was not maintained properly. That's why it broke."

"This is the first time that the SPS-40 has gone down since we left California. There was a surge on the incoming power line that blew an internal fuse. The fuse did its job and protected the equipment."

Darrow shrugged his shoulders. "I know. What about the Nixie?"

"I have no idea. Something failed in the transmission," I answered.

"Did you do the proper maintenance on that?"

I shook my head. "There is no maintenance for the winch. It's a depot-level overhaul requiring heavy equipment we don't have. My guess is that the civilian contractors screwed it up during our overhaul in Long Beach."

"And making an unauthorized change to the watch bill?"

I held up my hands in surrender. "Guilty. The bastard got me on that one. Rick's been up for two days straight. The man's a fucking zombie right now. If I don't get him some downtime, he's going to fall asleep while working on his equipment and zap himself. Master Chief, this is a safety thing."

Darrow agreed, "Yeah, that's a bad situation for him to be in. As usual, this is all bullshit. I'm not putting my name on a report chit for this."

"Thank you."

My master chief grabbed the watch bill and gave it a look. "Should I get someone down there to relieve Hammond now so he can get some rest?"

I glanced at my watch. It was 03:30. "At this point, why bother? It's going to be over in fifteen minutes anyway."

As if on cue, the IC line to the EMO started screaming. Even though I was the one on watch, Darrow answered it out of habit. He listened for a couple of seconds, and after responding with an "okay" and "I understand," he placed the handset back in its cradle. He then let out a long sigh of resignation and dropped his head into his hands. Something was wrong.

"What happened?" I asked.

My master chief shook his head. "The roving fire watch was patrolling the lower spaces. He caught Hammond asleep on his post."

Goddamn it! I told him not to fucking sit down!

"It's already been reported up the Engineering chain of command," Darrow continued. "Hammond's report chit will be on the captain's desk at reveille. There's nothing I can do about it."

*****

Darrow was right. There was nothing he could do. There was nothing any of us could do. Under the regime of Reaper Dick, sleeping on watch was a capital offense. If the Navy still allowed captains to keelhaul people for it, Darcy would have had Hammond dragged beneath the ship.

The captain's mast for Rick Hammond was held with industrial efficiency. Right after muster, Krause, Darrow, and I accompanied Hammond to the bridge where Darcy heard us out. I did most of the talking. I explained the day that Hammond had endured and my efforts to get him some rest by taking his watch. I emphasized, perhaps unwisely, Krause's role in undoing my efforts. Reaper Dick's expression never changed as I spoke. He sat in his chair like an Egyptian Pharaoh, staring at me with contemptuous eyes as I pled Rick's case for leniency.

"It sounds to me like you failed in managing your manpower, Petty Officer Murphy. If you'd been a better supervisor, you could have gotten your man the rest he should have had," the captain responded.

Fuck you. You're far more responsible for this than I am, you petty little prick. It took everything I had not to say that out loud.

Darcy was not a big man. He was on the short side for an officer and looked to be in his fifties. He had a gravelly voice and a wrinkled face. If Reaper Dick was not still a smoker, he had spent a lot of time as one. Unlike Captain Fleming, Darcy had never been an enlisted man. This surprised me because the way he carried himself was very blue-collar. The captain was a man who did not care about conversational niceties or projecting himself as refined. He cared only about being in charge and making sure everyone around him knew that he could destroy them on a whim. To press this point upon me, he leaned forward in his chair and said, "Maybe I should bust you instead of him."

It took a conscious effort, but I forced myself to stand my ground. "If it will help Petty Officer Hammond keep his rank, by all means, take mine."

Darrow glared at me, letting me know I was playing with fire. I already knew that, though. At that moment, I was tired of dealing with Krause and being responsible for other people. I was fine when I was an E-4. I knew I would be okay with being one again.

The captain squinted an eye at me. I caught sight of Krause trying to keep from smiling next to my master chief. He looked as if he were half-expecting the captain to order me flogged. "Would Radar Repair be a better shop if I took away one of your chevrons and fired your ass?"

"If you promoted Hammond in my place and put him in charge, it might."

"Because he's a better technician?" Captain Darcy asked.

I nodded. "Yes, sir. He absolutely is."

"How is he as a leader of men?"

"He's never been in a leadership position before," I answered, shrugging. "I'm sure he'd do fine. He sets a great example."

"Does he now?" the captain scoffed. "What kind of example does he set by sleeping on fucking watch?" Officers did not swear much in front of their subordinates. I had heard Reaper Dick did not practice much restraint in that regard, however. Now I knew it for a fact.

I tried to stammer out an answer, but Darcy cut me off. "Nice try, Murphy."

Reaper Dick stole a glance at the file the Master-At-Arms had given him. "Fireman Feeny!"

The young snipe who had stumbled across Hammond while on watch stepped forward. "Sir!"

“Tell me what happened with Petty Officer Hammond here.”

Feeny gave his report succinctly and without elaboration. He was all facts. FN Feeny climbed down the ladder and opened the hatch to aft steering. He saw Hammond sitting on the edge of the platform, resting his head in his hands. The fireman yelled out to him. Hammond did not answer. He waved his hand in front of Rick’s face. Hammond did not respond. He poked Hammond on the shoulder. Hammond leaned over against the bulkhead, still not recognizing the watch. When the fireman tried to shake him awake, Hammond opened his eyes briefly, then shut them again. Per his orders, Feeny called his watch supervisor and reported they had a man asleep on watch. Hammond was so out of it that he stayed asleep until HT1 Andrew Baker arrived to place him on report.

After Baker gave his account, the captain turned to Rick and asked if he had anything to add. Hammond replied, “No, sir. Everything’s been laid out exactly as it happened. I'd been awake for two days straight, and I fell asleep while on watch. That's all there is to it.”

As Hammond spoke, I could tell by his tone of voice that he sincerely believed nothing significant would happen to him. Yes, he had messed up. No man on that ship would have been able to stay awake on that watch after not sleeping for forty hours, though. I nearly dozed off after being awake for twenty. Darrow, Krause, and even the damn captain would have passed out down there under similar circumstances.

It was ludicrous that he had been on watch to begin with. Hammond could not comprehend that the captain would throw the book at him for not achieving the impossible.

“So, you take full responsibility for your actions?” asked Reaper Dick.

“I do,” answered Hammond.

“Okay. That’s commendable. Petty Officer Hammond, you are hereby reduced in rank to E3. You will forfeit half your pay for one month. I also sentence you to fifteen days restriction and fifteen days extra duty. You’re dismissed.” Rick’s reward for his honesty was being allowed to stay in the Navy. Reaper Dick threw the other men caught sleeping on watch right out of the service.

The sentence hit Hammond like a brick. He winced, tensed up, and looked like he would protest, but he was smart enough to know that doing so would only add to his troubles. He rendered the captain a crisp salute, dropped it when the captain reciprocated, then did an about-face and marched off the bridge with the Master-at-Arms. The rest of us walked out behind him.

I was pissed. Needing to lash out at someone, I turned to Fireman Feeny and mumbled, "Heaven help you if I ever catch you fucking up, asshole. You screwed over a damn good sailor."

Feeny stopped and turned to face me, waiting to speak until everyone else had passed. "What's your problem, dude? I did my job. I followed my orders, and I followed procedure. Hell, I tried to give him a break by shaking him awake, but he couldn't even come alive enough to realize he'd been caught. What if I'd left him there and somebody else nailed him? If he was so out of it that he didn't even remember me being there, well then, I'd be the one in front of the old man losing a hash mark for not doing my rounds."

"You could have…"

"I could have what? If the roles were reversed here and that guy caught me sleeping on watch under this captain's command, what would he have done?"

Feeny had me. If Hammond could not have awakened the guy, I would have told him to cover his ass and follow procedures. Especially with this captain. I could not give the young fireman an answer.

"Yeah, that's what I thought. If you want to blame someone for this, Murphy, blame your fucking lieutenant. He's the one that told me the guy down there was looking pretty tired and that I should check to make sure that he was still awake."

As Feeny stormed away, I stood there gobsmacked. The fireman was not responsible for what happened to my man. Krause was. As that realization sunk in, I felt myself starting to shake. Then my shock transformed into rage. There was no way that I was letting that son-of-a-bitch get away with what he did to Rick

Hammond. I realized for the first time that there was a high probability that I was not going to finish my enlistment without killing my division officer.

And I was angry enough at the time that I did not mean that figuratively.

*****

CHAPTER 5

Master Chief Darrow turned to me and asked, "How is Hammond doing?" We were in the SPN-35 dome, where no one could eavesdrop on us.

I shook my head in anger. "Not good. He's ruined. You know, that guy was a lifer. He was going to make a career out of the Navy. Rick would have gone far, too. Now, he's bitter. He wants off this ship and out of the Navy in the worst way possible."

Darrow frowned. "That's a fucking shame. You don't think he's going to get himself into any more trouble, do you? Pull some shit to get himself thrown out?"

Shrugging, I said, "I don't know. I don't think he'll want to jeopardize an honorable discharge, but I'm confident that we can kiss all of his extra-curricular initiatives goodbye. 'Hey Rick, we got a tough problem in Comm Repair. Can you take a look at this?' Fuck you. 'Hey Rick, the TV is on the fritz in the wardroom again. Can you check it out?' Fuck you. From now on, I'm betting that he'll only be working on his shit."

"That's really going to affect our readiness rating," my master chief groaned, shaking his head.

I nodded. “Yeah, it is. Hammond’s been carrying this division since he got here. I expect a twenty to thirty percent drop in equipment readiness almost immediately. Coupled with Reaper Dick knocking us down to three-section duty, I’m pretty sure it’s going to fall even further. Morale went right down the shitter as soon as we pulled back into Sasebo.”

Darrow took a long drag off of his cigarette. “Yeah, Krause hurt us big with that Hammond shit. The son-of-a-bitch is too stupid to realize that he hurt himself, too. Once he figures that out, I hope he’ll start backing off. The man's such a fucking idiot though that I'm not holding my breath on that prick wising up.” It was strange listening to my master chief disparage our division officer in front of me. Military men usually griped up the chain of command, not down it.

“Yeah, he ain’t backing off,” I quipped. “Now he’s riding Palazzo’s ass for kicks.”

“Palazzo?" Darrow grinned. "That must be fun to watch."

I shook my head again. “Not really. We still have work to do. Spanky is weak on the technical side, but he’s not hopeless. He’ll get the job done; it’s just going to take him three times longer than everyone else. Krause is rendering him completely useless, though. You know, the lieutenant busted in the other day and started screaming at Palazzo for his body fat. He ordered him to join the Fat Boys club and then dropped the guy to see if he could do enough sit-ups to pass PT.”

“Did he?” Darrow asked.

Shaking my head, I said, “Of course not. That sent Krause into hysterics again. He threatened to throw Spanky out of the service if he fails his fitness test in a couple of months. The lieutenant was slurring again, too. You ever check to see if he was hiding booze in the EMO?”

Darrow nodded. “I did. I couldn’t find anything, though. You know, I’m noticing it also, but I can’t smell it on his breath. If only he’d take those sunglasses off so I could see his eyes…”

“You think he’s drinking vodka?” I wondered.

“He could be.”

I caught myself gritting my teeth. "I swear, after what that son-of-a-bitch did to Rick, I'm going to fuck that guy over if it's the last thing I do."

Darrow glowered at me. "Look, Doyle, we need to change the subject and get you focused on the task at hand. Do NOT let yourself get distracted by that prick. You need to focus on what needs doing tonight. Do you understand? I'm sorry. I should never have brought it up."

My master chief slipped his gloves on and pulled an envelope out of his shirt. Not letting me touch it, he tucked it into the inside pocket of my motorcycle jacket. "This a new look for you. Nice coat."

I had a rather impressive collection of Hawaiian shirts. Generally, I would wear those with cargo shorts and deck shoes. Japan was a little colder than San Diego, however, so I reverted to my punk rock days of wearing denim and leather. "Yeah, this jacket's been through a lot with me."

"You have gloves? I wiped everything in that envelope down. I did the outside too. Don't get your fingerprints on anything."

"Yeah, you told me," I assured Darrow.

"The envelope contains everything they need to find a sample of what Tejada's trying to sell. Even if they don't speak English at all, it will lead them right to it. Whatever you do, don't let them open that envelope in front of you. You want to be able to deny knowing what we're dealing with here, so you don't want to know where I hid the thing. Okay?"

"Okay."

"What are you going to tell them?" Darrow asked.

"That a friend in the Philippines asked me to reach out to them. He says he has something that they may be interested in. I have a map to a sample, and after they've seen what I'm offering, I can arrange a meeting. I'll tell them I'm not authorized to negotiate. All I can do is set up the meeting with an interested party."

My master chief stared at me for a minute. "You ready for this?"

"Not really," I said. "But I've committed to it, so let's get it over with."

Darrow lifted himself to his feet with a nod and then held his hand out to help me up. "Yup. Let's get it over with. If this works out, we won't have to worry about that cocksucker Krause anymore."

"You know," I added. "If it doesn't work out, I won't have to worry about him either. We're going to have much bigger problems."

*****

"Doyle?" I was approaching Albuquerque Bridge when I heard Yukiko Fukuyama call out to me. "Is that you?"

I was still wincing when I turned toward her voice. I remembered the last time I saw her, cowering in a corner, naked and crying, screaming at me to get away from her. Four months had passed, but I still cringed when I thought about it. She looked better now, gorgeous as always, but tentative. Yukiko was usually full of confidence, but she was keeping her distance from me. "Hi, Yukiko," I called out to her. "How are you?"

Bobbing her head a couple of times, she told me that she was alright. Yukiko had spent significant time in the US, much of it as an exchange student at the University of Alabama. Her English was perfect but had an odd hint of a southern accent that was out of place in Japan. "How are you doing? Are you okay?"

"I am now," I said. I had not seen Yukiko since I attacked her in my sleep during one of my episodes. "Listen, Yukiko. I'm so sorry about what happened. I…"

"You know, I've been thinking about that a lot lately…"

I cringed again. "I can't stop thinking about it myself."

Yukiko crossed her arms. "Doyle, what was that?"

I let out a long sigh. "It's a long story. After what I did to you, I owe you an explanation, though. Can I buy you a drink?"

Yukiko looked like she was going to decline and make up an excuse to keep walking. Her curiosity won out over her apprehension, though. She agreed to sit down with me.

Bars in Japan were small, but there was one nearby large enough to have tables out of the barmaids' earshot. While there, I told Yukiko how my father murdered my family. Using generalities that would not violate any security classification, I also told her about the girl I got killed in El Salvador. After that, I described how I crippled Randy Green, causing his wife to return to a life of prostitution in the Philippines. I left out the part about Rafaela trying to have me murdered because of that and how I was forced to blow a young boy's brains out to protect myself. I also avoided letting her know that a Philippine policeman I was going into business with probably executed her for it.

I let Yukiko know how I almost got Warren Macklemore and myself killed by a corrupt police officer in Tijuana. I told her how bad they beat us in the desert. I spared her the details about how I watched that officer later get drowned by his rivals just offshore from the Coronado Islands. I did not have to tell her about David Miller getting beaten to death. She was there for that one.

"My master chief thinks I have PTSD, a form of shell shock," I said to Yukiko. "I've been dealing with the flashbacks my whole life. It was manageable when it was just my family, but it got worse after returning from Central America. It's getting even more difficult now. Look, I'm sorry I didn't have the time to explain all this to you before we spent the night together, but everything happened pretty fast. I didn't have time."

Yukiko stared at me like she could not believe what I had told her. "How is that possible? You're twenty-three years old! How does someone so young go through so much?"

Shrugging, I took a drink of my beer. "I've thought about that. It can all stem back to what my father did. What happened then was like a baptism of violence. It put this seed of rage in me that has to come out every once in a while. I guess it's my punishment for driving my old man to kill my family."

"You think you're responsible for that? That's ridiculous! You were only thirteen!"

I shrugged. "That man never laid a finger on my sister. He also doted on my baby brother. It was me that he took his demons out on. And my mother when she stepped in to stop him. What he did might not have been my fault, but that doesn't mean that I didn't have anything to do with it."

I shuddered as I thought back to El Salvador. "That girl in Central America, though? That shit was all me. When I saw what those soldiers were doing to her, I lost control. That led to her discovery and was the reason those animals needed to get rid of her."

Yukiko shook her head. "They would have killed her anyway. If you did anything, you shortened her suffering."

"I took away any chance she may have had to escape."

My hands were trembling. To calm them down, I downed over half of my beer in a single drink and ordered another. "Randy Green, I lost control again. That rage hit me while I was beating him, and I took it too far. Way too far. What happened to Rafaela was a direct result of that too." *So was the kid I killed in Olongapo.*

"And the boy we saw beat to death in the park last year?" Yukiko asked. "How was that your fault?"

I thought for a moment as one of the barmaids walked over with my beer. Shaking my head, I answered, "I guess that one was just dumb luck."

"Have you ever tried to get help for this stuff, Doyle? Have you been to a psychologist?"

Ill at ease, I again emptied the bottle before me of half its contents before placing it back on the table. "Nope. I wouldn't dare."

"Why not?"

"With the new captain that we have, they could construe it as malingering. Also, getting diagnosed with any psychological condition is an express ticket home."

Yukiko helped herself to one of my cigarettes. After lighting it, she asked, "You told me you were getting out of the Navy anyway. So what if they send you back to the US early?"

Leaning back in my seat, I said, "Who says I want to go back to the United States? I don't have anything back there but bad memories and an old motorcycle. I think I'd enjoy a whole new start in a whole new country."

"Here in Japan?"

I shook my head. "Nah, too expensive, and there's no way I would be comfortable here as a *gaijin*."

Yukiko nodded. "It's very difficult to be successful here as a foreigner. Do you have another place in mind?"

I did not think it prudent to tell Yukiko about my plans in the Philippines, so I said, "I'm keeping my options open."

Yukiko tried to bring the conversation back to getting me help. "Doyle, have you ever tried meditation? For your issues?"

Shaking my head, I said, "Not really. Isn't that a Buddhist thing?"

Yukiko nodded.

"No, thanks. After what happened to my family, I quit believing in God. If I'm wrong and He is out there in the cosmos somewhere, I don't fucking like Him."

"There is no god in Buddhism, Doyle."

That surprised me. "Seriously? A religion without a god?"

Yukiko took a sip of her beer. "You westerners call Buddhism a religion. We don't. It's a way of being, a way to find peace within chaos. Buddhists don't say whether there is a god or there isn't. It's irrelevant. For us, life is suffering, and the goal of Buddhism is to reduce suffering. We do this through meditation and mindfulness."

Finishing my beer, I showed Yukiko my empty bottle. "I do it with alcohol."

"Do you?" Yukiko asked. She knew what I said was a joke, but she sensed an opening. "Is it working?"

I looked at my bottle. "No, my beer is empty, and now I'm suffering."

Yukiko allowed herself to smile. "You know, there is no missionary tradition in Buddhism. There's no church to support, so there's no motivation for us to scare up converts to fill collection plates. I'm not trying to make you a Buddhist. I just want to help you, Doyle. I went to a *guru* after I saw that boy get killed in the park. It helped me a lot. It helped me to understand. Maybe it will help you too. Do you want to try?"

I looked at Yukiko. She was so pretty. It may have been the three beers I had, but I wanted her. If meditating with Yukiko increased my odds of sleeping with her again, I was all for it. "Sure," I said. "It can't hurt. I'd love to try."

Smiling, Yukiko gathered her things and stood up to leave. "I still have the number to the ship. I'll leave a message for you once I talk to my guy. Okay?" She then held her hand out to me.

"Do we have to do that?" I asked, still sitting down.

"Do what?"

"Shake hands. We've slept together. How about a hug?"

Yukiko's smile broadcasted a hint of mischief. She stuck her hand at me a little more forcefully, though. "We shake. I like you, Doyle, and I want to help you. For now, we're friends, okay?"

Her eyes said, *In other words, we'll give things another chance if I'm convinced that you won't try to kill me in my sleep again.*

I could not blame her. She had every reason to be cautious after what I had done to her. Standing up, I shook her hand and watched as she walked out of the bar. When she was gone, I sat down and had two more beers.

I still had some courage to work up before I tried to approach the *yakuza.*

*****

In southwest Detroit, there was a bowling alley in the middle of the city's vast industrial wasteland. It was one of the last remnants of what had once been a thriving Italian community that had been largely devoured by an ever-expanding oil refinery. An homage to the area's glory days of the 1950s, the Oakwood Blue Jackets had a bar in the back that catered to the lost sons of Europe's boot. Most of its customers were older men who had been going there for thirty years. I briefly worked there while attending high school. While the mafia did not exactly run the back bar, I knew who I could place illegal bets with there had I possessed the inclination.

If I learned one thing about mobsters back home, it was that they kept irregular hours. It was a trait shared by the Japanese mob. I found myself wondering if organized crime was a worldwide career path that catered to people who just had difficulty getting up in the morning. I waited for my *yakuza* men so long in the noodle restaurant across from the *pachinko* parlor that the shop closed on me. I ended up sitting on a bench, drinking beer from a vending machine, watching business after business shutter their doors.

I did not realize how suspicious I looked until I met the gaze of the *pachinko* parlor's cashier, who noticed me eye-balling his business. Watching for the mob from inside a noodle restaurant was discreet. Sitting on a bench across from the front door of the place, six beers in the bag and bloated from three servings of *yakisoba*, was not. As the cashier went back to his desk to make a phone call, I decided I had blown the job for the night and it was time to go home.

First, I needed a bathroom. That was a quest that ended in a KFC franchise open absurdly late for Japan, especially considering how far off the *ginza* it was. Still feeling the effects of all the beer I drank, I ended up lost, wandering around parts of Sasebo that I had never seen before. After forty minutes of trekking about the city's outskirts, I ended up almost back to where I started.

It was very late on a weekday, and though well lit, the ginza stood deserted. The only business open that time of night was the *pachinko* parlor. It was the closest thing to a casino Japan had. As I passed, I took a look inside and spotted a pair of *yakuza* men talking to the cashier I saw earlier. A bit overexcited, I stepped in and tried to get the gangsters' attention. "*Sumimasen*!" I called out, slurring the Japanese word for, "Excuse me." I startled them. They both briskly marched behind the counter and ducked into a back room.

As the mobsters disappeared, the cashier stepped forward to intercept me. "Solly! Solly!" he said in accented English. "No foreigners arrowed in here! Prease reave! Prease reave now!"

I tried to answer the cashier in Japanese but forgot the words. "Hey, can I ask those guys a couple of questions! I…"

"You go!" The cashier held up his hands and started guiding me towards the door. When I tried to dig my feet in to stop him, he gave me a shove.

"Hey!" I called out, stumbling backward. "Come on, man, I just want to talk!"

"No! You go now!" Before I could regain my balance, the cashier pushed me again, nearly sending me to the ground. I retreated a couple of steps to regroup and shove back, but I was far too predictable. The cashier picked up his gait and, while I was still hunched over, thrust his foot into my side hard enough to send me rolling out of the exit. Once I was lying on the ground outside, he slid the glass door closed and locked it. "You go! I carr porice!"

I rolled over and sat up, staring at the *pachinko* parlor in disbelief at how badly I fucked up my first attempt to meet a Japanese gangster. I nodded at the cashier and waved my hand at him. "Okay, okay. I'm going. I'm sorry. *Gomen nasai*."

After getting to my feet, I bowed low to show the proper amount of contrition. I then straightened up and tried to walk away, only to run into a young man standing to my side with his arms crossed. He said something in Japanese too fast for me to understand. I did pick out a part about "venerable elders" or something to that effect. I guessed he was chastising me for bothering the old people.

"Yeah, yeah," I said in response, trying to walk away from him. I was a little too drunk to understand Japanese. I just wanted to get home, but the kid was not going to let me.

I guessed the young man to be a few years younger than I was. Wearing jeans and a sweater, he dressed far more casually than most Japanese and was far more aggressive as well. If I stepped left, he jumped right in my way. When I stepped right, he did the same—chattering at me incessantly. After the fourth time dealing with this little guy blocking my retreat, I reached out and tried to move him out of my way. That was a painful mistake. In a flash, that kid had my wrist bent and my elbow twisted. He then knocked my feet out from beneath me and sent me hurtling toward the concrete face first.

"All right, goddammit," I told him as I picked myself up and dusted my clothes off. "I get it. I fucked up. I apologized, and now I'm on my way."

The kid stood firm. He crossed his arms, scowled at me, and asked, "*Nandeshou*?" Finally, it was something I understood. He asked me what I wanted.

"*Hanashitai*," I answered. I want to talk.

"*Nani ni tsuite hanashitaidesu ka*?"

I was not sure, but I thought he was asking me what I wanted to talk about. It became evident that the kid was associated with the *yakuza* men in some way. The problem was that the hoodlum looked like he was seventeen years old. It was hard to take him seriously. There was no way that I would divulge what I had to offer to someone who may not even have graduated high school yet. "*Īe, yakuza to no mi hanashimasu.*" I told him I would only talk to the mob.

The kid did not like this. He chattered some more stuff at me that I could not decipher. When I interrupted to tell him I did not understand, he slapped me across the face. I looked at him in shock and tried to warn him not to do that again. "*Nidoto suru...*"

Before I could finish, he slapped me again. Almost by instinct, I reached out and grabbed him by the shirt. I pulled him in close and slammed my forehead into his nose. That was the only hit I got in.

In a move that would be the envy of any major league hockey player, the kid grabbed my jacket and pulled it over my head so that I could not see. I could not move my arms either. I was defenseless, and the kid had his way with me. I took several brutal shots to the kidneys and got kicked in the knees so hard that I thought that they were going to snap. He also knocked the wind out of me several times over. There was nothing I could do about it. I took elbows to the temple, had my feet swept out from beneath me, and suffered a kick to the groin every time I tried to get back up.

The scary part about the whole ordeal was that the kid did not even sound angry. He was playing with me, having fun. For as much pain as he caused, he was not breaking any of my bones, nor was he doing any real damage. He was just getting off on showing the *gaijin*, a barbarian twice his size, who was boss.

Eventually, the cashier opened the door to the *pachinko* parlor and yelled at the kid to stop. That resulted in a terse exchange between the two that ended with my jacket getting ripped the rest of the way off so the punk could see me. As I was lying on the ground, gasping for breath, the kid laughed. "*Baka-yarō*," he told me. That was the Japanese equivalent of "Fuck you."

All I could do in response was pant and try to get my breath back.

Tired of waiting for me to reply, the kid lifted my jacket into the air as if it were a trophy before telling me, "*Sutekina jaketto*." Nice coat. It was the last thing he said before walking off with it.

Once the kid was gone, I sat myself up and tried to get my nose to stop bleeding. The cashier from the *pachinko* parlor threw me a small package of tissue paper. He looked surprised. "Where you coat?" he asked.

"With that fucking Kato kid," I snapped, wondering if they ever showed the Green Hornet in Japan for him to get the reference.

"He stear you coat?"

"Yeah, he stole my coat." I was a bit perplexed. The cashier did not seem fazed by me getting my ass kicked, but when it came to my stolen jacket, he was doing an awful lot of hand-wringing.

Then I remembered what was in my jacket. That kid now had the envelope that Master Chief Darrow had given me. That caused me to do an awful lot of hand-wringing myself.

*****

CHAPTER 6

At first, I was unsure if the expression on Master Chief Darrow's face was fear or anger. It was probably a combination of both. "You let him take the jacket?!?"

"I didn't let him do shit," I snapped back. "This kid was like a cross between Bruce Lee and Gordie Howe. I thought I was being mugged by some ninja power forward from the Detroit Red Wings. What are we going to do?"

Darrow began pacing around the SPN-35 dome. "That's a damn good question. What time did all this shit happen last night?"

"About eleven. Maybe midnight." I slid down the wall of the dome and took a seat on the floor. My knees were still sore from the abuse they took the night before.

Darrow looked relieved. "Then I doubt that they had time to do anything with it yet. I need to get out there and move it. I'll do that as soon as it gets dark."

"Do you need my help?" I asked.

The master chief shook his head. "Shit, I would love to have you out there watching my back, but I don't want you anywhere near the merchandise now."

"Master Chief," I asked. "What do you think is going to come of this?"

Darrow sighed. "Best case? That kid has no idea what he's looking at and throws everything away. He walks around town, impressing all the girls wearing your leather jacket."

"That kid was half my size. My jacket's going to wear like a dress on him."

"Who gives a fuck what he looks like," Darrow snapped. "You know what the worst-case scenario is? That kid's only a wannabee and he beat your ass to impress the big guys in the *pachinko* parlor. He opens the envelope, follows the clues, and finds the weapon I've stashed out there. Correctly guessing that he's in over his head, he goes to the fucking cops."

I buried my face in my hands. "Is there anything in between?"

Leaning up against the radar antenna, Darrow lost himself in thought for a few minutes. Shrugging, he then said, "Maybe the kid finds the weapon and turns it over to the *yakuza*. They accept it, no questions asked."

"You think that's possible?"

The master chief shook his head. "Hell no."

My heart sank. "We're fucked, aren't we?"

"Probably," Darrow told me. After a few more moments of thought, he added, "But maybe not. Look, if this kid is trying to impress the mob, or better yet, is already working with them, he's got a pretty serious piece of hardware now. He's not going to want to give it up. Or, if he turns it over to the *yakuza*, they're not going to want to get rid of it, either. Even if they're not interested in a deal, they're going to want the police to stay out of it."

"So, maybe we should cut our losses and let it go?"

Darrow shook his head. "No, I need to move it. We can't just throw a submachine gun onto Japan's streets and hope everything works out for the best. I'm going to take care of it. Tonight."

*****

Master Chief Darrow almost made it off of the ship. As he walked toward the quarterdeck, the Officer of the Deck strung a chain across the gangplank's entrance. He then held up his hand for everyone to stand fast. The Petty Officer of the Watch picked up the microphone and announced that liberty had been secured for the entire crew. Even the personnel already ashore were being called back.

Darrow walked over to the Officer of the Deck and asked what was going on. OSC Wallace shrugged his shoulders. "I don't know. Whatever it is, it's big. The captain's on his way back to the ship and everything's locked down until the Naval Investigative Service gets here." Though it had been renamed the Naval Criminal Investigative Service the year before, the agency's new name was not widely used in the fleet yet in 1993.

We had little information to go on for the next four hours. Darrow and I huddled in the radar dome, certain that we were screwed. We did our best to formulate a plan out of our predicament, but we came up empty. Finally, I told Darrow, "If they come after me, I'm just going to play stupid. This is why we kept the samples separate from setting up the meeting, isn't it? I don't know where anything was hidden, so no one can tie me to the location. I was never there, right?"

"Right," Darrow replied. "What are you going to say about the envelope?"

"What envelope? I don't know shit about any envelope," I responded, pretending to be under questioning.

My master chief ran with it. "Some kid said he pulled it out of your jacket." Darrow assumed the role of an interrogator.

"My jacket? I got mugged last night and some punk stole it."

"Mugged? In Japan?" the master chief laughed in disbelief. "There's no street crime here."

I lifted my shirt and showed Darrow the fresh bruises on my ribs. "Oh yeah? I beg to fucking differ."

Darrow winced. "Ouch. That kid did that to you?"

"Like I said, Master Chief, he was a pint-sized Bruce Lee."

"Explain the mugging," Darrow ordered, getting back into character.

"I had a lot to drink last night. I was walking through the *ginza,* and the only thing open was a *pachinko* parlor. I never played before, so I thought I'd give it a try. When I tried to ask the gentlemen up by the cash register how to play, though, they freaked and threw me out. They told me that foreigners weren't allowed…"

"You know," Darrow interrupted. "*Pachinko* parlors are off-limits to American military personnel."

I feigned surprise. "No shit? Why?"

"To discourage gambling."

"To discourage gambling? There're slot machines in the base club for Christ's sake!"

"The base is American territory. Gambling is illegal in Japan. *Pachinko* parlors are notorious for being tied to organized crime."

I looked quizzically at my master chief, cocking my head to one side. "You don't say?"

Darrow cracked up. "Doyle, if we get out of this, I'm going to see to it you get an Oscar. You're pretty good at this."

My actual screen test came at about midnight. One of the lower-ranking Masters-at-Arms pulled me out of my rack and led me to a ready room on the 04 Level. When I stepped inside, I was met by two stern federal agents. One was in a suit, the other in jeans and a polo shirt. At the sight of them, all the preparation I did with Master Chief Darrow flew right out the window. My knees went weak, my throat went dry, and I could feel my palms get clammy. After introducing myself, I was told to sit down.

Special Agent Koch, the one in the polo shirt, got right to the point. "I hear you have a reputation as something of a badass, Petty Officer Murphy. You like beating people up?"

"No," I answered.

Special Agent Bremmer was the one in the suit. He was holding my service record. "It says in your jacket that you nearly beat a man to death aboard this ship about a year and a half ago."

"You didn't ask if I ever beat someone up. You asked if I enjoyed it."

"Don't get smart, Murphy," Koch said. I suspected he was the one playing bad cop. "I heard from your division officer that there were likely others too. Men that you roughed up before the guy you almost killed."

"Krause reported aboard the *Belleau Wood* months after the incident with Randy Green. I don't know how he would have firsthand knowledge of that. I don't know how much time you spent around that man, but I would encourage getting to know him better. You're putting a lot of stock in his credibility."

"He said you were also involved in a couple of shootings in the Philippines," Bremmer told me.

Shaking my head, I replied, "And that would be my Exhibit A if I was laying out Krause's credibility issues in court. My master chief and I were in a bar that got held up by a meth addict. He was shot by an off-duty cop. There was also a gang shootout a few blocks from my apartment in Olongapo. That was close enough to where I lived that Krause thought I was involved in that one too." I swallowed uncomfortably. There would be many more questions raised if it came out that the same Philippine police sergeant was involved in both incidents.

It never did. After a half-hour of background questions, the two NCIS agents finally got to the point. "How do you feel about gay sailors, Petty Officer Murphy?" Agent Koch asked.

"Come again?" I had been bracing myself for questions about a submachine gun that somehow found its way to Sasebo from the Philippines. The last thing I was expecting was to be quizzed about my views on homosexuality.

Bremmer rephrased the question. "Do you have a problem with fags, Murphy?"

I shrugged. "I'm not sure how I feel about them. On one hand, thinking about what they do is disgusting. On the other, I've heard some straight guys bragging about what they did in the Philippines that made me queasy too." ET3 Kent had a story about some steel balls on a string that came to mind.

Agent Koch glowered at me. "Do you know RP3 Dwayne Banham, Petty Officer Murphy?"

I shook my head. An RP would have been a religious program specialist, an assistant to the ship's chaplain. There was not an area on that boat that I was less familiar with than the chapel. I did not even know where it was. I explained all that to the NCIS agents.

"Are you sure that you don't know Banham?" Agent Bremmer asked. "He's about five-foot-nine, blonde hair, super skinny, kind of effeminate?"

I shook my head. "There's nine-hundred men aboard this ship. I know a whole bunch of them, but not that one. I take it he's gay? And you think I have some knowledge of it? I'm pretty enthusiastically straight myself." Even if that man was a homosexual, being gay was hardly the level of offense that would warrant a lockdown of the crew and NCIS involvement.

"We have no evidence that he's queer. In fact, he's married and has a couple of kids," Koch told me. "I've met him, though. I can see how a group of guys could mistake him for a homosexual and start kicking his ass down in the chapel."

"What? A *group* of guys beat this kid up because they thought he was gay?" Being queer might not warrant the attention of the NCIS, but a hate crime would. "Five months after David Miller's murder? Are you serious?"

"Yeah, we're serious," Bremmer said. "And your lieutenant told us it sounded like something you would do."

I rolled my eyes. "Sir, are you aware that I was one of the people who found David Miller, the guy who got beat to death in Nimitz Park for being gay? I held his brains in his head while we carried him over the Albuquerque Bridge."

"I read that," Bremmer admitted. "We've got to cover all angles, though. Where were you at eighteen hundred hours today?"

"In my shop, working."

"Are there any witnesses?" Koch asked.

"Yeah, pretty much everybody. We were chasing our tails on PMS spot checks that the EMO was dissatisfied with. Every one of my men passed through the shop, asking if they could be excused long enough to go to chow. So did the entirety of my divisional chain of command, checking on our progress. That would be Chief Ramirez, Master Chief Darrow…"

I could not help myself. I started grinning. "…and even that idiot who suggested that this attack looked like something I would do. At 18:00, I was stuck on the 07 Level being screamed at by Lieutenant Junior Grade Krause."

The NCIS questioned me for over an hour before they were satisfied that I had nothing to do with the assault of RP3 Banham. I breezed through the interrogation, relieved that it had nothing to do with an automatic weapon or the Japanese mob. I was calm and collected throughout the entire ordeal. Master Chief Darrow, however, was a mess. Even though it was two a.m. before I made it back to the SPN-35 dome to decompress, he was there waiting for me.

"Thank fucking god," Darrow exhaled after I let him know that the lockdown of the *USS Belleau Wood* had nothing to do with us. Still, he only relaxed a little bit. "We're not completely out of the woods. I've got an MP5 I need to move, but I can't get off the fucking ship!"

That was something that was not going to be rectified soon. We figured out that locking down the *USS Belleau Wood* had little to do with the assault on RP3 Banham. It was more about controlling information. David Miller's murder made national headlines and resulted in the firing of Captain Fleming. Reaper Dick was taking no chances with having his career implode because word of this incident got out and created another journalistic maelstrom. No excuse on earth would get Darrow off of the ship to do what needed to be done.

According to Banham, he was beaten by five sailors wearing balaclavas and dungarees without name or rank insignias on them. He said that they did not speak much. Not only could Banham not identify his assailants by sight, but he could not identify them by voice, either. Still, by the time the sun rose, the NCIS had obtained confessions from two men and were working them over to figure out the identities of the other three.

Reaper Dick put out the call to his officers in the interim to shake the tree and shake it hard. He wanted all the rotten apples to fall from it. He sought to make life aboard the *USS Belleau Wood* so miserable that the other perpetrators would give themselves up to make it stop. It was a directive that Lieutenant Krause carried out with gusto.

*****

Breakfast was interrupted by an all-hands fire drill. Few of us got to eat. After quarters, Krause tore through our spaces, looking for discrepancies to gig us on. He was not able to find many, so he manufactured enough to justify his ill temperament. After a fire drill for the duty section, the lieutenant started giving more random PMS spot checks. He wanted to catch us gun-decking our maintenance records.

At sixteen hundred hours, we started making ourselves scarce. Because he had to climb ladders and access the weather decks to get to it, Krause usually overlooked the SPN-35 dome when hunting for people. Knowing this, Metaire, Hammond, Dixie, and I sought refuge there. ET3 Kent crawled through the porthole in the back of the radar repair shop and used test equipment padding to make himself a nice little bed back there. He then caught a couple of hours of shut-eye. Palazzo went to his fan room at the back of Radar Room One.

After dinner, Krause came looking for us. He first went to the shop and pounded on the door for several minutes. Kent never heard him over the din of the WSC-3 radios he was sleeping behind. Convinced that we were all ignoring him, the lieutenant called the chief's mess and had Ben Ramirez come all the way up with a key to prove that Radar Repair was empty. Krause then charged down to the berthing area to see if we were in our racks. Finding them unoccupied, he went to the well deck to check the Nixie spaces but found them secured. Infuriated, the lieutenant charged back up to the island structure, determined to make someone pay for forcing him to chase us.

He went to Radar Room Two on the 06 Level. There, Krause accused the fire control technicians of hiding us. The lieutenant then charged across the passageway and barged into Communications Repair. Our LPO got an earful about not keeping track of his radar technicians.

From there, Krause marched to the 07 Level to pound on the shop door one more time to make sure we had not come back. Bypassing Radar Room Three, he threw open the door to Radar One only to find it still unoccupied as well. Not wanting to leave any stone unturned, our lieutenant marched across the space to the fan room. With speed born of rage and fury, he ripped back the handle to disengage the watertight fitting and kicked open the hatch, rushing inside. There, he hit the jackpot.

Everybody in the Combat Systems Department knew that John Palazzo had issues. The men of the CSE division were even more familiar with them. We all knew what Palazzo tended to do to himself when he was under stress, and we were all aware of where he did it. You did not walk into the fan room at the back of Radar Room One without knocking first. Somehow, our EMO never got that message.

The way I heard it, Krause barged in on John Palazzo just as he was reaching the moment of truth. Palazzo was standing there monkey-faced with his pants around his knees and sweat pouring off his chin. He had his dick gripped tightly in his left hand, ready to blow. Startled, Spanky swung to his left to see who was walking in on him right when he started to climax.

Finding himself face-to-face with our division officer, Palazzo tried to hold everything in. That was biologically impossible, however, and all he did was build up an insane amount of pressure before letting everything go. When Spanky fired, he grossly overshot the tissue he was holding. The man squirted himself right up the side of the HVAC unit so hard that some of it ricocheted and landed on the lieutenant's trousers.

And just like that, I was no longer the primary focus of Lieutenant Krause's attention.

Now, getting caught masturbating by your division officer is never a good career move. Accidentally masturbating *on* your division officer is a criminal offense, however. That said, I'm not exactly sure which article of the Uniform Code of Military Justice that it was a violation of, but it did not matter. There was no way Spanky was getting away with that one.

The meltdown was epic. Krause's screaming could be heard all across three floors of the island structure. Chief Morris, who was in charge of the AGs next door to Radar Repair, ran in to intervene, convinced that there was a murder in progress. It was so loud that even Reaper Dick, who was on the bridge two decks below them, sent someone up to investigate.

Word of what happened spread like wildfire. The entire crew was on board, so all nine hundred men caught some version of the event before they went to bed that night. Even though we worked with Palazzo, I was one of the last people in my division to find out about it. Sequestered in the SPN-35 dome, listening to the radio and chain-smoking with my men, it was not until Master Chief Darrow tracked us down that I found out. Still, it took more than ten minutes for him even to begin to tell us what happened. He was laughing too hard to talk.

Darrow eventually got it out, and by the time he finished the account, all of us in the dome were roaring. I was in the fetal position on the floor, laughing so hard that no sound was coming out. My ribs, which that Kato kid had cracked a couple of nights before, were screaming in pain.

It took us at least fifteen minutes to settle down. Once we did, Darrow wiped the tears from his eyes and said, "Doyle, you've got to put Spanky on report."

"Under what charge?" I cried.

Darrow started cracking up once more, which set us all off again. "I have no fucking clue," the master chief admitted.

"I can't do it!" I exclaimed when I caught my breath.

"What? I thought you were waiting for a day like this," Darrow said.

"I was, but I can't bust Palazzo for cumming on the lieutenant. That's the kind of shit that deserves a fucking medal!"

*****

It took the NCIS another day to get a third confession in the assault of RP3 Dwayne Banham. Unsatisfied with the investigation's progress, Reaper Dick ordered the trio off of the ship in shackles. He allowed Banham the satisfaction of confronting the men before they disembarked, however. Confronted by the sight of three scared men, in handcuffs and facing years in a federal prison, Banham buckled. He confessed that the whole thing was a hoax. He told the NCIS that he made the story up, hoping to transfer to another command. He wanted to get as far away from Captain Darcy as he possibly could.

Banham got his wish. The command ensured that he was physically removed from the ship for his own protection before anyone knew what he had done. We never heard from him again. The captain made sure that the NCIS men were gone, too. Many of the *Belleau Wood's* sailors wondered how the agents got three men to confess to a crime that never even occurred.

Though the Banham incident never got to the press, word of the confessions got out around the base. After that, no one connected to the Sasebo naval station in any way would even consider talking to them without a lawyer present.

Free at last, I ordered Spanky to remove his pornography from the fan room once and for all. After it got dark, I then went for a walk, planning to meet my master chief at the *ginza* beer garden later. On my way there, I passed by a toy store and remembered that Mari had a birthday coming up. Walking in, I started looking at the Hello Kitty merchandise, wondering if that was a little young for a Filipina girl turning nine years old. After seeing a couple of young ladies in their twenties walking by in Hello Kitty tee-shirts, I guessed it was not.

Looking at the apparel, I was surprised by how much variety there was to the Hello Kitty franchise. There were shirts, skirts, shoes, backpacks, and jeans. In the back, I spotted what I assumed was Hello Kitty intimate apparel. I even saw the Hello Kitty boxer shorts that Darrow's girlfriend had given him back in Olongapo.

I smiled, thinking about that day. Bard and Darrow got into an argument over the merits of serving on surface ships versus submarines. Both were drunk, and during the disagreement, Darrow pantsed our LPO, tossing his shorts out into the street. Bard returned the favor and revealed our master chief's Hello Kitty boxers to the entire division. Darrow's girlfriend was beside herself in laughter. Lorna bought the underwear as a joke and only convinced her man to wear them that morning.

After spending nearly a hundred dollars on an outfit to ship back to Olongapo, I hiked back to the *ginza*. Despite trying not to, I glanced inside the *pachinko* parlor as I passed. A different cashier was working, and the Kato kid was nowhere to be seen. I got by it without incident.

When I arrived at the beer garden, Master Chief Darrow was already there. After getting myself a drink and an order of *tempura*, I took a seat across from him. "That was quick," I said. "Well?"

Darrow shook his head. "There was nothing for me to do. The weapon's gone."

I took a deep breath. "What does that mean? Is it good? Is it bad? Indifferent?"

Full of uncertainty and resigned to fate, my master chief shrugged. "Honestly, Doyle, I don't have the slightest idea."

*****

CHAPTER 7

From a career standpoint, ejaculating on a commissioned officer in the US Navy would be about as close as one could get to hitting rock bottom. John Palazzo had no idea how much further he had yet to sink, though. Reaper Dick did not fast-track Spanky's captain's mast like he did Rick Hammond's. Darcy let it simmer, making sure that the word got out around the men about what happened. The skipper then judged Palazzo during an open mast in the hangar bay, before the entire crew. His punishment was more about humiliation than about the loss of rank, money, or liberty.

Palazzo's mast was hard to watch. I had never been a fan of the guy, but I could not help but feel sorry for him. Everyone heard the story, so Spanky was standing before a massive audience. There, the captain forced him to describe in detail what happened in the radar fan room. The crew roared with laughter several times, especially when Krause delivered his account of what happened. There were times that even Reaper Dick could not keep a straight face.

Probably because the spectacle so entertained him, Darcy went easy on Spanky Palazzo. The old man only busted him down to an E-4 and spared him the usual restriction, extra duty, and forfeiture of pay. Palazzo did not feel lucky, though. He emerged from captain's mast a broken man. Incapable of curbing the behavior that landed him in so much trouble, he started abusing himself with even more gusto than before. It was his only source of comfort.

With that in mind, when I entered the fan room to do the filter maintenance, I knocked before I opened the hatch. Though relieved to find it unoccupied, I was irritated to discover that the space was still cluttered with the division's personal gear. Palazzo's porn was finally gone, but the compartment was full of clothing, sports gear, and even furniture from the Philippines. It was a major chore to get to the filter access panels on the HVAC's far side.

When I finally got to where I needed to be, I found that Spanky made himself a little hiding place behind all that junk, wholly hidden from view. There were foam cushions on the deck, a blanket, and even a pillow. Of course, there was also one small box of adult magazines within arm's reach, as well as a package of tissues. I sighed in disgust and frustration. Reaper Dick had been clear. He ordered Palazzo to remove all his smut from the division's spaces without exception.

I could have placed Spanky on report for disobeying Darcy's orders. The captain would have taken Palazzo's crow, stripping him of his status as a petty officer and reducing him to a seaman. That would have effectively ended his career. At that point, I concluded that the man needed help, though. I believed that more punishment would only exacerbate his condition. Deciding that I was only going to have Palazzo get rid of his smut, I tossed the box over the HVAC to the far side of the fan room. I also made a mental note to revisit the idea of sending him for a psych eval. Then, using only my thumb and forefinger, I picked up the blanket and tossed it out of my way. I kept the cushions in place to make it easier on my knees as I got to work.

HVAC filter maintenance was not complicated. The hardest part about it was fighting my way through all the clutter to get to them. Since it did not require being near any electrical connections, I did not even have to tag it out. All I had to do was unbolt the panel, remove the filter, and soak it in water to lift the contaminants out of it. When I finished that, I only needed to blow it dry and put it back. As I was pulling the filter out, the fan kicked on. I thought I heard something inside, like a piece of paper fluttering in the wind.

Using a penlight, I looked around for debris but saw nothing. The opening was too small for me to get my head into, so there were plenty of blind spots. Putting my light away, I stuck my arm inside to feel around. Eventually, my fingertips brushed across a manila envelope taped to the side of the steel wall. I ripped it off and pulled it outside. After looking it over, I opened it up and found nearly a dozen polaroid pictures inside.

My stomach turned. The photographs were of a young girl who looked to be about twelve or thirteen years old. A couple of the pictures showed her outdoors, and I recognized where she was from the background. She was in Pagsanjan, in the Philippines. The girl was standing in the slum where Darrow, Sergeant Tejada, and I tried to catch Krause accosting under-aged prostitutes. I cannot even begin to describe how the girl posed for the pictures taken of her indoors. Throwing the photos back into the envelope, I fought my way back through the fan room junk and charged toward my shop.

When I kicked open the door to Radar Repair, I had a full house. It was lunchtime, so Dixie, Metaire, and Kent were clowning around, shooting rubber bands at each other. Rick Hammond was perched upon the workbench, reading a book. John Palazzo was sitting back on a chair that he had leaned into a corner. His eyes were closed as he tried to take a quick nap. I heaved the manila envelope at him and screamed, "YOU FUCKING PRICK!"

The shop went silent. My men watched the envelope bounce off of Spanky's chest and spill the polaroid pictures out onto the floor.

Kent reached down to pick one of them up. After seeing the subject of the photos, Speedy grimaced and shook his head in disbelief. Turning to Palazzo, he said, "Dude, what the fuck?"

The rest of the shop crowded around Kent to check out what he was looking at. To a man, they all winced at what they saw. Palazzo was the last man to get a peek. When he saw what I found, his face went white. "G-g-guys," he stammered. "D-D-D-Doyle, th-th-those aren't mine!"

"BULLSHIT!" I screamed, reaching out to grab Spanky by his throat. Dixie and Metaire rushed in to hold me back before I could get a grip on him. "YOU AND ME, YOU MOTHERFUCKER! WE'RE TAKING A WALK! WE'RE GOING TO THE FUCKING NIXIE R…"

Metaire put his hand over my mouth. "No, you air noht!"

"Claude's right," Dixie said. "We're not going through this shit again! You can't afford another Randy Green incident! Neither can we!"

"MMMPH! MMMPH!"

"Palazzo! Get the fuck out of here!" Dixie ordered. "Make yourself scarce until I get Doyle calmed down. Don't go too far, though. I'm betting the Master-at-Arms is going to want a word with you."

Spanky reached out to grab the Polaroids from Kent, but Speedy pulled them back out of his grasp. "Fuck off," our booter growled at him.

After Palazzo left, Dixie and Metaire released me. Spinning around to face them, I promised, "I'm going to fucking kill him! I'm telling you, the next time we get underway, that motherfucker's going over the side!"

Dixie hauled off and smacked me across the face. He then grabbed me by the collar and slammed me against the filing cabinet. Sticking his finger in front of my nose, he snapped, "Shut the fuck up! Right now! You're going to keep your hands off of him and quit being stupid! Do you understand?!? When word gets out about this, guys'll be looking to put some hurt on that prick! If you don't quit shooting your trap off, you're going to be the prime suspect if something happens to him! You got that?!?"

I batted Dixie's arm to the side and pushed him away from me. "FUCK!" I shouted. I then turned around, cranked back, and planted my fist into the filing cabinet. With that out of my system, I said, "Yeah, Dixie, I got it."

"Good." Kevin swiped the pictures out of Kent's hands, put them back into the envelope, and shoved them into my chest. "Take those down to the EMO and give them to Darrow. Let him deal with that son-of-a-bitch!"

*****

It was still lunchtime, so my master chief was the only man in the EMO when I arrived. I realized I had messed up when he took the pictures from me. Darrow used a piece of paper towel to grab the Polaroids to avoid getting his fingerprints on them. "Who else has seen these?"

Swallowing hard, I had a feeling that the master chief was not going to like my answer. "Dixie, Metaire, Kent, Hammond, myself, and, of course, Palazzo."

"Who handled them?"

I swallowed again. "All of us."

Darrow let the pictures fall to his desk in frustration. "Seriously? You all handled them? You let your entire shop get their fingerprints all over this shit? Thanks, you fucking idiot! Now they're worthless!"

"What? They were in Spanky's fan room…"

"That everyone on the entire ship has access to."

"Maybe, but you know that that shit belongs to that fucking pervert!"

Darrow shook his head. "Do I? Did I see him put those pictures in the HVAC unit? Did you?"

"No, but…"

"But nothing. You've got a suspicion. You had evidence until you ruined it by letting every one of your men molest these pictures. Now, you ain't got shit!"

"Wait, you're not saying that he's going to get away with this!"

Darrow stood up to make sure I got his point. "Look, Doyle. You don't know that those pictures are Palazzo's. You think you do, but you don't. Anyone could have hidden those pictures in that fan unit." Darrow pointed his thumb at Lieutenant Krause's empty desk. "Even that son-of-a-bitch."

"But, Master Chief, we…"

"Look," Darrow interrupted. "Maybe these Polaroids are Palazzo's. He would definitely be my top suspect. I'm telling you from years of law enforcement experience, though, that there's nothing I can do with these now. Our best course of action is to destroy them. We don't want them turning up anywhere with *your* fingerprints on them, do we?"

I gulped. "No."

"That's what I thought." Darrow sat back down and lit a cigarette. He contemplated the situation in silence for a couple of moments. "Okay, here's what we're going to do. You're going to send Spanky to come speak with me in the dome. I'm going to let him know that I can't fuck him for this like I want to, but I've got my goddamn eyes on him. You're going up to your shop and telling…no, scratch that. You're going to *order* your men to never open their mouths about any of this shit to anyone. Especially that goddamn Metaire! That man gossips like a bloody prom queen. You got it?"

"No, I don't 'got it!'" I exclaimed. "We can still investigate this shit!"

"You fucked up all our evidence, Doyle! Don't tell me how we're supposed to proceed with an investigation now! If you've proved anything so far, it's that you sure as shit ain't no Sherlock Holmes!"

I glanced again at the photographs on Darrow's desk. I noticed something. "Wait! Look at the pictures, Master Chief! At the lower right-hand corner! There's a smudge or something there! There's something wrong with the camera! It's on every single Polaroid. If we search Palazzo's shit and find a camera in his stuff, all we have to do is take a picture with it. If it has that flaw in the corner, it'll prove that these came from that device! We'll have his ass!"

My master chief looked at the pictures and then at me. Breaking into a broad smile, Darrow nodded his head a couple of times, then said, "Fuckin' eh, Watson! If nothing else, you do have your moments!"

Darrow grabbed the handset of the IC line and passed it to me. "Get your men to hunt down Spanky and haul his ass up to Radar Repair to wait for me. Once he's up there, post guards on his rack and every place he stashes his shit. After we confiscate his keys, we'll go get our hands on that camera…"

Darrow paused to throw me another look of irritation. "At least we will if you didn't give him enough warning to toss the goddamn thing overboard first."

*****

While my master chief and Tony Bard went through Spanky's stuff, I stood guard over him in the radar repair shop. I had Palazzo sitting in a chair in the middle of the room. I sat facing him, my feet up on the garbage can, chain-smoking while I stared him down in silence. I never had a man sweat so much while under my gaze. To John's credit, he sat at the position of attention for more than a half-hour. After that, the tension became too much for him. "Can I use the head?" he finally asked me.

"No," I answered, blowing a lungful of smoke in his direction.

"I'm going to piss myself if…"

"Then you're going to piss yourself," I told him. "And you're going to sit in it until the master chief gets back. After that, you're going to mop up your mess before I let you change clothes. Cocksucker."

Spanky inhaled a large breath. "You know, Doyle, they're never going to find that camera. Or any more pictures."

I cocked an eyebrow. "Why not? Did you already get rid of it all?"

No," Palazzo said, shaking his head. "They ain't going to find it because I don't own a Polaroid camera. I never have. I didn't take those pictures, either."

"Bullshit."

"For Christ's sake, Doyle. You gotta believe me. I would never..."

"Oh, spare me. You would, too. We both know that, you sick fuck. Do you know what's going to happen to you, Spanky? Even if they don't find what we need to hang your fat ass for this shit? We're going to fuck you up. Some way, somehow, we're going to destroy you. You're finished, you little prick. You better hope you go to prison. Even if they make you Leavenworth's shower room belle, it ain't going to compare to the carnage we're going to unleash on you if you stay here. We're going to hurt you, John. We're going to *really* hurt you."

Palazzo had seen firsthand what I had done to Randy Green. He knew that I was not kidding. He hung his head, his shoulders slumped, and his gaze fell to the floor.

Master Chief Darrow walked into Radar Repair with Tony Bard and my men shortly after that. "Did you find it?" I asked.

Darrow shook his head. Jumping out of my seat, I marched over to Palazzo and stuck my finger in his face. "This isn't over, you piece of shit! It's only just...!"

"It *is* over!" Darrow barked, contradicting me. "Get back to your corner, Murphy! Now!"

Dixie grabbed me by my shirt and dragged me to my seat to ensure that I did what our master chief ordered.

When he was confident that he had everybody's attention, the master chief pointed at my men and me. "Let me be clear. We have *no* evidence, *zero* evidence, that those pictures were taken by, or belonged to, Petty Officer Palazzo. *None*. We have nothing that ties him to them aside from his reputation. Men, I've spent eight years in law enforcement during my military career. I've seen what can be wrought when men act upon assumptions instead of evidence. That is NOT going to happen here. Do you understand?"

The men nodded and murmured their agreement. That was not good enough for Darrow. "Do you understand!?!"

"YES, MASTER CHIEF!"

"No one is going to touch this man! No one's going to harass this man! No one is going to slander him, imply that he is into this shit, or do anything to make his life any more miserable than it already is! Is that clear!"

"YES, MASTER CHIEF!"

Darrow turned around and faced Palazzo. "That doesn't mean that I'm ordering you be his buddy, or be his pal, or share your deepest darkest secrets with him, either. But as long as we have no evidence against Petty Officer Palazzo, you're all going to leave him the fuck alone!"

The master chief bent over to look Spanky in the eye. "But son, heaven help you if we do find out that this is your particular brand of kink. If this really is the shit that you're into, hell, even Reaper Dick is likely to turn a blind eye to what these men will fucking do to you."

*****

After he dismissed my men, Darrow had me follow him to the SPN-35 dome. When he was sure we were alone, he turned to me and asked, "Is everything I said up there in your shop crystal clear, Doyle?"

"Of course," I told him.

Sensing I might only be humoring him, the master chief poked his finger into my chest. "I'm not fucking around here, Murphy. You need to drop this completely. With the shit we got going on, we can't afford *any* extra scrutiny around here. Do you understand?"

I had not even thought about the deal we were trying to work out for Sergeant Tejada. That put the Spanky situation into a whole new perspective. "I understand."

Darrow nodded. “Good. Now look, I have no idea whether those pictures were Palazzo’s or not. I want you to go up there and impress upon your guys that they need to keep their mouths shut about it, though. Not only to protect our thing with TJ, but in case those pictures actually weren’t Spanky’s. I don’t want word about this getting out and tipping off whoever did take those Polaroids. Keep it quiet. And keep your eyes open for anyone else regularly visiting that fan room besides Spanky.”

I nodded. “Aye aye.”

“Good.” Darrow reached into his pocket to grab his cigarettes. Instead of Lucky Strikes, however, he pulled a crumpled-up piece of paper out of his pocket. After looking at it, he flinched in surprise and handed it to me. “Shit, I almost forgot about this. I grabbed this from the quarterdeck this morning and was going to give it to you at quarters. Yukiko left you a message.”

Taking the paper from my master chief’s hand, I looked it over. It said to call her at the number written down in barely legible chicken scratch.

“I thought you burned that bridge,” Darrow mused.

“I pretty much did," I replied. "I ran into her last week, though. She offered to teach me how to meditate to try to get control of the shit going on in my head.”

“You gonna do it?”

I shrugged. “I might as well. It couldn’t hurt, could it?”

My master chief grinned. “You think it might work, or are you doing it to try to get back into her pants?”

“It wouldn’t be the weirdest thing I’ve ever done to get laid,” I told Darrow. “Not by a long shot."

*****

CHAPTER 8

When I set out to find a new *pachinko* parlor, and thus new mobsters to make a run at, it was a little cool for early April. The sun was out though, so as long as I had on a sweater and kept moving, it was bearable. Unable to read a Japanese telephone book or even the street signs, my search proved difficult. All I could do was wander around and hope to run into something.

I did manage to find several parlors, but none of them had a place nearby where I could inconspicuously sit and wait for *yakuza* men to show up. Before I came across a suitable candidate, the sun dropped below the horizon, the wind picked up, and it started pouring on me. That, combined with the chill already hanging in the air, made things miserable fast and I found myself really missing my motorcycle jacket. To make matters worse, not only was I a long way from base, I was in an area of the city where taxi service was scarce.

It took me forever to walk back to the *ginza* and I was close to clinical hypothermia when I finally arrived. I was shivering uncontrollably and my jaw was chattering so hard that I was afraid of chipping my teeth. The *ginza* offered little protection from the wind, but at least it put a roof over my head.

I contemplated ducking into my favorite noodle shop for some soup to temper the ice in my blood, but unfortunately, that was located right where the Kato kid had cleaned my clock a couple of weeks before. It was bad enough that I recognized the cashier in the *pachinko* parlor as I passed. Even worse was that the cashier looked up as I walked by and recognized me, too.

Cursing and picking up my pace, I hoped to clear the area before the guy called out another enforcer to see what I was up to. Before I took a dozen steps, however, the cashier was already outside yelling at me. "Hey! Yankee!"

I kept walking.

"*Gaijin*! Hey! You want you *jaketto* back?"

Still shivering, I stopped in my tracks and thought, *Yes. As a matter of fact, I do want my fucking jacket back.*

As I turned around, the cashier smiled and waved at me to join him. I let out a long sigh and walked up to the man. I doubted that returning my leather was the cashier's only motivation for grabbing my attention. He was either going to arrange my arrest, beating, murder, or an introduction to the people I wanted to connect with in the first place.

"You rook very cold," the man told me when I was close enough to hear him without being yelled at.

"I am," I said.

The cashier nodded sympathetically. "You go in *pachinko* stoah. Go door behind count-ah — that office. You take seat there. I bu-ring soup to you."

I bowed my head toward the man in gratitude, but I let the expression on my face tell him that I knew there was more in store for me than my coat.

The office in the back of the *pachinko* parlor was bigger than I thought it would be. It was also cluttered, loaded with boxes, loose papers, and overflowing file folders. There were two chairs, one at a desk and a cushioned armchair in the corner. Soaking wet, I did not want to take a seat in either.

When the cashier returned, he handed me a bowl of *karē*, a curry-flavored ramen topped with *chāshū*, a type of barbecued pork. It was what I usually ordered from the shop across the path. That proved to be an unsettling clue that the cashier knew more about me than I was comfortable with. Motioning his hand toward the armchair, he said, "Sit. Prease. *Dozo*."

I nodded to acknowledge his gesture but tried to decline. "I'm soaked. I don't want to get your furniture all wet."

"It okay. Prease, sit."

Once I was seated, the cashier leaned back against his desk. "My name is Kitamura Hideki."

"*Hajimemashita, Kitamura-san,*" I told him. Nice to meet you. "*Watashi no namae-wa Do-ru Mu-ru-pi.*" My name is Doyle Murphy.

"*Nihongo wa hanashemasu ka*?" Kitamura asked. Do you speak Japanese?

"*Sukoshi,*" I answered. A little.

"I speak Engrish, then. Okay?" Kitamura said. "I grow up around American soldier. My Engrish okay."

Nodding, I assured him that it was certainly better than my Japanese. "Is my jacket here?"

Kitamura frowned. "No. I make phone carr and they bring *jaketto* to you. Actuar-ree, they bring you to you *jaketto*. Mu-ru-pi-*san*, everyone very sorry about this. It very dishonorabu to stear in Japan. To be thief very dishonorabu and bring big shame to us. The boy who stear you *jaketto* be punish for his crime."

That surprised me. "By the police?"

Kitamura shook his head. "No. By other peo-po. You wirr see."

The "other people" arrived as I was finishing my soup. They were two men in black suits, *sans* ties, who ordered me up as soon as they walked into the office. Both were taller and stockier than what was typical for that part of the world. They reminded me more of Koreans than Japanese.

When I was back on my feet, one of them spun me around and roughly pushed me up against the wall. The other frisked me. Judging by how they were feeling me up, I suspected they were searching for wires more than weapons. One of them grabbed my wallet and rifled through it. He looked puzzled when he saw my military ID card and grunted a question to the cashier.

"Do-ru Mu-ru-pi," Kitamura told the man, showing him how to pronounce my name.

"*Hai*," the bruin nodded, indicating that he understood. He then looked at me and held his arm out towards the door. "*Mu-ru-pi*. Go!"

"*Iye,*" I told them, shaking my head. No. "*Mu-ru-pi-SAN*!" I then said, demanding that they address me properly. Being American, I preferred familiarity, but Japan was different. Dropping the honorary "*-san*" suffix from my name was a sign of disrespect. Had I allowed that, the men might have regarded me as subservient, maybe even submissive. Negotiating a deal to get the *yakuza* to the Philippines could not be done from a position of weakness.

To be clear, I harbored no illusions that I could best either of those men if we came to blows, let alone both at the same time. I needed to show them that if it came to that, though, I would go down fighting. I had to prove that I was willing to stand up to them before I accompanied them anywhere.

The hooligan that tried bossing me around did not take kindly to my challenge. His face contorted in anger as he took a menacing step my way. The bruiser looked ready to instruct me of my proper place within the Japanese underworld's social hierarchy. Judging by how far Kitamura backed away, I suspected that the cashier questioned the wisdom of my protest. The second thug might have enjoyed abusing a *gaijin* as much as his partner did, but he had instructions to bring me back unmolested. Fortunately for me, the goon took his orders seriously. He stopped his cohort from tearing me apart, then motioned me toward the exit. "Mu-ru-pi-*SAN*," he said, emphasizing his adherence to etiquette. "*Dozo*."

*****

NEPTUNE'S MARTYRS

The building the men took me to looked like it had once been a small factory. Far removed from residential areas, it was beyond the eyeshot of any busybodies inclined to report unusual comings and goings to the authorities. This was especially true at the time of night that we arrived. Aside from the three of us, the place appeared deserted.

When we got to the front of the facility, one of the hoodlums opened the door to let me in. The other stopped me from stepping across the threshold, however. Pointing at my feet, he said, "*Kutsu.*" Shoes.

People do not usually take their footwear off before entering a business in Japan. That was my first clue that the workshop was not what it seemed. The outside of the building appeared old and stained with a half-century's worth of industrial soot. The interior was by no means luxurious, but it was clean and maintained, if somewhat spartan. It was also warm and humid. Following my escorts, I started to shiver. The heat seemed to remind my body of how cold and uncomfortable I was in my sopping wet clothes.

Led down a narrow corridor of traditional *shoji* wood and paper walls, I could hear what sounded like people playing in water. Eventually, my *yakuza* escorts stopped and slid open a screen. Revealed was a steamy room containing several large tubs full of hot water, each about the size of a small swimming pool. Soaking within them were eight heavily tattooed men and a dozen young women, all buck naked and entirely unashamed of it.

One of the men grinned when he saw me, standing before him soaking wet but fully dressed. He said something in Japanese to the others that caused them to break out in laughter. I caught myself grinning at the ladies. They still covered their mouths with their hands when they laughed yet left everything else exposed. And I mean everything.

I could not completely understand what the joke was, but it went something like, "Look at the funny wet foreigner! He looks shocked to see us bathing together! They are such prudes that they shower with all their clothes on!"

In response, I looked at the man and said, "*Ame ga futta toki dake.*" Only when I get stuck in the rain.

The man and his retinue laughed again, not so much at my response, but at my poor language skills. "*Nihongo wa hanashemasu ka*?" I was again asked. I again answered that I spoke a little Japanese.

"I speak pretty good Engrish," the man told me. "My name is Furukawa Yasushi."

"I'm Doyle Murphy," I told him.

The Japanese all looked at each other in puzzlement, lost at how to pronounce my name. I had to katakanize it for them. "Do-ru Mu-ru-pi."

"Aaaaah," they all seemed to say in unison.

"Mu-ru-pi-*san*," Furukawa said as he waved his arms to show off the room. "Do you know what this is?"

A little unsure, I ventured a guess. "This is *onsen*?"

Grinning, Furukawa wagged his finger at me. "Good guess! But this no is *onsen. Onsen* is pubric bath that use water from hot spring. There no hot spring here. So this type of bath is carr *sentō.* A-so, this bath no is pubric." The gangster lifted his arms to show off his ink. "We no go to *sentō* because of tattoo. Tattoo forbidden in *sentō.* It okay for us, though. In pubric *sentō,* boy and girr have separate bath. In our *sentō*, boy and girr share same water. Is better, no?"

My grin stretched a little wider, looking at the young women among them. "*Hai*," I answered. Yes.

"S*entō* is tradition-oh way to talk in us business. In *sentō*, easy to see no one have weapon and no one wearing wire. You join us in bath, Mu-ru-pi-*san*? Or you too embarass?"

"No, I'm not embarrassed." At that point, I was grateful for any opportunity to get out of my cold, wet clothes. "Is there a locker room I should undress in?"

Furukawa waved his hand dismissively. "No, it okay. No sense to waste time." My host turned to one of the girls soaking at the side of his pool. "Katsumi-*chan*? You speak Engrish good, right?"

The girl nodded only once, but with great enthusiasm. "*Hai!*"

"Do you want to herp Mu-ru-pi-*san* get ready for *sentō*?"

Katsumi smiled at me and said, "*Hai!*" She then stood up and emerged from the water, revealing herself.

As the girl walked my way, Furukawa asked, "I understand you bother my boss a cou-po week ago. Why you bother my boss?"

Katsumi grabbed my soaked sweatshirt and lifted it over my head. She then folded it neatly and placed it on a plain wooden bench near the screen I passed through to enter the bath. As she unfastened the buttons of my shirt, I told Furukawa, "I was trying to set up a meeting between your people and someone I know with a business proposition."

"Business proposition? What kind business proposition?"

"I don't know," I said as the girl peeled my shirt off, folded it, and placed it atop my sweatshirt.

"You don't know?" Furukawa asked, sounding as if he doubted my sincerity.

Katsumi was removing my belt when I told him, "My job is strictly to arrange a meeting between your organization and my contact. Nothing more. I don't know what he is offering for sale or how much he's asking for it. The fact that I'm here tells me that you found the envelope in my coat. You now know what he's offering and you're interested enough to seek out more information. Am I wrong?"

Furukawa smiled at me. "The samp-poh you man leave for me...it very serious stuff. You man have a lot of this?"

I nodded as Katsumi pulled my jeans down to my ankles. As I stepped out of my pants and had my socks removed, I said, "My understanding is that he has several truckloads of it."

Furukawa inhaled deeply, looking pleasantly surprised. "Truck-roads? Truck-roads? This could be very big deal."

It was the moment of truth. Katsumi slipped her fingers around the waistband of my underwear and pulled them down, revealing me before my hosts. The girls started giggling, again covering their mouths with their hands. Furukawa chuckled himself. "You know, Japanese peo-po arways hear that *gaijin* have big prick. The radies are watching to see if this true. I sorry, but you no herping this image very much."

I shrugged. "Baby, it's cold outside."

Furukawa laughed out loud. "Yes. Yes, it is. It very cord outside for this time of year."

Suddenly anxious to get at least waist-deep in water, I took a step toward the bath. Katsumi stopped me. Giggling, she walked in front of me and pressed her entire body up against mine. Soft, wet, and warm, she felt so good. As she guided me to a corner of the room with a showerhead, she called out something I did not understand to no one in particular. At her command, however, the screen opened up and in marched a tiny elderly maid who grabbed my clothes and quickly disappeared with them.

"S*entō* in Japan is different than bath in America," Furukawa instructed me. "In America, a bath crean you body. In Japan, a bath crean you spirit. We use shower to wash ourserves, not bath."

I nodded. "That makes sense, I…" It was challenging to carry on a conversation while getting cleaned up in a *yakuza* s*entō*. Katsumi grabbed a bottle of liquid soap, but instead of squirting it on me, she put it on herself. Then, using her body as a washcloth, she rubbed me down from head to toe. It did not take long for my manhood to shake off the effects of the cold that had so embarrassed me a couple of moments before. In fact, because of the incredible job Katsumi was doing, I ended up impressing myself with how big I had become. Again, the girls giggled.

After Katsumi rinsed me off, she led me to the bath and guided me in as I took a seat on a submerged bench opposite my underworld host. She slid into the water, too, positioning herself between me and the side of the pool. Katsumi then wrapped her arms around my neck and her legs around my waist. For the rest of the time I spoke with Furukawa, she rubbed her breasts against my back. It wrought havoc upon my concentration.

"So Mu-ru-pi-*san*," Furukawa said as he offered me a cup of warm saké. "It is a preasure to meet you. Prease, I very appreciate if you terr me what you try to terr my boss a cou-po of weeks ago."

Taking the cup from my host, I bowed as low as Katsumi would let me, then took a long drink from my cup. It was rejuvenating. I nodded in approval and thanked the gangster for his hospitality. "Furukawa-*san*, my client has a large cache of merchandise in the Philippines. He is willing to let it go for quite a bargain if the buyer can arrange transportation out of the country. He can guarantee that your ship will be safe in the territorial waters of the Philippines. Of course, he has no control over your destination. He is also willing to process the product in whatever way you want to help get it past customs wherever you intend to send it."

"Guarantee?" Furukawa asked. "What is your guarantee? Your word?"

I shook my head. "Not *my* word. His. Like I said, Furukawa-*san*, he has all the details. Not me. My job is only to connect you and him."

Furukawa thought for a moment. "Mu-ru-pi-*san*, I appreciate you gesture, but without detairs of what you partner have, I think it big risk and reward maybe no be so much."

"Furukawa-*san*, I agree. You don't have many details. My offer is to take you to the man who can get you all the information you need. We get you to the Philippines where you meet my guy, see what he has to offer, and then decide if you want to proceed or not. If it doesn't work out, you get a free trip to the Philippines. You have nothing to lose."

That started the negotiations. From that point forward, we went back and forth about what the *yakuza* had to gain and why my proposal was worth their while. Despite the theatrics of resistance, the more we talked, the more I realized that I was speaking with the right guys. Furukawa and his men were Young Turks. They were upstarts, junior members of their organization anxious to make a name for themselves. They were hungry. The more reluctant they tried to appear, the more I could see that they wanted this transaction to work out almost more than I did. Pulling off an international arms deal was the kind of thing that could usher them into the big leagues. If we worked this out, they could leave their petty rackets to lesser men.

My biggest concern with Furukawa's gang was inexperience. They did not appear to know how to move arms from one country to another any more than I did. They knew people who could, though, and that was what was most important.

After a couple of hours of conversational tug-of-war, Furukawa leaned back in the bath and let out a long sigh. "Okay. We take trip to Phirippines to meet you guy. If this rook rike good deal, we take this to our boss." The gangster then held up his cup, which was immediately filled by one of the young ladies. Katsumi handed me mine, topped off with a fresh pour of piping hot saké. After toasting each other, Furukawa and I downed our drinks and concluded our business discussion.

Furukawa placed his cup down, then looked at the ink on my arm. He appeared intrigued by my Tequila Viking, the skull wearing a horned sailor cap placed before an anchor above a pair of liquor bottles crossed Jolly Roger-style. The gangster pushed his lips together and nodded in approval. Reading the script above and below my tattoo, the gangster asked me, "What is 'Tequira Viking?'"

I grinned. "A Tequila Viking's a sailor who does crazy things while drunk."

"Reary?" my new friend asked. "What you do to be a Tequira Viking?"

I told Furukawa how I got caught having sex by my date's husband and found myself forced to fight him naked in his front yard. Katsumi translated for the rest of the hooligans. She also described how I had to streak across half of San Diego to get away from the police before being rescued by Dixie. She must have done a great job telling the story as she had them all roaring with laughter.

Furukawa himself poured us both more saké after I finished my tale. "What erse you do?"

"God, what didn't we do? We went on epic week-long road trips in the desert, got into fights in Mexico, and caught food poisoning in the Philippines after picnicking with Communist guerillas. That was so bad that we almost had to abandon an apartment and sparked a stampede in a fish market. I even once got drunk and tried to set up a deal with the *yakuza* outside a *pachinko* parlor in the *ginza*. I got my ass kicked for that one."

The gangster laughed at that last line, but with much less humor than before. Pointing his index finger at his temple, he told me, "Yes, you did, didn't you? I armost forget. Shinzo!"

"*Hai*!" barked one of Furukawa's henchmen in response.

In Japanese, the gang leader told his man to fetch their little brother. Emerging from the water, Furukawa's minion wrapped a towel around himself and shuffled out of the bath. When he returned, he brought back the Kato kid I met a couple of weeks before. The boy was holding my jacket. Shinzo was carrying a small wooden tray upon which sat a *tantō* knife, a length of ribbon, and a white cloth.

With a great deal of ceremony, the Kato kid introduced himself as Ichiro Moriyama. He expressed his regret for what happened in the *ginza*, then presented my jacket to me. After that, he took his place behind the wooden tray and began rolling up his sleeves. Knowing what was about to take place, I turned to my host and said, "This isn't necessary, Furukawa-*san*. He won the fight we got into fair and square. I got my jacket back. No harm, no foul. I accept his apology."

Furukawa told me to relax. "This no about you. This about our code. The *yakuza* no is mafia. We are *ninkyō dantai,* a organization of honor. We have rures that arrow us to co-exist in society. We no harm civirians. We no dear in drugs. We no do drugs. We no stear. Our rittre brother break our code when he stear you jacket. He must atone for this. This about his honor as much as it about *yakuza* honor. To creanse himserf of this sin, he must make sacrifice. Trust me, Mu-ru-pi-*san*, he want do this. No one make him do *yubitsume*. He do this to regain his honor. To deny him this is to burden him with the shame of his mistake. He no want peo-po to think him thief."

By the time Furukawa finished explaining the *yubitsume* ritual to me, Ichiro had already finished tying off his pinky finger. He then positioned the knife above it, ready to perform the amputation. After a single nod from Furukawa, the boy pressed the blade down and removed the tip of the digit. The expression on Ichiro's face never changed. With an impressive display of stoicism, he then wrapped the severed appendage in a white cloth. When that was completed, the young boy stood up, bowed to the men gathered in the bath, and presented his flesh to his boss. Furukawa accepted it with a short speech, then dismissed the young man.

Once that unpleasantness was over, the saké once again began to flow. We drank and talked and allowed ourselves to be massaged by the ladies in attendance. At some point, late in the evening, people began pairing up and disappearing. Katsumi eventually followed their lead and led me to a room a few steps from the bath. Laying me down upon a futon, she asked, "You come back from Phirippines?"

Nodding, I answered, "Yeah, about four months ago."

Smiling, Katsumi pulled up a floor tile and retrieved a condom from a compartment beneath it. Growing up near an American naval base, she had a pretty good idea of what went on in Olongapo. There was no way she was going to pleasure me without protection.

And I can't say that I blamed her.

*****

American cars were rare in Japan, driven mainly by mobsters and, for some strange reason, dentists. Furukawa owned a black Lincoln, and when we finally decided to call it a night, he offered me a ride back to the base. Not wanting to get my freshly washed and dried clothes wet again, I accepted the offer.

Living dangerously, Furukawa drove with his sleeves rolled up to his elbows. His tattoos were fully exposed, advertising his standing in the Sasebo underworld. "How we get in touch with you?" he asked as we approached Nimitz Park.

Looking at Furukawa's arms, I thought it unwise to meet with him or his men in public. "Can you trust Katsumi?"

The gangster shrugged his shoulders. "She woman. She no work on business. She for preasure."

"Can she relay messages?" I asked. "It would be less suspicious if she was our go-between. No one bats an eye if a girl calls the ship. If I have any information for you, I can call her and arrange a meeting. If you want to meet, have her leave a message for me."

Furukawa laughed. "You want to fuck her again. Don't you?"

I grinned. "That's not my main goal, but if she offers, I'm certainly not going to deny her."

The gangster laughed again as I wrote down the number to the quarterdeck of the *USS Belleau Wood.* We were pulling up to the Albuquerque bridge as I finished. After he stopped his car on the side of the street, Furukawa and I shook hands and expressed our desire to work out a deal. I then opened the Lincoln's door and stepped outside, unexpectedly finding myself face-to-face with John Palazzo. He and his team were walking their Shore Patrol beat and happened to be in the perfect spot to see me get out of an American luxury vehicle.

Before I could close the door, Spanky stole a look inside Furukawa's ride. He undoubtedly caught sight of my new friend, tattooed arms and all. I watched Palazzo's jaw drop as he put two and two together. "Who the hell is that?" he asked as I blew past him, walking towards the bridge.

"None of your fucking business."

*****

CHAPTER 9

"Nice jacket!" Master Chief Darrow told me when we met up at the beer garden the day after I made contact with Furukawa Yasushi. With Krause constantly tearing through our spaces, we decided not to discuss our outreach to the *yakuza* aboard the ship anymore. Until he saw me in my bike leather, Darrow knew nothing about what had happened to me the day before.

"You like it?" I asked, spinning around in front of him like a woman showing off a new dress. "It doesn't make my ass look big, does it?"

"Trust me, Murphy," the master chief said. "There's nothing on this entire planet that could make you look like a bigger ass than you already are."

Over a half dozen bottles of Asahi, I filled Darrow in on everything that went down the previous night. He raised an eyebrow when I admitted to sleeping with Katsumi. "I thought you didn't fuck prostitutes."

"No, I don't pay for sex," I told him. "Considering my relationship with Tala in Olongapo, it's safe to say that I have, indeed, slept with a prostitute. Repeatedly. She just wouldn't take any money for it. Besides, Katsumi isn't a hooker. She's more like a groupie."

"The *yakuza* have groupies?"

I nodded. "Don't most gangsters? The Italians have molls in the US. What makes you think it'd be any different here? Some chicks like to live dangerously too, I guess." I paused to take a sip out of my beer. "So, we got a bite. What's next?"

Darrow took a bite of *gyoza* and shrugged. "We need to settle on a date to meet TJ that will work for all of us. There's not enough time to pull something together this month. We've got amphib workups in Okinawa and a trip to Hong Kong in May. You think we could swing a trip back to PI the first week of June? That'll give Tejada time to prepare, too."

Nodding, I said, "I still have forty-five days of leave on the books. I have the time. You just need to tell me when the command can cut me loose."

"I'll talk to TJ and get back to you. You going to tell Tala that you're going to be back in town?"

I cracked a grin as I rifled through my jacket for my cigarettes. "Hell yeah! Man, I can't wait to see Mari. She's been writing to me in English lately. She's learning it so fast."

"And Tala?"

"Yeah, her too."

My master chief looked at me with a strange expression on his face. "You know, you don't talk about Tala with half the enthusiasm you have when you talk about her daughter. What gives?"

Lighting the Marlboro I finally found, I shrugged. "I don't know, Master Chief. I don't understand it either. I love Mari to death. She's a kid, so I know there are no hidden agendas with her. I have no doubt whatsoever that she likes me for who I am. On my part, all I want is to be sure that she makes it through life without ever having to do what her mother did to survive. Our relationship is simple. We only want to make each other laugh."

I took a drag off of my cigarette and blew the smoke into the air. "What I have with Tala's more complicated. We've both survived some pretty horrific shit and emerged with serious issues as a result of it. I catch myself wondering if two people as damaged as we are can get together and make each other better. It seems far more likely that eventually, our mutual dysfunctions will feed upon each other until we self-destruct. Like it did between Randy Green and his wife."

My master chief shook his head. "Man, I thought you were doing good while you two were together."

"I was," I admitted to Darrow. "After everything that happened to me in the Philippines, I never had an episode when I was with Tala. Not one. I nearly got stabbed in Barrio Barretto. I saw that prick get shot in the throat on Magsaysay. I had those fuckers trying to blow my brains out in front of our apartment, even. I killed a kid, Master Chief! I shot a boy right in the fucking head! But still, no episodes. When I'm with her, I'm at ease and tranquil. Not to mention exhausted. That woman does shit in the bedroom that I could not possibly have imagined, and trust me, I've got a pretty broad imagination when it comes to that stuff."

Darrow laughed and took a drink of his beer.

"Tala's like a talisman for my sanity. When I'm with her, I'm alright. I'm afraid of getting used to that and then losing it, though. I got a feeling that there's no way this thing with Tala's going to last, so I'm having a hard time vesting myself in it. I'm willing to give it a shot when we get back to the Philippines, but I'm preparing myself to walk the instant I sense it going bad. For Mari's sake as much as for ours."

My master chief sighed again. Looking me in the eye, he said, "Do your best, Doyle. That's all you can do. Don't obsess about looking for Tala's faults, though. She's got plenty of them, just like you do. If it works, it works. If it doesn't, do what you got to do. Let me tell you something, though. If you go into this, or anything really, thinking it's not going to work, it probably won't. And the fault for it not working won't be hers. It'll be yours. You're setting it all up to fail."

I let out a long sigh. "I know. I did the same shit when we left the Philippines, too. I regretted it almost immediately. What about you, Master Chief? You going to go back and marry Lorna?"

Darrow shook his head. "I'm not getting married again. It ruins everything. I'm going to stay with Lorna, though. I'm going to raise my son with her. As long as we get this deal with the Japs worked out. Do you think there're any complications with this shit I should know about?"

I nodded. "Yeah, I got one. Palazzo."

"Oh, for fuck's sake," my master chief scoffed. "How on earth could Palazzo have any influence on this thing whatsoever?!?"

"Well," I answered. "He saw me get out of Furukawa's car when he dropped me off at the Albuquerque Bridge."

My master chief's jaw hit the table. "Furukawa dropped you off at the bridge?!? What the fuck, Doyle?!? Is this goddamn amateur hour?!? Why the hell did you let a Japanese gangster drive you to your front fucking door?!?"

"Look, I'm kind of new at this shit…"

"Yeah? Well, use your fuckin' head, for fuck's sake! Look, man, there isn't a learning curve for this kind of thing! One wrong step and we're gonna get our asses all locked up! Do you understand that?!?"

Fortunately, we were out in public. Had Darrow and I been having this conversation in the radar dome, he probably would have slugged me. Sitting in the beer garden, he had to keep his voice down to avoid attracting attention, though. "What are we going to do about this?"

I shrugged. "Nothing."

"What do you mean, nothing?" Darrow growled.

"Just what I said. I learned a lot about the *yakuza* last night. Do you know why the police tolerate them? Why they don't have to hide? It's because they make sure that there's no street crime. If you're breaking into houses, dealing dope, or holding up convenience stores, you better pray the cops get to you before the *yakuza* does. I got mugged and had my jacket stolen. The local hoodlums heard about it and made things right. That's the way things work around here."

"And you're going to sell that line of shit to Palazzo?"

Shaking my head, I said, "I ain't talking to that ass clown. The entire division heard about me getting my jacket ripped off. When I told my guys about how the mob got it back for me, they thought I was full of shit. To collaborate my story, I had them go ask Spanky whose car he saw me get out of last night."

Darrow winced in surprise. He looked impressed with the way I handled the issue. "You think Palazzo bought it?"

"Does it matter?" I asked. "That's my explanation. The next time I see Furukawa, I'll let him know the situation so that our stories match. It's easy to do because it's pretty damn close to what actually happened."

After taking another drink of beer, I added, "Besides, even if Spanky doesn't believe that's why I was in that car, who cares? After we found those pictures in the fan room, the man's become a pariah. Nobody gives a fuck what he thinks anymore."

*****

Losing a chevron during a captain's mast is tough on a man. It is not only about the drop in pay and privilege, but the drastic change in the military pecking order. After Palazzo got busted by Captain Darcy for dick spitting on our lieutenant, he not only became an E-4 once again. He became the junior E-4 of the entire department. It did not matter that the man was approaching eight years in rate. ET3 Kent, a kid who had not even hit his first anniversary at sea yet, was now senior to him. As a result, Spanky got every shit job that landed on our docket.

This grated on Palazzo's nerves. It wasn't only because he was lazy but also because he was not the lowest ranking man in our shop. Rick Hammond had only been a third-class petty officer when he had run afoul of the skipper. When he got busted, Rick ended up reduced in rank to an E-3, a seaman. By rights, he was the one who should have been taking on all of the dirty work.

Unlike Palazzo, though, Hammond enjoyed the respect of his shipmates. Even among the officers, the perception was that the kid had drawn an unbelievably raw deal. The crew's perception of Palazzo was of the other extreme. He had become the ship's laughingstock. For a man who got busted for ejaculating on an officer, most thought that he had gotten off easy. No pun intended.

Between his public humiliation and the belief that he was behind the Polaroids we found, Palazzo was an outcast. He was isolated, ridiculed, and shunned not only by the men of our shop but by the rest of the ship's crew as well. He had become an untouchable, something akin to a Hindu *Dalit.* Spanky found himself with no friends, no respect, no credibility, no porn, and, thus, no outlet for his frustration. The man was under a lot of strain, and it was only a matter of time before he snapped under the tension.

A few days after Darrow and I met, Palazzo was on duty. I spent the entire day with him spot-checking his equipment maintenance. Though I did not discover any evidence of gun-decking, I found plenty of examples of very sloppy workmanship. By the time we knocked off ship's work at 16:00, I was hoarse from screaming at the guy for almost eight solid hours. I would have kept going, but Spanky had watch until 20:00.

As Palazzo was getting relieved from his post, a pipe ruptured in one of the storerooms. The engineers got the flooding under control relatively fast, but there was a big mess to clean up and Radar Repair got tasked with supplying a man to the working party. I got word of the request while in the berthing area and called up to the shop to tell Palazzo to report to the damage control detail.

When he got off the phone with me, Spanky turned to Rick and said, "That was Murphy. He wanted me to tell you to report to the quarterdeck to help clean out the storeroom that got flooded."

"Bullshit," Hammond responded. He was lying on the workbench, reading a book. "He ordered *you* to report. I heard it all the way over here."

The color rushed into Spanky's face, maddened not only by being caught in a lie but by being called out on it by a lowly seaman. "I don't give a shit what you think you heard. They need a man down on the quarterdeck for a working party. Get off your ass and get down there."

Hammond turned a page. "Fuck you."

"Look, Hammond! I'm still a petty officer, and I'm giving you an…"

"You ain't shit."

Palazzo glowered at Rick, not believing what the seaman was telling him. "What did you say to me?"

Hammond closed his book, figuring that he would not be able to concentrate on it with Palazzo incessantly yapping at him. Rolling off the workbench, he said, "You heard me. You ain't shit. I'm going to bed. Enjoy your working party."

By the time Palazzo could get out of his chair, Rick was already in the passageway. Spanky had to run to catch him before he got to the ladder. Reaching out, he grabbed Rick by the shoulder and spun him around. "Now, you listen to me…!"

Hammond was not about to. Yelling at Spanky to get his hands off of him, Rick planted both of his palms into Palazzo's chest. He shoved the guy hard enough to send him hurtling into the fusebox beside the door of our shop. That made quite a racket and grabbed the attention of AG1 Pete Agnelli, who happened to be coming down the passageway at just the right moment to see it. As far as Agnelli was concerned, he had witnessed Rick assault a senior petty officer and immediately moved to write him up on the spot. Luckily, he gave me a courtesy call first.

I rushed up to the 07 Level as fast as I could and did everything in my power to keep Hammond from going to mast again. Seamen did not get three strikes aboard Reaper Dick's boat. Hell, even second chances were a rarity. If Rick Hammond went up before the old man again, he was a goner. Darcy would make him a civilian before sunrise if Rick was lucky. If he was not, he would end up in the brig.

For all the effort I put into keeping Hammond out of trouble, Palazzo worked twice as hard to bury him. Spanky was furious and wanted someone to suffer for his misfortunes. Rick was as good a candidate as anybody. In his rage, it appeared that Palazzo had forgotten his standing among us. He was shouting and interrupting me as if he were still a second-class petty officer and we were of equal rank. In the end, I had to order him to shut his mouth so that Agnelli could hear me out.

"Pete, man," I pled to the aerographer's mate. "It comes down to this: Seaman Hammond is the best technician we got. I'll tell you right now that he's probably the most squared-away sailor in our entire department as well. He's a seaman only because he got fucked for going above and beyond the call of duty so far that it came back to bite him. Rest assured, I'm doing everything I can to reverse what happened to the guy. All he ever wanted to do was make a career out of the Navy and trust me; the Navy's a better place for having him in it."

I turned around to look Palazzo right in the eye before I continued. "This son-of-a-bitch, however, is a fucking waste of skin. He blew a wad on a commissioned officer of the United States Navy, for Christ's sake! I can't think of a single redeeming feature about this miserable sack of shit. I'm going to do whatever's possible to cut this cancerous prick out of the military before he can do any more damage than he already has. Trust me, if Hammond put his hands on this asshole, there was a goddamn good reason for it."

Petty Officer Agnelli sat there staring at me for a long time before he said anything. When he did respond, he remained non-committal. "Alright, Doyle. I'll consider your points. I'll talk it over with Bard before I do anything."

I let out a long sigh of relief. Tony would say the same thing I did. There was no way that he wanted to lose a man like Hammond. Especially not on account of a shit stain like Gianni Palazzo. I shook Agnelli's hand, thanked him for thinking things over, then ordered my men back to Radar Repair.

Once we were in the passageway and out of earshot, I dismissed Hammond. "Don't you want to know what happened?" Rick asked me.

"Nope," I answered, turning an icy glare at Palazzo. "It's irrelevant."

I could see Spanky deflate as the enormity of his miscalculation began to sink in. He almost cost me my shop's greatest technical asset. That was not going to go unpunished. "I suppose you're going to want to talk with me?" John asked as we approached the shop door.

"No. Talking to you requires proximity and to be honest, being this close to you makes my skin crawl."

For a brief moment, Palazzo looked almost hopeful. "You're going to ignore me?"

I turned and took a couple of steps forward to invade the deviant's personal space. "Oh, I'm not ignoring you. I'm just going to carefully choose the time and place where I eventually deal with your sorry ass. Until then, I'm not wasting any energy on you. I'm saving it all up until the time is right for me to let it all out. Trust me. You're going to know goddamn well when I'm ready for you, you miserable little fuck."

Palazzo went white. He knew what I was implying. To remove any doubt, I spelled it out for him. "Man, trying to fuck over a guy who's already been screwed by Reaper Dick? That's quite a chickenshit move. You're not going to get away with it. Brace yourself. You're about to have yourself an 'accident,' Spanky."

*****

The orders that Master Chief Darrow gave us were crystal clear. No one was to talk about the Polaroids I had found in the fan room. Still, a rumor along those lines started spreading through the crew anyway. Palazzo was already a source of ridicule after what he had done to Lieutenant Krause. Once word got out that he might have had a taste for minors, he was openly despised.

A couple of days after the incident with Rick Hammond, I saw Palazzo walk into a packed galley at supper time. He slipped into the lone opening he could find at a table full of Air Department personnel. As soon as Spanky's butt hit the seat, the airmen all stopped eating and glared at him. Feeling their eyes boring into him, Spanky stared only at his tray as he ate. He knew nothing positive would come from making eye contact or conversation. Realizing that Gianni was not going to leave, the airmen stood up in unison and walked away from the table in silence, leaving him there to eat by himself.

Not long after that, a pair of surly boatswain's mates walked into the Combat Systems berthing area. Stopping in front of John's rack, they found him lying inside of it. "Are you Petty Officer Palazzo?" one of the men asked.

Sheepishly, Spanky nodded his head and said, "Yeah, can I help you with something?"

"This is where you sleep?" asked the other. "Rack fifty-seven?"

Palazzo again nodded. "Yes. Why?"

Breaking into an intimidating grin, the larger deck ape leaned in and said, "No reason. The guys in Deck Department were just wondering where they could find you. You know, in case we needed you for something."

There was nothing that a boatswain's mate would ever need an electronics technician for. The men were letting Spanky know that they could get to him whenever they wanted. That was when John Palazzo stopped sleeping.

Within a week or so, I could see that the man was starting to come unglued. Palazzo was under so much stress that his hands had developed tremors. He shook like he was suffering from alcohol withdrawal. He told Kent that he was afraid that the entire crew was out to get him and worried about 'falling' overboard the next time we got underway. Palazzo was heading toward a nervous breakdown. Then Metaire and Dixie caught Spanky in the radar shop all by himself one night.

"Get up," Dixie told him.

"Wh-wh-why?" Palazzo stammered, caught off guard by my henchmen barging into the shop like that after hours.

"We have a joab to do," Claude said. "We need to clean zhe Nixie room."

"Th-th-the Nixie room?" John glanced at his watch. "Now?"

Dixie nodded. "Right now."

Reminiscent of the day I nearly killed Randy Green, my men loaded Spanky's arms with cleaning supplies before leading him below. Before they reached the 05 Level, Palazzo's face was pouring sweat. He held few doubts about what lay in store for him.

Kevin told me that by the time they reached the 04 Level, he started trying to talk my men out of what he thought they were going to do to him. "Please, Dixie," Palazzo whimpered. "Please don't do this. I didn't do anything. Nothing that warrants this, anyway."

"Shut the fuck up and keep walking," Petty Officer Dixon told him.

"Claude…"

"Don't even try wiz me," Metaire snapped. "You've 'ad zhis coming vor a long time."

Palazzo was not a brave man. By the time they reached the 02 Level, he was shaking so hard that he could barely walk. His legs gave out at the foot of the ladder leading to the hangar bay. Spanky dropped his mop and bucket, sending them crashing to the deck along with him. No one extended a hand to help him up. Dixie and Metaire just stood over him and stared as he gathered his stuff and tried to get back to his feet. Feeling that he was stalling for time, the two of them started snapping at him to hurry up.

Spanky started to cry as they reached the catwalk leading to the Nixie Winch Room. Metaire mocked him for it. Dixie chuckled. "He sounds like Randy Green, doesn't he?"

Metaire nodded and laughed out loud. "He does! Onlay he zounds more lak a gorl zhan Green did!"

Palazzo tripped again and fell to the deck. "At least Randy could fucking walk, though," Dixie said.

"For a leetle while anyway. He wauz not walking much aftair Doyle feeneeshed wiz heem."

Kevin shook his head. "Walk? Hell, he was barely breathing." As Palazzo once again scurried around trying to gather his things, Dixie reminded him of Green's injuries. "Yeah, Doyle sure fucked that punk up, didn't he? Shattered ankle. Broken arm, How many of Randy's ribs did he end up cracking? Three? Four?"

"Please!" Palazzo sobbed. "Please! Don't do this! I didn't do anything! Please…"

"Man, Doyle broke his jaw. Cracked his skull. Busted his orbital socket. Well, at least he didn't split the prick's head wide open like Pruitt did to Miller…"

"Please! Claude! Dixie!"

"Shut the fuck up and get your shit. I don't have all fucking night, Spanky."

Palazzo was ugly-crying as he got back up and shuffled toward the hatch of the winch room. He stopped at the entrance, though, unable to bring himself to step inside. Dixie had to give him a little push.

"Hello, Spanky," I said as he stumbled through the hatch. For the third time, Palazzo dropped everything he was carrying and fell upon the deck. "It's time to pay the piper," I told him.

"NO!" Palazzo bawled as he crawled to the furthest corner of the space. "Noooooo! Please, Doyle! I didn't do anything to deserve this! Please don't hurt me!"

Claude closed the hatch to ensure that the well-deck camera could not record what was going on. Then we all slowly stepped toward where Palazzo was cowering. The man was hysterical. "Please! Pleeeeaaaaseeee," he cried. "I didn't do anything! I didn't hurt anyone! I'm not what you think I am! I'm just a loser! Okay! I said it! I'm a fucking loser! I'm worthless! I'm scum! Are you happy now?!? Plea-he-he-hease! Leave me alone! I don't want to end up like Randy Green! I never hurt any kids! I never did anyth…"

"Hey!" Dixie said, cracking a wide grin. "Can you guys hear that?"

I did. I caught it as Spanky inhaled to catch his breath. It sounded like running water. Reaching over, I unhooked the square yellow battle lantern from the inboard bulkhead. Turning it on, I pointed the beam of light right at Palazzo's crotch. Claude erupted into laughter. "Holee sheet!" he exclaimed. "You wore right! He deed peess hees pants!"

Kevin shook his head in disbelief as Spanky looked down at his zipper in shame and horror. "Oh my god. I thought that was only a figure of speech. I didn't think people actually got so scared that they literally pissed themselves. Have you ever seen this shit happen before, Doyle?"

I shook my head. "Nope. I figured if there was anyone who would do it, though, it would be this pussy." I held out my hand. "You got something for me, Dixie?"

"Yeah, hold on," Kevin said as he reached for his wallet. Pulling out a twenty-dollar bill, he slapped it into my outstretched palm. Turning to Metaire, I asked, "Claude?"

"*Oui*." Reaching into his dungarees, Metaire handed me twenty bucks as well.

With our bet settled, the three of us turned to walk out of the space. Before we left, I turned to Spanky and said, "Make sure you clean up your mess before you turn in. If I come down here tomorrow morning and smell piss, I'm going to have you scrubbing this place down with your fucking toothbrush. Understand?"

Palazzo nodded his head pathetically.

Before leaving, I could not help myself from laughing in Spanky's face one last time. When I finished, I said, "See, John? I told you that you were going to have yourself an accident."

*****

CHAPTER 10

As satisfying as watching John Palazzo wet himself down in the Nixie space was, it was not nearly enough to satiate my bloodlust. Every time I saw his face, my mind went to that little girl in the Polaroids I found in the fan room. I pictured what he must have done to her when he ran out of film. I wanted to hurt him. I wanted to hurt him worse than I had wanted to hurt Randy Green. My fantasies about what I could do to Spanky grew so violent that they were threatening to trigger one of my episodes.

I was descending into a very dark place. Filling with rage, I knew that sooner or later, I was going to blow. I needed help. Hoping to do something before I gave into my desire to seriously hurt Gianni Palazzo, I called Yukiko. Hearing the distress in my voice as I spoke to her, she made immediate arrangements to have me meet with her *guru*.

Shintaro Nishimura grew up in San Francisco, so, like Yukiko, his English was flawless. I also found his mannerisms far more American than Japanese. Casually dressed in a sweater and jeans, he was far from what I expected a Buddhist master to look like. Shaking my hand at the temple's entrance, Shintaro skipped the bow and asked, "So, you are the Doyle Murphy I heard so much about?"

Nodding, I answered, "I suppose I am."

"Yukiko tells me that you're interested in meditation. Is that true?"

I nodded again. "Yes."

"Why?" Shintaro asked. "What do you expect to achieve with meditation?"

I had no idea. I was there because Yukiko said that it could help me. Still, I needed to come up with something. "Uh, maybe some inner peace?"

The *guru* laughed. "If meditation could do that, the whole world would be Buddhist."

I was confused. "Then what does meditation do? Yukiko said that it could help me."

Shintaro shrugged. "Maybe it will. Maybe it won't. Look, Murphy-*san*, meditation is all about relaxation and mindfulness. It's about concentrating on the present moment, putting the past in its place, and suppressing anxiety about the future. It's about being here, in the now, the only place in time that you can do anything about. Your past is water under the bridge. Your future does not exist yet, but it is dependent on what you do here, in your present. Live for the now."

"And meditation will help me do that?"

"It will help you relax."

"How does relaxing help me?"

Shintaro frowned at me. "How does relaxing *not* help you? Yukiko tells me you have outbursts. A type of rage."

Disappointed that Yukiko did not keep that incident to herself, I said, "Yeah, my past hasn't been very kind to me. I get these episodes…"

"People do not generally lose their temper when they are relaxed, Murphy-*san*."

"Well, it's hard to relax when hallucinations of your dead family claw out of your frontal lobes to harsh your mellow on occasion."

Shintaro did not respond at first. He just stared at me, wondering what he was up against. Eventually, he nodded and said, "Well, let us see if we can fix that. The road to recovery has to start somewhere. Teaching you to relax will certainly not hurt you."

Leaving Yukiko behind, Shintaro led me down a temple corridor to a room devoid of furniture or decorations. It was just four walls of *shoji* wood and paper screens and a large *tatami* mat on the floor. For added ambiance, they piped in the sound of flowing water from somewhere in the background. It was supposed to be relaxing but all it did was make me want to urinate.

Following Shintaro's direction, I took a seat in the middle of the room with my legs crossed. He had me rest my forearms on my knees, touching the tips of my thumbs to the ends of my middle fingers. "Straighten your back," Shintaro told me. I immediately obeyed. "Now close your eyes and breathe, Murphy-*san*. In through your nose, out through your mouth. Concentrate on your breath. Notice how it feels as the air is pulled into your sinuses. Feel the sensation of it as it flows down the back of your throat. Your lungs. Feel them expand as you draw in the air…"

The *guru* lowered his voice in both octave and volume. "Hold it in. Yes, that's it. Feel the tingling in your chest…for just a little while. Now, let it out. Concentrate on the falling of your abdomen. Feel the compression of your lungs. Be aware of the air rising up through your throat…out through your mouth. Let it go. Now, do it again. Push all thought out of your mind, concentrating only on breathing. Breathing. Only breathing."

Shintaro went through this process several more times, not necessarily teaching me how to breathe, but how to be aware of it. He taught me how to appreciate and savor it. When he was satisfied that I could do that, he leaned in close to my ear and whispered, "I want you to relax your toes, now. Let your muscles release and let go. Good, good. Now your feet. Perfect. Relax your legs. Now your chest. Good. Now your shoulders. Yes, yes. Now your neck…let it go."

It was working. I felt warm and safe, teetering on the edge of sleep, yet not at all tired. Just calm. Relaxed. It was more like a trance. The constant noise in my head had dissipated, leaving me in a state of awe and wonder. I had not even realized it was there until Shintaro showed me how to make it go away. I wondered how long that racket had been…

"Don't worry about it," Shintaro told me.

"Worry about what?" I groggily asked.

"Whatever it is you're trying to think about right now. Concentrate only on your breathing. In through the nose, out through the mouth. Relax your body again, starting with your toes. Then your feet. Then your…"

And there it was again. It was dark but inviting, almost as if I was floating in some nurturing void. I felt myself starting to smile.

"Relax your face, Murphy-san. No smile. No frown. Clear all your thoughts. Only think of breathing. Now, relax your toes…"

I got there again. I was in that state of peace, but it was so hard to stay there. Nature abhors a vacuum. I discovered that the more I pushed my thoughts out of my head, the harder they fought to get back inside. I remembered something Dixie said to me once after he brought me out of one of my episodes.

Jesus Christ, Doyle! Put you in any kind of high-pressure situation, and you're the coolest cat I know. Leave you alone with your own thoughts for any more than fifteen minutes, though, and you fall apart!

"Relax, Murphy-*san*. Breathe."

I thought about that episode. It was brought on by a bad dream that revealed me to be the reason that my father murdered my family. It was my fault that those soldiers had executed that girl in El Salvador. My fault that Macklemore got thrown out of the Navy. That I had to kill that boy in Olongapo. That Tejada had Rafaela Green murdered. Rafaela. *Rafaela*. "Rafaela…"

"No, Murphy-*san*. Breathe. Concentrate on your breathing." Shintaro sounded far away. And underwater.

I was sweating, shaking. I wondered what they had done to Rafaela when they found her. Did they kill her quick, or did they make her suffer for trying to kill me? I had not thought of that since I left the Philippines. My subconscious was doing a great job at suppressing it. Now it was in my face, though, and I could not get away from it. I could see Rafaela, plain as day, pleading with her killers to let her see her son. It would have been the only thing she wanted to do. "Jesus Christ," I whimpered.

"Murphy-*san*!" I could tell Shintaro was yelling at me now, but I could barely hear him. He was so far away.

I could only imagine what Tejada's men might have done to Rafaela. I was sure that they had at least beat her. They might have raped her, too. After all, she was only a whore. The men she sent after me also shot Sergeant Tejada. For that, he might have taken a personal interest in watching her suffer. What TJ and his men had done to Rafaela, could they also do it to Tala if I ever crossed him? Mari? Suddenly, an image of Tejada's face filled my mind and I opened my eyes, only to see him reaching for me.

Letting out a scream, I lashed out, bunching up my fist and sending it hurtling toward Tejada's jaw. It connected perfectly, sending him hurtling backward onto the deck. Before he could retaliate, I was upon him with my fingers around his throat. I cranked my arm back and aimed a second blow toward the side of the policeman's head. I had every intention of taking his life.

*****

Besides being a Buddhist *guru*, Shintaro Nishimura was also a black belt in Shotokan Karate. I have no idea what he did, but everything went black before I could deliver a second punch to the man. The pain in my neck suggested that he put my lights out with some sort of chokehold.

I was not out long. When I came back, I was by myself but could hear Yukiko and Shintaro speaking in Japanese on the other side of the *shoji* wall. I could not understand the entire conversation, but I was able to get the gist of it.

"I am not saying this as a spiritual teacher, Yukiko-*chan*. I am speaking as a licensed psychologist now. That boy needs help. He is very dangerous."

"Uncle, he is a good man. He…"

I heard Shintaro sigh. "I am not arguing about his intentions. He has a sickness that expresses itself in violence. It's no surprise after what you told me about his family. How well do you think you would be if your father killed your mother and your sister? I am not saying that it is his fault that he is this way, only that he is."

"But, Uncle…"

"Yukiko, it is my job to see people like him all the time. Men like him hurt people. They don't want to, but they have no control over it. They get triggered and they snap. That boy is a walking time bomb, Yukiko. The odds are that when he blows, he is not going to hurt someone that deserves it. He's going to hurt someone that he cares about. I am begging you, Yukiko. Please do not let it be you. Do not get involved with this man."

After a brief pause, I heard Yukiko finally say, "*Hai*. I will not see him anymore, Uncle."

Shintaro breathed a long sigh of relief. "Good. That makes me feel much better. Take him home and beg him to get help. Mark my words, child. If he does not get this thing taken care of, that kid is going to kill somebody."

*****

A few days after my flirtation with Buddhism, Chief Ramirez pulled me out of my rack a little after midnight. "Were you out in town tonight?" he asked as I tried to shake some of the cobwebs out of my head.

"Yeah. Why?"

"Where'd you go?"

"Shooters. I also had a drink at the Suntory Tavern on Four Corners. What's this about?"

"Did you see Spanky out there?"

I shook my head. "Palazzo? Nope. Not at all. Did someone kick his teeth in or something?" I assumed somebody finally caught up to the man and gave the prick what he deserved. Obviously, I would be a prime suspect in a situation like that, but I was not concerned. My alibis were solid that night.

"I saw him," said AO2 Trevor Burke as he stuck his head out of his rack. "He got thrown out of the Panda Pub."

Chief Ramirez raised an eyebrow. "For what?"

Burke laughed. "The boy was all fucked up. One of the girls led him on all night and he dropped a wad of cash on her thinking she was going to go home with him."

The Panda Pub was a hostess bar that catered to Americans. That was the place's *modus operandi*. It was staffed with pretty young girls who did their best to convince sailors to buy them drinks for three times the usual price. They were good at making you think that they were interested in you, but they never were. No one ever got lucky out of that place. They just got their wallets lightened.

"Spanky got pissed when she backed out," Burke told us. "He made quite a scene."

I remembered what Palazzo did in Korea when a girl refused to sleep with him for money. "Did he get violent?" I asked.

"He didn't hit anybody, but he acted like he might slap his hostess around. He never got the chance, though. A couple of guys from the *Dubuque* pounced on him and threw his ass outside."

"Do you know where he went after that?" Ramirez asked. Burke shook his head.

"Do you?" I asked my chief.

Ramirez sighed. "I'm trying to put that together now. There was a disturbance at a soapland club…"

"A what?" Burke asked.

"A Turkish bath," I answered. "A type of brothel."

"Yeah," Chief Ramirez agreed. "But one that would be way out of Palazzo's price range even if they let foreigners use it. Someone matching Palazzo's description was pretty upset about being denied entrance."

I grinned. "What'd he do there?"

Ben shrugged. "Who knows? He did a lot of screaming. He probably leveled some threats. None of it mattered because no one there understood a word he said. They didn't speak English. After that, there's a couple hour gap where I can't account for him."

Raising my own eyebrow, I asked, "Why do you need to?"

Chief Ramirez sighed. "Because Shore Patrol found him passed out cold in Nimitz Park. As they were dragging him back through the main gate, the Japanese guards flagged him and brought him into the guard shack to put him in a lineup. A local woman tentatively ID'd him as a man who might have sexually assaulted her."

"What do you mean 'tentatively?'" I growled.

"It means she's not sure. You know, you white guys all look alike to the Japanese sometimes, just like they do to you. She flagged a half-dozen men that *might* have assaulted her. She's not able to pin any of them down as the one who *definitely* did."

"Goddammit!" I barked as I shot out of my rack. "I'm going to fucking kill him!"

Ramirez reached out and grabbed a handful of my t-shirt. "You are not! You're going to keep your hands to yourself, Doyle! Do you understand?!?"

"Why? So he can go out and molest more…"

"Shut it! That's a rumor that I am NOT going to let you spread!"

I was going to argue with Ramirez and let him know that I personally knew that the word going around the ship about Spanky was no rumor. Luckily, I realized that I would have confessed to destroying evidence had I blurted that out. I decided to try another tack. "Fine! What about all the porn?!? How about all the times we caught the son-of-a-bitch playing with himself?!? What do we have to do to stop this guy before he does something like…like…like this?!? We tried to get the prick off this ship before we left San Diego and no one would listen to us! What does he have to do before they listen to us now?!?"

"Doyle, look, the man has a reputation for being fond of smut," Ramirez snapped at me. "That leaves him vulnerable to accusations like this. It makes people like you want to jump to conclusions every time anyone insinuates something about the guy! I'm not throwing this man under the bus based upon accusations! We're going to let it play out. If this thing ends up having legs, I'm going to see to it myself that the man feels the full weight of the US Navy bearing down upon him. Until he's proven guilty, though, you're going to lay off of him!"

"He's guilty, Chief."

"You don't know that!"

"I do."

Ramirez was usually an even-keeled guy, but I was testing his patience. "Doyle, this thing you got with Palazzo, it's an awful lot like the thing that Krause has with you. Do you see me agreeing with him when he accuses you of being involved with that tweaker that got killed on Magsaysay when we were in Olongapo? Or when he insists you had something to do with that shootout that happened down the street from where you guys were staying? No. I give my men the benefit of the doubt until the evidence proves otherwise. This is what we, you and I, are going to do here. We're going to stand back and see where this thing with Palazzo goes."

Chief Ramirez was one of my favorite people aboard the *Belleau Wood.* Considering that I *was* involved in the junkie's death on Magsaysay *and* the gun battle on Harris Street, I did not have much faith in his instincts, though. Not when it came to stuff like this. "So we do nothing?" I asked. "When he gets back, we set him free until he rapes someone else?"

"Oh, no," Ben told me. "He's not going anywhere until this shit gets sorted out. Palazzo's confined to the ship until he's cleared. When they bring him back, you need to confiscate his ID card."

*****

Palazzo was standing in front of the entire shop, shaking. "I didn't do it," he said.

"Bullshit." Dixie was all smiles. "You know you're going to a Japanese prison for this, right?"

John shook his head. "No, I won't. There's the Status of Forces Agreement signed with Japan. They'll…"

"Read the SOFA, Spanky," I told him. "That only applies if a serviceman commits a crime against another American serviceman. If you commit a crime against a Japanese national, they get to keep your sorry ass."

"That's not true," Palazzo said, entirely without conviction.

"It is true," Dixie told him. "When I was on Shore Patrol a couple of months ago, I went with the Master-at-Arms to pick up a guy who just did fifteen years in a Jap jail for mugging a local taxi driver. A decade and a half. Apparently, they don't feed you very well in there, Spanky. Just rice, fish, and *miso* broth. Our guy looked like he got paroled from a concentration camp."

"I hear they like to fuck with foreigners in prison, too," Hammond said.

"Yep," Dixie answered. "Our guy said he was getting his ass beat by both the prisoners and the guards on the regular. He said that it was a pretty miserable way to spend fifteen years."

"Look at the bright side, Spanky," I told him. "After twenty years of rice and fish, you'll be coming out of the pokey a lean, mean, fighting machine. I bet you drop sixty pounds. And you'll be fluent in Japanese. Nobody on the inside here speaks English."

"You think this is funny?" Palazzo asked us.

I stood up and walked over to Spanky, grossly invading his personal space. "It's hilarious. This shit could not have happened to a better person. The only regret I have is that I won't be able to get my hands on you before your cellmates will. Twenty years, John. Twenty years. You'll be, what? Forty-six when you get out? Damn. It'll be too late to start a real career, not that anyone is going to hire you after you've spent most of your adult life behind bars."

"Not to menshun zhat you'll be a sex oaffendair," Claude added.

"No kidding," I laughed. "A sex offender. Man, that's an even heavier cross to bear. Your life is pretty much over, dude."

Unable to come up with a good response, Palazzo turned to me and said, "At least I'll be far away from you."

I laughed out loud. "You think so? I'm thinking that those guys who got me my jacket back might have some connections in prison. If I'm nice to them, you think they might help me make your life behind bars even more miserable than it already would be?"

I could see Spanky think back to the night he saw me get out of Furukawa's Lincoln at the foot of the Albuquerque Bridge. He probably thought that there might have been more to my interaction with the *yakuza* that night than a minor article of stolen property. Palazzo began to suspect that I really could get to him if he ended up in a Japanese prison. Knowing what I had done to Randy Green, it must have terrified him.

Close to tears, Palazzo stood up and stormed out of Radar Repair. He sprinted down the ladder to Comm Repair to find ET1 Bard. Our LPO was not there. Sergeant Fordson was. "What the fuck do you want?" the Marine snapped.

"I'm looking for Bard," John answered.

"Well, Spanky," Clay told him. "I'm pretty sure that Tony doesn't want to see you. Nor do I. Get the fuck out of my shop."

"Look, can I just wait here for Bard to get back?"

Bill Kramer was overjoyed to finally have someone in the division even more unpopular than he was. To score points and improve his standing even more, he got up out of his seat and stepped towards Palazzo. "No. You heard the sergeant. Get out of here. Now." When Cleveland and Willis stood to join Kramer, Palazzo retreated and left.

He tried the DS shop next. DS1 de Alba threw him out before he even got through the door. Palazzo then went to the calibration lab. ET1 Nevers told him to get lost also. The only place left for him to go was the EMO. Palazzo could count upon Master Chief Darrow to be indifferent to him and Chief Ramirez to have a sympathetic ear. All the chiefs were gone, though. Even Brennen, the division's RPPO, was absent. The only person occupying the Electronic Materials Office was LTJG Andrew Krause. The lieutenant shuddered when he saw Palazzo standing in front of him. "What the hell do you want, Petty Officer?"

Spanky paused for a second, thinking about what he was going to do. "I want to help you, sir."

Krause scoffed. "Help me with what? What do you think you can do for me?"

"I want to help you get Murphy, sir."

Laughing, the lieutenant spun his chair sideways. "And how does a known pervert under suspicion for a sexual assault expect to help me get Doyle Murphy?"

"I can tell the NIS that the attack on Randy Green was premeditated."

Krause raised an eyebrow. "And why would they believe you?"

"Because I know two other guys who Doyle beat in the Nixie winch room at the suggestion of Master Chief Darrow." Palazzo gulped as he said this. Conspiring against me was one thing. Crossing Darrow was something else altogether. He regretted uttering the master chief's name the instant it left his lips, but once it was gone, there was nothing he could do to take it back.

"The two names I can give you, they can corroborate that Murphy was known for doing that kind of stuff," Palazzo continued. "They're both out of the Navy now, but I'm sure that they'd leap at the opportunity to burn his thug ass."

Lieutenant Krause stood up in surprise. "Really? Who are these men?"

"Sir, I didn't do what that woman accused me of in town. I don't even know who she is or where I might've crossed paths with her at. I'm innocent."

"So? What does that have to do with Murphy? What are the names of the two men that…"

"Sir, get me out of this jam and I'll give you those names."

"How am I supposed to…?"

"Give me an alibi! Be a character witness for me! Have the NIS look harder into this shit! Something! For Christ's sake, sir…!"

Krause stuck his finger in Palazzo's face. "Don't you blaspheme in here, son! You do not take the Lord's name in vain in front of me!" After settling down, the lieutenant dropped his hand and asked, "Son, I hate to break this to you, but the accusation of a suspected sexual predator may not be enough to…"

"I saw Murphy in the company of a Japanese gangster, too!"

"What?" Krause asked, his mouth agape.

"I saw Murphy get out of a mobster's car! Please, sir! Help me!"

"How did you know it was a mobster's car?"

"It was a black Lincoln. The driver's arms were covered in tattoos! That's the mob here, isn't it?"

"It is," Krause said, pausing to think for a couple of minutes. "If Murphy's doing something with the mob around here, I'm sure he's not doing it on his own. Darrow's got to be involved."

The morsel Palazzo cooked up for the lieutenant was suddenly looking mighty juicy. Krause wanted to take a bite but had to consider the unsavory character of the chef. "How am I supposed to know whether you did anything to that woman or not?"

Spanky's shoulders slumped. "I guess you don't. I would just ask who you think is more dangerous. Would the greater good be served by taking me out of circulation or by putting Murphy and Darrow in the brig?"

Once Palazzo put it that way, Krause mulled his choices. "A disgusting pervert and a potential rapist, or the henchman to a military gangster? Alright, son. Let me see what I can do for you."

*****

CHAPTER 11

Our visit to Hong Kong had been scheduled long before Reaper Dick took command. If he could have, the captain likely would have canceled it to avoid giving his crew any time off. Hong Kong was a liberty port, visited with the mission of fostering goodwill amongst our allies. In this case, it was a show of solidarity with the English in the face of the Communist Chinese. Hong Kong was still a British colony in 1993.

Between what happened to Hammond, Krause's petty torments, and our skipper's incessant sadism, we desperately needed the time off. Morale was at an all-time low, and Master Chief Darrow knew it. As we pulled in from off of the South China Sea, he made sure we knew where to find a good time, giving us a tour of the city's impressive skyline from the flight deck. Waving his hand across the ship's starboard side, he said, "All these buildings over there are Hong Kong's business district. That white one there is the Asia House. That's where you need to go to change your money into Hong Kong dollars."

Looking around, Darrow spotted a smaller white building closer to the spot where we would moor. He made sure we all got a good look at it. "That building is the headquarters of the British Navy's Pacific Fleet here at HMS Tamar. That's where the English admiral sits. Off to its side is an impressive collection of rose bushes. Now, the English have a weird fetish when it comes to their roses, gentlemen. Do! Not! Get! Caught! Pissing! In! The! Admiral's! Rose bushes!" Turning his attention to Dixie and me, he punctuated his statement with, "Understand?"

It was an attempt at levity, but it fell flat. We were too tired and too demoralized to care. Darrow did not take it personally when no one laughed. "The Hong Kong side has some fun places and is loaded with pretty Chinese girls speaking with English accents, but things can get pretty pricey over there. If you want to hang out close to the ship, this area is chock full of Filipinas working here as domestics. They like to hang out at a place called the Pussycat Club, not far from where we'll be moored."

This brought a smile to Dixie's face, which Darrow quickly extinguished. "Despite its name Petty Officer Dixon, it's not a whorehouse. It's a regular old nightclub." Master Chief then walked us over to the port side of the flight deck. "Kowloon is the nightlife center of Hong Kong. There're all kinds of places over there filled with people from all over the world. It's a neat place, very international, and very cosmopolitan. It's also cheap."

Peering over the side, I was surprised to see a flotilla of junks, the traditional wooden Chinese vessels, floating about the waters around us. They looked like modern-day relics harkening back to the nineteenth century's opium wars.

I walked back over to the ship's starboard side and looked at the pier we were mooring against. I guessed space in Hong Kong was at a premium. Though we were officially docking at HMS Tamar, it did not look like much of a naval base. For starters, the *USS Belleau Wood* was the only ship there. Second, there was no security besides a pair of British MPs on walking patrol. Their rounds were sporadic at best. The only thing separating our ship from town was a waist-high chain link fence with unguarded gaps in it every fifty feet or so.

Hong Kong was one of the most densely populated places on the entire planet. On the other side of that little fence was a massive mob of humanity walking to whatever destination they were headed for. The only thing keeping them away from our ship was their lack of interest in it. I did not feel threatened by that at all, just surprised. In San Diego, we did not even trust our fellow Americans enough to give them that kind of access to our fleet. Hell, for all the scrutiny we had to go through just to get to work in the morning, the US Navy barely trusted its own sailors with it.

"You going to Kowloon with us?" Dixie asked, sliding up next to me.

"Not right away," I answered. "I need some sleep, Kevin. I'm wrecked."

"How about you, Claude?"

Metaire shook his head. "Not right now. I zhink zhat I might go fair a run or somezhing."

"Okay," Kevin said, shrugging his shoulders. "I guess it's up to me to keep the master chief out of trouble then."

I took my nap but did not sleep nearly as long as I thought I would. When I awoke, I went to the shop to catch up on some television but found Spanky up there. As he was restricted to the ship until the NIS concluded their investigation, Hong Kong was not a liberty port for him. I stayed long enough to give the man a list of chores to do while the rest of us enjoyed our time ashore. It was just a little more salt to rub into his wounds.

On my way back down from the island structure, I caught sight of some guys on the wharf playing basketball on a net set up on the side of one of the utility buildings. Metaire was among them, so I put on my PT gear and walked down to watch.

"Hey! Doyle!" Metaire called out when he spotted me. "You want to join us?"

I was the only white guy there. One of the men Claude was playing with, a towering flight line airman named Dre Jackson, laughed. "Shee-it! You gonna let this cracker play with us? Ain't you seen that movie that came out last year with Wesley Snipes, Frenchie? If you did, you'd know that white men can't jump!"

"I bet I can play basketball better than you can swim," I retorted.

The players all busted up laughing at that, none harder than Dre himself. "OK, Paleface," Jackson laughed. "Get your ass out here and show us what you got!"

I didn't have much. I could not shoot to save my life. I smoked too much to have any endurance and showed no inherent skill in dribbling, defense, or free throws. "God DAY-um," Jackson roared after seeing me at my worst. "You were lyin' your ass off when you told us you could play ball!"

"I never implied I could play ball," I told him. "I was just suggesting that you couldn't swim."

Jackson guffawed and slapped me on the back.

A short time later, a group of British soldiers showed up and looked a bit dismayed to find their court occupied. After trading some good-natured barbs with the Limeys, we found ourselves challenged to a friendly match by our hosts. We accepted and then proceeded to destroy them on the court. With little effort and no mercy at all, the *Belleau Wood* sailors ran the score up to the tune of eighty to ten within thirty minutes. Not surprisingly, there was a great deal of smack talk exchanged between the two sides. The ribbing intensified when the Yanks threatened to drive the score into triple digits, forcing the English to call the game.

One of the Brits tried to defend their honor by pointing out that they didn't grow up playing basketball as we Yanks did. They came up playing rugby, a brutal sport for real men. He promised that if we agreed to face them in a rugby match, we'd find out what true humiliation felt like. All that my basketball teammates could do was look at the puny pale Englishmen before us and laugh. We accepted their offer.

We marched off towards the Prince of Wales Barracks, which had a soccer field in the center of it. Our hosts told us to wait there while they disappeared back into their quarters. When they returned, they brought a rugby ball and a couple dozen spectators, both Chinese and English. They all looked like they were anticipating a really good time.

The Englishmen spent twenty minutes explaining the basic rules of the game. After that, they still had to help us, man by man, interlock our arms across our shoulders into something called a scrum. The British then took up a similar formation across from us while some Scotsman shoved a ball between the opposing groups of men. Immediately afterward, a whistle blew to unleash a brawl over who got to keep the ball.

Predictably, it was not the Americans who did. It was the English and we had to endure a flurry of body slams, elbows, trips, and tackles trying to get the ball. We never did. The Brits ran it right down the field and scored. That happened two more times in short order and to raucous applause from the spectators.

After the British scored for the third time, by some weird twist of fate, I saw the ball on the ground in front of me after one of those scrum things. Because I did not fully appreciate what happens in rugby when you have the ball, I reached down and scooped it up. I immediately looked behind me and saw three maniacal subjects of the British Crown racing in my direction at a full sprint. I could see by the expressions on their faces that they had nothing short of murder on their minds. I ran for my life at a speed that surprised everyone present, especially those who had seen me play basketball. To a man, my teammates started chanting, "Go, white boy! Go, white boy! Go! Go, white boy! Go, white boy! Go!" I appreciated the encouragement but found out the hard way that I would have appreciated some solid blocking even more.

I was so worried about the savages gaining ground behind me that I never saw the two blokes closing in from the front. When we collided, the wind got forced from my lungs by a knee I took to the stomach. The other man's elbow struck me above my eyebrows hard enough to push me almost into concussion territory. The three of us, inter-tangled and struggling for the ball, hurtled to the ground. When we landed, the pointy end of one of the men's cleats found its way into my crotch. A round of cheers erupted from the stands while gasps of horror burst from the mouths of my teammates. I ended up in the fetal position, writhing around in the grass.

A big Scottish sergeant by the name of Ian McCallister knelt beside me and exclaimed, "Jaysus! Wha' a bonkers hit! For shite's sake, man! Y'alright?"

I was lying there, holding my nuts in a death grip and unable to breathe. "No," I wheezed. "I'm pretty fucked up."

The sergeant stood up. "It's serious, mates! MEDIC!"

A little Chinese girl jumped from the stands and ran to me, lugging one of those black medical bags you used to see doctors carry in the 1970s. When she reached me, she asked, "Where you hurt?"

"My eye," I coughed. "My gut. And my balls."

She nodded. "Okay. I here to help." She opened up her bag, pulled out a bottle of Jameson, and poured me a shot. "Take this! Quickly!"

McCallister sat me upright so I could drink. Trying to be a good sport about everything, I grabbed the little shot glass and threw it back. I was never much of a whiskey drinker, so I winced at the burn. The girl helped with that by handing me an open bottle of Bass Ale. After chugging that down, I jumped to my feet and screamed, "It's a miracle! I'm cured! Hallelujah!"

The Brits all applauded and started walking toward us Yanks. The game was over. They proved their point. Now it was time to have a few beers and laugh about the whole thing. Two men named Nigel Turing and Nick Johnson sat with Sergeant McCallister and me to help us finish the bottle of whiskey. After that, it was back to the ship to clean up and grab a quick bite to eat before meeting our new friends in Kowloon at a place called The Watering Hole.

*****

The Watering Hole was a popular venue. It was full of expatriates and travelers from all over the world. The waitresses reflected the clientele. There were two from the UK, one from Germany, one from Japan, and one from Brazil. Oddly enough, I think the Chinese were the only nationality I did not see represented there. A quarter of the patrons that night were sailors and Marines from the *USS Belleau Wood*. Another quarter were business travelers or expatriates. The rest were tourists.

When we walked in, one of the British waitresses, a waif of a woman barely five feet tall and weighing about as much as an anorexic Lhasa Apso, bet a table full of hulking Marines that she could chug a pint of beer quicker than they could. After the drinks were lined up, she stretched her lips over the top of her glass. At the word "GO!" she threw her head back and sucked down the contents of the entire pint in a single gulp. The Marines had not even got their glasses to their mouths before she had finished. For that impressive display of drinking power, she earned $100 and two marriage proposals.

At one point in the evening, I walked up to the bar to refill our drinks when I noticed Darrow and Dixie were there. With a good buzz going, I slid in between them and slapped them on their backs. "Hey! Fancy seeing you two here!"

Darrow swung his head around to return the greeting but stopped when he saw my face. "Did you get into another goddamn fight?"

"No! Why?"

"It looks like you're getting a black eye."

I glanced up at the mirror behind the bar, but it was too far away for me to see anything. "If I am, it's from playing rugby with those savages over there…" I said while waving my arm at the table of Brits we were drinking with. "What have you guys been doing?"

Dixie raised his glass. "This is it. We figured we'd get our drunk on in Kowloon and then make our way back to Hong Kong. We're going to try our luck with the girls at the Pussycat Club. It's turning out to be a swell day!"

"Really? Why's that?" I asked.

"I had a long conversation with the department head earlier," Darrow told me.

"Yeah? What about?"

Darrow grinned. "Hammond. And Krause. You know, Doyle, there was no way the captain could have let Hammond skate for falling asleep on watch and kept his reputation as a disciplinarian. Winston knew this. That's why he wasn't there to stick up for the guy. He knew it'd be a waste of time. What struck Winston about that whole thing, though, was that you corrected the situation to get Hammond some sleep. Krause interfered with your solution and got the division's best technician busted to a seaman. In one fell swoop, he destroyed what little morale was left in the division. Winston was furious about that. You know, neither he nor I have ever seen a more destructive officer in all of our years in the Navy. I know for sure now that we'll be rid of him after the next evaluation cycle. Honestly, with this captain, I can see him getting fired even before then."

"Did he know that Krause had the engineering fire watch bust Hammond so no one could keep the report chit from getting to the old man?"

Darrow took a long drag off of his cigarette. "He does now."

"What did he say about that?"

Our master chief shrugged. "Not a damn thing. He didn't have to. That bright shade of crimson his face turned said it all. Like we predicted, Krause can't stop fucking himself. All we have to do is leave him to his own devices and he'll do our heavy lifting for us."

"Wonderful," I said. "Too bad we only had to sacrifice Rick's rank to get him to fall out of favor."

"We'll get Hammond's crow back," Darrow assured me. "I promise. By the way, we also talked about you offering up one of your chevrons to the captain so that Hammond could keep his."

I arched one of my eyebrows. "And?"

"We agreed that you're an idiot," Darrow told me. "Don't do that again. You know the Navy doesn't work that way. It looked like you're trying to be friends with your subordinates instead of being their boss. Understand?"

"Yes, Master Chief. I'm sorry but…"

"*Hallo*." I was interrupted by a female voice from behind. "Are you Doyle Murphy?"

I turned around to see a very cute brunette with bright green eyes smiling at me. "Yeah, I am. Who are you?"

"My name is Anneke. My friend and I are talking with Claude…" I looked behind her and saw Metaire sitting at a table with another pretty girl, a red-head who appeared as if she belonged to Anneke. When he saw me looking at them, he rose his glass up at me in salute and smiled wide. "…he said you talk about work too much with these guys. He thinks you should come back to the table with us."

Darrow grinned and introduced himself to Anneke. "Are you from Holland?"

"*Ja*."

"What part?"

"Eindhoven."

"Cool," my master chief said. "I love your accent. Anneke, Claude is right about Doyle. Me and Dixie are up here at the bar trying to forget about the ship, and he has to barge into our conversation and start talking shop. Could you please get him away from us?"

Anneke smiled at them all and then took my hand, leading me back to their table. We stayed at the Watering Hole for another couple of rounds. We learned that Anneke and Femke were touring the Far East as a graduation present from their parents. They had been to Bangkok, Hanoi, Jakarta, and now Hong Kong. They would soon be leaving to visit Seoul and Tokyo before returning home.

When we left The Watering Hole, we had a couple of drinks at Ned Kelley's across the street. We then walked along the waterfront to take in the skyline before riding the ferry back across the harbor to Hong Kong. There we had a light dinner of noodles and spent some time at an underground disco in Sheung Wan dancing to German techno music. At a quieter venue in Wan Chai, we coupled up when Anneke kissed me. The girls were staying in a hotel nearby, so they took us up to their room. Claude and Femke fell into one of the beds while Anneke practically threw me upon the other.

We learned relatively fast that there was nothing shy about Dutch girls. We were all in the same room, on two different beds just inches away from each other with the lights on. At first, I was not sure that I would be able to perform with an audience. After Anneke undressed and laid down on top of me, however, I could feel that stage fright would not be much of an issue. It certainly was no problem with the girls, who attacked us with enough enthusiasm that I am sure nobody on our floor slept for the next hour or so.

When we finished, Anneke and Femke turned off the lights and went into the bathroom together. Claude and I high-fived each other over the space between the beds and laughed over what we had just done. It was dark when the girls came out, but I could tell by the length of her hair that it was Femke who was getting into bed with me. "Uh, I think you have the wrong man…" I said as I felt her start rubbing my hip with the inside of her leg.

"No, I know where I am at," she purred.

"Wha…?"

"Anneke has never been with a black boy before, so she wanted to try Claude." Femke started kissing me on the chest and, with her tongue, traced a line that meandered all the way down below my beltline, forcing me to start reciting poetry in my head.

Decomposing manatees.
Eyeballs pierced with darts.
Richard Nixon naked blowing bloody liquid farts.

*****

While Claude and I were taking in the sights the following day with Anneke and Femke, Dixie met a local. Li Jing was one of those stunning Chinese girls who spoke flawless English with a British accent. While they were out and about, Kevin decided to impress her with a tour of the ship. It was a good move. Despite

Hong Kong being a busy port of call for American warships, Li Jing had never been aboard one before.

Dixie's date was impressed by the size of the hangar bay. The Harrier jump jets piqued her fascination and Kevin said that she was positively giddy to walk up and touch one. With one of the quartermasters' permission, Dixie even got her onto the bridge and took a picture of her sitting in the captain's chair.

The highlight of Li Jing's visit came when Dixie took her to the Radar Repair shop to show her where he worked. Dixie slid his key in the lock, turned the handle, and threw open the door only to catch John Palazzo with his pants around his knees, masturbating to a picture of Rick Hammond's wife that he pulled out of his shipmate's cabinet drawer.

Li Jing screamed. Dixie fell to the floor, laughing hysterically until he could regain his composure enough to escort his date off of the ship. When he told Claude and me the story at the end of our Hong Kong visit, the three of us laughed even harder. After that, we marched up to the Radar Repair shop together.

Palazzo was there by himself watching Star Trek on the BBC. Upon entering the shop, I walked over to the equipment racks and grabbed an empty cardboard bin. I then went to the workbench and opened up Spanky's personal drawer, pulling it completely out of its slot and dumping it into the box before Palazzo could do anything to stop me. "Hey!" he shouted, jumping to his feet. "That's my stuff! What do you think you're doing?!?"

I closed up the box then threw it into Spanky's chest. "Moving your shit out of here. Give me your key, John."

"What?!?" Palazzo gasped. "You can't do this! You can't just..."

"I can, and I did. Trying to get Hammond busted wasn't bad enough, so you went through his things to get a picture of his wife to jerk off to? You're fucking sick, man."

"I...I...I d-d-didn't..." Palazzo gave up trying to deny it when he looked over at Dixie, the man who caught him red-handed.

"You're not to be in here any more unsupervised, John. Give me your key."

"No," Spanky told me. I felt the heat of the blood rushing into my face and saw Dixie and Metaire maneuver themselves into a better position to get between us if I lost my temper.

"What did you just tell me?" I growled.

"No," Palazzo said as he set his box down and crossed his arms. He was standing firm. "I'm not giving you my key."

I took a step closer to Spanky. Dixie and Metaire took a step closer to me. Palazzo knew what they were doing and was emboldened by it. He knew that they were not going to let me hurt him. "I'm giving you a direct order, you pathetic piece of shit. Give me your key now!"

Spanky shook his head. "If you want it, come and get it."

I nearly did. I bunched up my fists, clenched my teeth, and was a hair away from launching myself at the punk. At the last instant, however, I realized that that was what Palazzo wanted me to do. If I struck him, I would be up in front of Reaper Dick that night. I would lose a chevron and find myself junior to Spanky once more. I did not take the bait. Instead, I decided that I would not wait for the Japanese to finish their investigation to end Palazzo's career. I was going to take it myself right there. "Fine, Palazzo. You're on report for insubordination."

Spanky's jaw dropped. Again, he grossly miscalculated my reaction. Frantically, he reached into his pocket to pull out his key ring. "Save it, dickhead," I snapped. "I've been waiting for an excuse to do this, and now I have one."

"Please, Doyle," Spanky pled.

"Go get fucked." I was pulling out a report chit but stopped to laugh in Palazzo's face. "Oh, but you can't, can you? That's too bad. You know, Claude and I got laid in Hong Kong. Did you get laid in Hong Kong, Dixie?"

Kevin nodded. "Yep."

"Hmmm, who didn't get laid in Hong Kong? I wonder…"

"I was restricted to the ship," Palazzo whined.

"Oh, like that would have made a difference!" I laughed as I sat down at my desk to fill out the form to send Spanky to captain's mast. "You don't get laid because you're pathetic, John. And now, you're going to be a civilian. Probably a prisoner, too."

Palazzo turned red and started shaking. It was no longer out of fear, however. It was rage. "Go ahead! Write me up, motherfucker! Burn me! I just want you all to know that I'm not going down alone! I'm taking every one of you pricks with me!"

Metaire scoffed. "Really? How do you zhink you're going to do zhat?"

"I don't *think* I'm going to do anything! I've already done it! I told Krause about Williams and Taylor, Doyle. He's going to relay it to the NIS! When they find out that you had a habit of beating up this division's problem children in the Nixie Room, they're going to look at what you did to Randy Green in a whole new light!"

Brian Taylor was a thief. We knew it but couldn't prove it. After we tuned him up a little, though, things stopped disappearing around our spaces. Scott Williams had an attitude problem. Again, after a little physical persuasion in a secluded part of the ship, his issues worked themselves out. Neither man even came close to getting beat into clinical epilepsy as Randy Green did, but if the NCIS got wind of what we did to them, it could reveal an awfully damning precedent.

Instead of me inching towards Spanky to wring his wretched little neck, Dixie did. "What did you do?" he snarled.

"You heard me! I fucking reported you! All of you! Once the NIS asks those two guys about what you did to them, they're going to re-open that investigation into Randy Green for sure!"

Claude looked at me. "Boaf of zhese guys are out of zhe Navy now. Can zhe NIS steell question zhem?"

I nodded. "The NIS are federal agents, just like the FBI. They can question anyone they want to. The question is, 'Will they?' Will it be worth it for them to re-open a closed case based upon the word of a suspected rapist and the biggest dipshit in the Navy's officer corps? I doubt it."

"Do you believe that?" Palazzo asked. "Do you think that the NIS is going to totally disregard a tip from a commissioned officer in the United States Navy?"

"Yes, I do," I lied. I stood up and walked over to Palazzo again. "And you should think about something before you go shooting your mouth off again. Do you really think it's a good idea to go up against a man like Master Chief Darrow, Olongapo Earp himself, when the only man you have in your corner is an idiot like Lieutenant Krause? Is that what you want?"

Palazzo swallowed uncomfortably. "It's not what I want, Doyle. It's the only option I have. What've I got to lose by taking the only shot I got?"

"You're about to find out, I imagine." Turning my back on Spanky, I sat back down at my desk and started filling out Palazzo's chit again.

"What?!?" Spanky gasped. "You're still putting me on report?!?"

"Why wouldn't I?" I asked.

"Because of what I know about you! Because of what I told the lieutenant!"

"You think that gives you leverage over me? You might have had some if you played those cards a little closer to your chest, but you've already shown your hand. You've blown your wad. Of course, I'm still putting you on report. What've *I* got to lose?"

*****

"Maybe I could throw his fat ass overboard."

"Are you serious?" Master Chief Darrow asked me. We were both sitting on the deck of the SPN-35 radar dome, smoking and contemplating what to do about Palazzo. "You want to drop him in the drink?"

I shrugged. "The man's a fucking pedophile and a rapist. If I didn't have the most obvious motive for wanting him out of the way, I'd seriously consider it."

Darrow stared at me for a couple of moments. It was hard to tell if he was concerned about what I had said or was impressed by it. "Yeah," my master chief finally said. "If anything, we need to make sure nothing happens to that son-of-a-bitch. If he so much as slips in the shower right now, the NIS is going to be on us like flies on shit."

"So, what do we do?" I asked.

Darrow took a long drag off of his cigarette and sighed as he exhaled. "You know, neither Palazzo nor Krause are reliable witnesses. Both have serious credibility issues. It's very possible that nothing comes of this. To be safe, though, it certainly wouldn't hurt us to compromise their credibility even more. What'd you do with those pictures you found in the fan room?"

"I tossed them overboard just like you told me to."

Darrow sighed and took another hit off of his Marlboro. "That's a shame. Those would have come in really handy right about now."

The two of us both sat and smoked in silence for a little while. Finally, Darrow interrupted it by saying, "You know, the ship got a report of two American sailors who were seen pissing in the admiral's rose bushes last night."

I grinned. "Yeah, that was me and Claude. The Limey MPs chased us right off of the pier. Luckily, we managed to blend into the crowd on the other side of the fence."

Master Chief Darrow shook his head and frowned. "I thought I told you not to get caught pissing in the admiral's rose bushes."

Shrugging my shoulders, I said, "You did. And we didn't. The Brits didn't catch us. We got away."

*****

CHAPTER 12

We were barely a day out of Hong Kong when the SPN-35 radar began acting up. The high voltage capacitor that started deteriorating in February was nearing the end of its life. Phantom returns were showing up all over the control indicators and current fluctuations wrought havoc upon the tuning crystals. They were not even lasting a third of their expected service life. I predicted that the radar would last two more weeks at best before it finally went down hard. Then I would end up in another argument with the EMO over the cost of getting it fixed.

It appeared that Lieutenant Krause was not willing to wait that long to have words with me, however. He stepped into the dome and interrupted me before I could shut down the radar's power to swap out its crystals. Lifting the report chit that I had written on Palazzo so that I could see it, the lieutenant tore it in half. He then let the pieces fall to the dome's deck. "I've had that happen to me enough on the chits I wrote on you that I figured you might enjoy knowing what it feels like."

I was not happy that Spanky was going to get away with disobeying a direct order. I was not going to give the EMO the satisfaction of knowing that, though. Dismissing it with a disinterested shrug, I said, "That's what I figured. Palazzo tells me the two of you are quite close now. Congratulations, sir. It looks like the start of a long and beautiful relationship. Have the two of you registered for china patterns or anything?"

Krause scowled. "You know, I came down here to make you an offer. If you're going to stand there and be a smart-aleck, though…"

I scoffed as I wiped my hands on a rag. "Offer? What kind of offer could you possibly have for me?"

"You're getting ready to go down in a big way, Murphy. A *big* way. I know that you and Darrow are reaching out to some unsavory characters back in Japan for something. The NIS is going to find out about that as soon as we reach Sasebo. They're going to hear about those boatswain's locker counseling sessions you used to conduct in the Nixie Winch Room, too. That's going to attract some new attention to what you guys did to Randy Green."

I laughed as I threw my rag back onto my workbench. I knew Krause had come to me hoping that I would give up something on Darrow. I decided to quash that idea before he even had the chance to ask. "You realize you don't know shit, right? You're being hoodwinked by a sick man lashing out in a moment of desperation."

"I know more than you think," the lieutenant assured me.

"No, sir," I countered. "You don't. That's because there's nothing to know. You have no idea what happened before you got here and this fantasy Palazzo's cooked up about us working with some 'unsavory characters' is hilarious! Does he think we're working with spies? The underworld? Whatever it is, you go right ahead and run to the NIS with that!"

I must have sounded more convincing than I felt. Krause looked like he suddenly had doubts about what Palazzo had told him. I was doing everything I could to keep him from seeing that my stomach was tying itself in knots. My lieutenant stood there, looking like he was giving my bluff some serious consideration. To break the standoff, I asked, "Well?"

"Well, what?" Krause almost sounded like he had forgotten what we were talking about.

"What are you going to do? Do you want me to go to the NIS with you when you report me?"

Krause looked taken aback by that suggestion. "Would you?"

"Are you kidding me? There's no way that I would want to miss that! I would love to sit at the table while you spun your little yarn just to see the look on the agents' faces when they realized how batshit crazy you really are."

Krause scowled at me with his mouth open, as if readying a retort. Unable to think of anything to say, though, he closed his piehole and shoved his index finger into my face. "I'm going to be watching you and Darrow real close from now on! If you two are up to something, I'll catch it! And when I do, I'm going to see to it that you're both strung up by your nutsacks!"

I had to laugh again. "Knock yourself out, Lieutenant."

"Do you honestly think you're capable of outsmarting me, boy?"

"God, I hope so, sir," I said. "Because even if I was up to something, if I still decided to go ahead with it after you came in here and told me that I'm going to be under surveillance, well, I'd have to be an extraordinary kind of idiot now, wouldn't I?"

Krause stammered for a moment before coming to grips with the fact that I was not going to admit to anything. Palazzo would need to sell him a better story. Seeing the futility in trying to force the issue, my lieutenant left the radar dome without ceremony and slammed the door behind him. Once he was gone, I let out a long sigh of exasperation.

The lieutenant had nothing on me but Palazzo's accusations. That was clear. Still, I had things that I needed to do in Japan that would be very difficult to pull off while being watched. Krause was plenty capable of foiling the plans Darrow and I had in the Philippines. We needed to neutralize our lieutenant, and we needed to do it fast.

In frustration, I hauled off and slapped the side of my radar's high voltage power supply. Upon impact, I heard a spark fire off inside the transmitter and watched my tuning dials spike with the current rush flooding the circuits. That made me grin. I had an idea.

I shut down the radar and detached the cover to the RT module. I then removed the high voltage unit enough to reach the capacitor that was destroying itself. Once I could touch it, I pressed the cap to slightly unseat it from its terminal slot. This increased the gap between the leads and worsened the arcing to the capacitor. When I re-energized the radar, it looked almost like I had installed a strobe light inside it. It would no longer be a matter of days before the capacitor finally gave out for good. It would be a matter of hours.

I grabbed a chair and put my Walkman on to keep me entertained while watching to ensure that my radar did not catch fire. Preparing for the chaos that I was about to unleash, I settled into my seat, listening to "Far Gone and Out" by the Jesus and Mary Chain.

*****

It took ninety minutes for the capacitor to burn up. When it did, the air boss went ballistic. He knew that it had been going for months, and he was beyond frustrated that it had not been fixed yet. Fortunately, Major Kowalski realized that I was not the obstacle to getting his gear back into working order. It was Krause. After his conversations with the EMO bore little fruit, the major had no desire to work with the man when the radar finally gave out. He went right to the captain.

Reaper Dick was not amused to learn that the ship's primary air traffic control radar was out of order. He was thrilled even less to discover that it had been failing for months without anything being done to fix it. The captain excoriated our department head for that. In return, LCDR Winston delivered his own tirade down upon Lieutenant Krause. Lieutenant Krause, of course, then tried to pass the pain on to me. Our EMO called me into the office and screamed for twenty minutes. Only after that did he finally ask what was wrong with my equipment.

"The high voltage capacitor finally went bad," I told the lieutenant.

"What high voltage capacitor?" Krause asked.

Darrow and I looked at each other. We found it hard to believe that Krause forgot about the argument we had had about the capacitors during the Team Spirit exercise in Korea. "The capacitor that was arcing and causing the phantom returns on the ATC control indicators. The one that costs $1500."

I could see by the look on Krause's face that he did not have a clue as to what I was talking about. "So, you know what's broken!"

"Yes, sir. It's been going bad for months."

"So, you can fix it?"

I nodded. "I can as long as you approved that requisition chit I gave you a couple of months ago." I already knew that he had not. I checked every other week to see if that part was on board. Unless the situation changed since we left Sasebo, I knew that what I needed was still sitting in some warehouse in California.

"Chit? What chit?"

I saw Darrow break into a grin. He knew where this was going. Chief Ramirez was shaking his head in disbelief. He knew where this was headed, too. The only person who had no idea what was going on was our division officer. To prod his memory, I started speaking very slow. "During Team Spirit, when the SPN-35 first started going bad, we gave you a requisition chit for two high voltage capacitors. You refused to sign them because it would mess up your budget. We went around and around about this."

I could not see through his sunglasses, but I imagined Krause's eyes were darting nervously about the space. "I don't remember that at all."

"I sure do," Master Chief Darrow said.

"So do I, sir," Ramirez said.

Krause shook his head, "Whatever. Give me a chit now and draw one out of the storeroom!"

I shook my head. "I would, sir, but there aren't any of these parts on board."

"What do you mean there're no parts on board?!? They have to be on board!"

I sighed. "Sir, again, we tried to get you to…"

"If the parts aren't on board, then that must not be the problem!"

Darrow could not help himself. He choked while trying to keep himself from laughing out loud. Chief Ramirez's eyes got as wide as dinner plates. That statement was one of the stupidest things Ben had ever heard. I could see that he was struggling to believe it came from the lips of a commissioned officer. As for myself, I did everything I could to keep my face neutral. My plan was working better than I had imagined it would.

"Sir?" I asked. I was hoping that he would dig himself an even deeper hole by explaining himself.

Krause took a step closer to me. "If that part was prone to breaking, the Navy would have made sure that all its ships had one aboard. It must be something else, Petty Officer Murphy."

"Sir, the goddamn thing is black with…"

"I'VE TOLD YOU BEFORE NOT TO BLASPHEME IN FRONT OF ME, MURPHY! NOW GET OUT OF MY SIGHT! GET BACK TO THAT RADAR DOME AND FIGURE OUT WHAT WENT WRONG WITH THE SPN-35! NOW!!!"

I had to keep myself from smiling as I did an about-face and marched out of the EMO office, wondering how far Lieutenant Krause was going to run with his delusions.

*****

It turned out that Krause ran as far with it as he could. I spent forty-eight hours in my dome with the parts of the RT Unit scattered across my workbench. It was just for show, though. There was no amount of wishful thinking on the lieutenant's side that would change what was wrong with the SPN-35. I made it look like I was working on it, but in reality, I was doing a lot of napping on the side of the radar not visible from the door.

As I did next to nothing in the dome, Krause sang tales of my incompetence to anyone who would listen. LCDR Winston paid particular attention to them. He took notes and promised that if it turned out that I had misdiagnosed the radar's failure, he would deal with me severely. The CSO knew better, though. I had a feeling that he was tiring of Krause and was feeding the man all the rope he needed to hang himself.

After dragging my name through the mud before the CSO, the air boss, and even Reaper Dick himself, Krause fired me as our primary SPN-35 technician. He went in front of the CSO and requested that we call in the Mobile Technical Training Unit, otherwise known as MOTTU.

MOTTU technicians were an electronics SEAL team. They were the best troubleshooters that the US Navy had and were on standby to fly out and assist anyone, anywhere on a moment's notice. When the *USS Belleau Wood* pulled in to offload our Marines in Okinawa, ETC Javier Acosta was already waiting for us on the pier.

Chief Acosta was one of those men who genuinely loved his job. When I went to the quarterdeck to escort him aboard, it seemed like there was nothing he would rather do than fly halfway around the globe to help me fix my gear. Born in Matamoros, Mexico, Acosta was also thrilled to learn that I spoke Spanish. That earned me bonus points with the man as I brought him up to speed while leading him to check in with the EMO.

"So, what's the story with the SPN-35, Murphy?"

"Back in February, the ACs started seeing phantom returns on the control indicator. The ghost targets got more common as time went on, and we started consuming tuning crystals like crazy as the problem got worse. While we were on our way to Okinawa, it finally went out completely."

Acosta gave me a weird look. "How long have you been working on this radar?"

"About three years."

"And you have no idea what's causing this?" he asked, sounding like he had a hard time believing that.

"It's capacitor C17 in the high voltage power supply," I answered.

The chief nodded as we stepped out of the hangar bay. He stopped in front of the ladder that would take us up into the island structure and said, "Yes, that's right. There's a manufacturing defect in those things that only gives them about a twelve-month lifespan. If you've been working with this model for any amount of time, you know what's going on. It's an easy problem to diagnose."

"I'll say. We've had this one in so long that it's burnt up the base from all the arcing."

"Did you show it to your EMO?"

Shaking my head, I said, "Nope. He has no interest in seeing it. I told him this would happen weeks ago, but he decided not to order the replacement caps. I think he's got a pretty good idea of how much trouble he's going to be in if that comes to light, though. Because of that, he's latched hold of this fantasy that it must be something else."

"Are you serious?"

"As a heart attack."

"Your EMO sounds like a serious work of art."

I chuckled. "Wait until you meet him."

Acosta nodded. "Well, let's go get that out of the way. Take me to your leader."

"Don't you want to see the radar first?" I asked.

The chief shook his head. "First? I don't think I need to see it at all. It sounds like you know what you're doing. Your EMO needs to learn to trust his techs."

The division office was packed when we arrived. Chiefs Ramirez and Moore were at their desks. The division's RPPO, Kyle Brennen, was tracking orders with Palazzo. Spanky had no legitimate purpose for being there. I suspected that he made up an excuse to speak with Brennen so that he could watch me get mauled by the MOTTU chief when he arrived. I took Acosta past them all and introduced him to our department head, LCDR Winston, and Master Chief Darrow. LTJG Krause needed no introduction.

"Andy?" Acosta asked him, laughing. "Andy Krause? How the hell are you, man? I'm sorry, I mean, 'sir.' You made lieutenant j.g? That's great!"

My heart sank. It appeared that the two men were old friends. That was not going to go well for me. I stole a glance back at Palazzo, who shot me an evil smirk in return. He knew I was screwed.

Turning my attention back to the EMO, however, I saw that maybe things were not as dire as they first seemed. Krause did not appear to share the chief's joy in the chance encounter with an old shipmate. I could not tell for sure because his eyes were hidden behind his sunglasses, but judging by the lieutenant's demeanor, it did not seem like the EMO recognized the chief at all. Krause leaned in and read his name tag. "Acosta?"

"Yes, sir. It's Javi! From the *Long Beach*!"

That did not seem to ring a bell. "Oh. Uh…good to see you again, chief. Do you have any ideas what might be going on with the SPN-35?"

No greeting. No, "you look great," nor "how's the family?" Just, "What's wrong with my radar?" The men may not have been as friendly as Acosta thought they were. I looked back at Palazzo again. He was no longer smirking.

"Yeah, I know what happened. Capacitor C17 burned up in the high voltage power supply."

"You know that already?" LCDR Winston asked. "You've been aboard the ship for ten minutes."

Acosta shrugged. "It's an easy and obvious defect. Any technician who's worked on this radar for more than a year knows those things go bad. The manufacturer built them with one of the leads biased away from the seating terminal. That causes arcing, which scores the leads, leading to more arcing. The cap gets progressively worse until the terminals fry off and stop working altogether."

"And you couldn't figure this out?!?" Krause snapped at me.

"He's talking about the same capacitor I told you about a couple of days ago. The one that you told me couldn't be the problem because it wasn't kept on board. The one I wanted you to order last February." It felt so good to say that right in front of the Combat Systems Officer.

Krause was rattled. I threw him right under the bus, right in front of his boss. He was not going to admit to his mistake. "Requested me to order in February? You didn't ask me to order any capacitors in February!" Listening to Krause say that, I realized how good of a liar he was. It sounded like he believed his own bullshit. Had we not all already been over the subject a couple of days before, he might have been more convincing.

I spelled the situation out again to ensure the CSO had the full story. "I did, sir. I initiated the chit and walked it through my chain of command. Chief Ramirez signed it. Master Chief Darrow signed it. You refused to approve it. You said it would mess up your budget."

"I DID NO SUCH THING!" Krause bellowed at me. "YOU LYING LITTLE…"

"Sir, the chit is probably still in the RPPO's files. I can show you…"

"IT IS NOT! IT CAN'T BE IN THERE BECAUSE IT DOESN'T EXIST!"

"Brennen!" Darrow called out. "Do you have a file for unapproved requisition chits over there?"

"Yes, Master Chief!" the RPPO answered.

"Go into it and bring me all the ones that Petty Officer Murphy has submitted."

Kyle Brennen was a very organized man. He passed Darrow the chit I filled out the previous February inside of a half minute. The master chief held it up for the lieutenant to see. "Does this ring a bell, sir?"

Krause's face flushed red. He glared at Darrow and then at me. "Did you plant that there?"

"Yes, sir," I answered. "In February. After you refused to approve it. Just like the procedure says I should."

"THAT'S A LIE! I…"

Darrow stood up to face the lieutenant as our department head took the requisition from his hand to read it for himself. "Sir, do you really want to question my integrity? You made a scene over this in front of everyone here except for the CSO."

I caught Winston looking over at Chief Ramirez, who gave him a nod in return, confirming what Darrow said. Our department head was seething now, but he was a very different man than Andrew Krause was. Outwardly, he kept his temper under control. He probably had doubts about how long he could keep that up if Krause kept talking, though. To prevent the EMO from digging himself a deeper hole in front of his subordinates by responding to Darrow, Winston turned to face me. "What do you need to get that radar back up and running?"

"I need to order a replacement capacitor."

"Actually," Chief Acosta chimed in. "You need to order three. One to get the radar running, one for the spare RT unit, and get one in stock to be safe. Some of those things are so bad that they burn out almost immediately."

Pulling a pen out of his pocket, Winston changed the quantity on the chit and signed it where our EMO typically would. It was a sign that the CSO did not trust Krause to get it done expeditiously or accurately. He then held it up for our RPPO. "Get this thing going now, Petty Officer Brennen."

"Aye aye, sir!"

Standing up, LCDR Winston shook Acosta's hand. "I appreciate your help, chief. I'm sorry to have to drag you halfway around the world for nothing."

"My pleasure, sir," Acosta said. "I like these nice and easy calls. It beats having to roll up my sleeves and get dirty for a couple of weeks."

"Well, we'll not be making a habit of this." Turning to the EMO, Winston asked, "Would you like to join me in the Combat Systems Office, Lieutenant?"

It may have sounded like an invitation, but it was an order. There was not a man who heard it that thought otherwise. Krause and Winston were about to have a very unpleasant conversation.

*****

"Yeah, I knew him," Acosta told me. "Back when he was a first-class. We served together aboard the *USS Long Beach*. He was a good man. Sharp, too. Not so much on the technical side, but he was damn good at all the Navy stuff. He was smart. Very smart. I don't know who that guy is I saw today, though. He looks like Andy Krause, but earning his commission must have sucked a shit ton of brain cells out of the poor guy. That is NOT the same man I knew back on the *Beach*. I mean, what's up with those sunglasses anyway? Does he think he's the second coming of Douglas-fucking-MacArthur or something?"

I laughed. Okinawa's White Beach was a tiny base. It was basically a pier and a small bar with a couple of slot machines to serve as an Enlisted Man's Club. There was a beautiful beach and scenic coral caves there, but they were off-limits. Besides the unexploded ordnance from World War II that would still periodically turn up, it was rumored that the caves held the remains of Japanese soldiers killed when the Marines invaded the island in 1945. Despite the pretty scenery, there was not a lot to do on White Beach except drink. That's what Chief Acosta and I were doing.

"I have no idea what the deal is with him and his sunglasses," I told Acosta. "That wasn't a thing with him when you knew the guy?"

The chief shook his head as he took a sip of his beer. "No, not at all. I don't think I ever saw him wearing any."

"I don't think I ever saw him without them," I said. "You know, it's hard for me to picture him as even barely competent in any former life. He's been something of a drooling imbecile the entire time I've known him."

"I guess he's just another casualty of the Peter Principle."

"The Peter Principle?"

Acosta nodded. "Yeah, it's when you get promoted to the point of your incompetence. As good as the guy was back when I knew him, Andy was always wound kind of tight. The fact that he's not making it as an officer must be driving him crazy or something. You can tell something's going on just looking at him. You never saw him in anything but an impeccable uniform with sharp military creases back on the *Beach*. Today it looked like he just threw those khakis on."

That had not dawned on me until Acosta mentioned it. When Krause first reported aboard the year before, he was all spit and polish. When I thought back to how he had been dressing lately, though, he looked ordinary. I would not call the lieutenant disheveled, but he was no longer putting in the effort on his appearance. It also seemed like his uniform was not fitting quite right, as if he was losing weight. I grinned. We were getting to him.

"Was he a drinker when you knew him, Chief?"

Shaking his head, Javi said, "No, he never drank back then. He's kind of religious. Is he drinking now?"

"I don't know. Sometimes, he seems kind of unsteady on his feet and slurs his words. He looks and sounds like he's been drinking, but I can never smell anything on his breath. I was kind of wondering if he might be an ex-alcoholic who's fallen off the wagon."

The chief shrugged. "If Andy was a lush, it would've been from before I met him. I've never known him to touch the stuff."

"Well, look at the two of you!" Master Chief Darrow said as he stepped through the door of the club. "You haven't known each other for four hours and you're already thick as thieves! I figured that you'd have caught the bus to Kadena to whoop it up with the rest of the boys."

I scooted over to make room for Darrow at our table. "Well, we dragged Chief Acosta all the way here from California for nothing. I figured the least I could do was buy him a beer."

"I don't know if it was for nothing," Darrow said as he ordered a round of drinks from a passing waitress. "I'm pretty happy with the way things turned out."

That caused me to perk up an eyebrow. "Really? Why's that?"

"Don't worry about it," the master chief told me. "I'll tell you later."

"So, Brad," Acosta started as he took his drink from the waitress. "When I was getting settled into the chief's mess, someone told me that you're Olongapo Earp. Is that right?"

Darrow nodded. "Yeah, that's right. I did three tours on the AFPD in Subic Bay."

The MOTTU chief laughed. "Yeah, you know, a buddy of mine had a run-in with you about a decade ago."

"Did he?" Darrow asked. "That's unfortunate. You looking for an apology?"

Acosta shook his head, still giggling. "Hardly. Actually, I may owe you one on his behalf. Now, according to my sources, you tried to apprehend my man Gary and a couple other of my shipmates. They got mouthy, so you started getting rough with them. I understand Gary made some comment about you not being so tough without that badge of yours. You responded by offering to drop your gun and shield to settle the issue man-to-man. If he lost, you said you'd add a charge of assaulting a superior. If he won, you said that you'd let them all go back to the ship without being charged with anything at all."

Darrow swallowed his first drink of beer, grinning. "Gary Narver? Is that your buddy's name?"

"Holy shit!" the chief exclaimed. "You remember that?!?"

"You're damn right, I do. Your boy Narver kicked my ass."

"You lost?" I gasped.

"I'm not Superman, Doyle. Yeah, I lost. That guy mopped the floor with me." Sensing that this was a teachable moment, Darrow turned to me and added, "It doesn't matter how tough you think you are, Murphy. There's always someone out there who's bigger and badder than you'll ever be. Always."

"So that actually happened?" Acosta asked. "Gary talked a lot of shit. He said he won the fight and you let him go."

Darrow nodded. "A deal's a deal. I gave them all a ride back to their boat and ran into your boy the following day when I was off duty. I bought him a few drinks and told him not to make a habit of doing that kind of shit. I let him know that the next chief he took a swing at would probably not share my sense of honor."

"He should've listened to your advice," Acosta said.

"What? Why?" Darrow asked. "What's Narver doing these days?"

"Five to ten at Fort Leavenworth for punching out an ensign that caught him sleeping with his wife."

"My kind of man," I told Chief Acosta. "He sounds like a real Tequila Viking."

*****

I was smashed when I got back to the ship. I was also too energized to sleep after the conversation I had with Master Chief Darrow. During our long walk up the pier, Darrow told me things that he probably should not have. Once I heard them, though, I knew that I would not be able to rest until I told someone else about them, too. I suspected that the person I most wanted to tell was still awake and hanging out in the Radar Repair Shop. John Palazzo was still on liberty risk restriction. He was not going anywhere.

Usually, I knew better than to touch Petty Officer Palazzo. The man was a sissy who would report me without hesitation. That night I was feeling invincible, however. Speeding up that capacitor's failure had worked better than I could have imagined in undercutting the threat that Krause posed to us. Once again, I was untouchable. I burst through the door of Radar Repair, grabbed Spanky by the shirt, and ripped him out of his chair. I then tossed him halfway across the room up against the port bulkhead. After that, I grabbed him by the throat and got into his face.

"You like that little show down in the EMO today, you little pervert? Huh? Did you really think that Krause calling in MOTTU was going to end badly for me?"

"I-I-I-I n-n-n-n-n..." Palazzo stammered.

"The CSO basically fired Krause today, you fucking cocksucker," I growled.

"Wh-wh-wha-what?"

"Krause has been trying to pull off whatever vendetta he has against me and Darrow for a year now. This time, it cost us a HUGE hit on our equipment readiness rating. It also caused the Navy to spend thousands of dollars to fly out a MOTTU chief for no reason whatsoever. Reaper Dick was livid about that and tore the CSO a new asshole. It appears that both Winston and the captain have lost confidence in Krause's ability to lead. He was told that he's not being recommended for advancement. They also informed him that he should prepare for separation from the Navy after the August promotion cycle. He's lost all his credibility."

Palazzo tried to swallow, but my hand around his neck made that difficult. I let go of him but kept our noses inches apart. "For all practical purposes, Master Chief Darrow is in charge of the division now. Krause has been told to stay out of his way and to leave us enlisted men alone. He was ordered to stay away from me in particular. In deference to Krause's years of service, the CSO isn't outright firing him, but he let the fucker know that if he screws up one more time, he's getting the boot. Do you know what this means, Spanky?"

Palazzo shook his head, so I spelled it out for him. "You lost your patron, motherfucker! He ain't going to the NIS with stories about Taylor and Williams getting beaten up in the Nixie. He ain't going to the NIS with fantasies about Darrow and me being in cahoots with the *yakuza,* either. He ain't going to be helping you with whatever you thought he could do to get you out of that shit you did in Japan. You're fucked, Spanky!"

"I didn't do any..."

I shoved Palazzo up against the wall so hard that I pushed myself backward a couple of steps in the process. I stumbled out of his personal space. "Whatever," I snapped as I recovered. "Save your pleas of innocence for the jurors, you little prick. Not that they'll understand you. By the way, 'I didn't do it' in Japanese is '*Watashi wa yatte inai.*' You better put your back into learning that shit."

A single tear fell out of Palazzo's right eye and rolled down his cheek. "Aw, what's the matter?" I was using baby talk to mock him now. "You don't want to go to jail? Huh? Is that it? Well, Spanky, you are. You're going away for fucking *years. YEARS!* And guess what? I do know the people that can get to you behind bars in Japan. You know, I would've been content to let you rot away in prison for whatever you did to that woman in Japan…"

"I didn't do it." Palazzo whimpered.

"Bullshit!" I retorted. "We both know you did and you're going to pay for it, Spanky. You're going to pay for what you did to that girl in the pictures I found in the fan room, too."

"I didn't do it." Palazzo was sobbing now.

"You're going to pay for trying to burn me for the low-lives I set straight in the Nixie…"

"I didn't do it!"

"…and for feeding Krause that line of shit about us working with the *yakuza.*"

"I DIDN'T DO IT!" Spanky screamed at me.

I busted out laughing. "Good lord, John. It almost sounds like you believe that. Too bad no one else ever will."

*****

CHAPTER 13

I had duty and the first watch the day after we pulled into Sasebo, so I turned down the offer to celebrate our return to our homeport. Instead, I took delivery of the high voltage capacitors I was waiting for, then spent the evening putting my radar back together. After that, I made a point of going to bed early and getting a good night's sleep.

At reveille, I woke up rejuvenated and refreshed. I got myself a good breakfast, showered and shaved, and then put on my dress whites to assume the Petty Officer of the Watch. As I walked through the hangar bay toward the quarterdeck, I saw that I would be relieving John Palazzo. He was not the man I felt like interacting with first thing in the morning, but taking over as the POOW required a pass-down of information and equipment. I had to listen to what Palazzo had to tell me and make sure that I properly took possession of the logbook, podium, and sidearm.

"Anything happen last night?" I asked as I looked over the communications kiosk to ensure that it was clean and in proper working order.

"Nope, not at all. It was quiet." Palazzo sounded much happier than he had any reason to be.

I walked over to the message board and scanned the pink slips of paper hanging from the Combat Systems clip. Right on top was a message for me from Katsumi. She left a number for me to call. I pulled it off the board and put it in my wallet. "Is the captain aboard yet?"

John shook his head, still smiling as I approached him at the podium. Something was up. No one was in that good of a mood at the tail end of the four to eight watch. "You ready to transfer the weapon?"

Palazzo nodded as he scribbled some last notes in the logbook. "Sure."

Spanky removed the .45 automatic from its holster and pulled back the slide to show me the empty chamber. That was per procedure. Removing a magazine from his ammo pouch, jamming it into the pistol's handle, then releasing the slide to lock and load it was not. That was a serious, not to mention illegal, breach of protocol. The sound of a round being chambered into a .45 is very distinct and it immediately caught the Officer of the Deck's attention. "Petty Officer Palazzo!" screamed Senior Chief Gorman. "What the fuck do you think you're doing?!? Drop that weapon right now!"

Disregarding the senior chief's commands, Palazzo pointed the pistol at my face. The two seamen that were on station turning over the roving watch took off running toward the mess decks. I assumed that they were heading toward the Master-at-Arms office to sound the alarm. Gorman slowly approached Palazzo from behind. Still smiling as if he was having the time of his life, Spanky said, "You don't want to come any closer, Senior Chief! The only guy here I want to shoot is Murphy. I don't want to shoot you, but if you get in my way, I will."

"What are you doing, John?" I asked. "What the fuck do you think you're doing?"

"I'm not going to a Japanese prison, Murphy. That's not going to happen."

"You think this is going to get you out of trouble?" I asked. "Seriously? John, you're putting yourself in a world of hurt here. Put that gun down before something happens that you can't take back."

"Take it back?" Palazzo scoffed. "I've already crossed the point of no return here, Doyle. I was fucked the moment I put the magazine in this weapon. If I could take anything back, it'd be signing up for the goddamn Navy in the first place. Christ, Doyle, my first command was awesome! If only there was some way that I could have stayed there! Getting stuck on this hellhole, though, well, this place is a fucking nightmare."

"Do you think going to the brig at Fort Leavenworth is going to be any better?" My voice cracked a bit as I posed the question. This was not the first time I had ever had a .45 pointed in my face. Darrow had aimed one at me when I returned from dragging Macklemore out of Mexico. That time, however, I knew there was no way that my master chief would pull the trigger. This time, I was pretty confident that Palazzo would.

"Leavenworth ain't going to be better than the *Belleau Wood*, Doyle. It's got to be better than spending a couple of decades doing time in Japan, though."

"John, at least if you go to a Japanese prison…"

The ship's 1MC system came to life and started screaming, "Security alert! Security alert! Away the security alert team! Away the backup alert force! All hands not involved in security alert stand fast! Reason for security alert: Armed man on quarterdeck! This is NOT a drill!" It sounded as if the rovers had made it to the MAA shack.

"Petty Officer Palazzo," Senior Chief Gorman pleaded. "That's it. You're going to be surrounded in about thirty seconds. If you don't put that weapon down right now, you're going to get yourself shot!"

"Back off, Senior Chief!" Palazzo barked.

"He's right, John. They're going to have you covered on all sides. Someone's going to take the shot if they see you holding a weapon on me."

Spanky shrugged. "You know, I'm part of the SAT and BAF teams just like you. They're going to be too afraid of getting into trouble to pull the trigger."

"For Christ's sake, Palazzo!" Gorman yelled. "They're going to be coming in hot this time! Put that goddamn gun down NOW!"

As Gorman was trying to convince Palazzo to give up, two security team members emerged from the mess deck passageway. They were both wearing dungarees and camouflaged flak jackets. One of them pointed an M-14 at Spanky and screamed, "DROP YOUR WEAPON AND PUT YOUR HANDS UP!"

Palazzo did not even bother to look at them. With his eyes remaining locked onto mine, he asked, "Aren't you going to beg me for your life?"

DS3 Stovic and a radioman stepped into the hangar bay from a passageway further aft. After seeing that he was dealing with Palazzo, Stovic pointed his shotgun at him and shouted out, "Come on, John! Don't be a fucking idiot! Put that gun down now!"

"Beg you for mercy?" I laughed at Palazzo. "Seriously? You may be overestimating just how much I have to live for."

"You want to die?" Spanky asked.

"Not particularly," I answered. "But if I do, it's not like I'm leaving much behind besides a lot of really bad memories."

Palazzo nodded. "Yeah, I can certainly appreciate that." It appeared as if the two of us were starting to find some common ground.

Two more SAT/BAF teams worked their way into the hangar bay. There were now eight men standing around us, pointing their weapons at Gianni Palazzo and screaming at him to give up his pistol. Both of us had them completely tuned out.

"There's no way out of this, Palazzo," I told him. "If you don't do something soon, one of those men is going to take that shot at you. We're far enough apart that they're not going to be worried about hitting me by mistake. It's time for you to either surrender your weapon or do whatever it is you decided to do. If you're going to shoot me, get it fucking over with."

I saw the muscles in Palazzo's hand tense up as he tried to squeeze the trigger, but nothing happened other than me damn near pissing my pants. I became acutely aware that the hole at the end of a pistol's barrel is really not all that large. Regardless, the object coming out of it would have wreaked havoc on the plans I made for the summer.

Stovic saw that Spanky nearly fired. "Goddammit, Palazzo! This is the last time I'm going to tell you! Put that motherfucking gun down! NOW!"

John averted his gaze toward Darren and gave the man a nod. He seemed to relax a bit as he transferred the pistol to his left hand. Looking me in the eye once again, he said, "I'm not going to kill you, Murphy. I'm not going to have my mother think I died a villain. I'm not the bad guy here. You are."

Spanky then unexpectedly snapped to attention and turned toward the flag. Rendering a crisp salute to the colors with his right arm, John lifted the .45 with his left and pressed the muzzle tight up against his temple.

"NOOOOOO!" I rushed to stop him but before I had taken two steps, Gianni Palazzo pulled the trigger.

The .45 ACP is a devastating round. Nobody would walk away from shooting themselves point-blank in the head with one. Had Palazzo left a little space between barrel and bone, however, he might have been able to enjoy an open-casket funeral. By pressing the weapon so hard against his temple, his death became particularly gruesome.

The bullet punched a hole in Palazzo's melon that was just slightly larger than the round's diameter. The gases propelling the projectile then rushed into the cavity between Spanky's ears and liquified his frontal lobe. The pressure and heat shredded and cooked the man's synapses until the bullet reached the other side of his mind. Once the slug compromised the opposite cranial wall, it gave the pressure a path to escape through. The right side of John's head popped like an over-inflated balloon, splattering everything within it all over me.

In an instant, my uniform turned from white to red. Strips of skin, scalp, and bone fragments landed in the top of my Dixie Cup cap. As Palazzo's lifeless body crumpled to the ground, I watched one of his eyes fall out of its socket and bounce off of the deck.

When David Miller was beaten to death, I felt his brains in my hands as I tried to hold his head together. It took months for me to shake the sensation that there were still pieces of Miller's gray matter hiding between my fingers. This time, I was facing Palazzo, screaming at the man, when he shot himself.

As difficult as it was to shake the feeling of holding tiny morsels of someone's cerebrum in my hands, it was infinitely easier than trying to forget the taste it could leave in your mouth.

*****

I shut down after witnessing John Palazzo kill himself. I was in shock. Unable to respond to the commands of the SAT/BAF team members or the medics, I had to be loaded onto a stretcher and carried down to sick bay. HM1 Bateman was at my side and roughly brushed Lieutenant Krause away when he rushed up to my gurney to call me a murderer. Since I could not answer their questions, the corpsmen had to cut away my uniform to see if I was injured or not. I had so much blood on me that they worried if Palazzo had shot me, too.

The state I was in was not exactly catatonia, but close. I could hear questions being asked but could only answer in unintelligible mumbling. The ship's corpsmen had to undress me, examine me, and clean me up without any help at all on my part. While trying to figure out what needed to be done next, they wheeled me into a back room for privacy and covered me with blankets to keep me warm. Bateman volunteered to keep watch. He was there when I finally broke down.

"You all right?" the corpsman asked after I pulled myself together a bit.

"I don't know, man. I don't know. He fucking killed himself."

"He was in your shop," Bateman said. "Were the two of you close?"

"No," I said. "I couldn't stand the prick. The man was sick. He couldn't quit playing with himself. He raped a woman..."

"Are you sure about that?" the corpsman asked.

"Yeah, I'm sure about that!" I snapped. "The Japanese police are investigating him for it!"

Bateman nodded sympathetically. "When we were getting you loaded onto the stretcher, the OOD was checking the logbook on the podium. The last thing Palazzo wrote in it was, 'I didn't do it.'"

I scoffed. "Yeah? Well, the man's a fucking liar, too."

Commander James Samuelson was the ship's Executive Officer. Back when Captain Fleming was the *USS Belleau Wood's* skipper, the XO was the most feared man aboard the vessel. He was the guy in charge of keeping order among the crew and walked through its passageways with the gait of a mafia don. After Reaper Dick assumed command, however, CDR Samuelson softened his tone. He figured someone needed to be on the side of the men. Within an hour of Palazzo's suicide, the XO walked into my room, shaking his head.

"It's always you, Murphy," Samuelson said as he approached my bedside. "Randy Green. Riots in Mexico. Warren Macklemore. David Miller. Shootings in the Philippines. And now, this. Every time something catastrophic occurs, you seem to be right in the middle of it. Why is that?"

When I answered the XO, I was not being flippant, nor was I cracking wise. I was as sincere as I could be. "I think I'm just cursed, sir. It started with my family when I was thirteen and hasn't ever let up."

"Well then, what do we have to do to break this curse, Murphy? Do I need to throw you off of my ship?"

I thought about that for a moment. I thought about it really hard. I then looked Commander Samuelson right in the eye and said, "You know, you just might, sir."

Then I broke down again. Bad. When I was able to speak, I wiped the tears out of my eyes and said, "If I had any idea how to stop this shit, I certainly would have done it by now."

*****

CHAPTER 14

I was not physically injured during Palazzo's suicide. So, less than two hours after Spanky splattered his brains all over my uniform, Doc Broward marched up beside my bed and, with a stroke of his pen, medically cleared me to return to work. This was entirely in character for our ship's medical officer. Broward generally treated enlisted men with Motrin no matter what their malady was. Short of losing a limb, it was virtually impossible for a crew member to expect any relief from duty. All an officer had to do to earn a week-long Sick-in-Quarters chit was show up outside of the doctor's office with a runny nose.

Typically, the caste system that Broward employed when doling out medical care infuriated me. This time, however, I was grateful for it. I did not need treatment right then. I needed privacy. I had a meltdown speeding my way, and I needed to hole up in my dome to ride it out. Having an episode in front of the entire *Belleau Wood* medical contingent would have earned me a psych discharge on the spot. I was only too happy to grab my stuff and flee from medical supervision at the earliest opportunity.

Unfortunately, HM1 Bateman was far more observant than LCDR Broward was. He knew something was wrong and was not willing to let me go. He voiced his objections several times, all of which the doctor dismissed out of hand. This resulted in an argument between the two men. Because of Bateman's effeminate mannerisms, they reminded me of a married couple squabbling over how to deal with an errant child's poor report card. No matter how adamantly Bateman pushed his case, the doctor refused to budge. Only when I tried to voice an opinion agreeing with him did Broward relent and order me to rest for a few more hours. Apparently, in the doctor's eyes, the only thing less credible than Bateman's medical opinion was mine.

When there was a lot of activity around me, I was distracted enough to keep my beasts at bay. Once Bateman settled in beside my bed and opened up his book, however, things began to unravel. It started with a flash of Palazzo's head exploding in front of me. My body tensed up and spasmed, causing the corpsman to look up from his reading. "You alright?" Bateman asked.

I nodded as my sweat pores began opening up.

Not here, Doyle! Not now! You've been able to control these things before. If there was ever a time to push one of your episodes into the very deepest recesses of your subconscious, it's now. Right now!

I still saw Palazzo's broken head lying on the quarterdeck, his eye slowly rolling out of its open socket once again.

Stop it! Clear your mind! Get that shit out of it before it's too late!

I recalled Yukiko's uncle teaching me how to suppress the noise ravaging through my synapses. "Close your eyes and breathe," I remembered Shintaro telling me. "In through your nose, out through your mouth. Concentrate on your breath. Notice how it feels as the air is pulled into your sinuses. Feel the sensation of it as it flows down the back of your throat. Your lungs. Feel them expand as you draw in the air..."

I did what he told me. I focused on drawing air in through my nose, holding it until I felt the tingling in my chest, then letting it out through my mouth. My visions of the gore seeping out of Spanky's skull began to subside. It was replaced with the memory of the boy I had killed in Olongapo.

My muscles went rigid and I gasped for another breath. *Come on, Doyle! You have to do this! Get it together and concentrate!*

"In through your nose, out through your mouth," Shintaro whispered to me once again. "Concentrate on your breath. Relax your toes. Let your muscles release and let go. Good, good. Now your feet. Perfect. Relax your legs. Now your chest. Good. Now your shoulders. Yes, yes. Now your neck…let it go. Clear your mind."

No! Wait! Don't clear your mind!

I remembered that brought on one of my episodes right inside of Shintaro's temple. *Don't clear your mind! Instead, fill it with something soothing! Something pleasant! Something...*

But what? I did not have a lot of soothing memories to draw upon. I did not have anything that was not marred by some sort of tragedy. I only had…

…Tala.

I drew a long breath in through my nose, held it inside of my lungs until I felt the tingle, then let it escape through my mouth. I felt my chest rise and fall. It was Tala's chest that I saw move, however. She was lying on her bed, in her apartment, not mine. It was the first time we made love. She was atop the sheets, naked, catching a little bit of sleep before Mari got home from school.

In through my nose, out through my mouth...

I was wide awake, lying next to her, studying the skin above her breasts. It was flawless, mocha-colored, and smooth. When I looked close enough, I could see tiny goosebumps from each of which emerged a single, fine, almost transparent hair that could only be seen if the light hit it just right.

In through my nose, out through my mouth. Let my muscles release and let go. Good, good. Now my feet. Perfect. Relax my legs. Now my chest. Good. Now my shoulders. Yes, yes. Now my neck...let it go.

I was back on the beach near Pundaquit, drinking a beer in the sand next to Dixie. I could see Tala and Mari playing in the surf. A wave emerged from the break and crested over Mari's head, knocking her down laughing into the water. God, how I missed them.

In through my nose, hold it in my lungs until I feel the tingling in my chest, then let it out through my mouth.

I was no longer on the *USS Belleau Wood.* I was back in the Philippines, where I belonged. That was my home. I was realizing that for the very first time. That was where I needed to be.

Tala was lying in the sand beside me now in San Felipe, where we were going to settle. She was smiling as if she had heard me say that I was coming back. "We need you too, Doyle. We need you to stay with us. Porever. You good man. You a pather to Mari. You a…you a…" Tala seemed like she was struggling to come up with the right words. "You a…"

*****

"…murderer."

Tala was gone. So was Bateman. Somehow, Krause had taken his place. He was standing over me, staring through his sunglasses, shaking with rage. "I don't know how you did it," my lieutenant snarled. "I don't know how you pulled it off, but you're not fooling me, you miserable, godless piece of shit! You killed that man, Murphy! Murdered him! Splattered his…"

"There were witnesses…" I countered, disoriented after emerging from my trance and unable to fully defend myself. "It happened right in front of the entire SAT and BAF teams…the Officer of the Deck…the Master-at-Arms…"

"I don't give a shit who you did it in front of. You're a crafty son-of-a-bitch, just like Satan himself! I don't know how you did it! Or how Darrow helped, but so help me God, I'm going to figure it out and…"

"Hey!" Bateman called out as he entered my room. "What do you think you're doing in here, Lieutenant? You're not authorized..."

"I'm an officer in the United States Navy, Petty Officer!" Krause barked. "I can be..."

"Pretty much anywhere but here!" the corpsman countered. "I'm in charge of this patient! Not you! You need to leave this bed right now!"

"YOU DON'T TELL ME WHAT TO DO! YOU HEAR THAT! YOU! DO! NOT! GIVE! ORDERS! TO! ME! DO YOU UNDERSTAND?!?"

Bateman stopped talking, but not out of fear. On the contrary, he put himself between the lieutenant and me to ensure that the EMO could not cause his patient any harm if he snapped. Then he went silent to let Krause continue his tirade.

"Palazzo was on to him!" Krause ranted. "He knew what they were up to! He knew about all the men that monster assaulted! His deals with Master Chief Darrow! The people the two of them killed in the Philippines! Palazzo knew they were in cahoots with the Japanese mob!"

Even though the lieutenant had no idea what he was talking about, excluding his belief that I had assassinated John Palazzo, the man was actually right. Yet he made it all sound so absurd. Watching Krause rage reversed my own descent into madness and cleared my head with remarkable speed. I caught myself marveling at how ridiculous he looked as he tried to describe me as some sort of international criminal mastermind.

Bateman turned his head and glanced at me as if to ask if he was hearing the lieutenant correctly. I shrugged my shoulders in response. "Yeah, according to the lieutenant here, I'm a regular Al Capone."

When the corpsman turned back to Krause, the EMO pointed his index finger at me. "You and Darrow had to get rid of him! He was going to rat you out! So you killed him! Murdered him! Shot him dead right on the fucking quarterdeck!"

"Sir," Bateman said softly. "Petty Officer Palazzo shot himself. Not only did he do it in front of more than a dozen witnesses, but before at least two cameras monitoring the hangar bay."

"That's what they're saying!" Krause slurred, sounding like he was on the verge of tears. "But those two, Murphy and Darrow, they seem to be able to make anybody say anything!"

"Sir," Bateman started to ask. "Why are you wearing your sunglasses right now?"

"What?"

"Your sunglasses. We're inside, the lights are turned low to help Murphy relax, and you're in here wearing some of the darkest shades I've ever seen." Bateman pulled a medical penlight from his shirt pocket. "Can you take your glasses off for me, sir?"

The EMO looked at the penlight and then back away from Bateman. "What for?"

"So I can see your eyes, sir. Are you experiencing any sort of light sensitivity?"

"What? No! Of course not!"

The corpsman sounded unconvinced. "Show me. Please, take off your sunglasses."

"I'm not taking off my sunglathes."

Krause's slur further piqued Bateman's interest. "Have you been drinking, sir?"

"I don't drink!" the lieutenant barked defensively.

"Then you wouldn't mind taking a breathalyzer?"

Unable to help myself, I grinned. Lieutenant Krause was not nearly as amused by the corpsman's curiosity as I was, though. He took a step into Bateman's personal space, looking even more perturbed in the face of the most effeminate man aboard the ship. Bateman remained immobile, though, fearlessly standing his ground. "You better watch yourself, Petty Officer," Krause growled. "You're treading into some dangerous water here wielding baseless accusations."

"I'm not accusing you of anything, Lieutenant. I'm trying to help you."

Krause took a step back and looked Bateman over with disgust. “I don’t need help. Especially not from the likes of you.” With that, the lieutenant turned his back on the corpsman and stormed out of sickbay.

*****

The main obstacle keeping LCDR Broward from being a good doctor was not incompetence. It was arrogance. Broward knew the books inside and out. He knew all the diseases and how to treat them. When required, he knew how to take a man apart and put him back together again. Broward was as skilled as a doctor could be. He lived to save the day whenever catastrophe struck. The banality of treating men for mundane maladies was beneath him, however. He was easily irritated and approached his enlisted patients with the assumption that each one was malingering, wasting his time fishing for an excuse to get out of work.

HM1 Bateman was the Yin to Broward’s Yang. Through years of experience as a combat medic, the corpsman was every bit as knowledgeable as the medical officer. He never managed to develop the doctor’s sense of contempt for the crew, though. The men of the *USS Belleau Wood* afforded Doc Broward the respect that military protocol required of them. The respect we bestowed upon Petty Officer Bateman was voluntary, however. And genuine.

That was a source of friction between the two men. Broward resented that the crew held a mere corpsman in such high esteem, especially considering that the man was obviously a homosexual. As far as the ship’s doc was concerned, Bateman had no business serving in the US Navy. The day that Palazzo died, I learned that the two men argued a lot. It also appeared that Broward tended to take the opposite opinion of Bateman for no other reason than to oppose him.

This seemed to be what the ship’s doctor was doing in the lieutenant commander’s office shortly after Lieutenant Krause left.

"I'm telling you, sir!" Bateman pled. "There's something wrong with the man!"

"Because he likes his sunglasses?" scoffed the doctor.

"I think he's got issues with light sensitivity."

"Did he complain about it?"

"No, but…"

"Then you're making assumptions. I'm not hauling Krause in for any kind of psych eval just because he wears sunglasses indoors. Rumor has it that Douglas MacArthur wore shades all the time, too."

"Lieutenant Krause is not Douglas MacArthur," the corpsman retorted.

"And you're not Sigmund Freud," Broward shot back.

"I don't have to be to tell that Krause is delusional."

The doctor let out a long sigh. "And what makes you think the EMO is delusional?"

"He thinks that Murphy is working with the *yakuza*, sir."

Broward laughed. "If I remember correctly, Petty Officer Murphy nearly beat a man to death aboard this ship a while back. Did you ever think that maybe he has a damn good reason for coming to a conclusion like that?"

"Krause also believes that Murphy murdered Palazzo on the quarterdeck. There's a dozen witnesses and videotape evidence that shows otherwise, sir."

There was a couple of moments of silence while Broward tried to work up a valid counterpoint. Failing to come up with anything, I heard him leave his office with the corpsman in tow. "Look, Bateman, drop it. Lieutenant Junior Grade Krause is an odd duck, but he's no lunatic."

"But, sir…"

I heard Broward stop and turn on the corpsman. "But nothing! I said drop it! Having an enlisted man question the mental fitness of an officer sets a really bad precedent. I'm not going to tolerate it."

"Sir, Krause could have a serious medical condition. It could be anything from untreated syphilis to…"

"For the last time, corpsman! Drop it! Do you understand?!? One more word out of you and I'll write you up for insubordination! Am I clear?!?"

"Crystal, sir."

"Good!" Perturbed, Doc Broward took a few dozen angry steps to the edge of my bed and barked, "Murphy!"

"Yes, sir!"

"Are you ready to get back to work?"

"Yes, sir!" I answered, hoping to regain the freedom to hide in my dome if it felt like my mind was going to turn on me again.

"Good!" Broward snapped. "Get your ass off of my floor then!"

*****

With my dress whites ruined and saturated with Palazzo's blood, I returned to my berthing area in a hospital gown. When I arrived, I found it secured by a quartermaster temporarily assigned to the Master-at-Arms. "We're collecting Palazzo's personal effects," Petty Officer Lawson told me when I asked what was going on.

"Come on, Dave. I really need to get cleaned up and into a set of dungarees. Can you at least let me get to my locker to get some clothes? I can shower in one of the Marine berthing spaces."

"Is that Murphy?" MA1 Carlton called out after hearing my voice at the top of the ladder.

"Yeah," Lawson answered.

"Let him in."

With the Master-at-Arms' permission, I descended the steps of the ladder. Carlton met me in the lounge. "You all right, Doyle?"

I shrugged. "I've been better."

Carlton nodded sympathetically. "I'm sure you have. We're almost done collecting Palazzo's stuff. Go ahead and get yourself cleaned up. I have to wait for you. When you're finished, I need to escort you to one of the ready rooms on the 04 level. The NIS is on board and needs to speak with you about what happened."

Surprised, I asked, "They're here already? Jesus Christ, do they have a detail assigned to Sasebo or something?"

Carlton shook his head. "No, they're based in Yokosuka. As luck would have it, they were already in the area on another issue. Obviously, this took precedence."

Special Agents Koch and Bremmer both recognized me as soon as I walked into the ready room. Koch never lifted his eyes off of me as I took my seat. "You know," he said as I settled in. "Ninety-nine percent of men who serve more than twenty-five years in the military go through their entire careers without ever having to speak to an NCIS agent, Petty Officer Murphy. You've been in the Navy for five years. This is your third time landing in front of us. Do you find that odd?"

With a shrug, I said, "To be fair, sir, the last time I was here, it was because my division officer accused me of participating in a crime that never even happened."

Bremmer nodded. "He's made some more accusations recently."

I was not surprised. "Yeah, I bet he did. He made some to me this morning, too."

"About what?" asked Koch.

I saw an opportunity presenting itself. I decided to take it. "He accused me of murdering John Palazzo on behalf of the Japanese mob."

Bremmer cocked one of his eyebrows. "Why would he do that?"

"Have you ever spoken with Lieutenant Krause, sir?"

"We spoke with him at length this morning," Koch told me.

"Okay then, sir. Look, I'm not trying to be disrespectful or insubordinate. I'm trying to be truthful. I don't think the man is well, and if you've talked to him, you've probably seen it for yourself."

"Do you think that Krause is fit for duty?" Bremmer asked.

"No," I answered. "I don't. But my opinion on my lieutenant's fitness to lead doesn't really matter, does it? That would be better left to a medical professional. You know, Petty Officer Bateman was there with me when Krause confronted me about Palazzo this morning. He might have a more objective idea about what's going on with the guy."

Koch shook his head. "We're not going to be doing anything to breach patient confidentiality, Petty Officer Murphy." The NCIS agent maintained his stoic demeanor. Despite this, I gathered that their lack of interest in approaching Bateman had little to do with protocol. It was probably because they had seen for themselves that Krause was a bit off. "Why would your lieutenant think you were working with the *yakuza*?"

I let out a long sigh. "Because Palazzo told him I was."

"Why would he do that?"

"You know," I started. "I used to walk the *ginza* here in Sasebo and try to strike up little conversations with people to improve my Japanese. Apparently, I picked the wrong two guys a couple of months ago. One of the local hoodlums took offense to me approaching a couple of older gentlemen and we had words. Eventually, the prick struck me. When I tried to hit him back, that kid kicked the living shit out of me while the older guys bounced. When he finished beating my ass, he took my jacket as a trophy."

I drew in a deep breath to carefully consider what I was about to say next. I was walking a tightrope and all it would take was one misspoken word to land me in a world of trouble.

"Now, beating the shit out of a foreigner is no big deal around here, but it appears that stealing is. It's taboo, even among criminals. A couple of weeks later, the guy running the *pachinko* parlor in the *ginza* recognized me walking by and stopped me, offering to get me my jacket back. He made a phone call and a couple of guys showed up to return what was taken from me. They brought the kid who beat my ass with them and made him apologize. It was raining that night, so one of them offered me a ride back to base. It felt rude to refuse it and those guys did not look like the kind of men that I wanted to offend, so I accepted. Spanky…I mean, Palazzo…saw me get out of the guy's Lincoln at the foot of the Albuquerque Bridge. He was on Shore Patrol that night."

Bremmer looked me over. "Did you notice anything different about the kid they made apologize to you?"

I nodded. "Yeah, they cut the tip of his pinky off."

Koch looked as if that was what he was expecting to hear. The agents asked a few more questions but seemed satisfied with my explanation. Both of them had been in Japan for a while. They knew how things worked there and my account rang true enough for them.

"So, because he saw you get out of a Lincoln, Palazzo assumes you were working with the Japanese mob?"

Shrugging, I answered, "I don't know if he believed it or not. He knew that he was probably going to prison for raping a woman out in town. He was desperate for someone to help get him out of that jam. He knew Krause had a hard-on for me, so he offered up that info to him in exchange for help fighting the accusation."

"How do you know this?"

"The EMO told me. He wanted me to incriminate Darrow for him. The lieutenant has it in for my master chief even more than he does for me."

"What did he want you to incriminate the master chief for?" Bremmer asked.

I shrugged. "Sir, I honestly have no idea. Like I said before, I don't think Krause is well. I don't have a fucking clue what fantasies were running around that man's head that day."

It was Koch's turn to sigh. "Murphy, Krause thinks you murdered Palazzo."

"I know. He thinks that despite a dozen people who saw it happen with their own eyes. Not to mention that there's videotape from the hangar bay cameras that'll probably show the whole thing. I never laid so much as a finger on that weapon, sir."

"Did you get along with Petty Officer Palazzo, Murphy?" Bremmer asked.

I shook my head again. "No. Not at all."

"Why not?"

"The man was a prick when he was in charge of Radar Repair. He was useless. He was also a pervert. We caught him playing with himself all over the place. He…" I nearly slipped and accused him of being a child molester, but I caught myself and pulled it back just in time. "…he…he raped a woman. The guy was a dirtbag."

"Palazzo didn't rape anybody," Koch said.

"Yeah, he did. The local cops have him under investigation for it."

Bremmer backed up his partner, shaking his head. "The woman had a hard time identifying her attacker. By her own admission, her IDs were suspect. She really didn't get a good look at the man who hurt her. While the *Belleau Wood* was away, however, the creep struck again. The cops caught him red-handed that time."

"But the porn…the pictures…" I mumbled. "It had to have been Palazzo."

"It wasn't, Murphy," Koch told me. "The suspect was not in the military. Hell, he wasn't even American. The son-of-a-bitch who attacked that lady was a merchant seaman out of Yugoslavia. He didn't even look much like Palazzo."

*****

I was reeling when I left the NCIS agents. I needed to be alone. Accessing the SPN-35 from the outside to avoid running into anybody, I was taken aback to find the dome already unlocked when I arrived. Master Chief Darrow was inside, sitting at my workbench waiting for me. "Are you okay?" he asked as I stepped through the door.

Shaking my head, I said, "No. I'm not. Can you leave me alone for a little while, Master Chief? Please? I need some time."

At that point, my knees went weak and gave out. Luckily, I was close enough to Darrow that he was able to catch me before I hit the deck. I thought about what I had done to Palazzo in the Nixie Room, how I scared the guy so badly that he wet himself in front of Dixie and Metaire. I thought about the threats I hurled at the man about getting to him in prison. I now had serious doubts if the pictures I had found in the fan room had been his. What if he was innocent of everything, and I drove him to suicide anyway? That would mean Krause was right. I *was* a murderer.

"He didn't do it!" I sobbed as Darrow laid me beside the radar. "He didn't do it!"

Thinking that I was in denial about something else, Darrow said, "He did, Doyle. The man shot himself. He's dead."

Wiping my eyes, I said, "Not that. The rape. He didn't rape that woman, Master Chief. Someone else did. He killed himself over it, though. Those pictures of that little girl probably weren't his, either. Just like you said."

"I didn't say they weren't his, Doyle. I only said that we couldn't prove they were."

"They weren't!" I argued.

"They could've been. We just couldn't…"

I grabbed Darrow by the collar. "THEY WEREN'T!"

My master chief hauled off and smacked me. He then yanked me up to my feet and threw me up against the bulkhead of the dome. Grabbing me by the throat, he said, "You need to get your shit together, Doyle! I know this is hard, but we don't have time for this right now. Not now! Do you hear me?!?"

I tried to break free, but Darrow's grip was unrelenting. "Give me a fucking break, Master Chief! A man just blew his brains into my face a little while ago! Into my fucking mouth! Don't you think that warrants a little time to myself?!?"

My master chief shook his head. "It does, Doyle, and I wish I could leave you alone for a while, but we don't have any time." Darrow reached into his pocket and pulled out a pink message slip from the quarterdeck. It was from Katsumi. Again, she left a number for me along with a short note that read, "Last Chance."

Darrow nodded at me one last time. "You need to pull yourself together. You need to get your shit straight enough to get past the quarterdeck watch and make it down to the pier. You need to make a goddamn phone call. Today."

*****

CHAPTER 15

I managed to make my phone call. Barely.

After an hour of trying to clear my mind of everything but Tala, I got myself together just enough to cross the quarterdeck and get to the payphones on the pier. I then explained to Katsumi what had happened and arranged to meet her at the Albuquerque Bridge the following evening.

When I turned around to go back aboard the ship, I noticed that the SPN-43 radar was rotating high upon the aft mast. That was unusual considering that we were in port. The only person who would have had any reason to turn that on would have been John Palazzo, who had by now assumed room temperature. As I watched Spanky's radar spin, I heard his voice in my head as if he were standing right in front of me. "I'm not the bad guy here," he said. "You are."

Those were his last words. Considering that I had just hung up the phone after making arrangements to meet with the Japanese mob, those words were closer to the truth than I was comfortable admitting.

Was I really the bad guy?

I tried to take stock. I had beaten Randy Green so badly that I left him a cripple. Had I not done that, however, I sincerely believe that he would have killed his wife. I saved Rafaela's life. I saved it long enough to end up seeing her forced back into prostitution until Tejada had someone put her out of her misery.

I winced at the thought of that and buried my face in my hands.

What a mess. I killed that poor woman. I might not have pulled the trigger, nor even wanted to, but I murdered her all the same. I butchered her while trying to save her from a monster.

It was the same with the girl in El Salvador. I tried to help her. I tried to protect her. In the end, though, all I did was get her killed.

She was dead anyway. Those soldiers were never going to let her live after everything they had done to her. I may not have saved her life, but at least I shortened her suffering.

And Hulagu? I got him killed, too.

That was a death that saved lives, though. Unmistakably. No. I'm not mourning that son-of-a-bitch. He had that shit coming.

The boy I shot in Olongapo?

I sighed. *I didn't want to do that. I had to do it. It was him or me. Him or Master Chief Darrow. Him or Tejada. Him or Tala. Or Mari. What was I supposed to do? Just let them kill me? I did what I had to.*

Palazzo?

I don't know. I drove him to suicide over a rape that he didn't commit. But those pictures, the ones I found in the fan room! They had to be his! He was the only one that hung out in that place. Everyone else knew what Spanky did in there and stayed away from it. Those pictures had to be his!

They had to be!

They had to.

I pulled my palms from my eyes and looked back up at the SPN-43. "You're not pinning this shit on me, you son-of-a-bitch," I said to it. "I'm not the bad guy. I wasn't the guy taking pictures of little girls in Pagsanjan. You might not have hurt that woman here in Japan, but you got what you had coming to you, you miserable sack of shit."

Of course, the radar did not answer. It just kept spinning, counting off the seconds until Palazzo's time bomb finally went off.

Tick. Tock.

Tick.

*****

When I left the pier, I went to the SPN-35 dome, my refuge, and let my mind have its way with me. All. Night. Long. I showed up to quarters the following day red-eyed, unshaven, and barely able to stand. "You all right?" Tony Bard asked when he arrived to take roll call.

"What do you think?" I asked in return.

I planned to go directly back to my dome after we were dismissed. As luck would have it, though, it was our division's turn to report to medical for our semi-annual HIV test. We spent the morning in sickbay waiting for the corpsmen to get their crap together so that we could get our blood drawn. By the time they finished with us, the galley was open so I got something to eat before climbing up to my dome for a nap.

I only meant to sleep through lunch but I did not wake up until just before the call to knock off ship's work. I made my way back to the berthing area, showered, put on civilian clothes, and started working my way toward town to meet Katsumi.

Sasebo is not a large base. There is only one path to take to get off of it. I had no choice but to pass by one of the base clubs and the diner next door to it. That diner was the ideal place to lie in wait for someone walking by. It was where Krause was waiting for me.

Unlike Master Chief Darrow, I was never trained to detect someone was following me. Fortunately, Krause was never trained how to tail someone, either. I made him as I was passing through the gate. He was so bad at surveillance that I had to make a special effort not to let on that I had spotted him. He trailed me right across Nimitz Park and hid beside the restroom where David Miller was killed when I stopped at Sasebogawa Street.

Lighting up a cigarette, I leaned on the guardrail to look at the koi swimming in the Sasebo River. I occasionally stole a glance back at Nimitz Park to see if Krause was still there. He was. He never moved until a yellow Daihatsu Mira pulled up behind me and honked its horn. Spotting Katsumi behind the wheel, I flicked my cigarette into the water below and hopped into the Mira's passenger seat.

As we pulled away from the Albuquerque Bridge, my lieutenant bolted from his hiding spot. He sprinted through the park and across the bridge. When he reached the east bank, the EMO looked up and down Sasebogawa Street in a panic, hoping to flag down a taxi. He was out of luck. There were none to be had.

Katsumi caught me looking back at Krause and asked, "Who is that?"

Turning around and fastening my seat belt, I smiled. "Quite possibly the stupidest man I have ever known."

*****

For such an economic powerhouse, Japan is a country with few natural resources. It does not even have much in the way of flat land. It is nearly all mountains, so level ground is at a premium. People are packed very tightly together and generally live in small, single-room apartments built right on top of one another. There is little privacy, even within one's own household where the bedrooms, living room, and dining area are all the same space. Unless one has exhibitionist tendencies, this makes indulging in physical intimacy a problem.

The solution is the Japanese institution of love hotels. Rented out hourly, they provide a very discreet way for couples to get together. The entire process of obtaining a room in one of these establishments is done without ever interacting with another human being. In the one that Katsumi took me to, a vending machine in the lobby displayed pictures of the rooms they offered. Available chambers were illuminated. Occupied suites were not. To get a key, you fed your money into the machine and pressed the button of the room you wanted. It was like ordering a soft drink back in the US. We did not have to do any of this, however. Katsumi had already secured a room before she picked me up.

As I passed the key machine, I stopped to take a closer look. The rooms all had different themes. Half of them looked like traditional honeymoon suites. A couple looked like classrooms. One looked like a prison cell; another had a spaceship theme going on. I pointed at one occupied chamber that looked equipped with some pretty fearsome-looking bondage gear. Getting Katsumi's attention, I asked, "The key you have wouldn't be for this one, would it?"

Katsumi walked back to me to see what I was pointing at. Giggling, she told me, "No, I no think we need something rike that unress you meeting no go so good."

I suspected that my reunion with Furukawa would not go very well the moment Katsumi ushered me into our room. She did not stay with us.

The last time I had met with Yasushi Furukawa, we were naked in a public bath. This time he wore a black suit, white shirt, and a black tie. The man he brought with him was dressed the same. Furukawa was tall by Japanese standards. And lithe. His companion was shorter and more rotund. Together, the two of them looked like they moonlighted as Asian Blues Brothers impersonators when the extortion rackets got slow.

On the other hand, I looked like I had recently lost my gig as a roadie for Jimmy Buffet. I was wearing my typical liberty attire: Hawaiian shirt thrown over a Billabong tee, cargo shorts, and loafers *sans* socks. This did not go unnoticed by the older gentleman who turned his head and snapped at Furukawa about wasting his time with some *gaijin* beach bum.

"*Gomen nasai*," I apologized. Continuing in the best Japanese I knew, I then said, "I am an enlisted man in the United States Navy. If I left my ship in a suit, it would create suspicions. This is the way my shipmates are used to seeing me. My intent on meeting you dressed like this is discretion, not disrespect."

Hearing me try to speak in his native language softened the older man's tone. He grunted. "You speak Japanese?"

"Poorly," I answered.

"Are you more comfortable speaking in English?"

I nodded. "That would be best. I have only been in Japan for a short time. I am doing my best to learn the language and customs, but I risk offending you with my ignorance. I would prefer to have Furukawa-*san* smooth out my rough edges."

With another grunt to indicate his agreement, the older man sat on the edge of the bed and let Furukawa do the introductions. When I had met him at the *sentō,* Furukawa radiated nothing but confidence. There, he was the master of his domain and acted the part. Here, in a mid-scale Japanese love hotel, Furukawa looked and behaved like a man who was very much out of his league. He was nervous, sweaty, and fidgeted when he spoke. He began by explaining to me the relationship between him and the older gentleman.

In *yakuza* parlance, Furukawa was what they called an "*aniki,*" or an "older brother." He ran a crew consisting of "*wakashu,*" or "younger brothers." Though he may have been the big fish among the men I met in the *sentō,* in the organization as a whole, Furukawa was still a low man on the totem pole. The gentleman seated on the bed was not. He was a "*shatei gashira,*" a lieutenant, a man only one layer away from the very head of the syndicate. He was so high up that I could not be trusted with his name. In front of me, he would only be referred to as *Otōsan*. Father.

After explaining to his boss who I was, Furukawa asked me who my contact was in the Philippines. "A policeman," I answered. "A federal policeman."

"Does he have a name?"

I nodded. "Yes, but he will have to give that to you himself. I am not going to reveal his identity without his permission."

Otōsan did not like that answer at all. It set off a heated round of enthusiastic conversation that threatened to derail the entire deal before it even got started. Finally, I told them, "Look, would you want me to reveal your identities to my guy in the Philippines? No, you wouldn't, and I'm not going to. My job here is to arrange a meeting. That's all. Once you and he are in a room together, you can reveal to each other whatever it is you are comfortable admitting."

"And you have no idea how much product this man has to offer us?" Furukawa translated.

"To be clear, I want to remind you that I have no idea what he is selling," I lied. "But what I do know is that he has several truckloads of it that was officially lost in the eruption of Mount Pinatubo and that he has a wide variety of what he offered you."

"So you say. How do we know this for sure?"

I pulled a key out of my pocket that my master chief had given me before I left. Passing it to Furukawa, I told him, "This is to one of the lockers in the *ginza* near the *pachinko* parlor where we first made contact. My understanding is that there are more samples there."

As Furukawa took the key from me, he rubbed his fingers. "Why is key so sticky?"

"I wrapped it in duct tape," I told him. "The glue residue will make it impossible to lift fingerprints from it."

Furukawa looked impressed. "Did they teach you that in Navy?"

I shook my head. "No, I saw it on *The Godfather*."

I saw *Otōsan* grin. *The son-of-a-bitch speaks English.*

Furukawa walked over and picked up the phone. He dialed a number and asked Katsumi to come back to the room. When she arrived, he gave her the key and asked her to check it out. After she left, Furukawa went to the mini-fridge and retrieved a few bottles of beer, pouring glasses for all three of us.

Our negotiations were now in limbo while we waited for Katsumi to recover whatever Master Chief Darrow had left for them. The conversation turned to the news in the US and, in particular, what had recently occurred in Waco, Texas. A few weeks before, federal agents had raided the Branch Davidian compound there, resulting in the deaths of seventy-six people. It was still big news all over the world, and Furukawa seemed fascinated by it.

We were not far from the *ginza,* so Katsumi called the room within forty-five minutes. She found the package. "What's in it?" the gangster asked.

When Katsumi answered, Furukawa's eyes went wide. "*Painappuru*?!?" he gasped.

Otōsan's eyes went wide, too. "*Painappuru*?!?" he repeated.

Both men then turned to me, and the demeanor of our negotiations changed dramatically. Whatever "*painappuru*" meant, the gangsters were impressed enough to meet our man in Olongapo. It was no longer a matter of *if* they should meet Tejada. It was a matter of when. Furukawa appeared ready to leave immediately.

"I can't go that soon," I told the gangsters. "I have to get my leave approved."

"We can not wait too rong," Furukawa pled. "You ship reaving for rong time soon, right?"

I was surprised to hear that the *yakuza* knew the deployment schedule of the *USS Belleau Wood.* "Yes, we're going on a WESTPAC deployment in July. I'll be gone for a few months."

"We must meet your man before you go!" *Otōsan* insisted through Furukawa.

"I'll tell you what," I told the men. "The earliest I think I will be able to go is the second week of June. Let me run my leave chit, and once I get it approved, I'll make the arrangements with my man. Sound good?" I was getting excited myself. I would soon see Tala and Mari again.

The rush of air that *Otōsan* sucked in through his clenched teeth suggested that it did not. "Or go without me," I told them. "I'll have him meet you at the airport. My job is only to arrange the meeting. I don't have to attend it to get my commission."

Neither Furukawa nor *Otōsan* were keen on that suggestion. Reluctantly, they agreed to shoot for June to meet Tejada. As they stood up to leave, we bowed to one another, shook hands, and decided that we would all communicate through Katsumi from that point forward.

Fifteen minutes after the men left, Katsumi returned, smiling broadly. "Furukawa-*san* say meeting go very well," she said, lifting her shirt off as she closed the door behind her. "He say I should take very good care of you."

And she did. When she finished with me, we laid in bed while she told me things about the *yakuza* that I would have already known had I been able to read the newspapers. I learned that the island of Kyushu was to Japan what Sicily was to the Italians. It was where the *yakuza* was born and was the place that most Japanese gangsters considered home.

Katsumi also told me that Furukawa's organization was at war with a larger group based out of Kobe. Furukawa's syndicate was both out-manned and out-gunned, but they had better leadership and tougher men. Against the odds, they were holding their own against the Kobe gang. They knew that their position was not sustainable against a family with so many more resources than they had, however. I learned that they were desperate to get their hands on something that would turn the tide in their favor.

I also learned that *painappuru* was the Japanese word for "pineapple." Katsumi told me it was *yakuza* slang for hand grenades.

*****

The Combat Systems Officer conceded that, after witnessing Palazzo's suicide, I could use a break. He also thought it was a good idea if Master Chief Darrow went with me. LCDR Winston fast-tracked both of our leave chits and had them back to us in just over a week.

Soon after that, Darrow called Tejada from a payphone near the beer garden to make the rest of our arrangements. As an added surprise, TJ had Tala and Mari come to his house to speak to me as well. "You really coming back to Olongapo!?!" Tala squealed into the phone as soon as I got on the line.

"I am," I told her. "For two weeks this time."

"Oh my God!" Tala gasped. "I can't wait! I miss you so much!"

"I miss you too," I said. "I need you, Tala. You're the only one who seems to know how to put me back together."

I told Tala about what happened with Palazzo. I also let her know that thinking of her was the only thing keeping me from slipping into a full-blown psychotic break.

Hearing that caused Tala's voice to crack. "Doyle, you no have to say it back to me, but I tell you now. I love you. I need you to know dat. Okay? You can tell me dat back when you ready. Ip you ever be ready. I just want to make sure you know dat. Okay?"

"Okay."

"Mari want talk to now, okay? She very excited. I see you soon!"

"Hello, Doyle!" Mari screamed at me when she took the phone from her mother. "I learning English! In school!"

"So I hear!" I laughed. For the next five minutes, Mari chattered non-stop. She told me all about her new school, her new friends, and her new life. She told me that everything changed after she met me, just the way that she thought it would.

When we finally hung up, I was shaking. "You alright?" Darrow asked me.

"Yeah," I answered. "I will be anyway. The moment we get back to the Philippines."

"What about that *yakuza* girl you're banging?"

"What about her?"

"Is there anything going on there?"

I laughed. "Besides her keeping an eye on me for the mob? No, there's nothing there. She's doing what she's doing to keep tabs on me. I'm going along with it so that I don't raise any suspicions. And because it's a hell of a lot of fun."

Speaking with Tala kept me out of episodes for another week. Things were coming together and the horror of Palazzo's suicide got pushed to the back of my mind. Then, near the end of May, I was in my dome when I received a call to report immediately back to the shop for an all-hands meeting of Radar Repair. When I arrived, Chief Ramirez turned toward Darrow and said, "That's everybody. We can get started."

Looking at my men, I noticed that Claude Metaire was absent. As the only black guy in my shop, his absence was conspicuous. "Wait," I said, interrupting my chief. "Where's Claude?"

Darrow cast his eyes toward the deck. "Claude's not coming, Doyle. He's gone."

The shop gasped in unison. "Claude's dead?!?" I exclaimed.

Ramirez shook his head and held up his hands. "No, no! He's alright for now! He's on medical hold. Metaire's being taken off the ship to be sent to a medical command back in the US. Because of privacy rules, they couldn't tell us why. They could only say that he's not coming back."

Even though the medical department could not reveal anything about Metaire's condition, we put two and two together. At least I did, and I was terrified. When our meeting was over, I went back to my dome and chain-smoked a half pack of cigarettes to get my hands to stop shaking. After that, I made my way to sickbay and tracked down HM1 Bateman. "Metaire tested positive for HIV, didn't he?" I asked when I found the corpsman.

"You know that I can't tell you that," Bateman shot back at me.

"I need to know, Petty Officer…"

"At this point, we've been through enough together that you can call me Dylan."

"Dylan, I need to know. I need to know if I have to get tested again."

Bateman stopped dead in his tracks and turned around to face me. He had a look of earth-shattering surprise on his face. "Seriously?!? You and Metaire were…"

"Oh! No! For Christ's sake! We weren't screwing around with each other…"

"Then why would you think you needed to be tested if he popped positive for HIV?"

After a long sigh, I explained to the corpsman what happened between Claude, me, and two Dutch girls in Hong Kong.

"And none of you used protection?" the corpsman asked.

"No."

Bateman brought his hand up to cover his face, shaking his head. "Have you got a death wish, Doyle?"

"Not particularly. I think I'm just an idiot."

"I *know* you're an idiot. Look, you've just been tested. You're negative, but, goddammit, you've got to stop all this reckless behavior! One of these days you're going to get hit by a bullet you can't dodge!"

"I know, I know! Do you think Claude could have caught it from one of those Dutch girls, though?"

"I'm not confirming that he caught anything…"

"Come on, man! Okay, let's say, theoretically, if Claude got HIV, could he have caught it in Hong Kong?"

Bateman did the math in his head. "Probably not. There's a pretty damn good chance that he passed it along to them, though!"

"So, if he was with a girl first and then I was with her…"

"Jesus Christ, Doyle! Yeah, you put yourself at a huge risk. However, if he caught something and you didn't, I would suspect that the girls you met were not the ones that gave it to him. I would bet my next paycheck that he probably passed it along, though. Think about that for a moment, Murphy. Think about it *really* hard! What the two of you did that night could very well have sentenced those two women to long, slow, and lonely deaths. Do you have any way of getting in touch with those girls?"

I shook my head.

Bateman glowered at me for a long time. Finally, he turned around and said, "Follow me."

I gulped. "To where?"

"To draw some blood. By God's grace alone, you're probably negative, but it won't hurt to check again. I'll put a rush on it."

*****

CHAPTER 16

I was fired from the position of work center supervisor of Radar Repair almost as soon as we flipped the calendar to June. If anything was surprising about that, it was that I lasted as long as I had. Still, losing my job did not happen quite the way that I would have expected it to.

The *USS Belleau Wood* was six weeks away from a three-month deployment. Within the space of twenty days, we had lost two men, one of whom was our only IFF technician. The captain was not willing to risk getting underway while being so critically undermanned. He moved heaven and earth to ensure replacements were on station before we left, and both of them reported for duty a few days before I flew out for the Philippines.

The Navy replaced Palazzo with another Italian. His name was Brian Garibaldi, but he told us his friends usually just called him Baldy for short. That was funny considering that he was the hairiest man that I had ever met. Competent, empathetic, and possessing a sensational sense of humor, he was the morale boost that Radar Repair needed. As an ET1, Baldy outranked me, so he got the job as shop supervisor, and I was more than delighted to turn it over to him.

Metaire's replacement was ET3 Trevor Simpson. He was a quiet, studious kid who was a kindred spirit to Rick Hammond, though far more introverted. Simpson appeared to be a sound technician, but he seemed to have little stomach for all the military stuff that went along with serving in the US Navy. He was also kind of moody, but since he kept to himself and never made any effort to pass his funk on to anyone else, the rest of the shop was happy to let him be. We welcomed Simpson into the conversation whenever he expressed an interest in it, but we were also okay with leaving him alone when he didn't.

"What's the story with Hammond?" Baldy asked me once we found ourselves alone in the shop.

"He got screwed over by the lieutenant," I answered. I then explained how Krause had made the extra effort to bust Rick since he had been so unsuccessful in prosecuting me. "Hammond's the best technician on the ship. I would have considered him one of the best sailors too, but for obvious reasons, his attitude's suffered a bit after he lost his crow."

Baldy nodded in understanding. "You think we can fix his attitude if we get his rank back?"

I shrugged. "I don't know. The man was a lifer before he went to captain's mast. Now, he just wants to go home."

Shaking his head, my new boss said, "It'd be a shame to send a man like that back as an E-3. I'm going to make it job one to get that kid his rank back."

"Good," I told him. "I've been working on it as well but don't see it happening until Krause is out of the way. Still, keep pushing it. If we build up enough documentation, the next guy'll have more evidence to go off of."

"Anything I need to know about Dixie?"

I shook my head. "Not really. He's a good man to have in your corner, especially in a bar fight. Be ready to step in when his blood's up, though. Keep him away from Kramer downstairs in Comm Repair."

"Kent?"

"He's alright. Professionally, I don't have any complaints about the guy. On a personal level, he's never really fit in with the rest of us, though. Part of his problem is he's trying too hard. He used to hang around with Palazzo, but he'd put some distance between them of late. Well before the man killed himself."

Baldy sat there looking at me for a moment. "How are you doing with all this stuff? With Palazzo? I heard he shot himself right in front of you."

"Yeah, he ruined my dress whites. I had to buy a whole new set. I'm fine, though. The guy was a dirtbag."

Petty Officer Garibaldi raised an eyebrow. "I heard he was cleared of that assault in Japan."

"Can I tell you something off the record?"

"Sure."

"The scuttlebutt was that he was into little girls. I found some pictures in the fan room where he liked to hang out with his porn. I'm pretty certain they were his."

"Jesus Christ."

I pulled out my pack of cigarettes, offering one to Baldy. He waved it off, telling me that he did not smoke. "We couldn't prove Palazzo brought those Polaroids aboard," I told my boss as I lit up. "So Palazzo got away with it. Word got around anyway, though. He was pretty much a pariah after that. That's why Kent stopped hangin' with him."

"You know, there's a lot of scuttlebutt going around the ship about you, too."

I nodded. "I'm sure there is."

"I'm not going to ask you about Randy Green. I know how things happen under an old-school master chief, so I'm not going to put you in a position where you have to lie to me. I want to be clear to you, though. I'm not going to tolerate any of that stuff under my watch. If you lay your hands on anyone aboard this ship, I'll take you right to the old man. No hesitation. If Darrow tells you to do anything along those lines, I expect you to come to me first. Understood?"

Smiling, I said, "Understood. Navy policy regarding the physical punishment of subordinates was reinforced to me and Darrow in the wake of the Green incident. You're never going to have to worry about that kind of shit while you're here."

"I wish I shared your confidence about that," Baldy told me. "You know, Darrow and Ramirez speak very highly of you. So does the LPO and the Combat Systems Officer. They say you're a natural leader, a great technician, and very cool under pressure. I noticed that under your guidance, though, Radar Repair has had a freaky high casualty rate. You lost a guy because he assaulted a shipmate in front of several television cameras. You had a man busted for sleeping on watch. Another guy got put on medical hold, and one blew his brains out right in front of you. I understand that you were also mixed up with that kid who was beaten to death in the park last year."

Nodding my head once more, I said, "Yeah, it's kind of my thing. While we're on the subject of bad karma, my father murdered my entire family when I was thirteen. A guy also tried to hold up a bar in Olongapo and got gunned down by an off-duty cop right in front of me and the master chief."

"Good God," Baldy gasped. Still, he looked as if he had already been told about that. I think that he was more surprised to hear me drop the information about my family so casually. "Krause told me that he thinks you were more of an active participant in the Olongapo shooting."

"Well, in case you haven't noticed, Krause is off his fucking head. Did he also tell you his theory that I murdered Palazzo to cover up my involvement with the Japanese mob?"

"No, but if I'm going to be honest with you, if he had, it wouldn't have been the craziest shit he said while I was down in the EMO. As a first-class petty officer, I shouldn't be saying this to you, but something's not quite right about that guy."

"Trust me, that's not news from my end. I've been dealing with him a lot longer than you have."

Leaning back in his chair, Baldy took his hands and put them behind his head. "Well, Murphy, I'm a big believer in the chain of command. You shouldn't be having much direct contact with the man anymore. As your supervisor, it's now my pleasure to deal with the prick."

I appreciated Baldy's intentions, but there was little the man could do to insulate me from our division officer. Not while it was still that prick's pleasure to keep dealing with me.

*****

CHAPTER 17

Through Katsumi, Furukawa and I decided upon a flight we would take to Manila. We also agreed not to interact in any way until we landed in the Philippines. Even then, we suppressed any outward display of familiarity.

I sat next to Darrow during our flight. We worked together. Had anyone been watching us, it would have been odd had we acted like we did not know each other. Still, we split up after we landed. Lorna and little Bradley met Darrow after we cleared customs and he traveled to their village near Porac to give us a reason to separate. I continued walking until I reached a line of jeepneys outside of the airport and found the one that went to the Sea Orchid Resort in Barrio Barretto.

I gave the jeepney driver my ticket and climbed aboard with my luggage. A short time later, Furukawa and one of his men did the same, taking seats all the way in the back of the vehicle. Ten minutes after that, Sergeant Tejada, satisfied that no one in the crowd had taken an interest in us, pulled himself into the jeepney too. He took a seat across the aisle and sat facing me. The driver made a show of waiting a little longer for another fare that he knew would never arrive, then pulled out of the queue to take us toward Subic Bay.

As we drove, TJ scanned the cars around us for a tail. Once we escaped metro-Manila traffic, the roads cleared out. When Tejada convinced himself that no one was interested in who we were or what we were doing, he gave me the nod.

Turning towards the back of the jeepney, I looked at the *yakuza* men, smiled, and said, "Welcome to the Philippines, Furukawa-san!"

"*Domo arigato, Do-ru san*!" Furukawa responded, smiling broadly. "You are taking us to a resort?"

I laughed. "I wouldn't call the Sea Orchid a resort. It's just a place to stay that's out of the way and unlikely to draw attention from anybody. It's actually kind of a dump."

"Hey!" the jeepney driver protested. "Dat my place you talk about!"

"Now, now, Renato," Sergeant Tejada said, leaning over to pat the man on the shoulder. "Even you admit dat you place can use new paint, more purniture, and no so much bugs." Turning back to our guests, TJ added, "But we make sure you get da good rooms! Da VIP suites! No bugs in dere!"

The sergeant then leaned over and slapped me across the arm. "We put all you bugs in Doyle's room!"

Laughing, Furukawa told me, "That okay, Do-ru-*san.* If bugs too much for you, I ret you sreep in my room."

I appreciated Furukawa's offer but had to decline. "We're not going to see each other again once we leave this jeepney," I let him know. Pointing at Tejada, I said, "My job is only to introduce you to this man. I don't know his business, nor do I want to. That's to protect me, him, and you. Now that I've put the two of you together, my work here's done." Though seated, I bowed towards Furukawa and his bodyguard. "I wish you the greatest success in your business together."

Furukawa bowed back. "And I thank you for your herp in making this happen, Do-ru-*san.* I wirr miss having you with us. What are you going to do once you reave us?"

I shrugged. "I'm sure I'll think of something."

*****

Mari screamed when she answered the door of her new apartment. She then pushed it open so hard that she nearly broke my nose when it hit me in the face. Jumping up into my arms, she collapsed into sobs as she buried her face into my neck. Tala was happy to see me, too, but she had better control of her impulses than her nine-year-old daughter. Tala just walked up, hugged us both, and said, "Welcome home, Doyle."

I had lived twenty-two years in the United States. I had been living in Japan for eight months. I had spent only four weeks in the Philippines. Tala was right, though. Olongapo felt like home. It was the only place on the entire planet where anyone was waiting for me to return.

The first thing we did was pile into the old Jeep I rented and took Mari to dinner at Jollibee. We then drove out to Pundaquit and played in the ocean. After that, we went back home, put Mari to bed, and retired to Tala's room for a few hours of wild monkey loving. When we finished, we fixed ourselves a couple of cold drinks and then sat out on the balcony. Rocking back and forth in a hammock, we took in the view overlooking the Santa Rita River.

We talked about what we had done in the seven months since we had last seen each other. After falling into a comfortable lull in the conversation, Tala turned to me and asked, "Doyle, what you doing here?"

"Coming to see you and Mari," I answered.

Tala smiled. "Besides dat. Lorna tell me dat da master chiep here, too. She say he workin' on somet'ing dat maybe bring him back to Olongapo to stay. Are you working wid da master chiep?"

I grinned. "Maybe."

Tala's eyes got wide and she rolled over to face me. "What?!? You coming back here to stay?!?"

"I'm trying, Tala. I'm trying."

"To be wid me and Mari?"

"That's my plan," I told her. "Remember when we went to the beach in San Felipe? Where I went surfing?"

Tala nodded her head.

"We're going to try to turn that into a little beach resort for wave jockeys."

"Por what?"

"Surfers, Tala. Surfers. We want to put some little cabanas on the beach and open a bar on the other side of the road. We'll also try to open a snack shack right next to it to sell street food and, if things go well, maybe even open a hotel. Nothing too big. We don't want to ruin the natural beauty of the place."

Tala looked at me as if I was telling her some sort of fairy tale. "And you live dere?"

"Not right there, no. I'm thinking after things get going, maybe we'll build a house a little way up the mountain."

"We? You mean you and da master chiep?"

I grinned. "No, I mean you, me, and Mari."

Tala gasped and brought her hand up to cover her mouth. "You mean it?!? Da t'ree op us?!?"

"Well, maybe four."

"What you mean pour?"

I took a sip from my drink. "Tala, do you still work with Children's Hope Ministries?"

"Sometimes. No so much as bepore, but when I have day opp and Mari at school, sometime I go dere to see ip I can help."

"Is Manny Green still there?"

Tala nodded.

"If this thing works out, what do you think about us pulling him out of that place and taking care of him?"

Gasping again, Tala nodded her head with such enthusiasm that she was rocking the hammock. "Doyle! He such a good boy! It no pair what happen to him! It no pair at all! Ip he stay in da orpanage, he gonna grow up and have a bery rough lipe! We can save him, Doyle! We be so good por him! He be a little brodda por Mari!"

Smiling, I told her, "Then that's what we're going to do."

Tala was shaking now. "When? When you t'ink dis gonna happen?"

I shrugged. "My enlistment is up in thirteen months. Master Chief retires two months after that. Once we're here, it's just a matter of TJ putting together the deal to buy the land."

"TJ? Sergeant Tejada?" Tala seemed to cool off a little.

"Is that okay?"

Tala smiled, but in the fake way that she used to when I first met her. "TJ very good to me and Lorna. When da base close, he get both op us bery good jobs patrolling da port. He a bery good priend to us, and to you and da master chiep. Ip you his priend, he da best priend you ever going to have. Ip you his enemy, dough, he be very scary."

"Well, luckily, I'm not his enemy."

"No, you not," Tala said. "But what ip you hab a argument? What ip business go bad, and you get bad peelings wit TJ? Dis no is America, Doyle. Dis Philippines. Ip you go to court, TJ hab all da connections. All da power. You no win. Ip TJ no want to go to court, he can do anyt'ing he want to you and you hab no way to pight back. He hab gun. And men. You hab da master chiep. Only da master chiep. And dere no American base here anymore to help you out. You can't win. Doyle, TJ is a powerpul man. He make Manny's modda disappear. She gone. He can make any op us disappear. He good priend to have, but many priends become enemy apter dey do business together. You no want TJ to ever be you enemy. Not here in da Philippines."

"I'm not worried about TJ, Tala. Master Chief trusts him, and I trust my master chief. Darrow's a chess player. He's always thinking several moves ahead. I'm sure that he's got a contingency plan set up for if things ever go sour with Tejada."

Tala looked unconvinced. "Doyle, dat good por da master chiep. I no sure it good por you, dough. How many move ahead are *you* t'inking?"

*****

"Can you still get to that gun that I gave you after those pricks tried to kill us?"

That was Darrow's answer when I asked him what we should do if things ever went bad between us and Sergeant Tejada. I nodded in response.

"Well, then, that's what it's going to take to get him off your ass. My words of wisdom to you is never to let it get to that point. Period."

We were in Lorna's village, out near Porac. The girls were inside cooking. The kids were out in the rice paddies playing with the other children. Darrow and I were discussing the drastic change our lives were on the precipice of making. "Tala's right," my master chief told me. "You always have to think several steps ahead. Not just with stuff like this, but with everything in life. You need a Plan B. And a Plan C. And a D. And an E…"

"What is your Plan B if things ever go bad with Tejada?"

Darrow raised his arms and waved them over the area around us. "Right here, Doyle. Right here. This is NPA country. These rice paddies are lousy with communist guerillas. There's no way that Tejada would chase me out here. Not without the army at his back. Paco Villa would love to have a crack at a sergeant in the PNP. Especially someone with Tejada's reputation. Look, I'm not expecting to ever have any trouble with TJ, Doyle. The man is like a brother to me. I'd never double-cross him, and I can't imagine any situation where he'd ever cross me. That doesn't mean I haven't ever thought about what I'd do if things came to that, though. I'd be negligent if I hadn't."

I let out a long sigh. "So, what do I do if I don't have an NPA sanctuary to fall back on?"

"You got one, Doyle. If things were to go bad, I'd bring you out here with me." After lighting a cigarette, my master chief added, "Of course, if something happens to me, you'd better have some other solution."

I laughed. "Like anything's ever going to happen to you."

Darrow gave me a side-eyed glare. "I appreciate your confidence in me, son, but even Superman had Kryptonite. You know, the Philippines can be a dangerous place and I've got more enemies here than I even want to think about. I take comfort in the fact that I've got some pretty solid friends, though, too. Look, man, if I'm making plans for if something ever happens to me, you should be also."

"What kind of plans are you making?" I asked.

"Well, I'm glad you asked," Darrow said. "In case I get myself arrested, murdered, or plain old just have a heart attack one morning, I want you to make sure my share of this deal goes to Lorna and Bradley."

"What?" I gulped. "Are you serious?"

"Damn right I am."

"But what about Tejada? You've known that man for decades. You've only known me for a couple of years, Master Chief."

Darrow took a drag off of his smoke. "I'd trust TJ with my life, Doyle. I'd trust him with my family's lives. He could trust his family's lives with me. Money's a different story, though. Especially when you find yourself as a loose end that someone else needs to tie up. When that happens, a man has to take care of his own."

"You think that's going to happen to us?"

He laughed. "This thing with the Japs is me and TJ's last caper, Doyle. Our very last one. We've taken all our experience, all our abilities, and did everything we could to make sure nothing went wrong. You were our biggest risk, and I'm not going to lie; you were sloppy. Getting your ass kicked, letting that guy give you a ride to base so that Palazzo could spot you, that could have brought everything down. You must have had beginner's luck on your side, though. It looks like we may be on the verge of pulling this off."

Darrow paused to take a drag off of his smoke. "But say these guys take the weapons we're selling them and catch a bus full of school kids in their crossfire? People are going to want to know where they got all that firepower. If one of them sings, we could find ourselves in a lot of trouble years after this deal goes down. That's the risk we're taking. To be blunt, if Tejada thinks I, or you, have become a risk to him and his family, he'll take us out. If I feel that he's become a risk to me or my family, I'll take him out, too. It'll kill us to have to do it, Doyle, but both of us understand the situation."

"And you don't think I'd turn on you if things get tough?"

"You've already proved that you won't," Darrow told me. "When you nearly killed Randy Green, you were going to prison, Doyle. For life if that fucker didn't make it. You were hauled off the ship in cuffs, thrown in a cage, and worked over for three days by the NIS. If you were going to turn on me to save your own ass, you would have done it then. You didn't, though. You stuck to your story and kept both of us out of jail.

"And then there was Macklemore. You risked your life to save that sorry son-of-a-bitch. Damn near got yourself killed. You could've gotten yourself iced in El Salvador trying to stick up for that poor girl down there, too. You're a good man, Doyle. I know if something happens to me that you'll do the right thing. When we get our money, we're going to put it in safety deposit boxes. I'm giving you one of the keys to mine. If something happens to me, you make sure that cash gets to Lorna and my boy. Okay?"

I nodded. "You think anything's going to happen?"

Darrow shook his head. "Naw. The dangerous part was what we did in Japan. We're practically safe at home plate now. It's just smart to be prepared if it does, son."

"In case something happens to me," I started to ask. "Will you take one of my keys?"

My master chief shook his head once more. "Nope. If something goes down, they'll be coming for me first. You keep one of those keys on you and you put the other where whoever you care about can find it."

I turned my head toward one of the huts. Tala and Mari were coming out of it to set a table for dinner.

"Thatta boy," Darrow told me. "Hide it where Tala can get it. Figure out a way that you can get in touch with her quickly, too. If shit ever does go south, it's going to happen fast. You're going to want her to know right where to go so she can get that cash and run."

Darrow lifted a bottle of San Miguel beer to his lips and took a long drink. "And Doyle, if you ever give Tejada a reason to think that you've double-crossed him, or me for that matter, you better tell Tala how to get her hands on that gun we were just talking about, too. She's gonna need it."

*****

"What we doing here?" Tala asked as we stepped out of the trike outside of our old apartment complex.

"Playing chess," I told her. "Like we talked about. In case something ever goes wrong."

We squeezed ourselves between the walls that separated our former apartment building from the neighbors. When we were finally in the jungle behind it, we started walking uphill. It was hot and humid, as it always was, and it took no time at all for me to become drenched in my own sweat. "Do you remember the night those guys tried to kill us?" I asked Tala as we marched upwards.

"How you t'ink I ever be able to porget?"

Breathing hard from the exertion, I said, "Master Chief gave me a pistol he found that night. I buried it in front of a Banaba tree and marked it with a big rock…"

I stopped. I found the tree I was looking for. And the rock. The problem was that one of those *matsing* monkeys was sitting on it when we got there. "Shit."

"Oh no," Tala said when she arrived at my side. "Is dat da rock you looking por?"

I nodded. "It sure is."

"Okay. I see it. We can go now."

"No, I need to dig it up and make sure everything's okay in there."

Tala shook her head. "Den come back later. When da monkey no here."

I reached down and grabbed a big stick from off of the ground. "There's only one of them this time. I can chase it away."

"No, Doyle," Tala pled. "Please don't. You no know dose t'ings like we do. Dey nasty. Leave it alone bepore you make it angry."

"I don't want to hurt it; just shoo it away." I reached down to the ground again and picked up a stone.

"What you t'ink you gonna do wid dat?"

"Throw it at him. See if it'll scare it off."

"Doyle! No!" Stomping her foot down to get my attention, she asked, "Do you know dey call dese t'ings 'rock apes' in Cubi Point? You know why dey call dem dat?"

I shrugged. "Because they live around rocks?"

"No! Because dey t'row da rocks really hard! Harder dan you can! And dey always hit what dey aiming por! Leave it alone, Doyle! Let's go!"

"But…"

In exasperation, Tala threw her hands up into the air and started walking back down the hill. "You do what you want! I getting da hell outta here!"

Remembering what those things did to Claude, I guessed Tala was right. I turned around to follow her back to the street.

I cannot explain the complexities of simian communication. Like humans, certain behaviors can provoke particular reactions from them. I knew that I was not supposed to make eye contact with the monkeys because they could interpret it as a challenge and attack. I learned that day you should not turn your back on them, either. I am still unclear on the psychology behind what happened, but the instant I turned to leave, that little shit leapt off my rock and charged.

I heard the monkey coming, so before he could get his grubby little paws on me, I instinctively swung the stick I was carrying. The creature jumped back and screamed. I shouted back at it, not out of aggression but from fear. I was doing my best to convey that I was conceding defeat and that if it would let me get away, there was nothing that I would rather do than leave it alone.

The monkey did not get the hint. It darted at me again, and out of nothing but sheer impulse, I chucked my rock at it as hard as I could, missing my target by a mile. I swear, the monkey then stopped and looked at me with an expression on its face that perfectly conveyed, "Oh? We're playing *that* game, little man? Well then, allow me to retort."

Seeming to produce a stone from nothing but thin air, that midget monster heaved it at me with a level of speed and accuracy that defied comprehension. I was amazed that something a little larger than a house cat could have Nolan Ryan's pitching arm. The rock caught me just above my right eye so hard that for a split second, I appreciated how Goliath must have felt. I doubled over, gripped my face with my free hand, and shrieked, "Motherfucker!"

Then I got hit on the left cheek. With feces. Now I was pissed. I was not so much angered at the insult as I was frustrated by my inability to defecate on command and respond in kind. I let go of my face, turned toward my adversary, and shouted, "You dick!" I then grabbed my stick like it was a Louisville slugger and prepared to launch that little bastard into orbit if it took another step in my direction.

Undeterred, the monkey bared its teeth and charged at me once more. I swung my stick and missed. The *matsing* changed direction, snorted, then came at me from another angle. I swung there too and missed again.

"Doyle!" Tala screamed at me. She was near the street by then. "Come on! Get down here!"

I was trying, but at this point, I was under a full-frontal assault. I was backing away as fast as I could. Claude Metaire was far more athletic than I would ever be, and if he could not outrun one of those things, I did not have a prayer of doing it. If I turned and ran, that son-of-a-bitch would be on my shoulders inside of two steps. All I could do was back my way down the slope and swing my stick left, right, up, down, diagonally, and in any other direction that would keep the creature at bay. "HEEEEELLLLLLPPPPP!" I screamed as I tried to pick up the pace of my retreat.

"Run, Doyle!" Tala screamed back. She was past the old apartment and yelling at me from the street now. "I got a trike! Come on! Hurry!"

That was when I finally connected. The monkey leapt at me while I was mid-swing and my stick caught it right in the ribs. The blow sent its hairy ass flying head over heels through the air until it landed in the bush, howling in shock and pain.

Having always been something of an animal lover and growing up with a fascination toward monkeys in particular, I felt sorry for the poor thing at first. "Oh my God!" I gasped. "I'm sorry! I'm sorry!"

Then I heard the creature's henchmen answer its cries of distress from somewhere up the hill in the distance. As they called out again, I could tell they were quickly getting closer. When they were near enough that I could hear the bush rustling, I dropped my stick and ran for my life.

When I cleared the jungle and emerged onto the street, I had at least twenty chattering primates hot on my heels and I was screaming bloody murder. When the trike driver saw us heading his way, he screamed too. Tala jumped into the sidecar just as he gunned the engine and tore away, leaving me there by myself. Luckily, another trike passed me from behind and I hopped into the sidecar while he was still doing at least fifteen miles an hour. The impact knocked the wind out of me and nearly caused the driver to crash. Seeing Harris Street rapidly filling with a dozen pissed-off rock apes, however, the driver took it in stride.

Opening up the throttle, my chauffeur veered right and passed the jeepney in front of us by driving on the sidewalk. Behind us, cars slammed on their brakes, swerved, and blared their horns to scatter the monkeys out of the road before they got hit.

When we were back on the street, my driver stepped on the gas to put more distance between us and the chaos in his mirror, then breathed a long sigh of relief. "Where we going, boss?"

Shaking my head while fighting for air, I gasped, "I don't care. Just get me as far away from those fucking things as you can for now."

*****

I had been in the Philippines a little over a week when Darrow got word to me to meet him at Lorna's apartment. When I got there, Tejada was sitting with my master chief waiting for me. Both of them were all smiles. "I take it everything is going well?"

TJ kicked a chair out away from Lorna's kitchen table for me to take a seat upon. "It no going well. It done. It done good. Everyt'ing pinished."

"And?" I asked.

"Da Japs already going home. Dey pay half op da money to make sure we no sell to anyone else. When dey people come back to pick up da guns, dey gonna gib us da rest." Tejada reached under the table and pulled out the two duffle bags he brought with him. He set one in front of Darrow and one in front of me.

In too much shock to open mine, I looked up at TJ and asked, "How much?"

The sergeant grinned. "Dere two hundred and twelve t'ousand dollars in dose bags. US."

"They got it to you that quick?" Darrow asked.

"Yeah, sure," Tejada said. "Dey hab a lot of money here in da Philippines already. Dey get a loan prom men here recruiting girls to work in Japan."

"Jesus Christ," I said. "Trafficking girls to hook in Japan?"

Tejada shrugged. "Dey doing the same t'ings in Tokyo dat dey doing in Barrio Barretto, only making lot more money doing it. When dose girls come back here, dey set up better dan da girls dat stay."

"When do they expect to get the guns and close the rest of the deal?" Darrow asked.

A couple months at least," Tejada shrugged. "Maybe August. Dey very motivated to get dis stupp back to Japan. Dey really want dose hand grenades."

"We're going to be at sea in August," I told Darrow.

Nodding, my master chief said, "Yep. It looks like we'll have to come back in October."

"So how do we go about buying the land we need? How do we get this money to you when you need it?"

Tejada shook his head. "You no buying any land, Doyle. Poreigners can no buy land in the Philippines. I buy da land. You and da master chiep be using you money to build da business. You keep dat money sape until it time por you to come back and start. When you guys getting out op da Navy again?"

Darrow and I looked at each other. "Next summer," I told him.

Tejada raised his bottle of beer in salute. "Den we drink to next summer!"

Clinking our bottles together, the three of us cheered and toasted, "Next summer!"

After slamming what remained of his beer, Darrow banged the empty bottle of San Miguel on the table. "But we'll be back in October for the rest of our money."

*****

The following morning Darrow loaded our duffel bags into our Jeep and drove up to Manila. There, we split up to put my cut into a safety deposit box of one bank while Darrow put his into another. With our money safe and secure, we drove back to Olongapo. I dropped Darrow off at Lorna's place, then drove to a hardware store to buy a machete. I needed to get to the gun I had buried in the jungle, and if I came across those monkeys again, I wanted to be appropriately armed this time.

Fortunately, the *matsing* were nowhere to be found. Still, I was so anxious about the prospect of the little beasts catching me there that I worked myself up enough to nearly trigger one of my episodes. I dug up that tin in record time. After inspecting the weapon to ensure that it still looked to be in working order, I replaced it and buried it again, along with a safety deposit box key and a little more cash tucked inside a Ziplock bag to protect it from the humidity.

Confident that my arrangements were made, I went back to enjoying life with Tala and Mari for the next few days. I spent most of our afternoons teaching Mari to surf on one of the calmer stretches of our San Felipe beach. During the day, I made sure that Tala had everything she needed to start the process of taking custody of Manny Green. I also had a telephone installed in Tala's apartment so that I could call her at any time. To be extra safe, I also bought her an answering machine in case there was an emergency and she was not around to pick up.

When it was time for me to leave at the end of the week, it was sad, but not nearly as devastating as it was the year before. This time we knew our separation was only temporary. I would be back in Olongapo before the Day of the Dead celebrations.

When I returned to Japan, I was a new man. Palazzo and his suicide were far behind me, and the time I had spent with Tala and Mari seemed to have purged all the other horrors that plagued me as well. I was relaxed. I was at peace. And, at least as far as I was concerned, I was rich. I had more than a quarter-million dollars stashed between Panama and the Philippines. Back where I was from, that was more money than I had heard of anyone ever having. With that much cash, I did not even care if Krause somehow gained the upper hand and busted my ass anymore.

Hell, by the time we left on our WESTPAC deployment, I was wishing that he would. The faster he tossed me out of the fleet, the quicker I could get back to Subic Bay and my girls.

*****

CHAPTER 18

The *USS Belleau Wood* left Sasebo the first week of July. We traveled to Okinawa to load up our Marines and their equipment, then set sail to rendezvous with the flotilla that arrived in theater from the US. Linking up with ships from Japan, Korea, Britain, Australia, and New Zealand, we then commenced patrolling the South China Sea.

For the next few weeks, we spread out on exercises to make our presence known off the coasts of Taiwan, the Philippines, and Vietnam. We then pulled into Hong Kong for a few days of rest and to resupply. While most of the crew were content to booze it up in the nightclubs of Kowloon, Dixie and I caught a catamaran to the Portuguese colony of Macao. We lost our asses in the casinos there.

The next leg of the WESTPAC exercise was brutal. Sailing from China, we steamed past the north coast of Luzon into the Philippine Sea on our way to the Northern Marianas. There, we spent more than a week reenacting the invasions of Tinian and Saipan. We spent almost the entire time on station at General

Quarters. We barely slept until we pulled into Guam at the beginning of August.

Technically, Guam was a working port. Since we had performed so well, though, the captain stepped out of character. He granted us Cinderella liberty, allowing us to leave the ship after knock-off but requiring us to return before the stroke of midnight. That gave Dixie and me eight hours to get as drunk as we could.

The enlisted man's club on Guam was much larger than the one on White Beach in Okinawa, but it was housed in an old World War II-era building that had seen better days. Not that we cared. It had cold beer, and that was good enough for us. Dixie and I took seats at an empty table and started throwing back pitchers of flat Budweiser and shots of Jim Beam.

Sometime around ten that evening, I left to refill our drinks. When I returned, a petite blonde Australian girl was sitting on Dixie's lap. She had her arms wrapped around Kevin's head, and her tongue was shoved so deep into his mouth that she could tickle his tonsils. She was very attractive and even more intoxicated. The lady did not even seem to notice me when I retook my seat. "Wow. This's got to be a record," I told Kevin. "What kind of line did you use on this one?"

When the woman pulled her lips away from Dixie's to begin gnawing on his neck, he looked at me with an expression of total surprise. "Dude! I was sitting here waiting for my beer, and she just jumped in my lap and started doing this shit!"

The woman lifted her head and put her mouth up to Kevin's ear. "Let's get out of here," she whispered.

Looking up at me, Dixie asked, "What do I do?"

I poured myself a beer. "Well, think about this for a second. We've got a little over an hour before we have to start heading back to the ship. You don't have a whole lot of time to enjoy yourself. Also, she's smashed out of her mind. That's asking for trouble. Third, we're on a military base and she sounds about as Australian as a girl can. Since it's not likely that she's in the American Navy with an accent like that, I'm guessing she's a dependent. She's probably somebody's wife. Getting caught in base housing with her would be a *really* bad idea."

"Let's get out of here," she suggested again, still oblivious to my presence.

Dixie thought for a moment and then shook his head. "Look," he told the girl. "I'm flattered. We have to get back to our ship after this pitcher, though. I just don't have the time."

"Okay," The woman slurred. She then stood up and took a boozy sway to her right, nearly falling over onto our table. I reached out to steady her. As soon as we touched, she turned to me, smiled, and sat down upon *my* lap. She then grabbed my head and slipped her tongue into my mouth like she had done to Dixie a moment before.

Kevin erupted into laughter as I spread my arms out into a "what the bloody hell?" gesture. Of course, that was the moment her husband walked in.

The blonde's old man was in a chief's uniform and on duty. Not only did he outrank me, but he was also wearing the Special Warfare insignia above the left pocket of his khaki shirt. He had been a Navy SEAL.

Seeing as how he was stationed in Guam and shared the physique of most forty-year-old senior chiefs, it did not appear that he was still on a team. That did not matter one bit, though. If a man made it through SEAL training, it showed that pain did not affect him a whole lot. If we came to blows, he was going to hurt me.

"GODDAMMIT ELIZA!" he roared as he ripped the woman off of my lap, causing the entire bar to go silent. He then went on to create quite the spectacle dragging her out into the parking lot.

Once the senior chief was gone, AG2 Gott, who was on Shore Patrol, rushed over to our table with his partner. "Did you see that, Doyle?"

I could not have thought of a more stupid question. "See what?" I asked, my voice cracking in fear. "Did I miss something?"

"Dude! That guy was a fucking SEAL!"

"No shit?" I answered while chugging the rest of my Budweiser. "I did not notice that." My trembling hands suggested otherwise.

"Doyle! You need to get the hell out of here before that guy gets back!"

It was sage advice, and I intended to heed it, but I did not want to cross paths with that man in a dark parking lot. I wanted to give him time to clear the club. I also wanted to finish the beer I had just bought to settle my nerves.

Dixie and I were almost done with our pitcher when the senior chief returned. Once again, the bar fell silent, and the crowd parted to clear a path between the woman's husband and myself. The two of us locked eyes. Being an orphan, I was relieved that my impending death would not ruin many people's Christmas plans.

"What are we going to do?" Dixie asked me. "There's two of us. Do you think we can take him?"

I shook my head. "Even if we did, we'd still end up in the brig for assaulting a senior chief."

"So, what the hell are we going to do?"

"Run!"

As if someone suddenly fired a starter pistol, Dixie and I simultaneously slammed the shots of whiskey still lying on our table. We then bolted in different directions. Kevin ran screaming out of one door of the club while I dashed out of another, screaming even louder. Both of us went our separate ways, sprinting into the night, too drunk to remember exactly where the pier was that our ship was moored to.

*****

I got lost on base. It took me an hour to figure out how to get back to the *Belleau Wood.* Still, I crossed the quarterdeck with ten minutes to spare before curfew. I discovered from the Petty Officer of the Watch that Dixie never made it. Unable to go back out and look for him, I sadly stumbled to my rack. I was confident that

Kevin had landed himself on thirty days of Liberty Risk and would spend the rest of our WESTPAC confined to the ship.

I woke up the following morning with a brutal hangover and the realization that we were still missing a sailor. I began to fear that the SEAL had caught him. At roll call, I told Darrow what had happened and he initiated a frantic series of phone calls to Guam's shore facilities. No one had heard from our missing man. We wondered if he went for a drunken swim on the way back to the boat. The ocean currents around Guam were notoriously treacherous. He could have gotten himself caught in a riptide and drowned.

When the tugboats finished pushing the *USS Peleliu* out to sea, they came back for us. We pulled in our lines, pushed off from the pier, and started heading for the equator without Dixie. I went back to Radar Repair, wondering what the hell had happened to him. I had already lost Claude. I was not sure I could handle losing Kevin, too.

It was not long before ET1 Garibaldi walked into the shop and announced that they had found him. "Where is he?" I asked.

Baldy grinned. "Follow me."

As we marched out of the shop, I heard the 1MC come alive. "Flight Quarters! Flight Quarters! Set condition 1-alpha for flight operations!" That was odd. I was not expecting any air ops until much later in the afternoon.

My new supervisor took me to the flight deck staging area where the master-at-arms was waiting for us. "You want to tell me what's going on?" I asked MA1 Carlton.

"Nope," the master-at-arms told me. "Not sure that you'd believe me if I did. This is something you have to see for yourself."

Within five minutes, a helicopter touched down upon our flight deck. Out of it stepped ET3 Kevin Dixon, still wearing the clothes I last saw him in. "What the hell?" I gasped.

Baldy laughed, shaking his head. Patting me on the shoulder, he said, "Let's get him up to the bridge and get this over with.

Darrow assured me that Reaper Dick's probably going to take his crow. Let's hope that he doesn't take one of your stripes, too."

There is usually a process for sending someone to mast, but justice was swift under Captain Darcy. He did not even give Dixie time to change into uniform. We went right to the bridge where Krause, Darrow, and LCDR Winston were waiting for us.

Dispensing with all ceremony, Reaper Dick tore into Dixie the moment he laid eyes upon him. "What the hell is the matter with you, son! Do you understand that you're up here accused of missing ship's movement?"

Dixie appeared surprised at Reaper Dick's insinuation. "Missing ship's movement?!? Sir, I didn't miss ship's movement?"

Darcy looked shocked. "Are you serious? How the hell do you explain that helicopter ride you just took?"

Kevin cleared his throat. "Sir, I was running back to the ship last night when the base police stopped me to see why I was in such a hurry. After I told them a SEAL was trying to kill me…"

"A seal? You talking a frogman or a sea lion?"

"A frogman, sir. A commando."

"Son, why was a SEAL trying to kill you?"

"Because he caught Petty Officer Murphy making out with his wife, sir."

Reaper Dick turned to face me. "You were making out with a SEAL's wife?"

"No, sir," I answered. "She was making out with me." I paused awkwardly while the captain kept his glare focused in my direction. "I did not consent to be made out with, sir. I'd press charges, but she was kind of hot. I'll let it go this time."

The captain shook his head and told Dixie to continue. "Well, sir, after I explained the situation to the base police, they offered to give me a ride back to my ship, which I accepted. I asked them to take me to the *Belleau Wood*. Apparently, they misunderstood me and took me to the *Peleliu,* on the other side of the pier, instead." Until Kevin said that out loud, I never realized how close to each other our ships' names sounded.

"Sir, both vessels are amphibious assault ships. They're LHAs. They're exactly the same. I went right to where my berthing area would be, right to where my rack would be, and climbed into where my bed would be. Then I crashed. I'm a deep sleeper, sir, but my body's trained to wake up to an alarm clock I keep under my pillow. I didn't have that, so I slept through Reveille. Since the rack I was in was supposed to be empty, no one bothered to pull the curtains open to wake me up. I didn't open my eyes until the guys came down to clean the berthing area, and by then, the *Peleliu* had already left Guam."

"That's your excuse?" the captain balked. "You got confused over what ship you were supposed to be on? That's how you intend to defend yourself for getting left on the beach?"

Dixie looked at the skipper, appearing genuinely outraged. "No one left *me* on the beach, sir! I left *you* there! Now, if we're going to charge into the rest of this WESTPAC kicking ass and taking names, you guys are going to have to learn to keep up!"

The collective jaws of Dixie's entire chain of command dropped open, and the captain's head looked like it was ready to explode. He took an angry step toward Kevin as if he was about to bust him in the kisser, but stopped shy of the young petty officer. "Son, are you fucking drunk?"

Dixie shook his head. "No, sir. Not any more."

"Master-at-Arms!" Darcy barked. "Do you have a breathalyzer on you?"

"Yes, sir!" Carlton responded. That was a standard request from Reaper Dick. The master-at-arms was prepared.

"Then check and see if this young man is lying to me."

The master-at-arms pulled his breathalyzer out of his pocket and had Dixie breathe into it. Not believing the results, he repeated the process two more times. Growing impatient, the captain snapped, "What'd he blow?"

Carlton shook his head. "Nothing, sir. The man's stone-cold sober."

The captain looked enraged when he turned back to Dixie, but before he could say anything, he chuckled. He tried to suppress it but then laughed again. Then, shaking his head, he gave in and completely cracked up. Unsure if he was laughing with hilarity or malice, no one else dared to laugh with him. When Reaper Dick regained his composure, he looked back at Dixie and laughed once more. "You got any tattoos, Dixon?"

Kevin nodded. "Yes, sir. On my arm."

"Let me see it," the captain ordered.

Dixie pushed his tee-shirt sleeve up and showed off his ink. It was the same one that I had: a skull in a horned sailor cap before an old anchor. Below it was a pair of crossed liquor bottles.

"So that's the Tequila Viking that I was told so much about?"

Kevin nodded. "Yes, sir."

Reaper Dick seemed to approve. "Alright, son. You win this one. Get off my bridge, get your uniform on, and get to work. We'll do our best to keep up with you."

And that was it. To my knowledge, Dixie was the only man to ever go before Reaper Dick and walk off of the bridge without dropping a paygrade.

*****

CHAPTER 19

I had heard that the ritual performed when a ship crosses the equator had its origins in ancient Phoenicia. I also understood that those ancient ceremonies involved human sacrifice. The American Navy incorporated the rite pretty much at its inception, though it had mellowed somewhat since the pagan era. Nobody got killed doing it by the early 1990s, though the saltier men aboard the *Belleau Wood* did everything in their power to make some of the greener sailors wish they were dead.

"OUTTA YER RACK YE SCURVY POLLIWOG!" ET1 Garibaldi bellowed as he grabbed me by my hair and ripped me out of my rack. That morning he had modified his uniform to reflect something of a pirate theme. Baldy cut his dungarees into shorts and tied his tee-shirt up in front to expose his naval. He even wore a patch over his left eye and had his Dixie Cup cover cocked far to the back of his head.

Baldy was also armed with a shillelagh. That was a three-foot section of fire hose with one end wound with tape to make it easier to grip. The men used them to whip the uninitiated, those heinous wastes of humanity, otherwise known as "wogs." Baldy had crossed the equator before and paid his penance. Therefore, he was a "Trusty Shellback" and duty-bound to inflict a similar degree of suffering upon lesser men so that they too could be reborn as true mariners.

Throwing me down to the deck onto my hands and knees, my shellback supervisor took his shillelagh and cracked me across my ass. I am not going to lie. That first blow hurt like hell.

Staying in character, Baldy got down into my face. "It's yer day to bow before his high majesty King Neptune and the high priest of the deep, the right honorable Davey Jones!" The berthing area erupted into pandemonium. Our department's other shellbacks broke out into a chorus of screaming while pulling the rest of us wogs out of our racks.

The *Belleau Wood* was no longer an American warship. The ensign had been lowered and the Jolly Roger, the skull and crossbones of the pirate nation, was raised in its place. For several hours, Captain Darcy would be suspending his insistence on order and discipline to let the shellbacks run amok.

"Petty Officer Murpheeeeeeeee!" screamed Baldy. "Do you wish to engage in the test of the times? Do you consider yourself to be worthy of Neptune's favors and blessings? Do you wish for the honor of proving yourself worthy of being named a Trusty Shellback?"

I jumped to my feet and snapped to attention as I was taught to do in boot camp. "Yes! This unworthy wog seeks Neptune's blessing!"

"Blasphemy!" cried Baldy. "No wog is allowed on his feet on this blessed day! Get down upon your knees, cur!" Again grabbing me by my hair, Baldy forced me back down upon all fours. He then screamed for his enforcer, AO2 Stinson. "This filthy wog needs two eggs and a sardine!"

Stinson reached into the bag he was carrying and pulled out what Baldy had ordered, two eggs and a sardine. My boss dropped all three of them down the back of my underwear. After that, he yelled, "Clear!" He wound up his shillelagh, then flogged me across my backside so hard that my scrotum got peppered with eggshell shrapnel. I lost sensation of the sardine completely. I suspected that it ran up my digestive tract until it came to rest somewhere in the neighborhood of my prostate.

The sound of the shillelagh striking my backside, that "SWACK!" sound, reverberated throughout the berthing area. Each crack of the hose hitting a dirty wog's rump was followed by some unfortunate sailor's screams. It was a little overplayed, however. The shillelagh's bark was much worse than its bite. Many of us exaggerated the agony it caused to avoid getting hit again. This terrified the men who had not experienced it yet

SWACK! SWACK! SWACK! "DO YOU SEEK NEPTUNE'S BLESSING?!?"

"I DO!" SWACK!

SWACK! SWACK! "DO YOU WANNA BE A SHELLBACK?!?"

"YEEEEEES!"

SWACK!

"HOW ABOUT YOU, WOG?!? ARE YOU PREPARED TO STAND BEFORE DAVY JONES?!?"

It was almost imperceptible through the chaos, but somewhere through the racket, we heard someone whimper a "no." Everything came to a grinding halt. "Who said that? Who was that?" asked DS1 de Alba.

Over here!" GM2 Fred Long called out, cracking up. "It's fucking Kramer!"

The shellbacks roared with laughter. Bill Kramer had been considered a tough guy at one time. His shipmates now regarded him as something of a coward. Chickening out of the shellback rite was not going to help his reputation. "Kramer!" DS1 de Alba yelled. "Get the fuck out of here! Get dressed and report to MS1 Velazquez on the mess decks for the day! Move it!"

As Kramer put his uniform on and fled the berthing area, he was jeered by wog and shellback alike. Once he was gone, the carnage resumed.

After each wog had declared that we were voluntarily participating in the shellback initiation, we were lined up on all fours, still in our underwear. Each man's nose was resting between the ass cheeks of the man before him. Only an eighth of an inch of white cotton separated us from making direct contact. From there, we crawled through the berthing area and up the ladders to the mess deck. The shillelaghs punished us for any infraction of initiation decorum. That proved painful considering none of us really knew what the decorum even was.

When we reached the mess decks, we were not allowed to witness the inquisition taking place inside. As we inched closer to the front of the line, the shellbacks blindfolded us. When it was our turn for questioning, we were dragged into the galley and thrown into a metal folding chair. We had to spread our legs so that another wog could kneel between them, facing us.

Those of us in the chair were then asked questions that we very likely did not know the answer to. "What is your fifth general order?" I was asked. This was something I had forgotten almost immediately after leaving boot camp. I would have bet good money that the guy questioning me did not know the answer to it either.

Of course, I answered incorrectly. As punishment, I had to drink what I suspected was a mixture of Tabasco, milk, lemon juice, Worcestershire Sauce, coffee grounds, and pureed avocado. It was one of the most offensive things I have ever swallowed, and it came right back up immediately, spewing out all over the man kneeling in front of me. Then we had to switch positions.

Once finished with the inquisition, we were allowed back to the berthing area to prepare for the gauntlet. We could not shower, but we could at least get dressed. We put on our worst pair of dungaree pants (padding our butts and the back of our thighs with whatever we could to protect them from the shillelaghs). We also duct-taped shower shoes to our knees in preparation for spending the rest of the day crawling around the flight deck. The non-skid surface there would eat the skin right off of any bare joint that came into contact with it.

When ready, we were herded onto the flight deck to meet the Court of the Deep. First out before us was Davy Jones, who was played by our chaplain of all people. He emerged from the island structure wearing clerical robes, an old-style pancake cover, and a hockey mask. He looked every bit like some horror movie serial killer who found himself some Jesus. He was escorted by Master Chief Darrow, dressed in pirate attire. He held the leash of two Devil Dogs, a pair of the biggest wogs on the ship dressed as French Poodles. They were forced to do tricks at Davy Jones' command. While we all knelt before him, Jones berated us, spending at least twenty minutes letting us know just how much of a stain upon the sea we were. He doubted any of us would ever prove worthy of the honor of becoming a shellback.

King Neptune then emerged to give us all hope. Dressed in white with golden locks and brandishing a massive trident, our executive officer offered us salvation by trial and tribulation. If we could complete the tasks before us, our names would be recorded in the annals of the deep. We would be forever remembered as worthy and righteous men of the sea. When the ship's whistle blew, the hazing began in earnest.

SWACK! SWACK! SWACK! The shillelaghs went flying, crashing down upon our backs. I was herded toward a line of a half dozen of the ship's most obese chief petty officers. They were pale living Buddhas perched in folding chairs, shirtless, and with their ample abdomens slathered in mess deck lard. "What do you think you are, sailor?" yelled one of the chiefs when I got close enough.

"What?" I asked. SWACK! I did not cry out, but I definitely clenched my teeth.

"What are you, sailor?!?"

"I'm a wog, Chief!"

"You're goddamn right you are, you worthless piece of shit!" The chief reached into a bucket beside him and pulled out an olive. After inserting it as deep into his navel as he could push it, he barked, "Get that fuckin' olive out of my belly button, wog!"

Now, it is only natural to look at a man like he's lost his mind when he asks you to pull an hors d'oeuvre out of an orifice. It is an outlandish request in virtually any setting other than a shellback initiation. While I was trying to figure out the mechanics of what the chief was telling me to do, some snipe brought his shillelagh down across my ass. SWACK!

I yelped in pain and then reached out to grab the olive.

SWACK! I got hit again. "Keep your grubby mitts off of the chief, wog!" yelled the snipe.

"Then how am I supposed to…"

SWACK!

"Aaaaaiiiiiieeeee! Fuck! That…"

The chief grabbed me by the ears and pulled my face into his greased-up beer belly. "Grab it with your teeth, wog!"

I tried, but my nose and chin were preventing my teeth from getting anywhere near it. As my nostrils began filling with lard, I had to work it out with my tongue. Once the olive was in my mouth, another blow from the snipe's shillelagh expelled it from my lips and sent it flying across the flight deck. "You got your treat, wog! Now get the fuck out of here and give someone else a turn!"

Still on all fours, I tried to scurry away before I got hit again. I got snagged by a supply clerk before I made it five feet. Grabbing me by the neck, he forced my face to the deck. "Someone got shit in my pad eye!"

A pad eye was a divot in the flight deck. It was a depression over which a small cross of metal rods were welded for the aircraft chains to hook to. Contrary to what the clerk had said, it did not appear that anyone put feces in his pad eye. It smelled more like urine. "Blow that shit out of there!"

I tried. After blowing into it four or five times, though, someone else came by and started screaming at me for laying down on the flight deck. SWACK! "What do you think you are!"

"I'm a wog!"

"You're god damn right you are! Go kiss the wog queen's foot!" This shellback put me in a line to crawl before Neptune's court. At the far end of them, I had to lick peanut butter from between the toes of a Marine dressed in drag for the occasion.

SWACK! Next, we were led to a row of large metal bowls. They were filled with wet garbage from the mess decks that was allowed to putrefy for days in the equatorial sun solely for this occasion. We had to stick our faces in it and blow bubbles.

SWACK! We dove into a large plastic box full of lemon water to freshen up.

SWACK! We were ordered to sing bawdy songs. SWACK! We had to make up lewd nursery rhymes. SWACK! We were pushed onto a large tarp full of wet garbage for impromptu wrestling matches with other wogs. I got teamed up against a Marine that had me turned upside down and pinned inside of a minute. For losing, a shellback branded me with a black "S" on my forehead that singled me out for "Special Treatment."

SWACK! I was sent scrambling towards the island structure. Once there, an airman turned a fire hose on me that rolled me across the non-skid while it blew some of my funk off. When the airman manning the hose turned it off, he opened a hatch and told me to get in.

It was a dark space. Once I was inside, I got hit again. SWACK! "Who are you?" screamed one of the men inside.

"I'm a wog!"

SWACK! "I asked who you are! Not what you are!"

"I'm Petty Officer Doyle Murphy!"

My ears were full of water from the fire hose. I could hear one man tell the other to take a break but could not recognize who it was. Once we were alone, I got hit again, but this time it was different. There was something in the shillelagh. Something heavy. SWACK! The blow struck me across my lower back, knocking my pelvis to the ground. I did not know what they sealed inside of that hose, but whatever it was, it turned the shillelagh into a three-foot-long blackjack.

"Hey!" I protested, only to be rocked by another blow across the shoulders. That one buckled my elbows and laid me flat across the deck. "What the fuck are you doing?!?"

SWACK! "Giving you what you deserve!" Lieutenant Krause snarled. "You're not getting away with murdering Palazzo, Murphy! If I can't make you pay for it the Navy way, I'll give you a taste of your own fuckin' medicine! Welcome to *my* Nixie room, you son-of-a-bitch!"

I brought my arms up to cover my head in the nick of time. SWACK! SWACK! I took two blows across my forearms that were aimed at my melon. SWACK! I then took a brutal one across the gut that took my breath away. SWACK! My knees. SWACK! Back to my shoulders. SWACK! SWACK! Two to the ribs. The second blow felt like it snapped one of them, causing me to howl in pain.

"You happy now?!" Krause asked. "You still feel lak a big mun…d'ya?" The lieutenant was so worked up that he was having trouble getting his words out. My hands were down along my side nursing my broken rib when he struck again. SWACK! It was right across the side of my head.

The blow smacked me senseless. It bloodied my nose and filled my ears with a ringing that drowned out everything else. It knocked me right into my underwater world, the one I was in when I crippled Randy Green. The state I was in when I nearly killed the Hockey Mullet Frat Guy in Ocean Beach. The frame of mind that I needed to be in to beat the very life out of Lieutenant Krause.

Leaping to my feet, I grabbed Krause's weapon and ripped it out of his hands. I then planted my fist into his gut with everything I had. Grabbing him by the throat, I threw him up against the bulkhead and pulled my arm back, readying to bash his face in. I was entirely consumed by my rage now, the one that I could not control. I was in a dark room, alone with my victim. Claude and Dixie were not there to stop me this time. Neither were Dreadlock John or Warren Macklemore. There was no one there to restrain me from beating my division officer to death.

Except for Tala.

Before I had the chance to murder Andrew Krause, I saw what would become of Tala if I did not return to the Philippines. I envisioned her going back to work in the bars. I imagined Mari forced to follow in her footsteps. As much as I wanted to destroy Krause, as much as I wanted even to take his life, I could not bring myself to do it knowing what could become of my girls in Olongapo.

"Get your hands off of me!" Krause gasped. "I'm an officer!"

I pulled Krause away from the bulkhead, then slammed him back into it as hard as I could, making the steel ring. After that, I took my knee and drove it into his crotch before dropping him to the deck.

"An officer?!?" I screamed at him. "You ain't shit!" Wiping my hand across my face, I was surprised by how much blood it was covered in.

Krause broke into a coughing fit as he tried to catch his breath. Grinning at me, he gasped, "You assaulted an officer! I'm going to have you put in the stockade!"

"You assaulted *me*, bitch," I told him. Holding up my hand to show him the blood dripping off of it, I then said, "And because you're too stupid to know any better, you left all kinds of evidence on me. At least I knew to hit you in places where it wouldn't leave a mark."

The look on Krause's face showed that he realized I had him by the balls. I smiled at him. "Relax. I'm not going to turn you in. In fact, I don't want anyone to know I have a motive for doing the things I'm going to put you through the first chance I get."

I stumbled backward, still a little dizzy from the shot I took to the head. When I recovered, I steadied myself and asked the lieutenant, "Do you really think I'm working with the *yakuza*, Krause?"

My lieutenant nodded in defiance.

"Then, if I was, how wise do you think it is to keep pursuing this little vendetta that you have against the master chief and me? If you're right, you may find yourself inside of a dark room with me someday that I won't let you walk out of." At that, I turned my back on my lieutenant and walked out toward the flight deck.

When I stepped outside, I was about to get hit with a blast of pressurized seawater again. When the airman manning it saw my bloodied face, however, he dropped his hose and ran over to me. "Jesus Christ! What happened to you?"

"Special Treatment. Remember?"

"That's not special treatment!" the airman exclaimed. "That's fucking assault! I'm getting the master-at-arms. This's bullshit!"

I grabbed the airman by the arm. "Let it go."

Master Chief Darrow spotted me from his spot on Neptune's court and jogged over my way. Parroting the airman's reaction, he too asked what had happened.

"An accident," I answered.

"Bullshit," Darrow growled.

"Are you okay?" the airman asked. "Is it just a bloody nose, or is anything else hurt too."

"I think I broke a rib."

"Jesus Christ," Darrow said. "What happened?"

The airman and Darrow had their backs to the island, so they did not see Krause step out of the space behind them. He was carrying his modified shillelagh with him, no doubt to chuck it into the Pacific when he got near enough to the side. "I was a little too close to the guy in front of me. Some deck ape went to whip the kid's ass, missed, and caught me in the face instead. The rib thing happened while wrestling."

I now knew how unstable Krause was. I realized the lengths he was willing to go to hold me accountable for Palazzo's death. If it got to the point where I had to kill that man, I did not want to broadcast that I had a reason to do it. I was not worried about Darrow. My lies were for the airman's benefit.

The master chief grabbed me by the arm. "All right. Let's get you to medical."

I wriggled out of Darrow's grip. "No. Master Chief, I just want to finish this thing. I'm almost done."

My master chief nodded and turned to the airman. "Take him to the tunnel. Tell the guys running it that they're not to use any more shillelaghs on him. It looks like he's taken far more than he should have already. Secure your hose first before someone trips on it."

After the airman ran to put away his gear, Darrow leaned in closer to me. “I’m not an idiot, Doyle. Is the person who did this who I think it is?”

I nodded.

Darrow thought for a moment. “Then the lieutenant’s completely lost his fucking mind. I’m not sure if that’s a good thing or a bad thing at this point. You know, I can bury him for this. If I do that, though, he’s going to push that shit about the *yakuza* again. The NIS isn’t going to take him seriously, but they may have to investigate it anyway to check all their boxes. I don’t care about the NIS. Krause doesn’t know enough to give them anything useful. The *yakuza*, though, that’s another story. If the NIS goes asking around about the lieutenant’s claims, it doesn’t matter how little they know. They could still spook our friends in Sasebo. The Japs could kill our deal…”

“…or us.” I interrupted.

Darrow nodded. “Or us. We gotta let this go for now. I promise you, though, Doyle. I’m going to get that little fucker for this shit. If it’s the last thing I do.”

*****

The tunnel was a long section of canvas tube full of the same putrid wet garbage that was everywhere else on the flight deck. We had to crawl fifty feet through this nastiness, retching and vomiting the entire way. Outside, men continually screamed, “WHAT ARE YOU?!?” They expected us to answer that we were wogs.

When I emerged from the other end, I was standing before a large pool that had been set up on the aft end of the deck and filled with seawater. A second class AE then stood me up on my feet for the first time and screamed the question at me again. “WHAT ARE YOU?!?”

“I’m a wog!”

“You’re goddamn right you are!” He pushed me backward into the pool and ordered me to swim to the other side.

I did what I was told. Emerging on the far end, I was met by a boiler tech screaming, "WHAT ARE YOU?!?"

"I'M A GODDAMN SHELLBACK!" I screamed back at him.

The BT shook my hand and patted me on the shoulder. "You sure are. Congratulations, sailor."

The guy behind me did not get the message. When the BT asked him what he was, he shouted that he was a wog again. He got pulled from the pool and sent to the back of the line to start all over.

After all that we had been through, the clothes we had worn were unfit for service. All we could do was take our garbage, oil, blood, and vomit-stained uniforms off and toss them to the deck. Then, as naked as the day we were born, we stood in line to be sprayed down by a couple of airmen manning firehoses.

Once we were cleaned enough to go back inside, we filed past a table staffed by the pansies who had refused to go through the initiation. They were trying to serve us food. Among them was Kramer, who stuck out a sandwich sealed in a Ziploc bag. "You want a ham and cheese, Doyle?" he sheepishly asked. The man looked sufficiently humiliated.

The guy behind me managed to save a fistful of garbage from the final tunnel in his hand. He threw it right into Kramer's face. "Shut your fucking pie hole, wog!"

A young seaman behind him added, "Yeah, we ain't eatin' shit that's been touched by your little wog rat fingers, ya pussies!" Another man spat at the pathetic-looking group as he passed. This had been going on before I got there and went on for the entire ceremony after I left. The vitriol directed at those men far exceeded anything we newly-minted shellbacks had just endured.

I heard HM1 Bateman yell from behind me as soon as I entered the island structure. "Petty Officer Murphy!" I had to admit that his effeminate voice calling out to me while I was buck naked made me a tad bit uncomfortable. "Doyle! Master Chief Darrow told me what happened. Come see me right after you clean up so we can get your ribs looked at."

I nodded and kept going without saying a word. Internally, I was struggling. I was buoyed by what I had accomplished, but I was still seething at a low burn. I was unable to put out of my mind what Krause had done to me. Once the adrenaline from the line-crossing ceremony wore off, I suspected it would be replaced with one of my episodes. It would be my first one since leaving for the Philippines.

I nearly lost it in the shower. The hot water cleared my head and allowed me to think. Instead of focusing on something soothing, however, my mind went right to visions of me stomping Krause's head in like Pruitt had done to Miller. This transported me back to Nimitz Park, where I relived the night of the radioman's murder.

I was about to break down when I felt something alien tickling me between my legs. It was so out of place with the visceral scenes playing out in my head that it shook me out of my episode. I had to reach down to see what it was.

It turned out to be the sardine that ET1 Garibaldi had dropped down my shorts that morning. I could not believe that it had managed to hang on wedged between the cheeks of my ass after all I had been through that day. It struck me as hilarious. I laughed so hard that I was brought back from the precipice of my episode. "I was wondering where you went to," I told the sardine.

Returning to my locker, I passed by the rack that Claude Metaire had once occupied. Dixie was leaning over it, resting his head upon the bare mattress. When he sensed me staring at him, he straightened up and looked at me with reddened eyes. "Claude should've been here for this, Doyle."

Stepping over to pat him on the shoulder, I nodded. I could feel my own eyes starting to sting. "Yeah, Kevin. He certainly should have. It's not fair that he wasn't. Not at all."

*****

CHAPTER 20

After our experience in Guam, Dixie and I decided to do something a little different when we pulled into Perth, Australia. Instead of our usual routine of pushing our blood alcohol levels past the threshold that would kill lesser men, we vowed to stay sober. When Kevin expressed an interest in learning to scuba dive, I was ecstatic. I got on the phone as soon as we hit the pier and booked him a PADI course at a dive school in the northern suburb of Hillarys.

Swimming with a broken rib is not particularly wise, but Australia was a once-in-a-lifetime underwater destination. There was no way that I was going to pass it up. While Dixie was in training, I slid myself into it by spending a couple of days diving easy around Garden Island. I got through it with minimal discomfort and was rewarded with a sighting of a tiny, but deadly, blue-ringed octopus for my efforts. My guide told me that it was a rarity in those waters.

Once Dixie was legal, we invested in a trip to Rottnest Island, the pearl of Western Australia as far as scuba diving was concerned. Unfortunately, visibility was poor on our first dive of the day. Besides a solitary blue devil we spotted lumbering about the limestone reef, the divers were the most exciting things in the water. At least that was the consensus of the fur seals darting in and around us as we looked for other marine life. Enjoying the seals far more than the reef, Dixie and I rose from the ocean floor and suspended ourselves in open water to let them play around us. That turned out to be a huge mistake.

A large sea lion swooshed in to check us out. He circled Dixie two or three times and then swam my way, sticking his snout right up to my goggles as if he were about to kiss me. I was laughing at it when I suddenly felt as if I had been struck by a runaway freight train.

The impact spun me cartwheeling through the water, knocking my regulator out of my mouth and ripping my mask off my face. I was not by any means the world's most experienced diver. Still, I was able to feel out my regulator and get it back into my mouth almost by automation. My mask was a lost cause, though. It was gone.

I was blind in the water and feeling the rib that Krause had fractured. I was also terrified. Though I never saw what hit us, I knew what it was. It was a shark, and a *really* big shark at that. And it was still out there somewhere.

No matter how well trained you are, when you get hit by something that massive underwater, your instinct is to haul ass to the surface. You need to get the hell out of the ocean. I would have done precisely that and taken my chances with decompression sickness, but my dive buddy was missing. If he was not coming to my aid, I guessed that he might have needed me to come to his. Despite having no mask on, I forced my eyes open to try to find him.

There was nothing to see but a massive cloud of crimson that I was floating right in the middle of. Fearing that the blood would attract even more sharks, I kicked as hard as I could to avoid ending up an entrée in the middle of a feeding frenzy. Once clear, I opened my eyes again. I was alone. There were no more sea lions,

I lost track of the other divers of our group, and I could not find Dixie.

Eventually, I spotted a massive shadow just below me. It was dark and blurry, but I could see it thrashing. Suspecting that it had my shipmate in its jaws, I turned to chase it, but was grabbed from above by one of the guides. He was trying to force me up.

I did my best to fight him, but he was experienced dealing with hysterical divers. Controlling our ascent, he got us both to the surface.

"I gotta get back down there!" I shouted as soon as I could get the regulator out of my mouth. "That fucking thing's got my buddy!"

The guide shook his head. "No, mate! You got to get yer arse into the bleedin' boat! Quick!"

"I can't!" I screamed back. "We've got to do something! We can't leave him there!"

"Get in the feckin' boat, mate! NOW!"

"But…!"

"DOYLE! GET IN THE GODDAMN BOAT!"

I swung my head around, shocked to see Kevin already aboard our craft, reaching his hand out to help pull me in. Bursting out into laughter, I cried out, "Dixie! How the hell did…"

"BLOODY HELL, YOU FUCKING NITWIT!" our guide screamed at me. "FIGURE IT OUT AFTER WE GET THE HELL OUTTA THE WATER!"

When we were safely inside of our vessel, I turned to Kevin and asked, "How did you get up here?!? I thought you were a goner!"

Dixie nodded. "Christ, Doyle! I thought I was, too! I never saw it coming! I didn't see anything, I…" Dixie paused, trying to get his shaking under control.

Our guide was quaking as bad as we were. "I saw the whole bloody thing. Jayus Christ! That beast came out of nowhere from below and cut that bloody sea lion that was playing with ya right in half! I've been diving this place for ten years and I ain't ever seen nothing like it! Bloody feckin' hell!"

"W-w-w-w-was it a g-g-g-great white?" one of the other divers stammered.

The guide shook his head. "Naw. It wasn't no white shark. It was a tiger. Blimey!"

"A tiger?!?" asked the boat's pilot. "Are you sure?"

Our guide nodded. "Yeah, Steve. I'm sure."

"Are tiger sharks rare here or something?" I asked.

"Rare?" the guide asked back. "Naw, they're common enough in these waters. What's rare is seeing one in the daytime. They usually only hunt at night."

Another diver of our group looked very concerned. "We're not staying here for our second dive, are we?"

Dixie turned and looked at me with an expression of panic on his face. Shaking his head vigorously, he said, "I ain't going on a second dive, Doyle! Not here! Not ever!"

*****

It turned out that nobody was going back into the water that day. Once the authorities got wind of a potential man-eater lurking about beneath the waves, they called in all the diving charters. They closed the island's beaches, too.

None of our group was particularly keen about re-entering the water after what we had witnessed anyway. Still, our guides must have felt that they owed us a consolation prize for our canceled dive. They decided to pull into Rottnest and show us something far more soothing than a tiger shark ripping a sea lion in half. They introduced us to an animal called a quokka.

A small marsupial, the quokka looks like a cross between a guinea pig and a tiny kangaroo. Quokkas were famous in Australia for bearing a permanent grin etched upon their furry little faces. Having little fear of humans, they were very photogenic and would come right up to you to have their pictures taken.

"That could be the cutest animal on the entire planet," I told our guide.

"Yeah, they sure are," Mike responded. "People go bonkers over those bloody things. Especially the sheilas. I often wondered how much they'd love those little critters if they bloody well knew how the females protected themselves from predators, though."

Lighting myself a cigarette, I asked, "How do they do that?"

"They throw their bloody joeys at whatever's chasing them and let the beasts eat their babies instead of them. Not exactly mother of the year material, are they?"

After the obligatory quokka sighting, Mike led us to the real reason we pulled into Rottnest Island. He wanted us to calm our shattered nerves at the nearest watering hole. The bar he took us to was a rustic wooden shack, looking much like a set piece from an American Western. It even had a donkey hitched to a post outside.

"Watch out for that bloody thing," Mike warned Dixie and me as we approached. "You think that shark had a vicious bite? It ain't nothing compared to what that nasty bastard will do to you if you get too close."

"It bites?" Kevin asked. "Then why do they keep it there, then?"

"*They* don't," Mike answered. "It belongs to one of the locals. There's no cars on Rottnest Island, so that's a bloke's main means of transport. Most of the folks around here ride bikes, but that bloody bogan comes drinkin' on that fuckin' thing. A bloody wombat, he is."

We saw the donkey's owner, an ornery, overweight, and hairy fellow drinking by himself at the far end of the bar. He looked like he shared the same sunny disposition as his donkey, so we left him alone. "A schooner of piss for me mates, keep," our guide ordered as we took our seats. "We could use a few blasts of the hard stuff, too. We had a run-in with a tiger shark out by Roe Reef."

"Blimey! That was you?" asked the barkeep. "Everybody all right?"

Mike nodded. "Yeah, just had a bit of a fright is all. Jaysus. It was a big bugger, too."

Our guide told our tender the whole story, while Dixie and I added color commentary from our perspective. Sympathetic of our ordeal, that first round was on the house.

A couple of tourists wandered in toward the end of our tale and asked us to repeat it. We did, and ended up with another round of drinks for our troubles. When they left, another group came in, having heard the survivors of the shark attack were inside. We recounted the story once more and again got our drinks paid for. The three of us looked at one another. We were detecting a pattern.

For the next couple of hours, we told the story of our tiger shark encounter over and over, each time scoring ourselves free drinks. When our boat's pilot came to collect us to go back home, we were positively pie-eyed, or "pissed," as they like to call it in the local parlance. We waved our captain off and said we'd catch the ferry back to Freemantle when we finished.

Not long after our ride departed, a new group came in and caught wind of what happened at Roe's Reef. Before we had the chance to tell them the story, however, the owner of the mule stood up and said, "Jaysus! Would you bludgers give it a bloody rest! We all heard the story a dozen fuckin' times now! I ain't want to hear it no feckin' more!"

"Eh! Settle down, ya bleedin' drongo!" Mike responded. "What're ya gittin' yer panties all bunched up fer?"

This set off an exchange between the two men that, though allegedly conducted in English, was overladen with Australian slang. Neither Dixie nor I could tell what the hell was being said. We did not get the gist of what was going on until Mike finally crossed a line that the mule man would not suffer. Stumbling forward, the cretin tried to take a swing at our guide, who dotted him on the nose and knocked him onto his butt.

Mule Man got up, ready to do battle. Mike stepped forward to meet the challenge. Dixie and I both rushed in to keep the men apart, but we ended up getting cut off and tossed outside anyway for our efforts. Once we were back under daylight, the mule man took another crack at Mike. Again, I stepped in to separate them but got turned around and shoved out of the fray. Too drunk to maintain my balance, I stumbled backward until I caught myself on a porch rail. Again, I felt my broken rib. Then I received a fresh bolt of agony from near my neck as the troll's donkey sunk its teeth into my shoulder.

I screamed. The mule man laughed. "That's it, Tommy! Git the wanker!"

"Let go!" I cried out. "OW! OW! Owowowowowowowowow! Jesus Christ!"

While Mike fought the mule man, Dixie tried to help me. He ended up tripping over his own feet, though, and landed face-down in the dirt.

"Goddammit! Let me go!" I shouted at the mule. By now, I was trying to smack the damned thing into releasing me but having no effect. I then tried punching the beast over my shoulder, but it was too awkward to make much of a difference either. Finally, I clenched my teeth and wrenched myself free, screaming bloody murder. There was quite a crowd watching all this go down by now.

When I turned to face the donkey, it brayed and lurched forward, startling me. Entirely by instinct, I threw a punch that caught it hard across the nose. The beast then swung its head and hit me back. My legs got twisted around one another, and I ended up joining Dixie in the dust. The donkey was going nuts at this point and spun around to kick me. I jumped to my feet with my fists raised. I did not want to hit the animal again, despite how big of a dick it was being, but I didn't want to get my skull caved in either. My intent was only to back away with my guard up.

It proved to be a poor optical. When the cops showed up, Mike was beating up a fat old drunk guy. Dixie was on the ground laughing hysterically at the absurdity of the situation. I looked like I had just challenged an agitated farm animal to a boxing match.

Not surprisingly, I ended up getting arrested.

*****

Reaper Dick was enjoying himself in Australia. He did not return to the *Belleau Wood* until we were ready to pull out, and we were a couple of days at sea before I ended up standing before him at captain's mast. Amazingly, despite all the misadventures of my Navy career, that was my very first time standing at mast under charges. I made it five years. It was quite a run.

Our captain could only shake his head as he read the incident report. When he finished, he looked up at me and asked, "You got into a fight with a donkey?"

Standing at the position of attention with my eyes staring straight ahead, I answered, "Yes, sir."

Reaper Dick glowered at me in disbelief. "For God's sake, son. Why?"

"It was being an ass, sir."

I found that far funnier than the skipper did. He busted me down to an E-4 and sentenced me to thirty days of restriction and extra duty. He also took a half month's pay from me.

"Finally," Lieutenant Krause gloated after we had left the podium. "It's about time."

I grinned. "Well, sir, if only you had half of the brains that that donkey did. You could have gotten this shit done a lot sooner."

*****

CHAPTER 21

"Did you learn your lesson?" Baldy asked me. We had pulled into Singapore. My boss and I were leaning on the rail at the top of the island structure, admiring the skyline. He was on duty and I was on restriction. Everyone else was getting ready to go on liberty.

"About what? Goofing off while on liberty?" I could not help but grin. "Oh, hell no."

Darrow had heard from Tejada while we were in Australia. The Japanese had been desperate to complete the deal for his weapons. Not only was everything paid for, but a sizeable shipment of armaments was already headed to Japan. The rest had been sold to a third party that Darrow guessed to be one of the Golden Triangle's opium cartels. The remainder of our money was waiting for us in Olongapo.

Knowing that I was good for almost half a million dollars now made the Navy seem like an albatross around my neck. It had become an inconvenience, and I wanted out. "When it comes to raising hell on the beach," I told Baldy. "I'm just getting started."

My supervisor laughed. "So, you're going to be in a state of open rebellion then? Is that what I have to look forward to?"

I shook my head. "Naw, you don't have anything to worry about. Look, I've soured on the Navy, but I haven't on my shipmates at all. While I'm aboard this ship, nothing's changed. If I were you, I'd stay out of my way while we're in town, though. If I go down, I don't want to take any of you with me."

After a little laugh, Baldy said, "I'll take that under advisement. You know, this's too bad. Don't get me wrong, you earned your mast, Doyle. You got what you deserved. Still, you're a smart guy and a natural leader. Hell, besides Hammond, you're the junior man in this shop, yet every time I give an order, the guys all look at you to make sure it's the right thing to do first. Even Simpson does, and, goddammit, I got here before he did!"

"I'm not going to contradict your orders, Baldy. You're a good man. You know what you're doing. I'd be an idiot to try to undermine you."

Garibaldi waved me off. "Naw, I'm not worried about that. I'm pretty happy having you around. What I was trying to say here is that you have the respect of the men. They know you have experience, they know that you've protected them from Krause as best you could, and they know you'll always have their backs. You're a good sailor. It's too bad you got caught up in all this Tequila Viking bullshit. You could've had a great career in the Navy."

Smiling, I countered, "I guess that depends upon how you measure the success of a career. Mine's been pretty damn eventful. I accomplished what I wanted to. Now it feels like I'm just biding time, though."

"You going to try to get yourself thrown out?"

I shrugged. "Actively? No. If it happens, though, it happens. I'll be the happiest man in the holding company. The sooner, the better. It's beginning to feel like my luck is starting to run out around here."

"Maybe it is." Baldy turned around and looked up at the SPN-43 radar on the aft mast. "You think that thing's been spinning long enough? We've been out here five minutes, right?"

I looked at my watch. Since I had nothing better to do, I was helping Baldy do his maintenance. "Ten, actually. I'll go shut it down. You keep your eye on it to make sure it glides to a rest."

As I turned toward the hatch to go back down below, I thought I heard a metallic tapping noise coming from on high. I took another look up at the SPN-43 and tried to concentrate. It took a while, but eventually, I heard it again. I stopped to focus on it.

"What's going on?" Baldy asked when he saw me pause.

"You hear that?"

My boss stopped and stood quiet for a few moments. "Hear what?"

"That clicking noise."

Baldy shook his head. "Not really. But I like listening to my heavy metal loud and proud. You picking up on something we should be concerned about?"

I listened a bit longer. The noise was there but did not sound all that ominous or offensive. It was just something I never noticed before. Then again, the SPN-43 was Palazzo's gear. I did not spend a whole lot of time listening to it. "It's probably nothing."

But it was something and happened about once per revolution. Click…click…click…click…tick…tock…tick..tock. Tick.

Tock.

*****

I missed visiting Hong Kong again, but I was okay with that. I also missed Okinawa. In fact, we were back home in Sasebo for two weeks before I finally got off of the ship. Since underway time did not count as time served on restriction, it was two and a half months before my feet had hit dry land.

The first thing I did was take a long walk. I strolled the *ginza* a few times before taking a seat at my favorite noodle restaurant across from the *pachinko* parlor. After I finished eating and was settling my bill, the cashier told me that I should go to the beer garden. I thanked her for the suggestion with no intention of actually going until she grabbed my arm and said, "No. You go beer garden. That message from friend. Go now."

Having a fair idea of who that friend might be, I did as she asked.

The beer garden was nearly deserted when I arrived, and I did not recognize anyone there at first. As I cracked open my second beer, Katsumi showed up and took a seat across from me. She was friendly but not as bubbly as usual. "How did you know I was here?"

"The man at *pachinko* prace see you go to nood-oh restaurant. He carr our friend, who carr me."

"Are we going to meet our friend?"

Katsumi smiled and shook her head. "No. He just want to give you message. He say thank you for everyt'ing you do. He very happy with the resu't. His boss very happy, too. He get big promotion."

"Will it help them win their little war?" I asked.

Katsumi shrugged. "They no win war. They too few. What they have now wirr herp make sure they no roose war, though. They get attacked in Fukuoka one week ago. The men from Kobe come with pist-oh, but Fukuoka men have machine gun and *painappuru.* The Kobe men no coming back."

I looked around nervously, hoping that no one was close enough to overhear us. "You think you should be telling me this?"

With a puzzled look on her face, Katsumi answered, "Why I no terr you about that? It in newspaper. If you read *kanji*, you could find out for yourserf."

After pausing to take a drink of beer, Katsumi reached into her purse and slid me a piece of paper with a phone number on it. "Our friend say he owe you big favor. He say if you ever need his herp, to carr him anytime. He rike you very much Do-ru-*san*. Because of you, he going up in organization."

"How about you?" I asked Katsumi. "Can I call you sometime?" I had been at sea for quite a while and was unsure when I would get to see Tala again. I would have enjoyed having a little more fun with Katsumi.

"I no think that good idea," she said, shutting me down. "It now time to put distance between you and our friends. This is, how you say? Our break up?" Katsumi stood up and held out her hand. "Goodbye, Do-ru-*san*. I hope you have good rife."

Following her lead, I rose to my feet and shook Katsumi's hand. "You know, in America, we would give each other a hug to wish each other well during a good break-up."

Still smiling, Katsumi reminded me, "This no is America."

*****

Sailors who do not have any family to go back to tend to build up a lot of leave time. My September Leave and Earnings Statement showed that I still had over sixty days on the books. I had to either use them or lose them. Despite Krause's resistance to granting me anything, our department head over-ruled him. I was allowed to go back to the Philippines near the end of October.

Deciding it was safer for us to go separately this time, Darrow went first to collect our cash from Sergeant Tejada. He put my share in the safety deposit box that I already had the key to. When he got back to Japan, it was my turn to go.

As soon as I landed in Manila, I picked up my share from Darrow's box and placed it in a different bank. Tala did not know about the key buried with the gun, but if she ever found out, I did not want her to have access to everything I owned. Tala was a good woman, but she was still a former bar girl. If she knew that she had access to a couple hundred thousand dollars, she might run with it. All she had ever known was poverty and that kind of cash would forever change her life. I could not blame her if the temptation proved too much. That is why I split the risk.

After driving to Olongapo, I knocked on the door to Tala's apartment. I was stunned when it was opened by Manny Green. I was so surprised I could barely speak. "Y-y-you remember me, little man?"

Manny nodded. "You're Murphy." Manny Green grew up in California. He was more at ease speaking English than Tagalog. That was good because so was I.

Smiling, I told him, "That's right. How are you doing? Is everything okay? Do you like living here with Tala?"

Manny beamed back and nodded. "It's better than the orphanage and Tala and Mari are really nice. I still miss my mom, though."

I sighed. "I bet you do. You know what, Manny? That's okay. I lost my mother ten years ago and I still miss her, too."

Before I could say anything else, Mari heard my voice and ran screaming into my arms. Tala was not far behind.

We bundled up the kids and drove out to San Felipe, parking along a deserted stretch of beach. I strung a hammock up between two palm trees and while the kids played in the shallows, Tala and I laid back and talked.

"How on earth did you get custody of Manny so fast?" I asked her.

"Dere so many kids in da orpanage dat dey's begging people to come get dem. When I say I t'inking about taking Manny, dey practically t'rew him at me. I work dere and dey know me, so Manny come home wit me da same day I ask. Dey let da paperwork catch up."

"Are you able to afford him?"

Tala shrugged. "It no easy. He extra mouth to peed, but he sweetheart and I love him to death."

"How about school?"

Tala inhaled sharply. "I t'ink dat I have to pull Mari out op her school so dat I can appord…"

I shook my head. "No, don't do that. Tell me how much you need and I'll pay tuition for both."

Tala's smile stretched from ear to ear. "You really coming back, aren't you?"

"I am. When I get back to Japan, we're leaving for the Cobra Gold exercise in Thailand. After that, our operations tempo slows down dramatically. I'm hoping to come back at Christmas, and maybe one other time in the spring. Next July, I'm discharged. I'll be back in the Philippines for good."

"Seriously?" Tala gasped. "Porever?"

I nodded. "Forever."

*****

While I was in Subic Bay, LCDR Winston's son was driving home to San Diego from college in Los Angeles. It was a late-night trip and sometime around three in the morning, he fell asleep at the wheel. His Plymouth Sundance drifted onto the left shoulder, crossed the median, and flipped over before being struck by an oncoming vehicle. The Plymouth rolled over several more times before it finally came to a rest.

It was a horrific wreck. Against all odds, both drivers survived, but for a while, the doctors were not sure if Sammy Winston was going to make it. Things were touch and go for weeks. Our department head was granted family emergency leave to fly back to the US to be with his only son. He would not be participating in Cobra Gold with us.

The captain made Lieutenant Junior Grade Krause the acting Combat Systems Officer in Mr. Winston's absence.

That did not go very well.

*****

CHAPTER 22

We were conducting air operations in the Gulf of Thailand, somewhere near the border of Vietnam and Cambodia, when Palazzo's time bomb finally went off.

Tick…tock…tick…tock…tick…SNAP! CRUNCH! SMASH! POW! CRASH! GRRRRrrrrrrrrrrRRRRRR!!! GRIND! CLINK! CLUNKCLUNKCLUNK! Kerrrrrrrrr-CHUNK!

When Palazzo did the annual check on the radar's lubricant, he squeezed more grease onto the outside of the gearbox than he put inside of it. Literally. The gears were never adequately covered, and the resulting friction produced metal shavings that gummed up the gears until one of the teeth finally broke off. That started a chain reaction that tore up the entire train.

Reaper Dick just happened to be standing on top of the island structure when the SPN-43's gearbox started destroying itself. The sounds the radar made as it came apart were hideous enough to convince the captain that the entire antenna was about to come crashing down off of the mast. He got very excited.

So did the signalmen. SM2 Noel Ocaña called down to Radar Repair while Captain Darcy was melting down thirty feet in front of him. "You better get up here, Doyle," Ocaña told me when I answered the phone. "Your radar just shit the bed big. The captain saw it happen and he's losing his fucking mind. I hate to tell you this, buddy, but I'm thinking you guys are about to be in a world of hurt."

"Roger that," I responded as I put down the handset of the IC line. No sooner had I turned off the talk button when it started to ring again. Picking the handset right back up, I answered, "Radar Repair. This is Petty Officer Murphy speaking."

"Hey, Doyle," it was AC2 Cory Boggess. "You might want to come down here to ATC. I think that the SPN-43 is down."

"I heard. We're getting ready to check it out now."

"What's going on?" Baldy asked.

"It sounds like the SPN-43 went…" The IC line went off again.

"WHAT IS GOING ON WITH YOUR RADAR UP THERE, MURPHY?!? ARE YOU…"

It was the EMO. I pulled the handset away from my ear and turned back to Baldy. "ET1, it'd be a good idea if you went up and tried to see what's going on topside. I'll go down and secure everything in ATC for you, then I'll run interference on Krause…"

"WHAT?!?" my lieutenant screamed out of my handset. He overheard what I said and was not happy about it. "RUN INTERFERENCE ON ME?!? WHO DO YOU THINK…"

"Rick!" I called out, ignoring my division officer. "This one sounds pretty serious. Baldy might need that big brain of yours. Shadow him and make sure he has everything he needs."

"Aye aye, Doyle."

"Dixie!"

"Yeah?"

I reached into Baldy's desk and pulled out the required paperwork. Handing it to Kevin, I said, "By the sounds of it, we're going to have to go up the mast. You're running the man aloft chit."

"DAMMIT, MURPHY! I'M TALKING TO YOU! GET BACK ON THE HORN THIS INSTANT BEFORE I…!"

Baldy broke out laughing, "You know you're not in charge of this shop anymore, right?"

I grinned at my new supervisor. "Would you rather I try to go up there and figure out what's wrong with equipment I've never been trained on while *you* ran interference on Krause?"

"WILL YOU PEOPLE STOP TALKING ABOUT RUNNING INTERFERENCE…!"

Baldy put his hand on my shoulder. "No. I wouldn't. Thank you for your service. I'll make sure everyone knows that you died with dignity and honor."

When I put the handset back to my ear, Krause came unglued. He screamed at me so loud and for so long that I had no idea how he kept himself from passing out. The EMO was still at it when Garibaldi returned. He looked shaken. "What's up?"

"The dish lurched down enough so that the waveguide caught the platform rail. It ripped the damn thing right off and sent shit flying everywhere. A piece almost hit the captain and he's raving about the safety implications. Rightfully so."

"Oh my god," I gasped. Cobra Gold had proved deadly already. While the Marines were on the beach with their Royal Thai counterparts, a bolt of lightning struck a squad. Six men got sent to the hospital and one to the morgue. Another died after suffering a severe reaction from some sort of bug bite. Reaper Dick could not be blamed for those, but a sailor getting killed by a piece of metal falling off the mast would not have looked good on his fitrep.

"I'm going up the mast," Baldy told me. "Did Dixon get that chit run yet?"

"Nope, but it's in process."

"Do you want to tag out the SPN-43 for me?"

"Not really." I looked down at the IC handset lying on the desk. The acting CSO was still screaming through it, completely unaware that I was not even listening to him. "The red tag log is in the Combat Systems Office. That's where Krause is. I'll have to see him in person."

Grinning, I looked back up at Baldy. "Do you think if I went down there right now that he'd still be screaming at me over the phone when I walked through the door?"

Baldy smiled back. "If he is, the drinks are on me when we hit the beach in Thailand."

*****

He wasn't. When I walked into the CSO office to get to the red tag log, my lieutenant was on the phone with the captain. I could hear that Reaper Dick was giving Krause the exact same treatment he had been giving me. The skipper's tirade was brutal but brief. I was filling out my tag when the captain cut out. Once freed, the EMO turned his fury my way once again, screaming at me to hurry up and figure out what was wrong with the radar. I held up the red tag I was filling out. "Sir, we can't even begin to get started until you sign this."

Red Tags are sacrosanct. Only the person who signed it out is ever allowed to remove it. Not even the captain can order it bypassed unless in a combat situation or where a greater loss of life will occur if the equipment remains out of service. They are so important that there is a very precise procedure involved in putting them on and taking them off a piece of equipment. Krause was so agitated after the tongue-lashing he endured that I struggled to get him to focus enough to follow the sign-out procedure. This was not something that I should have had to do with someone who had spent two decades in the fleet. It should have been instinctive to him by now.

I ran into Master Chief Darrow as I was walking out. When he saw what I had in my hand, he exclaimed, "You still haven't tagged out the SPN-43? What the hell's taking you so goddamn long?"

Without slowing my stride, I pointed my thumb back towards the CSO while Darrow quickened his gait to keep up. "Some people have more interest in screaming at us instead of letting us do our jobs. If Krause would give his mouth a rest and let us have a chance to work, we'd have an idea of what's going on by now."

Darrow scoffed. "You know, the captain's on the warpath."

"So, I've heard."

"He wants that radar up and running now."

Still walking as fast as I could, I said, "Yeah, I got the message."

"The longer that radar is down, the more pissed off the old man is going to get and the more miserable he's going to make us."

Frustrated, I snapped, "I'm doing what I can!"

Darrow grabbed me by the shoulder, spun me around, and pushed me up against the bulkhead. "You're not listening to me, Doyle. The longer it takes you to do this, the more ballistic the captain is going to get. Now, shit rolls downhill, right? The captain follows the chain of command. Whose life is Reaper Dick going to make the most miserable?"

I looked over towards the Combat Systems Office. *Krause's*. I grinned.

My master chief put his hand in front of my face, his thumb and forefinger a half-inch apart from one another. "That man is *this* close to cracking under the pressure, Doyle. This close! I'll bet you my paycheck that he can't take the kind of heat that Reaper Dick's going to lay on his sorry ass over this. I'm not telling you to drag your feet. I've seen how bad that thing's fucked up. This's not going to be an easy fix. I'm telling you to take your time and do this shit right and safe, not quick. Do you understand?"

Boy, did I ever. "Aye aye, Master Chief."

*****

When Baldy came down from the mast, Darrow and I were waiting for him. "What's the prognosis?" the master chief asked.

The new Radar Repair supervisor shook his head. "Not good. The gears are all messed up. To fix them, we're going to need to lift the entire antenna to relieve the tension on them. They can't be removed otherwise. The waveguides are also trashed. This isn't getting fixed out at sea. It's going to be a depot-level repair."

"WHAT?!?" Krause bellowed when we gave him the news in the EMO office. "It can't be a depot level repair! I already told the captain that we would have it up in twenty-four hours!"

Chief Ramirez dropped his face into his hands and shook his head. "Then you lied, sir. There's no way we can do this underway."

We all saw Krause starting to shake. He was beside himself and he began pacing the office like a caged animal.

"Sir," Baldy said. "The ACs have the SPN-35 and the SPS-40. This is why we have redundant systems. The 43 going down is not going to affect our mission at all."

"The ACs? THE ACs?!? I don't give a fuck about the ACs! This is about the successful completion of Cobra Gold! This is about...about..." Krause was trying to figure out a way to spin his anxiety. He did not want to come right out and say that this was his last chance to prove himself worthy of promotion. If the lieutenant did not seize it, he would be retired. He needed to show the captain that he could rise to the occasion and motivate his men to make the SPN-43 work again. Accepting that the radar required a depot level repair was not an option. Not this time.

Nor was it for me. If we gave up, the captain would go on to his next crisis. I wanted to see Krause crack. I wanted everyone to see that the man was as unhinged as I knew he was. I needed to keep the wrath of Reaper Dick focused upon him.

"You know, we can do this," I said. "I know the waveguide segments are on board. I've had to order them before. If they're not, there's a flexible waveguide on the SPN-35 that I could make work. The gears are fifty-fifty. We may be able to find close alternatives. If not, if some are not damaged too bad, we might be able to get some machinists to fabricate them for us."

Baldy shook his head, "But lifting that radar antenna..."

"We don't have to take it all the way out. We just have to lift it enough to relieve the pressure on the train. As long as the output shaft doesn't clear the sleeve bearing, it won't swing. I'm sure we can get the boatswain's mates to rig something up to lift the antenna."

Chief Ramirez did not like my idea at all. "It takes too much precision, far more than we can manage while rolling on the ocean. If you guys over-compensate, that antenna is going to swing like the pendulum on a grandfather clock. It'll knock every one of you off of the mast. It's dangerous."

"It is," I agreed. "It's my idea, though, so I'll take the risk. I'll be the guy who goes up there."

"No, Doyle. It's way too risky," Chief Ramirez said.

He was right. LCDR Winston would never have approved what I was proposing. However, Krause was desperate and delusional. "Do it," he told me. "How long will it take you to figure out if we have the parts available?"

"Two hours?"

"You have one."

*****

I took three. Then Krause wasted another forty-five minutes screaming at me for being tardy.

We had all the gears onboard except two. By cross-referencing the part numbers, I determined that one could be found in a rarely used auxiliary hoist. We could cannibalize that to get a suitable replacement.

The second gear was trickier. It was utterly destroyed with no replacement to be found in the storeroom. Again, by cross-referencing the part numbers, I found the same gear in my SPN-35 that was much easier to get to. During a break in air operations, I pulled it and ran it down to the machine shop to be measured. When they finished, I put the gear back where it belonged while the MRs made me a new one.

All this took time. We wouldn't know if anything would be feasible until we could verify that the gear the MRs made for us would work. With nothing to do, we all hit the rack that night, which drove the EMO into a conniption.

The following day, the captain was not at all satisfied with Krause's progress report and let him have it. In return, Krause screamed at us for our laziness. That delayed us for another hour.

The pinion gear the MRs fabricated turned out great, so we got the boatswain's mates to work on rigging us a hoist. That took time as well. The Deck Department Officer needed to be convinced that what we were trying to do was a good idea. That proved a tall order considering it was one of the stupidest plans I had ever come up with. I was shocked that it had gotten as far as it had. I was secretly hoping that someone would come to their senses and stop us before we dropped a radar dish right through the roof of the island structure.

Krause got his ass chewed out by the captain again at lunch. Then he ran looking for me to share the pain. He caught me atop the island, watching the boatswain's mates rig the tackle we would use to lift the antenna. He was enraged to see me standing idle and demanded to know where everyone else was. "THIS IS AN ALL HANDS EFFORT!" the lieutenant bellowed at me.

"And all hands are involved, sir. ET1 Garibaldi is planning the repair and training Simpson to help him get those gears in place as quickly as possible. Hammond is modifying the flexible waveguide from the 35 to fit the 43. Dixon is studying how to calibrate the positioning cams in case they got knocked out of wack when the antenna crashed. Kent is up there with the deck apes stringing up the rigging. The only one of us in the shop not doing something useful right now is me."

"And why aren't you doing your share?" Krause barked.

"Because I'm talking to you, sir."

The lieutenant exploded on me. He demanded I round up everyone in Radar Repair and bring them up to him. He wanted to personally demand the proper level of respect out of us that he felt he had earned.

It took a half-hour for me to gather the troops. Then Krause berated us for another twenty minutes. He would have gone on longer, but the captain came up to check the progress of the repair. When he found us all standing about being yelled at instead of working on his problem, he was less than thrilled. We went back to work after Darcy ordered our division officer below for a meeting to clarify his expectations. We heard later that Reaper Dick had unloaded on Krause worse than anyone had ever seen.

That was the point where everything took on an entirely different dynamic.

The captain's tirades were no longer about the progress of our efforts. After speaking with Master Chief Darrow, Reaper Dick knew that what we were attempting was extraordinary. It required a great deal of precision and expertise to pull something like this off while underway. What the captain realized was that Krause was not aiding our progress. He was hindering it, and Reaper Dick was making him pay dearly for that.

Krause attempted to berate us once more before the team went up the mast, but it fell flat. The lieutenant was incoherent and non-sensical. He was not angry; he was scared.

As dangerous as it is to rebuild a gearbox aloft and while underway, Baldy did it masterfully. True to my word, I went up to direct the lifting of the antenna and make sure we did not take it too far. After we steadied and locked the dish at the correct height, my boss got to work putting all the pieces back in order. I held on to the antenna for dear life to ensure that it did not move enough to break free and swing. That was nerve-wracking. I would have had less anxiety prancing through the packed shower of a federal penitentiary wearing a pair of pink leather hot pants. One wrong move and we would find ourselves eight stories above the flight deck dodging an out-of-control wrecking ball.

Baldy worked like a heart surgeon. Piece by piece and gear by gear, he methodically rebuilt what Palazzo's incompetence had destroyed. It was a job that required precision and time, the latter something that our EMO refused to allow. Krause could not keep himself from giving the captain unrealistic projections of when we would finish. In return, he kept getting brutalized for failing to meet them. He never learned his lesson.

Finally, after three hours of meticulous work, Baldy leaned back and let out a long sigh of exhaustion. Nodding at me, he said, "Okay. You can lower it now."

*****

The hard part was done, but the job was still a long way from completion. After we secured the antenna and took down the rigging, I told Baldy that we should take a break and report our progress to Darrow and the EMO. "Why don't you go ahead and do that," ET1 Garibaldi told me. "I just want to get this shit done."

"Aye aye." I collected my gear and made my way to the ladder to work my way down. Before I left, I double-checked the safety interlock switch that cut all power to the SPN-43. "Fucking Palazzo," I muttered under my breath when I saw it. The salt build-up on the handle showed that he had not done the maintenance on it. Because I was obsessive about those things, I double-checked to ensure it was in the correct position to keep the radar from energizing. Only when I was convinced that it was, did I continue my descent.

When I got to the deck, Krause and Darrow were coming up through the hatch to greet me. "You got a status report, Martin?" the lieutenant asked.

"Murphy, sir."

"What?"

"You called me Martin. My name's Murphy."

Krause looked exasperated, "I don't care what your name is! You going to tell me what's going on up there or what?"

"Well, the hard part's finished..."

"Great! Did it work?"

"It seems to have..."

"Perfect!" At that, Krause turned on his heel and marched away from us, not bothering to hear the rest.

"...so far." As Darrow and I watched the lieutenant disappear through the door to the 07 Level, I shook my head. "He's marching right down to the captain to dig himself a deeper hole, isn't he?"

My master chief could hardly believe it either. "Yep. My god. It's like he's totally incapable of processing anything but what he wants to hear. Even after it blows up on him time after time after time. I've never seen anything like it. I don't think the captain has either. I keep thinking that sooner or later, Reaper Dick's going to put him out of his misery. Anyway, what's the real story up there?"

"The gears are in place. We need to manually rotate the antenna a few times to make sure the train is moving smoothly, then pack it full of grease. Properly this time. After that, we'll power it up and see how we did."

"You think this's going to work?"

I shrugged. "It looks good. Better than I expected it to, for sure. Granted, this wasn't done under optimal conditions. I'd have the contractors come out and give it a good look when we get back to Sasebo. I think we should be able to complete Cobra Gold, though. No problem."

Darrow patted me on the shoulder. "That's amazing work. From all of you. I mean it. How much time do you think it's going to take to wrap this up?"

"Maybe an hour. It'll take thirty minutes after that to power it up and make sure everything's okay. If those positioning cams got knocked out of whack, though, it's going to be a bitch to recalibrate them. We're going to need targets in the air to zero in on. Let's hope it doesn't come to that."

*****

AC2 Boggess was the only person in the Air Traffic Control center when I walked in. "How's it going up there, Murphy?"

"We're done. Just cleaning up now. Hey, when're you guys doing air ops again? We'd like to compare range acquisition data between the 35 and the 43 to see if they're compatible. We want to make sure we didn't knock any of our positioning cams out of position."

Boggess leaned back in his seat to check the clipboard hanging above his head. "Looks like we'll be extracting the Marines from Phetchaburi at around seventeen hundred. That work for you guys?"

"Works for me. Thanks, Cory."

From ATC, I went back up to the shop to sit down and enjoy a cigarette for the first time in hours. After that, I climbed back topside to see how clean-up was going. Darrow was up there already. "They finished?" he asked me.

I nodded. "Almost. They're just cleaning up now. Once they're down, I'll remove…"

I was interrupted by the sound of power hitting the SPN-43 rotors, bringing it to life. Our men aloft instantly froze in place, simultaneously turning their heads toward the radar to stare at it in fear and disbelief. Then the antenna slowly started its rotation, heading right for ET3 Simpson. Trevor backed up as fast as he could to get out of the way but quickly ran out of room. Eventually, he stepped off of the platform into oblivion and fell off of the mast.

Simpson's lanyard was fastened to the safety rail, so he was not seriously hurt. He did find himself dangling fifty feet above the deck, however. Understandably, the man was terrified and screaming bloody murder. Hammond was too scared even to speak, let alone scream. He had to throw himself down onto the sub-platform and get as low as he could. With the radar spinning inches above him, if he dared to lift his head to see what was going on, he would have been decapitated.

Baldy was in an equally dire predicament. His safety lanyard was secured to the rail on the opposite side of the platform from which he had fallen, stretched tight just below the spinning dish. If the antenna caught the strap attached to Baldy's safety harness, it would rip him right off of his feet, blend him up, then spit him over the side.

"Oh my god!" I cried out as I bolted to the mast, scurrying up the ladder. Master Chief Darrow was right behind me.

Lieutenant Brigham, the Signals Officer, came running after us. “Hey!” he screamed, “Stop! You can’t go up there without a safety harness!”

Both of us ignored him, tearing up the mast in record time. I stopped before the safety interlock switch. That was the device that was supposed to prevent things like this from happening. I was shocked to see that it was indeed in the proper position. The antenna should not have been rotating. I grabbed the switch and wrenched it, trying to re-engage the contacts so that I could break them again. I discovered it was so corroded that, while the handle was rotating, the shaft that turned the circuit off was not.

I went up a couple of more steps to see if they had any tools up there that I could use. As I was doing that, the *USS Belleau Wood* took a starboard roll. The gyroscope signal transmitting to the antenna caused it to tilt to port to compensate. That dropped it enough to barely skim the tops of Hammond’s fingers that he was covering his head with. Rick screamed out in terror.

Baldy looked horrified as well. “Help, Doyle! Please!”

“I’m doing what I can!” I rifled through the aloft bag for something I could use on the safety cut-off. Finding a pair of large channel locks, I went back down the ladder and started beating on the interlock switch. With each blow, I could see the salt and oxidized metal falling out of it. Had Palazzo not already been dead, I would have killed him for gun decking that check.

Finally, the handle to the switch gave away and fell off, dropping to the deck below. Now that it was exposed, I gripped the shaft as tight as I could with my channel locks and wrenched it counter-clockwise. The circuit broke and the SPN-43 finally slowed to a stop.

Baldy collapsed in relief. Hammond lifted himself up and looked at me with an expression of disbelief. Simpson remained suspended mid-air below us, shrieking himself hoarse. I went to try to pull him up, but Baldy stopped me. “Get off of my mast without a safety harness, Doyle! Now!” Darrow was coming up to the platform when Baldy stopped him also. “You too, Master Chief! Get the fuck off of my mast! I’m not surviving that shitshow just to watch you two fall to your deaths. Get out of here!" Turning back to me, Baldy pointed his finger into my face and screamed, "You get down to ATC and secure my fucking gear! You got that?!?"

ET1 Garibaldi was pissed, but not nearly as much as I was. Following his orders, I practically leapt off of the mast and ran down to Air Traffic Control. When I got there, I found it empty. I stepped over to the control console and slapped the master switch back to the "Off" position. I was turning around to leave when Cory Boggess stepped through the door. "Hey, Doyle, what's going on up…"

Enraged, I grabbed Boggess by the shirt and lifted him off of his feet, pushing him up against the bulkhead, "What the fuck do you think you're doing?!? That was MY red tag you removed!"

Trying to defend himself, Cory kneed me in the chest, but I was too pumped up to feel it. "Get your hands off of me! I didn't remove shit!"

"THEN WHO DID?!?"

Master Chief Darrow burst in the door next and pulled me off of Boggess. As he was man-handling me into my corner of the ring, I shouted out, "You nearly got us killed up there! Three of us! One of my men got knocked off of the fucking mast!"

"I didn't remove your goddamn red tag, Murphy! I'm not that stupid! Why don't you check with that frickin' drooler you work for? He was in here right after you were! I left him here to wait for the air boss!"

"Krause?!?" Darrow asked.

"Yeah!" Boggess snapped, rubbing his neck. "Your lieutenant!"

I looked at Darrow in disbelief. "He couldn't have!"

Darrow scoffed. "You don't think so? Who else would?"

Powered by an adrenaline surge, I planted my hands into my master chief's chest and shoved him away from me. He stumbled backward a couple of steps, tripped over a chair, and landed on his ass. "No!" he shouted at me as I bolted for the door. "No! Murphy! Stand fast! No! No! Nonononononono!"

By the time Darrow got to his feet, I was already running through the Combat Information Center, heading for the EMO office. The Operations Officer, alerted by the commotion in the middle of CIC, was in pursuit, trying to figure out what was going on. Darrow almost took him out when he burst through the door after me.

When I reached the EMO, it was already a scene of utter chaos. Krause was standing in the middle of the office, trying to give orders but making no sense. DSC Moore was standing in front of him, trying to discern what he was saying. Chief Ramirez was on the IC line. He pulled the handset away from his ear for a moment to scream, "Sir! The Ops Officer is on the horn about a fight in CIC! He needs to talk to you now!"

Tony Bard was on the other line at Darrow's desk with a bigger problem. "Lieutenant Krause! The Officer of the Deck's telling me the captain's on his way here right now! You need to snap out of this!"

"I'll snap that son-of-a-bitch out of it!" I growled right before I charged.

"Oh shit!" Ramirez dropped the IC line. For a man who never in his life had ever laced a pair of ice skates onto his feet, he hit me with a perfect hockey rink cross-check. He knocked me right off of my trajectory and onto the RPPO's desk. Moore jumped in front of Krause to put himself between the lieutenant and me. As I was recovering to take another run at Krause, Darrow burst into the office and took me to the deck.

"You nearly killed us!" I screamed at the lieutenant.

"What are you talking about?!?" Chief Moore screamed back.

"MURPHY!" Darrow bellowed at me. "SETTLE THE FUCK DOWN! IT'S OVER!"

"Guys!" yelled Bard, trying to be heard over the fray. "The captain's coming! He's on his way!"

"What'd you do, Lieutenant?" Ramirez barked at the EMO.

"I-I-I d-d-d-didn't do it. I-I-I didn't do a-a-a-anything…"

"You did, too!" I yelled. "You…!"

"IT'S OVER, MURPHY! STOP!" Then, in a much quieter voice, Darrow put his mouth up to my ear and said, "Let it go. We got him."

I relaxed and took in the scene before me. Lieutenant Krause was standing in the middle of the office, quaking and staring off into space. He looked like he was mentally checking out. Chief Moore was yelling at the man, trying to bring him back. Krause knew he messed up in a spectacular fashion. He realized that he was ruined. Ramirez kept the Operations Officer at bay on the IC line while trying to get Krause to explain what he had done. Tony Bard was behind the EMO, screaming for us all to get our shit together before the captain arrived. Suddenly becoming an island of tranquility amid a tempest of pandemonium, I let Darrow help me to my feet as I watched everything unfold. Then I heard Petty Officer Brennen yell out, "ATTENTION ON DECK!"

The bickering came to an abrupt halt as everyone in the office fell silent and snapped to attention. Reaper Dick stormed into the EMO, his face a shade of crimson that I had never seen before. He looked like he was premeditating his very first murder. "What in the unholy FUCK is going on in here?!?" Reaper Dick snarled. "And what the FUCK happened up there on the mast just now?!?"

When nobody answered, the captain lost his mind, "I AM NOT LISTENING TO MYSELF SPEAK HERE, GENTLEMEN! SOMEONE BETTER STEP FORWARD RIGHT NOW AND TELL ME WHAT THE HELL IS GOING ON!!!"

Having long passed the point of caring about my Navy career, I was the one who stuck my neck out. Pointing my finger at Lieutenant Junior Grade Krause, I growled, "That son-of-a-bitch tried to…"

"YOU WATCH YOUR FUCKING TONGUE, SON!" the skipper screamed at me. "THAT IS AN OFFICER IN THE UNITED STATES NAVY! YOU PUT YOURSELF BACK AT ATTENTION AND ADDRESS ME AS YOU WERE TAUGHT IN BOOT CAMP, SAILOR!" Reaper Dick then lowered his tone while upping the degree of menace in his voice. "Someone's going to hang for this, kid. You'd better get your temper under control and tread very lightly if you don't want it to be you."

"Yes, sir," I answered. "Lieutenant Krause tried to kill us, sir. He removed the red tag that I attached to the SPN-43 control console and powered up the radar while my men were still aloft. When the antenna started rotating, it knocked ET3 Simpson off the mast. It nearly decapitated Seaman Hammond and could have splattered ET1 Garibaldi all over the flight deck."

Reaper Dick's eyes opened freakishly wide. "Bullshit! You better have some damn good evidence backing that accusation up, son. Nobody's that fucking stupid."

"Sir, he…"

"Think really hard about this, Murphy. Are you *sure* that Mister Krause removed your red tag and powered up the SPN-43?"

Wilting under Reaper Dick's glare, I suddenly wasn't. I had not seen Krause remove it with my own eyes. Still, I could not think of anyone else who would have done it.

Sensing my hesitation, the captain turned towards the EMO. "Mister Krause? Did you remove the red tag from the SPN-43 and turn it on?"

"N-n-n-no. I don't think so. No! I d-didn't. But it was ready. The p-p-petty officer told me they w-w-w-were done. The radar was ready. I-i-it was finished. Ready t-t-to go! I…"

The lieutenant was not very convincing. With his jaw dropping open, the captain asked, "What? Krause, I asked you a yes or no question. Did you remove that red tag?"

"I-I-I don't think so. No. I did…maybe I could have…I don't know. I…"

As Krause stammered through his answer, Tony Bard noticed a length of thick black string protruding from the lieutenant's back pocket. He recognized it as the type we used to tie the red tags to our gear. Breaking the position of attention, Bard stepped toward the lieutenant and pulled on it. Sliding the evidence we needed right out the back of the EMO's khakis, Tony lifted my red tag up into the air and held it up for the rest of us to see.

That effectively ended the naval career of Lieutenant Junior Grade Andrew Krause right on the spot. He was finished. His decades of service were obliterated in disgrace right before our eyes. There was no way for him to salvage it now. He was beyond redemption.

I felt a great weight lifted from my shoulders. Our war with Krause was over. We won. Darrow and I were home free. All we had to do now was skate through our last year of service and then retire to a bum's life in Olongapo. We were out of enemies.

Or so I thought. I had no way of knowing it then, but Lieutenant Junior Grade Andrew Krause was far from being our last casualty of Cobra Gold.

*****

CHAPTER 23

There was no pier in Pattaya Beach, Thailand. That meant the crew disembarked for shore leave via "liberty launches." We lined up, descended a flight of stairs down the side of the ship, and leapt into a smaller craft that held about sixty hands. It was crowded and uncomfortable, but the boat's pilot gave us beer, so we were good with it

Heading towards shore, the water got shallow fast, so the first boat could only go so far. It stopped about a third of the way in and split us between smaller boats that held fifteen men apiece. This was inconvenient, but they had beer too, so everything was still cool. These boats took us about another third of the way in toward the beach. They then dumped us into dugout canoes equipped with outboard motors. They did not give us beer, so Dixie and I ditched them once the water was only waist-deep. It was not that we were impatient. We were just already five beers in the bag, and the ocean was the closest thing to a urinal that we could get to.

While wading towards shore, Dixie and I were stunned by how beautiful Thailand was. The turquoise ocean met emerald green jungle everywhere we looked, the two separated only by a thin white line of pristine beach.

Pattaya was as busy as it was vibrant. There was a lot of traffic. The two-lane highway behind the beach seemed to accommodate every type of vehicle known to man. There were jeepneys, motorcycles, taxis, bicycles, and even the occasional beast of burden. Long before we reached town, we had a pretty clear picture of how chaotic the place was.

In 1993, Thailand was an HIV hotspot, and Claude Metaire testing positive was a wake-up call for Dixie and me. To ensure we did not fall victim to the same fate as our friend, we shared a hotel room to keep each other from doing anything stupid. We were staying at the Asia Pattaya, which was clear across town. It was a long walk, and we decided to take in a Thai kickboxing match and have another beer before we started on it.

As raunchy as Olongapo had been, it was nothing compared to Pattaya Beach. Everywhere we turned, sex was being thrown in our faces. Even at the kickboxing match, our drinks seemed to come with a pair of stunning young women. The ladies stood beside us, rubbing our chests and whispering obscene proposals into our ears while we tried to watch the fight.

The match did not keep our attention long. Even without the distraction of the girls, the boxers battled with little enthusiasm. They barely even feigned interest. They approached each other as if they were a pair of moody youngsters who were only there because they were forced to take boxing lessons by their old men.

There were a couple of Marines sitting ringside, heckling the combatants. The announcer got tired of them by the third match and asked the leathernecks if they could do better. The burliest of them claimed that he could, and his American comrades erupted into cheers and jeers to egg him into the ring.

At that point, I had put my seventh beer into an empty stomach. I was smashed, yet even I could still tell that the announcer was working the crowd. I got the sense that he had done this a thousand times before. "You dink you beat my gai?" he asked the jarhead. "You goink to come in heyah and proob it?"

"Fuck yeah!" the Marine screamed out, encouraged by his buddies.

"You gonna put big money where big mout' is?"

At that point, the bruin's friends reached for their wallets. They were willing to bet huge that their man would emerge the victor. As large as their wager was, the announcer had no problem matching it. One of the locals next to us turned to Kevin and tried to place his own bet on one of the native champions. Noting that the man spoke flawless English, I shook my head and laughed. I thought it too obvious that he was in cahoots with the house. "They're totally trying to set us up," I told Dixie.

"What?" asked an offended Marine on the other side of our table. "You don't think our guy can do this? You some kind of traitor?"

"No," I laughed. "I just have a pretty good eye for when I'm being conned. You think this doesn't happen every time the fleet pulls into this place? That skinny little bundle of lethargy up there is going to find a whole new sense of purpose when he's fighting for real. Mark my word."

"A hundred bucks says you're wrong," the Marine said.

"Look, man, I ain't looking to profit off this. I'm trying to warn you that you're being set up. Save your money. Get your buddy back over here to sit down, and I'll buy you all a beer."

The jarhead smiled at me with a scary degree of overconfidence. "That dude's the toughest guy I know. These midgets don't stand a chance against him. I'll bet you two-hundred!"

I laughed again, shaking my head in disbelief that these poor schmucks could not see what I did. I reached for my wallet and took a look inside, separating the American bills from the baht notes. "How about we make it three?"

The Marine whistled, signaling that three hundred bucks was a bit rich for his blood. His buddies jumped in to pick up the slack, however. Before I knew it, we had six hundred dollars sitting in the pot on our table. The Thai man that first tried to wager with us shot me a look of extreme displeasure for cutting in on his action.

The bout barely lasted a single round. Once the opening bell sounded, the Marine realized how quick a short, skinny Siamese man can be. The leatherneck could not even touch him, let alone catch him. Had the guy ever been able to land a blow, he might have crippled his opponent. The only thing the Marine seemed to be able to hit with any efficiency was the mat, though. After his fourth trip to the floor, he had to be helped up and the referee called the match.

I collected my cash and stuffed it into my pockets as quickly as I could. I then ordered a round of drinks for the men I had just won my money from to thank them for doing business with me before we left. One of the guys was something of a sore loser and got a little belligerent with me. One of his companions, a man with the voice and bearing of an infantry sergeant, said, "Knock it off. The squid tried to warn you what was going on. It's not his fault you weren't smart enough to listen."

Dixie and I made it about a block down from the kickboxing bar before we hit the stretch of Beach Road with all the sex shows for which Thailand was famous. The streets there were packed. We had to push our way through the crowd. At one point, someone roughly pushed me back. I got knocked sideways, stumbling into the narrow space between two buildings. Dixie ducked behind me to help me out, but when we turned around, we found that our route back to the street was blocked. A trio of rough-looking young men stood between us and the sidewalk. As they approached us, the ruffians picked up a couple of large pieces of wood from the ground and brandished them as clubs. "Uh oh," I said as I realized what was happening.

Dixie held his hands up in a gesture of surrender. "Hey guys, we don't want any trouble."

The ringleader was in front of Kevin. "We no wan' trouble too. We want money."

Kevin pulled out a handful of crumpled-up baht notes from his pocket and held it out to the thug. The hooligan batted it away, knocking it to the ground. "We no wan' you money. We wan' his money!" He was pointing at me.

The three hoodlums stepped towards us. In response, we backpedaled to keep our distance. When I turned around to see where I was headed, I discovered that we were being herded towards a dark alley. Deciding that was the last place I wanted to end up, I planted my feet and began looking for a weapon of my own. Before I could find anything, however, the passageway filled with battle cries echoing off the walls. The Marines from the bar were charging our would-be muggers from behind.

Unlike the boxing match, this one was not much of a fight. The Americans outnumbered the street thugs three-to-one. The Thais split as soon as they saw how over-matched they were and bolted past Dixie and me to the alley they had been pushing us toward.

The Marines tried to pursue them, but Dixie and I held them back. "Hey! Hey! Hey!" I yelled. "You don't know what's in that place. Let them go. They didn't get anything. We're good, and they're gone. Let's get back into daylight and find a bar. Drinks are on me!"

As we filed back onto the street, I recognized the guy who threatened me for betting against a fellow *gringo*. I reached out to shake his hand. "Thanks, man, you saved our asses."

The Marine laughed. "Those guys were on your tail as soon as you walked away from your table. We knew you were getting rolled. You're still an asshole, but we couldn't stand by and let you get stuck in the gut for your wallet."

"I appreciate that. My name's Doyle Murphy, by the way." Grabbing my shipmate by the shoulder, I added, "And this is Kevin Dixon."

The Marine shook our hands. "I'm Rudy Lund. Good to meet you." He then introduced us to the others.

Back on the sidewalk, one of the bar hustlers shoved a card into a lance corporal's hand. He meant to glance it over and throw it away, but something caught his eye that stopped him in his tracks. He grabbed Lund and showed him the item he saw on the card. "Can girls actually do that?"

Rudy appeared to be a man who knew his way around women, but he looked stumped. He grabbed the card and showed it to me.

"I don't know. What do you think, squid? You think that's physically possible?"

Now, strip bars are not my thing. I had never been drawn to them out of any desire to agitate my libido. That day, however, I discovered that morbid curiosity could be a more formidable force to resist than sexual arousal. If the things printed on that card were true, they had to be seen to be believed. We had no choice but to go inside.

*****

Dixie and I departed that bar unable to believe what we had seen. We were both left far more impressed, and a little scared, of what the female body could do. Both of us concluded that we were done with that kind of stuff for the night, though. We beelined to the Asia Pattaya hotel, checked in, then headed back into town.

We ran into Tony Bard and Clay Fordson within an hour, then met up with Kent, Baldy, and Hammond shortly after that. Before long, Tony Bard and most of the Comm Repair guys also joined our pack. When we spotted our division's DSs hanging out in a place called Siamese George's, we joined them. Master Chief Darrow, Chief Ramirez, and DSC Moore found us a little after sundown. By then, we had almost taken over the entire bar and turned it into a division party.

The George was a traditional British pub that catered to retired English expatriates. We crashed their refuge during what was supposed to have been their trivia night and kind of overwhelmed them. "Sorry about that," I apologized. I was sitting next to a rotund older gentleman and his wife. Both of them were from Manchester and were being pretty good sports about the situation.

"Don't worry about it, mate!" the old man told me, slapping me on the shoulder. "I did thirty years in Her Majesty's Navy myself! I'm bloody thrilled to see you young men here havin' a good time about the place! So's good ole George! That bloody bugger's rakin' in all kinds of lucre tonight off o' you blokes!"

"You're an old sailor?" I asked. "When were you in?"

"I went in 1950, came out in 1982, just after the Falklands War."

"He wanted to stay in," the old man's wife said to me. "But after I saw that his ship got sunk out from under him, he had to choose either the Navy or me."

I was a little awe-struck. That was the second man I had ever met who had lost a ship. "You were on the *Sheffield*?"

"Aye, I was," he told me. "And let me tell you, the water in the South Atlantic is pretty bloody cold. After that, Margaret did not have to try too hard to get me out. I vowed that I'd never live in a place where the water freezes again! So, here I am, getting sunburned on the regular and making me livin' selling meat pies to all the hotels around here catering to English travelers."

I got on excellent with Nigel and Margaret from Manchester. We spent a large chunk of time exchanging sea stories over several rounds that I insisted on paying for. When I offered to give the couple a tour of the *USS Belleau Wood*, they were touched and leapt at the offer. After that, they insisted on buying all of my drinks.

The George was not a typical Pattaya bar. That meant that there were no prostitutes inside. There were only sailors and English people, both of whom were world-renown for their drinking prowess. By eleven that night, both the British and their former subjects were in rare form. At some point, one of us told a hilarious story highlighting the ineptitude of our recently fired division officer. One of the Englishmen lifted a glass to toast that "fucking cunt, Lieutenant Krause!"

For a while, that became something of a battle cry. A short time later, some Limey passerby heard us shouting out the EMO's virtues and popped his head into the open window. "Who's Krause?" he asked.

Almost in unison, the entire occupancy of Siamese George's screamed out, "A FUCKING CUNT!"

Not only did The George then erupt into hysterical laughter, but so did the go-go bar across the street. Then the guys at the go-go bar yelled out, "Who's Krause?" Again we shouted out, "A

FUCKING CUNT!" Then one of our guys yelled out to them, "Who's Krause?" and they screamed back, "A FUCKING CUNT!" In no time at all, random people passing Siamese George's would yell out the question, causing us to respond in kind. At one point, when someone from within the George shouted out, "Who's Krause?" the entire street shrieked the answer back to us.

It became a great game until one poor soul stumbled into the bar around midnight and slurred, "Who's Krause?" A few of the Brits jumped right out of their seats and screamed, "A FUCKING CUNT!" All of the Americans stood fast, however.

Nigel leaned over to me, laughing. "Don't tell me! That's the actual wanker you were all talking about, isn't it?"

I nodded and took a drink of my beer. "Yep. It sure is."

Krause tripped as he walked further into The George and had to catch himself. He was clearly drunk this time. Plastered. Pissed. And impotent. Technically, he was still an officer in the United States Navy, but any power he might have held over us had evaporated a few days before. He was not even a part of the ship's company at that point. He was likely just quartered in town until he could catch a flight back stateside. "Good evening, gentlemen!" Krause called out after he recovered. "Are you men having a pleasant evening?"

Hammond busted out into laughter. That was out of character for him, but he was insanely drunk and Krause had destroyed Rick's career. No one could blame him for finding hilarity at karma striking our lieutenant back in spades. "Yeah, it's been a great evening, sir!" he spat out. "And it's only getting better!"

"You think this is funny?!?" the lieutenant asked, incredulous at the shade being thrown at him by a lowly seaman.

"It's fucking hilarious!" Hammond gasped.

Krause stepped forward like he was going to slap some sense into the young man. That was enough to propel Darrow right out of his seat. "Go ahead, Krause!" he shouted out from the back of the bar. Marching forward with his fists clenched, our master chief then growled, "I dare you! If you so much as lay one finger on that kid, I'll have every excuse I need to swab the street with your sorry ass! Do it!"

Krause stopped in his tracks, turning to look at Darrow with burning contempt.

"I don't think he's going to do it, mate," one of the Brits joked to Darrow. "But if ye wanna fuck 'im up anyway, there ain't a one of us in 'ere that's not gonna back ye up an' say that bloody bugger took a swing o' ye first."

The master chief looked like he was considering the man's offer but glanced up and guessed that the entire street could see inside Siamese George's. There was bound to be somebody out there who would not stick to the story.

"What's the matter, Master Chief?" Krause asked. "Go ahead and take a shot at me."

Darrow grinned menacingly. "You know I'm smarter than that."

"What? You don't want to go at it? Just you and me? I won't say anything. I promise. I give you my word of honor."

"Your word isn't worth a single bead of sweat rolling off a wharf rat's balls."

Krause swallowed hard. "Oh, but you're a man of unquestionable integrity, aren't you? AREN'T YOU?!?"

The lieutenant went to take a step towards Darrow and stumbled again. "I know what you are, Darrow. You're a gangster! A whoremonger! An assassin! I know what you did in Olongapo, you fucking piece of shit! I know you killed that man on Magsaysay!"

The entire bar shifted their gaze to Darrow upon that accusation, but he laughed it off. "That man was robbing a bar and was shot by an off-duty police officer. You're delusional."

"Those others that got blown away on Harris Street…"

"That was a gang shooting blocks from where we were. Seriously, you need help, Lieutenant."

Pointing at me, Krause broke into tears and cried out, "And you! You son-of-a-bitch! You murdered Palazzo!"

Darren Stovic leaned back in his seat. "Spanky blew his own brains out in front of a dozen witnesses, you moron. I was one of them."

The lieutenant ignored him. Still looking at me, he shouted, "You did it for the *yakuza*!"

"Oh my god!" Margaret said beside me. "He's gone completely off his head now, hasn't he?"

"The bloke's mental," her husband agreed. "Bonkers."

Spinning back around to face the master chief, Krause snarled, "I know about Pagsanjan, Darrow!"

"Of course you do, you sick fuck. We went there looking for you!"

Krause was now ugly-crying, "I know about Lieutenant Commander Egan! I know about everything, you rotten bastard! I'm not letting you get away with it! I'm going to the NCIS! I'm taking you down! You and your little minion!"

Of all the people in that room that night, I probably knew Darrow the best. No one else noticed it, but I saw the master chief tense up when the lieutenant said Egan's name. I had never heard it spoken before, but I suspected that I knew who it was.

The master chief maintained a perfect air of nonchalance in the face of Krause's accusation. "Whatever," Darrow said, blowing the lieutenant off. "You're crazy. You need to leave, Krause. Now."

"I'm an officer! You don't tell me what to do!" the lieutenant bawled.

"Yeah?" called out one of the Englishmen, getting up out of his seat. "Then let *me* tell you what to do, mate. Get your bloody arse outta here! Back on the street wit' ya!"

"Who the hell do *you* think you are?" Krause asked. Even through his tears, the lieutenant's words dripped with condescension.

The Englishman did not appreciate our former division officer's tone at all. "I'm the bloody owner o' this joint," he answered, grabbing the lieutenant by the shirt.

Krause tried to bat the bar's owner away from him. "Get your hands off of me!"

It was a bad move. The proprietor was a former rugby player. He belted Krause across the jaw, kneed him in the stomach, then dragged him out into the street by his hair. There, he planted his foot three more times into the lieutenant's gut hard enough to make him vomit. "Now! Get the feck outta here, ya wanker! If ye ain't gone in ten minutes, I'm calling the coppers, and trust me, mate, you don't want them comin' after ye around this place! They ain't nice like me!"

As the Englishman walked back into his bar, we could hear Krause sobbing in the gutter. "This isn't over!" he screamed as he tried to get back to his feet. "You're not getting away with this! Keep laughing at me!"

At that point, no one thought this was funny. It was pathetic. "I'm going to get you!" Krause continued. "All of you! I don't deserve this! I served my country! I served my God! I did everything I was supposed to do! I dedicated my entire life to the Navy! All of it! And you took it from me! You bastards took it from me!"

Darrow and I walked to the front door of Siamese George's and watched Krause stumble down the street. He was hunched over and holding his abdomen. He had fallen to the lowest point of his entire life. The lieutenant had been discarded by the Navy, beaten, humiliated, and was now wandering a foreign port of call all alone. I thought I would have felt better about having witnessed that petty little man finally get what was coming to him. I was having a hard time gloating about it, though.

Turning to my master chief, I asked, "Is Lieutenant Commander Egan who I think it is?"

Darrow nodded. "That's who Fleming's wife was married to before she met him."

That's what I figured. "How'd he know about that?"

"My guess? I think Krause was running Pagsanjan when I nailed that creep. Maybe he and Egan got chummy in that missionary group they both used to cover up their kink. I just never connected the two of them. That place was full of perverts back then. There were too many to all land on my radar."

"Is this something you need to worry about?"

Darrow shrugged. "No more so than that *yakuza* stuff he's been pushing about you. My tracks are covered. Still, I'm pretty sure that I can bury that fucker once and for all now."

"How?"

Sticking his chin out towards the lieutenant, Darrow said, "Look at that poor son-of-a-bitch. When a man's fallen that low, he goes looking for comfort. If he's of the same ilk as Lieutenant Commander Egan, I know where he's going to try to find it."

I shuddered. The streets of Pattaya were full of kids aggressively offering intimate favors in exchange for hard currency. "You need help?"

Darrow shook his head. "Nope. Not this time. I'm doing this one alone."

*****

For most people, passing out means your night is pretty much over. When you are in the Navy, however, it could just be the beginning. After I lost consciousness, I was carried from Siamese George's to one of the many bars along the ocean-side strip. There I ended up on stage and, while in the throes of a Singha coma, was used as a prop in several different stage shows. The guys found this hilarious and took plenty of pictures. The photos were of the kind that would still turn up on the eleven o'clock news should I ever decide to run for public office.

Eventually, I sobered up enough to realize that I needed to get to bed. Feeling it would take too much energy to tell my shipmates I was leaving, I slipped out when nobody was looking. This set off a considerable panic hours later when my inebriated friends tried to remember where they had left me.

I may have been able to move, but I was nowhere near sober enough to know where I was going. I just remember walking. Forever. At some point, I reunited with the Marines from the kickboxing bar. I ended up being carried with my arms over the shoulders of a pair of my new jarhead friends while two others marched behind us, bearing a case of beer.

We eventually turned a corner and walked into an alley that we had mistaken for a street, finding ourselves face-to-face with what I thought was an acid flashback from the LSD I took in Las Vegas. It was no figment of my boozy imagination, however. It was a real live elephant we found well within Pattaya's city limits.

At first, the beast scared the hell out of us. The animal's minder, a boy who looked to be no more than fifteen years old, had to quiet us down so that we did not startle the creature. The young man spoke decent English and explained that the elephant performed at one of the nearby resorts. None of us had ever been that close to an animal that large before and we were somewhat awe-struck. We pet it and the kid allowed us to feed it a little. After discovering that my hotel was not far away, the boy offered to give us a ride to the Asia Pattaya if we could cough up a few hundred baht. I closed that deal myself inside of ten seconds.

Climbing atop a pachyderm without a ladder is as complicated as it sounds. It is exponentially more difficult when dangerously intoxicated. We nearly all fell off when the elephant stood up. Once we got the hang of it, though, we rode majestically through the alleys of Pattaya City, whooping it up and hollering with delight.

On the third block, we hit a hitch. Somehow, the elephant tripped over a bicycle chained to a utility pole. The animal destroyed it, stumbling enough in the process to dump both beer and my brethren ten feet onto the ground below. I landed in a pile of garbage that broke my fall. A couple of the Marines were not so lucky. They ended curled into a ball on the ground, moaning in agony.

Before long, we were surrounded by several irate residents chattering at us in a language we could not understand. They were pretty pissed to find that we were joy-riding an elephant through their neighborhood in the middle of the night. A man we assumed to be the owner of the bicycle was particularly distraught. Most

Americans would think he was overreacting, but a bike in Thailand is akin to a Chevy in the United States. The Royal Thai police eventually turned up to straighten things out.

The situation deteriorated and several animated conversations erupted around us. We could not decipher any of them. At some point in the argument, the elephant's handler nodded my way.

"You!" one of the policemen called out while pointing at me. "You drive the elephant?"

"What?!?" I gasped. "I wasn't driving shit!" At the time, I weighed about a hundred and seventy pounds. An Asian elephant clocks in at four tons. I was not driving that beast. It was going wherever the hell it wanted to.

"You sit on neck! You steer elephant!" the police officer insisted.

"I wasn't steering the elephant! I wasn't even touching the elephant! My hands were up in the air!" I then raised my arms as people do on rollercoasters. "Weeeeeeeeeeeeee!"

"That reckless driving! Would you take hands off wheel of car?!?" At this point, the officer had walked up close enough to smell my breath. "You be drinking?"

He had me there. *Yeah, I be drinking*. I did not want to come right out and confess that, though. I needed another explanation of why my breath reeked of stale Singha. When I caught sight of the elephant's trunk probing the ground where the Marines dropped the case of beer, I thought I found an out. Pointing at the pachyderm, I shouted out, "Look! The elephant's drinking! I bet that fucker's stoned!"

"You give elephant beer?!?" the officer retorted. "That against law! You ever see drunk elephant! Drunk elephant is angry elephant!"

"Well, he seemed cool enough to me…"

When one of the policemen pulled out a pair of handcuffs, I decided to change tactics. "Alright," I moaned. "What's the score here? What is it going to cost me to make this all better?"

The policeman engaged the owner of the bike. "It cost 1,250 baht to get him a new bicycle."

I reached into my wallet and gave the man fifteen hundred. He was the only person there genuinely aggrieved by the situation, so he deserved a tip.

"Each of the residents get two hundred fifty baht for disturbing their rest."

The crowd around us dispersed after I shelled out more bills. When they were gone, the policeman then said, "Two thousand baht fine for creating trouble."

I was not surprised that the police would take the largest cut of all. Once I paid their bribes, the officers pointed us towards the street and told us to go home. "We see you again tonight, you get big trouble!"

When the cops were gone, one of the Marines slapped me on the shoulder. "Dude! I think you just got a drunk driving ticket while riding an elephant! That's fuckin' EPIC!"

*****

I have no memory of walking back up to my hotel room that night, nor of undressing or climbing into bed. The first thing I can remember after the elephant is the ring of a telephone pulling me out of a deep sleep. I sat up to answer it. "Hello?"

"Mistah Murpee! Are you okay?"

"Yeah. I think so. Am I?" I flipped the switch of the lamp on the nightstand and screamed as I jumped out of my skin. Dixie was sitting on the edge of the other bed, staring at me in the dark. When I started freaking out, he did, too.

"Mistah Murpee! You okay?!? Da police is on dey way up! Dey help you! I coming too! Hang on!"

"The police? Wha…No! Don't send the police! It was a misunderstanding!" It did not sound like it, though. Dixie was still screaming. Then he started laughing. "Hello? Hello?" I asked into the phone. Nobody answered back. The line was dead.

Hanging up the phone, I turned back to Dixie. "The police are coming."

"I don't fucking believe this!" Dixie said. He was extremely drunk. Even drunker than I was. He was just more animated. "I pounded on that door for like twenty minutes," he slurred. "You didn't answer. When Tony came out of his room down the hall to tell me to shut up, I rushed in and, starting from their place, jumped balconies all the way to our room. By the way, the guy next door has three girls he's doing at the same time. I watched that for a little while. Anyway, I was standing on our balcony pounding on the door wall, trying to wake you up. You never even moved. Since you had your back to me, I couldn't see you and was wondering if you had thrown up and drowned in it or something."

"Why didn't you just ask the concierge for the key?"

"Because asshole! You never put my name on the fucking room!"

"I didn't? Seriously? Oops."

"Yeah. *Oops*! You also told the guy at the desk not to let anyone in. You were worried about some girls you gave your room number to. Anyway, I'm thinking you might be dead, right? I told the guy at the desk that either he was going to let me in to see if you were okay, or I was going to break the fuckin' door down."

"So he let you in?"

"No goddammit! I broke the fucking door down! You slept right through it! Never even moved! As soon as the phone rings, though, you sit right up and answer it like it's nothing! Jesus Christ!"

"Petty Officer Dixon! Can we please see you out in the hallway?" I recognized that voice. It was Chief Newberry from the Air Department. He was on Shore Patrol that night.

"Shit! Don't let anyone know I'm here!" Dixie exclaimed, plenty loud enough to be heard in Bangkok, let alone from the hallway, fifteen feet away. He rolled over onto the bed and put a pillow over his head. He apparently learned the fine art of camouflage from a cartoon ostrich.

I stood up and walked to the door in my underwear. It was ajar, and I noticed a large rectangular shape busted out of where the handle should have been. After pulling it open, I spotted Newberry and a second-class aviation boatswain's mate standing out in the hall. They were with the same two police officers I had bribed earlier. "Hi! How can I be of service to you gentlemen?"

Chief Newberry was not amused. "You're not Dixon, Doyle."

"Dixie's not here right now."

"So I heard." Newberry handed me the missing piece from the door, with the handle and lock still attached to it. The door looked like it had been made out of hollow balsa wood. "Stop trying to be funny and go get him."

I walked back into the room. "Hey, Dixie. Chief Newberry wants to see you."

"Dammit!" Dixie jumped out of bed and stumbled to the door. He immediately started arguing with Shore Patrol, the police, and the hotel manager when he got there. He was outraged, pressing his case that he only broke the door down because he thought I was in danger.

When it sounded like Kevin would be heading to jail, I walked back into the hallway to intervene. Turning to the hotel manager, I asked, "How much will it cost to fix the door?"

The manager shrugged. "Maybe two thousand baht."

That seemed excessive, but it was hard to barter from a position of strength when you are standing in public wearing only a pair of tighty-whiteys. "Add it to my bill."

"Okay," the manager said. He then pointed his index finger at my roommate. "But he go home now!"

"No way! I paid half for this room!" Dixie protested.

"Kevin, I don't think this is going to be negotiable," I said.

"It's not," Chief Newberry agreed. "You're done for the night. Get your shit and go back to the ship, Dixon."

"Aw, fuck this!" Kevin yelled, turning on his feet and walking away. "Fuck this whole hotel!" Turning to the manager, he exclaimed, "Fuck you too, Hotel Guy!"

I did not know it until the following day, but Dixie worked himself up so much that he got sick in the lobby. He barfed right into the aquarium as a final "fuck you" to the Asia Pattaya night staff. I had to pay for that when I checked out the following day. It was a damn good thing that I won all that money from the Marines.

With Dixie gone, the hotel manager left with Shore Patrol. The two Thai policemen stayed behind, staring at me with smiles on their faces, making me feel *really* under-dressed for the occasion. "Don't tell me," I said to them. "It's going to be two thousand baht for creating trouble."

"Three thousand," the English-speaking policeman answered. "It you second offense."

*****

CHAPTER 24

I woke up just before checkout time. I was in horrible shape. Still drunk, yet at the same time viciously hungover, I spent the remainder of my morning vomiting. I had reservations to go on a tour of the Bridge on the River Kwai, but there was no way that I was going to make it. All I could do was wolf down a plate of chicken pad prik at the hotel's restaurant and guzzle crazy amounts of ice water before I left. I needed something in my stomach to throw up during the long journey back to the *USS Belleau Wood.*

When I finally reached my rack in the early afternoon, I passed out and did not wake up again until right before sunrise on the following day. By some miracle, I remembered that I had promised Nigel and Margaret from Manchester a tour of the ship that morning.

After a ravenous breakfast, I got ready and caught the first boat to shore, finding the British couple waiting for me on the beach just like they said they would be.

I had more fun giving my English friends a tour of the ship than they had taking it. It was the first time that Nigel had ever been aboard an American warship and he was positively giddy. I took them from the hangar bay to the top of the island structure. I got them onto the bridge, where they were a hit among the duty crew. As a special treat, I even took them down to my SPN-35 dome. "Here it is," I told them. "The United States Navy's highly classified super-secret death ray."

Margaret eyed my radar monstrosity with wonder. "Is it really a death ray?"

I grinned and shook my head. "No, but that's what I used to tell the girls I brought up here in San Diego when I was trying to get lucky."

Margaret turned and looked at her husband with a horrified expression on her face. With typical British deadpan, Nigel told her, "Don't look at me like that, love. I'm pretty certain he does not want me to be the one giving him a shag in here."

Having shown them everything I could, I escorted my guests back to the beach. I thanked them for being so enjoyable and told them I hoped to run into them again sometime. As I turned to go back to the *Belleau Wood*, Margaret cried out, "What? You're not going back to the ship, are you?"

"Yeah, my first night in town kind of wiped me out," I admitted. "I'm broke."

Nigel seemed almost offended. "No, no, no, son! We're having none of that! I have to deliver my meat pies soon, but you have to let us buy you dinner or something. It's the least we can do for you for taking us on such a delightful tour!"

"That's not necessary," I told them. "It was my pleas…"

"Rubbish! It is necessary! Look, make your way back to Siamese George's," Nigel said as he pulled his wallet out, "Take this and buy yourself…"

I threw my hands up in the air. "I am NOT taking that!"

"You bloody well will!" Nigel insisted.

"I bloody well won't!" I countered, mimicking his accent.

"Then please, hang out at George's for a while and wait for us," Margaret begged. "We're doing trivia again tonight. We're going to have a great crowd there, and they're going to find you lovely!

We'll buy dinner. You're a smart chap. You got a fair chance of winning, playing against us driveling idiots."

After we parted ways, I sighed and made my way down the street to an ATM. I took out a cash advance on my already stressed credit card for a few thousand baht. Having refilled my wallet, I then made my way to Siamese George's.

This time, there were few sailors to be seen in the place. It was all expatriates, a few of whom I recognized from my first time there. They asked what I had done so far in Pattaya, so I told them all about my misadventures of the other day. They found the story of my accident with the elephant particularly hilarious.

Nigel and Margaret showed up at about three, walking through the front door with the Siamese George's owner. He was the man who had bounced Krause out of the bar in front of us. "You know, mate," the owner told me. "That shit bird lieutenant of yours came back yesterday askin' if any of ye had been back."

"Christ! That reminds me!" Nigel said. "I just saw the bastard too! While I was doing my delivery a little while ago! I spotted him creeping about S̄nām Dĕk Lèn."

"Seriously?" Nick spat, shaking his head in disgust. "Doesn't surprise me a bit. No doubt there was something off about that cunt."

"What's that?" I asked. "Whatever it was you said?"

"S̄nām Dĕk Lèn?" It rolled right off of Nigel's tongue. As good as I was with languages, what he said sounded hopelessly unpronounceable to me. "It means 'playground' in Thai. It's what we call a bunch of decrepit bamboo huts on the beach south of here. It's where ye go to find drugs and junkie hookers so desperate for dope money that they'll do *anything* you ask them to. The big draw there is the kids, though. The place is full o' urchins lookin' to make a buck off o' ye. You have to be a special kind of sick bastard to be lurking about that place."

I looked at Nigel, stunned. *Darrow was right!*

"Hey!" I shouted out to Siamese George's owner. "Where can I get one of those disposable 35mm cameras?"

"Pretty much anywhere, mate," he responded. "Any street kiosk has them."

"Great. Then how do I get to this 'playground' place?"

"Son," Nigel told me. "Take my advice. Let this go. You don't want to find yourself alone in S̄nām Dĕk Lèn. It's nasty. Really nasty."

"That man ruined the career of my best guy," I told Nigel. "He nearly killed a few of my men up on the mast. You know the man that Krause accused me of murdering? Palazzo? He killed himself because of some pictures of little girls I found hidden in a fan room. The guy was a pervert, so I thought they belonged to him. If that lieutenant's out there prowling this playground place, though, they were probably his."

My hands were shaking. To get them to stop, I lit myself a cigarette. "I accused Palazzo of taking those pictures." My voice cracked. "I didn't kill that man, but I bear a pretty big piece of responsibility for what he did to himself. I burned the wrong guy. You gotta help me make this right. Help me take down the right one. Where the hell is this playground?"

Nigel thought for a moment, then nodded to let me know that he understood. "Just get in a cab and ask, son. Trust me, they all know where it is."

*****

Before I got there, I pictured S̄nām Dĕk Lèn as a few beach shacks being misappropriated by sexual deviants. When I stepped out of the taxi, I found that it was more like a palm-frond shantytown. It was busy and crowded. The demand for what S̄nām Dĕk Lèn offered was so high, the locals kept building more shacks to accommodate it. It felt like Pagsanjan, but not nearly as discreet. It was also bigger. I had been picturing a few dozen hovels on my ride in. What I got was a small city within itself.

As I was paying the cab driver, I was propositioned by a woman who at least looked to be about the same age as I was. She was gorgeous if you looked at her from her left profile. Her right side was a different story. She was disfigured by a scar that ran over her eye, turning the lens milky white. She offered herself to me for less than five American dollars.

Feeling sorry for the girl, I gave her double her asking price while refusing her services. That proved to be a mistake. I got swarmed by a mob of street kids looking for similar charity and had to run away to escape them.

When I stopped, a couple of hooligans tried to sell me heroin before I could even catch my breath. As I shook my head to turn them down, I noticed a group of young boys sitting on a pile of wood nearby. They looked to be between ten and twelve years old, wearing make-up and sharing a cigarette. I watched a pear-shaped geriatric walk up to one of them, show them his money, then let a boy lead him back toward the huts. My blood started to boil. Instinctively, I turned to follow the geezer. I wanted to beat him but noticed that the toughs peddling dope were eyeing me with suspicion. Remembering the trouble I once landed myself in Pagsanjan, I decided to move on.

The scale of S̄nām Dĕk Lèn was overwhelming. Time after time, I crossed paths with people I wanted to deal with harshly, but I could do nothing about it. There were too many of them. As much as I wanted to, I could not take them all on. I needed to focus, or else I would not even be able to take down the one I had come there for. Swallowing the bile in my mouth, I trudged forward in search of Krause.

Not all the people selling themselves in S̄nām Dĕk Lèn were children. Most of the prostitutes working that area looked to be of consenting age. There were men, women, and men dressed as women. Many were junkies, too enslaved to their addictions to work in town. Others appeared mentally ill. Some had compromised health in other ways, as if they might have been exiled to S̄nām Dĕk Lèn when their HIV status progressed into AIDS. For many, the Playground looked to be the last desperate stop of a career in prostitution.

For others, however, it was the first. Though a minority, there were still many more children working S̄nām Dĕk Lèn than I imagined possible. It was a sickening, not to mention infuriating, sight. If it was even possible to have a silver lining in a cloud like the Playground, it was that I did not see a single serviceman prowling the area besides me. That was comforting on one level, but on another, it made me feel vulnerable. I stood out like a sore thumb.

One of the shacks lining the path had been converted into a beer hut. There was a window through which you could order a cold bottle of Singha or a simple cocktail. A picnic table was placed nearby where you could enjoy it. After a fruitless hour of wandering S̄nām Dĕk Lèn, I needed to temper my disgust with a drink. As dangerous as it was, I sat with my back to the shacks, unable to look at them anymore.

Before long, a man sat across from me. Though not as old as most of the other creeps out that day, he was still considerably older than I was. He looked to be in his mid-fifties and spoke with a Texan accent. Flashing me the toothy smile of a used car salesman, he said, "Man, is this place crazy or what!?! What a blast! You from one of the ships, friend? You a Marine?"

I felt no obligation to show the man even a hint of cordiality. "No, I'm not a Marine, and I'm not your friend either, bumpkin. If you know what's good for you, you'll fuck off."

The man looked indignant. "Well, that's uncalled for, you self-loathing piece of…" I tuned him out with a sigh, irritated that he was not fucking off like I told him to. Since I could not find Krause, I considered beating him into epilepsy as a consolation prize.

My eyes zeroed in on the Texan's nose and I balled my right hand into a fist. As I was standing up to plant it right in the middle of the bastard's face, I heard a disturbance break out behind me. It was too far away for me to tell what was going on, but just close enough for me to pick out one of the voices. It was someone I recognized. It was Krause.

I left the Texan and ran for the beach huts. When I was in the center of them, I stopped to get my bearings. I was a little closer to the commotion, but not much. I could not pick out Krause's voice anymore, but I could hear the chatter of a crowd forming to my right.

Tearing through the narrow spaces around the cabanas, I ran north and spotted Krause sprinting right at me. His polo shirt was ripped at the neck and splattered with the blood streaming out of his nose. He was screaming for help and running as if his life depended on it. When I saw Darrow fly out of the broken door of one of the huts behind him, I had little reason to doubt that it did.

As surprised as I was to see Krause, Master Chief Darrow shocked me even more. Dressed only in a bathing suit, he was screaming, too. He wanted to make sure that his victim knew what he was going to do to him once he got his hands on him.

Krause was making good time for a man his age, but he was hurt and limping. He could not run as fast as he normally could. The gathering crowd also slowed his escape. He did not make it far before Darrow pounced and took him down into the sand. My master chief pounded him twice in the back of the head. He then rolled him over, straddled his chest, and started throttling him in the face. The lieutenant was begging the master chief to stop, but the fourth or fifth blow Darrow landed shut him up. Still, my master chief kept going. He was not in a rage like I got into on occasion. Darrow was landing his blows with premeditation and precision.

"Master Chief!" I yelled, piercing the split second of silence that fell upon the crowd once Krause went quiet.

My sudden appearance startled Darrow. He leapt off of Krause and fell backward, looking at me as if he thought I was some sort of apparition. "Doyle! What the hell are you doing out here?"

I glanced down at Krause, unable to believe what I was seeing. The man was messed up. His face was bloodied and already bruising. Once Darrow was off of him, he gurgled something, sobbed, then rolled over onto his stomach. He was attempting to crawl away.

Looking back at my master chief, I said, "One of the guys at Siamese George's said he saw Krause out this way. I came out here to catch him."

Darrow nodded. He was panting, trying to catch his breath. "Yeah, so did I. I've been staking out this place for two days. I finally caught the little prick."

The master chief's words made sense, but the situation did not. Darrow did not look dressed for a stakeout. He was in a bathing suit. "Where?"

"What?" Darrow asked. "What do you mean where?"

"Where did you catch him?" I asked again.

"What does it matter? I caught him…" Krause was crawling a little further away than the master chief was comfortable with, so he reached out to grab the lieutenant's leg. My former division officer panicked and mumbled something, but it was unintelligible coming out of his broken mouth.

I was trying to process the scene around me, but my head was spinning. Nothing was adding up, probably because I desperately did not want it to.

"Master Chief, what was Krause doing when you caught him and where was he?"

"I told you I was staking out…"

"In your bathing suit?"

Darrow pointed at the ocean. There were plenty of people in the water. "When you stake shit out, you try to blend in. People like us stand out walking around a place like this. Our haircuts and the gait we move with screams that we're military men. If you're on a beach in a suit, no one gives you a second look."

"Hep," Krause gasped, weakly struggling to free his leg from Darrow's grip. "Hep me…"

"Where did you find him?"

Darrow's face flushed red. He did not like my tone and was indignant that I dared to question him. "Who the fuck do you think you are, Murphy?!? Huh?!? You don't think I know what I'm doing? Who the…"

I spun around and marched toward the hut I saw Darrow emerge from. The master chief rolled over and pummeled Krause in the back of the head hard enough to knock him out. He then got up and took off after me.

When I burst through the cabana's shattered door, I saw that the place had been completely ransacked. It looked like the commotion I first heard at the beer shack started right there. It was ground zero. A small duffel bag full of clothes had been tossed over, and within the laundry, I spotted a pair of Hello Kitty boxer shorts. They were the pair that Lorna had bought my master chief in Olongapo. Krause had not been staying in that hut. It was Darrow's place.

Starting to hyperventilate, I paced the room, turning over the debris inside. When I rolled over a demolished end table, I found Polaroid photographs lying face down upon the sand floor beneath it. Picking them up, I gasped. They were shots of a young boy, naked and wearing make-up like the group of kids I had seen earlier. There was also a smudge on the lower right-hand corner of the photos. They were all taken with the same camera as the ones I had discovered in the fan room. When I picked up Darrow's duffel bag, I found the device that took them.

"Lieutenant Commander Egan was a homosexual. Just like I told you," Darrow said when he entered the hut. "If Krause was so worked up about what happened to him that he was obsessed with punishing me for it, I figured he must be gay, too. They probably had something going on. Pictures of little girls wouldn't have worked with that piece of shit. As disgusting as it was, I had to get one of those little boys in here to pose for me."

I couldn't breathe. "Why?" I gasped. "Krause was gone! He was…"

"He was going to the NIS, Doyle. Yeah, he didn't know shit about our deal with the Japs or any of that stuff that went down with Randy Green, but I'm not sure what he knows about Egan. If the NIS goes poking around there, it could sink us all. Especially if they question Fleming's wife again. If she hears I was making pictures like this to burn Krause, she might question the ones she found in her husband's shit. Especially considering that I was the one who convinced her to look for them."

I looked at the Polaroids again and wanted to gag. "What'd you do to Egan? You frame him?" I threw the photos into Darrow's face. "With shit like this?!?"

My master chief grimaced. What happened with Egan did not appear to be a very proud moment for him. "He left me no choice, Doyle. It was him or me…"

"Over what?!?" I yelled. "What'd he have on you?!?"

"A mistake, Doyle! It was an accident! I didn't know how old she was!"

"Oh, Christ," I cried, covering my ears with my hands.

"I wasn't taking advantage of her! I loved her, Doyle! I still do! Lorna looked twice her age when I met her! I didn't know that she was only…"

"Goddammit! Stop!" I sobbed. "You motherfucker! You hid those pictures in the fan room! To frame Krause! I remember when we were in the Philippines and the captain told us he was referring the lieutenant to the NIS. I asked you what you were going to do about it. You told me if the NIS came looking for dirt on Krause, you were going to make sure that they fucking found it. Is that what you meant?!? That you were going to frame him?!?"

"At the time, I thought the son-of-a-bitch was trying to kill me!"

"But you let me blame Palazzo for that shit!"

"Hey!" Darrow screamed at me. "I tried to fucking tell you to back off, but you kept on pushing that poor guy! You wouldn't let it go! That shit's on you!"

"You could have stopped it! You could've just told me that…"

"What?!?" Darrow exclaimed. "That I was going to frame a commissioned officer in the United States Navy for being a pederast?!? You'd have gone along with that?!?"

"I would've talked you out of…"

"Oh, BULL-shit, Doyle! You're nowhere near leveling up to that kind of shit, son! No way! Look at you now! You're crying like a fuckin' baby over some worthless chicken-chokin' tub of pig lard! That kid was a loser, Doyle! He was a coward! He was a pervert! He was…"

"…innocent," I said. "He was innocent! And so is Krause! You didn't come out here to catch him. You came out here to manufacture evidence against him."

"Yeah, well, when you're in the big leagues, you have to make tough choices sometimes, kid. Look, speaking of that motherfucker, we need to get out there and take care of the prick before we both land ourselves in Leavenworth. Let's go."

"To kill him?"

"No, Doyle. We're going to ask him really nicely not to go to the NIS and tell them what I was doing out here. Come on! We've got shit to clean up outside!"

"No," I told Darrow.

The master chief turned on me. "This isn't fucking negotiable, Doyle. Get out here and help me…"

"You're not doing this," I growled.

"The fuck I ain't!"

"That man's the biggest prick I've ever met, but I ain't going to murder an innocent…"

"Aw, fuck you, Doyle!" Darrow snapped. "We don't have time for this shit! I'll do it myself!"

"In front of all these witnesses?!?" I asked.

Darrow scoffed. "These motherfuckers are out here pimping their own kids! What makes you think they care if a couple of pale round-eyes beat each other to death in this shit pit?!? You saw what went down here already! You hear any cop sirens in the distance heading this way to put things back in order? This is the part of town where people get put down, son. I'll tell you right now, for a couple of hundred bucks, I can get a few of these folks to take care of the body after I finish that sorry sack of shit off!" At that, Darrow turned to walk out of the hut.

"Stop!" I screamed at him.

"Fuck you!"

Minutes before, I was a man who often fantasized about all the ways I could inflict pain upon Lieutenant Junior Grade Krause. Now, I was compelled to hurt the closest thing to a father I ever had to save the prick. Thinking that Darrow would ever follow one of my orders was laughably ridiculous. A man like my master chief could only be made to do something through force. I did not order him to halt a second time. I charged.

My intent was to tackle Master Chief Darrow and take him to the ground. What I managed to do was body-slam him into the doorjamb so hard that he split open his brow. Enraged, Darrow spun and swung at me.

Had my master chief landed that blow, the fight would have ended right there. I ducked fast enough for him to miss me, however, and he struck the wooden post in the center of the hut with everything he had. The entire structure shook, Darrow's knuckles cracked, then the man bellowed out in pain. Before he could recover, I let him have it in the gut, cutting off his scream as I forced the air out of his lungs.

My master chief was off balance and I did everything I could to take advantage of that. I planted my left fist into his wounded eye, then took my right and buried it into his jaw. When I brought my left in again to take out his other peeper, he managed to twist enough to deflect the blow off of his shoulder. He then caught me in the chest with his elbow, throwing me off my stance before he barrelled his right fist into my temple. That was supposedly Darrow's broken hand, but even injured, he hit me hard enough to drive me right to the deck.

He gave me no time to retaliate. The instant I lifted my face out of the sand, Darrow pummeled me in the back of the head. My nose got driven so hard back into the beach that blood gushed out of both nostrils and poured over my upper lip. He followed it up with a pair of kicks to the ribs that forced me onto my back. The master chief then dropped his knees down onto my chest, knocking the wind out of me. As I struggled for air, he wrapped the fingers of his good hand around my neck.

"Stop it, Doyle!" Darrow barked at me as I suffocated under his weight. He sounded close to tears. "What the hell's the matter with you?!? You're like a son to me! Don't make me do this!"

"Let…l-l-let…let me go!" I gasped.

"Are you going to come to your senses and stop this shit?"

"I can't...I can't...I can't let you kill him..."

Darrow sobbed. "Why not?!? For Christ's sake, man! If we let him go, he's going to put us both away! My boy'll grow up an outcast in the Philippines! Tala will have to go back to selling herself in bikini bars! Mari will end up there, too! This is madness, Doyle! Stop it! Stop it, right now! Let's just get this shit over with and go home!"

"I can't!" I could barely speak now and I felt like I was blacking out. "I can't murder an innocent man."

"God damn it!" Darrow cried, dropping his head in grief. He broke down for a few seconds, then wrapped his bad hand around my throat, too. "I'm sorry, son. I'm so sorry."

As Darrow started to squeeze, I choked out, "Tala! Tal..."

My master chief nodded. "I know, Doyle. I'll have TJ take care of her and Mari."

Darrow's words were meant to soothe me. I took his promise to "take care of" Tala in an entirely different context than he intended it, however. He was trying to tell me that they would be alright after I was gone. I knew better, though. Tala knew we were going into business together. If the master chief was forced to kill me, Tejada would consider her a loose end. He would not know how much I had told her about how I got my money. TJ would take care of Tala, all right. He might even take care of Mari, too. Picturing what Tejada would do to them sent a surge of adrenaline coursing through my system. Though barely conscious, I grabbed a handful of sand and threw it into Darrow's face.

It did nothing. "Shhhhhh. Let go, Doyle. Let it go. Everything's going to be over soon. It'll be all..."

With the last reserve of energy I had, I took my thumb and jammed it into Darrow's eye as hard as I could. Surprising myself, it felt like I forced it in past the knuckle. I could have popped it right out of the socket had I possessed just a little more strength. Even with what I had, though, I half-blinded the man. More importantly, I forced him to release his grip. My master chief howled in a way I had never heard before. He released my neck, clutched his face with both hands, and fell off of my chest, shrieking in agony.

I rolled towards the door, grabbing my throat and struggling to force air back into my lungs. It still felt as if I was dangerously close to passing out, but I was terrified of what would happen to Tala and Mari if I did. I could not let Darrow win, but I did not know if I could take him either. I needed a weapon.

Nearly hysterical, I scampered about the hut on my hands and knees, looking for something I could use as a weapon. When I came across the destroyed end table that I found the photos beneath, I picked up one of the legs. I was relieved to feel it was heavier than it looked. Without any time to hesitate, I jumped to my feet, turned around, and smashed it across the back of Darrow's head as hard as I could.

A blow like that would have killed a lesser man. All it did to Darrow was piss him off. He jumped to his feet and throttled me in the jaw, knocking me back against the wall. As he charged me, I managed to bring up the leg and club him again, dropping him to his knees. Still, the master chief would not give up. He threw his left arm out and grabbed me between my legs, squeezing my testicles until I screamed. To force him to let go, I hit him again so hard that the chunk of wood bounced off of his skull and went flying out of my grip, landing far out of reach.

My master chief collapsed into the sand, but incredibly, he was still reaching for me. I fell upon him and began throttling the man with everything I could muster, left after right and right after left. My rage started welling up, and I began descending back into my underwater world once more as I landed blow after blow after blow. On the precipice of a full-blown episode, I was pulled back from the brink with a single word. "Stop."

I pulled my last punch and paused to force my head back together. Looking down at my master chief, I was suddenly appalled by what I had done to him. His eyes were already swollen shut. His lips were mangled and pouring blood down his cheeks. I had broken his teeth right out of his mouth. The man had been beaten beyond recognition and was bawling beneath me. "Stop!

Please! You're killing me. Go do whatever it is you have to do. Just get off of me."

I jumped from Darrow's chest and scampered away, not quite believing that I had beaten him. Seeing him on the ground, I knew that he was broken, but the truth was that the man still terrified me. I got up and bolted outside, intending to collect Krause and get him to safety before the master chief came to his senses.

Pushing my way through the crowd that had gathered around the hut, I jogged as fast as I could to where we had left the lieutenant. When I got there, however, the man was gone. For a second, I thought about following the blood trail to see if he was okay, but I did not have that kind of energy. Instead, I staggered back to the hut.

*****

"What the fuck are you doing here?" Darrow wheezed when I returned.

I collapsed upon the bed, still trying to get my breath back. "Krause's gone. He got away. He's safe."

Darrow grimaced. "Good for you. You win. So, what are you doing here?"

"I'm getting you to a hospital."

The master chief started to laugh, but the pain set him groaning instead. "I ain't going to no fuckin' hospital. I'm going to prison, Doyle. Krause is going to burn me for what he caught me doing out here."

I nodded and lit a couple of smashed cigarettes that I fished out of my pocket. I held one out for Darrow, but he couldn't extend his arm to grab it. I had to bend down and put it between his bloody lips. "He caught you?"

Darrow nodded weakly as he inhaled the smoke. His lungs sucked in some blood, too, and he broke into a violent coughing fit. When that passed, I asked, "How did he catch you?"

"He took pictures of me with that boy."

I shook my head in disgust. "You fucking deserve this shit, Master Chief." After a long sigh, I told him, "I guess I do, too."

Darrow shook his head. "No, you don't. You're a good man, Doyle." His voice was so soft that I had to lean in to hear him. "I'm going down, Doyle. There's nothing I can do about that now. I'm not taking you with me, though. You did the right thing. Now, get out of here before it's too late. I'll cover for you. I'll tell them you did this to keep me from killing Krause. You're going to be a fuckin' hero."

"The hell with that. I'm no hero, Master Chief. It's time for me to pay the piper now, too. I drove Palazzo to..."

"Stop it!" Darrow cried. "I fucked that up! I could've stopped you. I should've stopped you. I didn't. Get out of here, Doyle. I need you to leave. Just...just promise me that you'll do good by Lorna and my son. Make sure they get my cut. Make sure they get out of the Philippines. Go. Get out of here."

I sucked in another lungful of smoke and blew it out toward the ceiling. Then I laughed. "Where am I going to go? What am I supposed to do? Become a fugitive in Thailand?"

"I don't care! Just get the hell out of here."

"I can't leave you like this, Master Chief. You're hurt, man. Bad. I gotta get you some help."

Darrow mumbled something too quietly for me to decipher. When I leaned in to hear better, he reached up and grabbed me by the shirt. "Goddammit, Doyle! Get out of here so I can take care of this! Make sure Lorna and Bradly are taken care of and for Christ's sake, man, make sure that TJ doesn't get his hands on Tala and the kid."

Tala!

Remembering the threat that Tejada posed to Tala and Mari, I forced myself off the bed and ran outside. Again, I pushed my way through the people gathered on the beach and limped all the way out of S̄nām Dĕk Lèn. Despite the rough shape that I was in, I kept going for a couple of miles up Beach Road, not daring to stop until I reached a bank of payphones. Using my international phone card, I dialed the number I had memorized. When Tala answered the phone, I instantly burst into tears. After I finally pulled myself together, I told her to run. “Go to where I buried the gun,” I blabbered. “There’s money there. I also left a key and instructions on how to get more cash out of a safety deposit box. Run, Tala. Take Mari and Manny, and run.”

Before she had a chance to respond, I hung up the phone and collapsed onto the sidewalk. When I finally got myself together, I walked away, determined to get as drunk as I could before Shore Patrol caught up with me.

*****

CHAPTER 25

As an aspiring alcoholic, there was nothing remarkable about regaining consciousness face down at the beach. In fact, I would be hard-pressed to name a sandy stretch of ocean-side real estate between Los Angeles and Ensenada on which I had not awakened.

Though not technically a beach, I often used Spanish Landing, a park overlooking San Diego Bay, as a landing pad after a Tijuana tequila bender in BE/E School. Their irrigation system was timed to go off at 5:30 am. I could easily sleep through reveille back at the barracks. There was no way I was going to slumber through getting doused with an icy blast of sprinkler water right before sunrise. With the added bonus of showering while screaming my way through the freezing droplets, I never failed to make roll call on time. I would also be well exercised, wide awake, and stone sober.

I was not sober the time I woke up overlooking the Gulf of Thailand. I was plastered, brutalized, and nauseous. Since I was supposed to have been on duty that day, I was also away without leave. Not that I cared. When compared to the severity of the other crimes I knew I would be charged with, being AWOL and drunk on duty seemed almost inconsequential.

Darrow told me that he was not taking me down with him, but the way I saw it, there was no way I was getting away with beating an E-9 the way that I had. I also told the crowd at Siamese George's that I was going to S̄nām Dĕk Lèn with the explicit intent of catching a commissioned officer molesting children. That made me sound more like Darrow's accomplice than his adversary. Besides, once they got to that hut and found the pictures that I left there with him, my master chief was going to have a BIG credibility problem. I was doomed no matter what angle I looked at it from.

With the prospect of a decade's worth of hard time staring me in the face, I did not see any sense in heading back to the *Belleau Wood* to report for duty. It seemed like a much better idea to go back to drinking.

It was hard to continue being festive while horizontal and sleeping with the sand fleas. I was also blocks away from any venue serving booze. I needed to get up and find my way to a dockside watering hole, but my body did not seem willing to go along with the plan.

My head was screaming at me. I was used to waking up hungover. Waking up hungover and drunk was much less common, but still well within my skill set. Waking up hungover, drunk, and with a concussion was uncharted territory. It was really harshing the mellow of an otherwise serene Siamese sunrise.

As I lifted my swollen melon off the beach, the world spun around me like a hyper-driven roulette wheel. That added a whole new level of difficulty to keeping the rancid mixture of spicy seafood and Thai beer in my stomach. The blow that gave me the concussion also left my right eye swollen shut. That cut in half my ability to see what else was wrong with me.

I did not need my sight to figure out the shape my hands were in. I could feel how bruised my knuckles were. As I struggled to sit upright, it felt as if my fingers were shattered when I tried to steady myself from falling over. I let out a short scream while making that discovery.

When I was able to sit up, I looked over my clothes. The red tropical shirt I picked up in Honolulu was shredded and torn, but it was the perfect color to hide bloodstains. The Hard Rock Café t-shirt I bought in Hong Kong was not. It also sustained substantial damage. When I looked through the rips in it, I saw scores of claw marks dug deep into my chest. It looked like I might have tried to molest a large jungle cat. The injuries on my shoulders suggested that the cat might have tried to molest me back.

I tried to get to my feet without using my right hand. It took several attempts, each one more complicated than the last. They all involved superhuman feats of balance, determination, and quietly slurred words of self-encouragement. After twenty minutes of exhausting effort, however, I found myself finally upright. I was standing with the poise of a drunken ostrich trying to keep its balance on a pair of broken roller skates, but upright.

Up to that point, I had not noticed a trio of Thai fishermen leaning against their boats on the beach thirty feet behind me. They sure noticed me, though. They had been watching me the whole time and burst into a polite round of applause once I finally made it to my feet. Startled, I spun around to face them. Then, inspired by their appreciation of my efforts, I smiled and tried to take a bow. That was a rookie mistake. The second my head dropped below my stomach, I got sick, fell forward, and planted my face right in the middle of a puddle of my own vomit. I then gasped a couple of choice expletives and blacked out again.

*****

I was awakened by a familiar voice a couple of hours later. "Petty Officer Murphy. Wake up. Petty Officer Doyle Murphy! Wake! Up! Goddammit, Doyle! Wake UP!" It was my chief, Ben Ramirez. I opened my one good eye and saw him kneeling above me in uniform with an SP armband wrapped around his left bicep. Had I made it back to the ship on time, I would have been on

Shore Patrol with him. It appeared that BM3 Danny Gibson, the knuckle-dragger that was with me when Miller was murdered, took my place. Once Ramirez saw me open an eye, he leaned in closer. "You with us, Doyle? You alright?"

I nodded my head. "Yeah. Kinda."

"It's about time," Ben told me. "Are you okay? How do you feel?"

"Like shit," I answered. "How do I look?"

Chief Ramirez paused for a moment before answering, "About the same as you feel."

"Yeah, well, you should see the other guy."

There was a brief pause before Ben responded. He stayed where he was, nodding and unable to convey anything in response. Eventually, he just said, "I have."

"You did?" I asked. "How bad did I fuck him up?"

"Pretty bad, Doyle," Ben started as he tried to find the words. He stammered a few times before he finally said, "Doyle…he…he didn't make it."

My jaw dropped open. With the shock of Ben's news suppressing the discomfort of my injuries, I sat myself up as if I had been spring-loaded. "What?!? What do you mean he didn't make it?!?"

Ben's shoulders slumped, and he broke eye contact with me. Casting his gaze to the ground, he said, "Doyle, Master Chief Darrow's dead."

*****

CHAPTER 26

For the first few weeks, I plodded through all the interrogations and legal briefings I was subjected to as if I was moving through a dream. The NCIS agents thought I was drugged. My JAG attorney was questioning my sanity. Then he showed me pictures of the crime scene in S̄nām Dĕk Lèn. After that, he was convinced that I had lost my mind.

The picture showed Darrow lying upon the sand floor of the hut we had fought in. His face had been reduced to a bloody pulp, looking even worse than I remembered it being when I left him. Some of the damage had been inflicted with the table leg lying next to my master chief's head in the photograph. Most of it, though, had been caused with my own bare hands. When I saw what I had done, I lost it. I slipped into my underwater world and did not come out for weeks.

The Navy transferred me from the brig in Yokosuka, Japan, to the Mental Health Unit at Balboa Hospital in San Diego. Once deemed competent enough to assist in my own defense, I was remanded to the consolidated brig in Miramar to await court-martial.

The JAG officer assigned to defend me called my case one of the most complicated he had ever worked. The military prosecutors suspected me of doing a lot of stuff. They caught rumors of me clashing with cartel men in Tijuana. My name also came up in connection with the shootings in Olongapo. Investigators also heard all about my alleged involvement with the Japanese mob. They deemed the source of those accusations as wildly unreliable, however. The only thing they could corroborate for sure was my participation in a couple of acts of corporal punishment down in the Nixie Winch Room. No one seemed to deem that worthy of a court-martial, though.

Still, the Navy had a master chief petty officer seemingly beaten to death at the hands of a long-time collaborator. The authorities could hardly allow that to go unpunished, even if the evidence pointed to me acting in defense of myself and Lieutenant Krause. They knew I was guilty of something. They were just having a hard time figuring out what it was.

It did not help that the deeper they dug into Darrow, the more unsavory the man became. The investigation into the master chief also yielded some embarrassing dirt that Darrow had on a couple of high-ranking military officers and one politician. Afraid that continuing the inquest could get even more uncomfortable, the powers that be decided it was in everyone's best interests if the issue just quietly faded away.

The Navy wanted to avoid a court-martial that could grab the press's attention. To that end, they offered me a plea deal for some pretty absurd charges. My attorney found the prosecution's offer laughable and was prepared to fight them. At that point, though, I wanted the investigation over just as much as the Navy did. The longer it went on, the higher the risk was of them finding something *really* damning against me. It was better to quit while I was ahead. I pled to some weird "conduct unbecoming" bullshit and got sentenced to four years confinement.

Due to my episodes, I did most of my time in the psych ward at Balboa Hospital. Between my attorney's efforts to get my sentence reduced and the time off I earned for good behavior, I served less than twenty-four months.

The first thing I did after walking out of Balboa Hospital was find a payphone and call the number that Katsumi had given me in Japan.

*****

Lorna was startled. I could hardly blame her, though. She had just walked into her dark apartment and turned on the light. I grabbed her from behind and put a gloved hand over her mouth to keep her from screaming. She must have thought I was there to kill her. "Shhhhhhh," I whispered into her ear. "I'm not here to hurt you, Lorna. I'm here to keep a promise I made to Master Chief Darrow. I'm here to make sure that neither you nor little Bradley ever want for anything ever again. Understand?"

When Lorna nodded her head, I let her go and directed her to take a seat at the kitchen table. I then sat down myself, placing the revolver I was carrying between us. "Ip you no going to hurt me, why you bring dat t'ing into my house?" she asked.

Motioning my arm towards the duffel bag lying on her couch, I told her, "There's more than $400,000 over there. I'm not walking around a place like Olongapo with that kind of cash and not have a way to keep people from stealing it."

Lorna's eyes opened wide. "What you do with dat kind op money?" she gasped.

"Giving it to you," I told her.

"Why?"

"It's what the master chief wanted."

Lorna sobbed. "Why you care what Bradley wanted? You kill him!"

As a tear rolled down my own cheek, I told her, "I didn't mean to, Lorna. I was only trying to keep him from killing me. Even after our fight was over, I wanted to get him to a hospital, but he refused to go."

Shaking her head, Lorna cried, "You t'ink I supposed to porgive you? I not, Murpee. I not! I wit dat man por a long time!"

"I know. Since you were thirteen."

Lorna looked shocked. "How you know dat?"

"I saw your birth date on the statement you gave to the NCIS investigators. You're only five years older than I am. You met Darrow during his second tour on the AFPD. That was in 1978."

"I pourteen, when I meet him," Lorna corrected me. "I no meet him when he pirst get here. I meet him in 1979."

"My bad," I said. "Thirteen, fourteen, whatever. You were still a child."

"It not his pault. I tell him dat I eighteen. When we meet, he t'ink I am woman, not a girl."

I shrugged. "But Lieutenant Commander Egan knew your age after pulling you out of Pagsanjan. He knew how young you were. He told Darrow, too. But even after he knew your age, he kept seeing you."

Lorna sobbed. "Because he love me…"

Nodding, I said, "He did. He couldn't stay away. Egan tried to get the command to do something about it, but Darrow had dirt on a lot of high-ranking people in Olongapo. They were afraid to cross him. He even found the skeletons in Egan's closet. That was enough to get the lieutenant commander to back off of the military channels but not enough to keep him from going to Darrow's wife. Once she found out the master chief was involved with a child, she packed up her daughters and made sure that their father never saw them again."

As Lorna cried, I struggled to keep my own composure. "Darrow retaliated," I went on. "Egan's wife already knew he was gay. So, Darrow made sure she found pictures of naked boys in the man's own home. He also started circulating the word about Egan's sexual preferences around the base, killing Egan's credibility. After that, the poor guy snapped and got himself killed by his wife's lover. Christ, Darrow even came out on top cleaning that shit up."

"How you know all dis?"

I shrugged. "Darrow told me some of it. Sergeant Tejada told me the rest."

"You know, TJ gonna kill you por what you do to Bradley."

I shook my head. "Tejada's not going to be killing anyone anymore."

Lorna gasped, bringing her hand up to her mouth. "You kill him?"

"Did I personally pull the trigger?" I asked, shaking my head. "No, I didn't. I paid the man who did, though."

Struck by the realization that Rico Tejada was dead, Lorna lunged for the revolver on the table. I let her grab it and point it right at my face. She pulled the trigger twice. Click! Click!

"Sorry, I only had two bullets," I apologized. "I had to make sure that TJ was dead, so I had my guy use them both." I held out my hand, beckoning for Lorna to give me my gun back.

Lorna meekly put the weapon in my hand. "Your fingerprints are now on the weapon used to kill a sergeant of the Philippine National Police. If you don't want it turning up where the cops will find it, I suggest you do what I say. Take that money I'm leaving you. Get the hell out of the Philippines and go to Hawaii or something. Start over with little Bradley. Forget that I was ever here. There's no record of me coming into the country and there won't be one of me leaving it. You won't be able to ever prove I was here, anyway. Besides that, I have friends in Japan setting me up with a pretty airtight alibi."

I sat in silence and watched Lorna cry for a little while. After she pulled herself together, I asked, "Are we good?"

Lorna nodded.

"Good." I gathered my things and stood up to leave. Placing my hand on Lorna's shoulder, I said, "I loved the man, too. I'm going to miss him. The last thing I wanted was for any of this to happen."

I departed Olongapo and headed back up to the Port of Manila to catch my freighter back to Japan. Before I left, I found a payphone and called the number to a house deep in the Cagayan Valley. The Cagayan was a hotbed of NPA activity, and somewhere Tejada would never dare go without the army watching his flank. It was where Mahal Legarda was raised.

"Hello?" Tala answered.

I drew in a deep breath to keep from breaking down. "Hi, Tala. It's done. You're safe. Take the money and the kids and go."

Starting to cry, she asked, "Are you sure dat we no can be wit you?"

Even though she could not see me over the phone, I nodded. "I'm a mess, Tala. They threw me out of the Navy with a Big Chicken Dinner…"

"A what?"

I chuckled humorlessly. Tala spent a lot of time around sailors when she was working the bars. Still, I was not surprised that she never picked up that particular piece of Navy slang. "A BCD. A Bad Conduct Discharge. It's a scarlet letter in my record that'll keep me from ever holding down a decent job back home. I'm not going to be living in the US, Tala."

"We go anywhere wit you."

"I know, but I'm not going to let you. I've ruined enough people. I'm not going to ruin you, too." I let that sink in for a moment before I asked, "Is he a nice guy, Tala?"

"He old," she answered. "But, yes. He bery nice. He bery good to Mari and Manny, too. He sending dem gifts all da time."

"Then that's the best," I told her. It wasn't, but being a mail-order bride was far better than hooking to feed a child. "Don't let him know about the money you have, though. If he doesn't turn out to be who you think he is, you use it as an insurance policy to get the hell out of there. Okay?"

"Okay." There was a long period of silence while the two of us just stood there, listening to each other breathe. Finally, Tala asked, "Do you wanna speak to Mari?"

It was a question that hit me like a gut punch. I broke down and my legs gave out, causing me to fall against the wall of the phone booth to stay upright. "I can't," I sobbed. "When she's older, please tell her that I love her and explain why everything had to be this way. Please don't let her hate me for leaving."

"I never let dat happen, Doyle," Tala assured me. "Never."

I could not get out an answer to that. Eventually, I just thanked her. At that point, I had all of that conversation that I was emotionally equipped to handle. "I have to go," I told her. "I..."

"No! Doyle! Don't go! Not yet! How Mari and me ever repay you por what you do por us?!? How we…?"

"You can repay me by taking care of Manny and being as happy as you all can possibly be for the rest of your lives. Repay me by not worrying about me, by enjoying a happy marriage to that geezer in Florida, and doing everything you ever dreamed of doing. Repay me by watching your kids grow up without ever experiencing one bit of the pain we had to endure when we were children. Do that, and as far as I'm concerned, you're square with the house. I love you, Tala. Never forget that. That's why I'm doing this. Good-bye."

I hung up the phone before she had a chance to answer. I then took some time to collect myself before calling the United States. "Hello?" Dylan Bateman, by now a chief petty officer, answered.

I was relieved that the corpsman was not on duty at Balboa. "Hi, Dylan. It's Murphy. How's he doing?"

"Not good. If you want to see him, you'd better plan on being here soon. It's not going to be long."

*****

One of the things I learned while under investigation was that Lieutenant Krause was not gay. Nor was he an idiot. He was just a man doing the best he could with a lemon-sized tumor eating away at his cerebral cortex. Ironically, Darrow's attempt to kill the man ended up saving his life. Well, for a couple of years, anyway. The doctors discovered the cancer while trying to figure out what to do about his cracked skull. With some pretty aggressive treatment, Krause was able to buy himself another thirty months, much of it spent in great discomfort.

After my ship docked in Fukuoka, I rushed to the airport and caught the first plane I could back to San Diego. I then raced to

Balboa Hospital, where I found Andrew Krause in hospice care, dying alone.

A couple of years before, that was what I had wished for the man. Not anymore. I realized that the sadist that tormented us aboard the *USS Belleau Wood* was not the real Andrew Krause. That was a monster driven by the malignancy wreaking havoc just behind his eyes. I did not forgive the lieutenant for what he had done to my men and me, but I did not feel that he deserved to leave this mortal coil all alone, either.

Looking at me with pure disgust when I entered his room, Krause groaned, "What the hell are you doing here, Murphy? Can't you let me die in peace?"

I have to admit that I took some pleasure in Krause's reaction to seeing me again. Knowing that I was the last person the man wanted to see in his final hours only made me want to stay longer. I pulled up a chair and took a seat beside his bed. "Is that any way to talk to the guy who saved your life?"

Krause scoffed. "You didn't save my life. I saved my own."

"If I hadn't shown up when I did, the man would've killed you," I argued.

"Whatever," the lieutenant groaned. "It's not like you pulled him off of me or anything."

"I kept him from coming back for you."

"Yeah?" Krause exclaimed. "I was long gone by then."

I had to laugh. *I doubt it. If you knew that Darrow was coming back after you, you had to have been close enough to hear us arguing.*

"What do you want, Murphy?"

"Just to keep you company, sir."

"Bullshit. You want to watch me die."

"Watching you die is not the reason I came here, sir," I assured the lieutenant. "It's just a perk."

Krause let out a weary sigh. "What do I have to do to get you to leave?"

"You want to answer a couple of my questions?"

"No."

I grinned. "Then how about we talk about the great philosophers? You know, I heard that when Voltaire was on his deathbed, his priest started reading him his last rights. When the padre asked Voltaire if he renounced Satan, he refused, insisting that it probably was not a good time to start making new enemies…"

The lieutenant surrendered. "Alright, Murphy. You win. What do you want to know?"

"Just a couple of things, sir. First, do you remember when we were in Olongapo, and that guy got shot in the bar?"

Krause nodded.

"How did you know that we were there?"

"The Butterfly Express."

"The what?"

My former lieutenant smiled. "The kids that hang around the bridge over the Shit River. The girls pay them to keep track of where their *honey-kos* go when they leave the base. They want to know if their men are sleeping around on them. You know, fluttering from flower to flower, like a butterfly. The kids that spy on them for a few coins…" Krause paused to cough. "They're called the Butterfly Express. They're better operatives than the KGB. I had them keeping tabs on what Darrow was up to. Is that it?"

I shook my head. "What about Commander Egan? What was your relationship with him?"

"There was no relationship. We worked together with Children's Hope Ministries. We were trying to get the kids off the streets in Pagsanjan. He was a good man, Murphy. He was dedicated to those children. All he wanted to do was help them. And Master Chief Darrow killed him for it. The son-of-a-bitch sent a street assassin after him. And he got away with it for years."

That was the official story. With Darrow's manipulation, the reports all said that Egan was killed during a home invasion. He was shot with a .45 automatic that had been misappropriated from the base armory. Krause had no idea that he got shot during the struggle for his gun after he pulled it on Captain Fleming. I saw no reason to set the record straight now.

"Just out of curiosity," I asked next. "Did you know that Lieutenant Commander Egan was gay?"

"He wasn't," the lieutenant snapped.

"He was. Even his widow knew it. The investigation into Darrow confirmed it." Knowing all about Krause's bigotries, I asked, "Does that change your opinion of him?"

"Well, Murphy," Krause snarled. "If Egan was a sodomite, then I guess he got what was coming to him, didn't he? Just like that poor sinner you tried to save in Nimitz Park."

God, you're still a miserable bastard.

I would have liked to have stayed and tormented Krause some more, but I had my fill of the bitter little man. "Alright, Lieutenant," I said as I stood up to take my leave. "You win. Godspeed, and may you rest in peace."

"Go to hell."

I paused and looked at Krause in disgust. "Do you regret anything you did back on the *Belleau Wood*? Busting Hammond? Breaking my ribs? Almost killing those men on the mast?"

"I don't regret a damn thing. None of you suffered enough as far as I'm concerned."

Letting out a sigh, I realized that though the tumor was gone, the monster it created got left behind. In a flash of malice, I turned around and walked back to Krause's bed. Bending over, I put my lips up next to his ear and whispered, "I have a small confession to make. You were right, Krause. I *was* working with the Japanese mob. I also made a lot of money doing it, and you know what?" I snarled. "I fucking got away with it."

Krause turned his head toward me and smiled broadly. "I have a confession to make also, Murphy. You didn't kill Darrow, you cock-sucking son-of-a-bitch. I did. I beat him with that table leg you left behind after you left. And you know what? I fucking got away with it, too."

At that, Krause closed his eyes and went to sleep while I stared at him, stunned. As far as I know, those were the last words he ever uttered. Bateman told me the lieutenant never woke up after I left. He slipped into a coma and passed away a couple of days later.

I left the hospital gob-smacked, replaying the fight in my head between Darrow and me in that little hut in S̄nām Dĕk Lèn. I remembered my master chief charging me. I struck him in the head so hard that day the table leg flew out of my hand and sailed out of my reach. *Way* out of my reach. That's why I was beating him with my hands.

Then I visualized the photograph I was shown of the crime scene when I was in the brig at Yokosuka. The table leg was clearly shown right next to Darrow's lifeless body.

Son-of-a-bitch! I thought to myself. *He did kill Darrow! He must have returned after I left! He did the crime! Then the bastard let me do the time!*

In a weird sort of way, I was impressed. After everything that had happened, it appeared that Krause managed to find a way to out-villain us all.

*****

I pulled my motorcycle out of storage near the end of May. I then drove due north until I left California. I crossed Oregon and Washington State, then passed through British Columbia. After taking a ferry to Ketchikan, Alaska, I motored up to a place called Clover Pass. There I met up with Warren Macklemore. He was still as goofy as I remembered him being and, now that he made his living processing fish, smelled even worse. Macklemore and Oksana had two young boys, and the four of them were happier than I could have imagined them being.

When I left, I motored down to New Orleans. I tried to find Claude Metaire but failed. I spent the next couple of months biking across the country, not crossing the border into Mexico until late August.

Despite the anxiety I had of getting caught down there, I took my time working my way south. It was almost September when I crossed into Guatemala. I had mechanical trouble near the capital, but luckily, I fixed it before getting to the next frontier. The ride through Honduras was harrowing due to all of the gang violence wracking the country back then. Traversing across Nicaragua was no picnic either. The roads and the weather took a toll on my motorcycle. I limped into Costa Rica and wrote off my bike in the city of Liberia. I arrived in Bocas del Toro, Panama, by bus.

I was there a month before I crossed paths with Carlo Finnegan. Finn was the man who told me about Bocas del Toro when we were in El Salvador together. He helped me buy a boat and set up a modest business running scuba charters around the islands. It did not earn me a lot of money, but the thing about Bocas del Toro is that you don't need a lot when you know how to live right.

My boat was my home. At night, I anchored near a clump of saltwater mangrove trees just offshore of the mainland. This allowed me to sleep outside in the cooler ocean air without being bothered by mosquitos. I learned to play an acoustic guitar and joined a reggae band. We only made tip money from tourists, but we drank for free, saving even more money.

A few of us kept a flock of chickens on a small island owned by an eccentric hippy anthropologist known as Acid Jack. That kept us in eggs and drumsticks as long as we could harvest them before the snakes did. The ocean provided us with fish and shrimp. Fruits and vegetables were abundant all over the place. You only needed to know where to find them. Marijuana grew wild on Isla Solarte, so I did not even have to pay for the dope I used to keep my episodes at bay.

The only thing I spent money on was rice, beans, tortillas, and fuel. With what would be considered starvation wages back home, I was banking money. I would not call my life in Bocas del Toro a happy ending, but I was making it. I was still damaged, and I was still regularly getting rocked by my psychoses, but I was getting by. Six years after arriving in Panama, I felt as if I was where I needed to be.

NEPTUNE'S MARTYRS

Hell, near the end of 2002, I had reached a point where I could say that I was doing all right. I was sitting in the Big Tuna Café, drinking a beer with Acid Jack with one eye on the television. It had only been a year since the September 11th attacks, and another group had bombed the Indonesian resort of Bali. The BBC was interviewing a survivor of the carnage. He could barely keep his composure.

"We were at the Sari Club," the New Zealander said. He was speaking from a makeshift triage center at a local hotel. "We felt the explosion over at Paddy's and saw all of these people running out into the street. Many of them were just burned bloody awful. I told my partner to stay put while I ran over to help."

"Didn't you think it possible that the terrorists could strike again?" asked the BBC correspondent.

"At Paddy's?" the man answered. "Nah. There was no one in there but dead and wounded. Why would they hit that place, ya know? They didn't, did they?" the man said, breaking down into heaving sobs.

"They didn't," a female BBC commentator cut in. "A Mitsubishi van loaded with explosives went off in the street. When the lorry exploded, it was surrounded by people trying to escape the carnage at Paddy's Pub. The blast was tremendous. It left a gaping three-meter crater in the street and shattered windows for several blocks in every direction. The car bomb leveled the Sari Club and caused most of the more than two hundred fatalities connected to the attack. Among the dead was Stephen Poore's partner, thirty-two-year-old Hannah Baxter, whose body was pulled from the debris…"

The instant the picture of my former fiancé was flashed up on the television screen, I felt all the progress I thought I had made unravel into a tangled mess. I was cursed. Anyone I ever cared about died. It was only a matter of time before it got to Tala, Mari, and Manny. I had to end it.

Knowing I had an episode coming on, I fled the bar, leaving Acid Jack with the tab. I stumbled down Avenida H through the rain until I got to Carlo Finnegan's apartment, then I fought my way up the stairs to his front door. I did not knock. I pounded upon it, screaming his name, "Finn! Finn! Open up! FINN!"

When the former Green Beret opened the door, I fell inside, sobbing.

"Jesus Christ, man! Are you alright?" Finn understood my condition more than most. Thanks to his time in Special Forces, he was fighting even more demons than I was. "What do you need, man! What can I do!"

"Can you still get me a gun?" I bawled.

"Of course I can!" Finn answered. "But what do you need it for? Is someone after you? Do you need it for someone in particular?"

Nodding my head, I cried, "Yes! For Christ's sake! I gotta make it stop! Please! Please! I need it for *me*!"

End

Thus ends the Tequila Vikings Trilogy, but look for Doyle Murphy to return in the novel "Darien Gap" in 2023.

Author's Note – Did you enjoy this story? If so, I invite you to *please* leave a review on Amazon.com! Good reviews not only raise the visibility of an author's work; they massage our fragile egos. It keeps us from priming our muses with absinthe and psychosis.

Acknowledgments

No great task is ever undertaken alone, and this was certainly no exception. There were plenty of people who offered me their encouragement and support in getting this, and the subsequent books of this series, written.

The first people I have to thank are my family. This has been a LONG effort, three years in the making, and there was a lot of time taken away from my wife and children to get this done. So, to Patrina, Regan, Mason, Carson, Fairen, and Linden, I love you and thank you for your patience, enthusiasm, and support.

Second, I have to thank the men I served with aboard the *USS Belleau Wood* in the early 1990s. The *Tequila Viking* series is absolutely a work of fiction, but it was inspired by the diverse cast of colorful characters I was in the Navy with.

As usual, I also need to thank the authors of the Grand Blanc Authors Meetup who have continually read, critiqued, and listened to my work for three years now. Doug Allyn, Boyd Craven, Gloria Goldsmith, Brenda Hasse, Stephen Foster, Richard Drummer, Mike Asselin, Kathleen Rollins, Jo Macek, and anyone I may have missed, THANK YOU!

And, of course, my beta readers! Deann D'Onofrio, Mikki Domine, Rich Sorgenfrei, and Tim Geniac, thank you so much for your help and invaluable assistance in helping me get this done.

And, of course, to you, the reader, thank you so much for continuing through the third book in the Tequila Viking saga. I hope I earned the opportunity to have you continue to Book 4 – *Darien Gap*

Appendix I
Slang and Abbreviations

1MC -	The ship's public address system.
Aft -	In the direction of the stern of a ship.
AFPD	Armed Forces Police Department – An American military law enforcement organization tasked with keeping order in Olongapo, Philippines
Airedales -	Sailors assigned in roles to support air operations.
A School -	Navy school that teaches a recruit how to do their job.
BCD	Bad Conduct Discharge. Also known as a "Big Chicken Dinner."
BE/E School -	Basic Electricity and Electronics School. This is the first phase of training for US Navy electronics rates for ET, FC, ST.
Blanket Party -	(or "Bosun Locker Counseling Session" or "Fan Room Counseling Session") Unauthorized, and illegal, disciplinary action involving violence to adjust a crew member's behavior or mete out revenge if a man could not be held accountable through normal channels.

Booter –	Green, new sailor. Fresh out of boot camp or A School.
Brig -	The ship's jail.
Bow -	The front of a ship.
Bulkhead -	Wall on a ship.
Captain's Mast -	Non-judicial punishment for relatively minor (misdemeanor) offenses. Sentences can range from restriction, loss of pay, confinement with bread and water, or discharge from service (known as Article 15 in other services).
C School -	Technical school that teaches a sailor how to perform a specific task or repair a particular piece of equipment. Training that allows a sailor to become a specialist within their rate.
CIC -	Combat Information Center. The place on a ship where the crew monitors the radar, sonar, and other detection systems. It is a dark room with a lot of electronics gear.
CSE -	Combat Systems (Electronics). A division of the Combat Systems Department in charge of maintaining radar and communications equipment.
CSO -	Combat Systems Office -or- Combat Systems Officer. Is used interchangeably as a space or a person. The CSO person is located in the CSO location.
CO -	Commanding Officer.
Deck -	The floor or the ground on a ship.
Deck Apes -	Boatswain's Mates, sailors assigned to the Deck Department charged with maintaining the appearance and working order of ship's surfaces.
EMO -	Electronics Materials Office -or-

Electronics Materials Officer. Is used interchangeably as a space or a person. The EMO person is located in the EMO location.

Field Day - Deep cleaning of a ship's spaces.

Fore - In the direction of the bow of a ship.

Gedunk - Junk food.

GI Shower - (or "The Scrub") When the sailors pull a crew member with hygiene issues into the shower to clean him up with wire brushes, scalding water, and industrial abrasives.

Gundecking - Signing off work as complete despite not actually doing it.

Head - Bathroom.

Helm - The wheel used to steer the ship.

IC Line - Ship's internal telephone system.

JAG Judge Advocate General – A Navy lawyer

Ladder - Stairs.

LBFM - Little Brown Fucking Machine. Slang for Filipina bar girls (not derogatory. It is a complimentary, if vulgar, term – bar girls would often refer to themselves as an LBFM).

Liberty Drip - Venereal Disease.

Master-at-Arms - Navy version of an MP (Military Policeman).

NIS - Naval Investigative Service. The US Navy's version of the FBI. At the time of this story, the NIS had just been renamed as the NCIS (Naval Criminal Investigative Service), but the change was new, and the sailors of the fleet still usually referred to it by its old name.

OOD - Officer of the Deck. This watch controls

	access to the ship and is in charge of the quarterdeck while in port.
Overhead -	The ceiling on a ship.
Passageways -	Hallways on a ship.
Pecker Checkers -	Hospital Corpsmen, the ship's medical personnel.
PI -	The Philippines.
PMS -	Preventative Maintenance Schedule. This dictates the frequency and timing of equipment maintenance tasks.
POOW -	Petty Officer of the Watch. Mans the podium on the quarterdeck while in port, armed with a pistol. Makes the announcements over the 1MC, logs activity about the ship.
Port -	The left side of a ship when facing forward.
Rank -	Paygrade of a sailor, his place in the command hierarchy.
Rate -	The job a sailor is trained to perform aboard a ship.
RPPO	Repair Parts Petty Officer – the technician on temporary duty to requisition parts for the division.
Sand Dog -	San Diego
Scuttlebutt -	A rumor or a drinking fountain.
Shellback -	A sailor that has gone through the Shellback initiation ritual while crossing the equator – a tradition hundreds of years old.
Skating -	Avoiding work, goofing off (also skylarking).
Space -	A room or a compartment on a ship.
Snipes -	Engineers. Sailors charged with the propulsion of ship and essential services such as electricity, water, and fuel.

SP –	Shore Patrol. US Navy version of MP, but composed of duty personnel, not professional military police personnel.
Starboard -	The right side of a ship when facing forward.
Stern -	The back end of a ship.
TJ -	Tijuana, Mexico
Trons -	Electronics
Twidgets -	Technicians, sailors working in technical rates.
UCMJ -	Uniform Code of Military Justice. This is the list of laws and regulations that apply to military personnel, violations of which can be punished under a Captain's Mast or court-martial.
Wog -	A sailor who has never crossed the equator and has not taken part in the Shellback initiation rite.
XO -	Executive Officer (ship's second in command).

Appendix II

Rates and Rank

Officers

Naval officer ranks are straightforward, progressing from the lowest officer paygrade (O-1) to the highest (O-10).

O-1	Ensign (ENS)
O-2	Lieutenant Junior Grade (LTJG)
O-3	Lieutenant (LT)
O-4	Lieutenant Commander (LCDR)
O-5	Commander (CDR)
O-6	Captain (CAP)
O-7	Rear Admiral Lower Half (RADM)
O-8	Rear Admiral Upper Half (RADM)
O-9	Vice Admiral (VADM)
O-10	Admiral (ADM)

Enlisted Rates and Rank

Rank

Enlisted ranks are among the most complicated of any US military branch. A typical enlisted rank consists of a two or three-letter rate designation followed by letters or numbers that identify a sailor's paygrade. For instance, the rank "ET2" means that a sailor is an E-5, a second-class electronics technician. The "ET" signifies that the sailor is an Electronics Technician. The "2" indicates that their paygrade is E-5. An ETSN would be a junior Electronics Technician whose paygrade was E-3. An ETCM would be a Master Chief Electronics Technician (paygrade E-9).

Junior enlisted ranks are identified by hash marks on the right arm, the color of which designates which general function of the ship's contingent they work for.

Seaman (White Hash Marks) – General seamanship duties
Airman (Green Hash Marks) – General aviation duties
Fireman (Red Hash Marks) – General engineering duties

E-1	Seaman / Airman / Fireman Recruit (SR, AR, FR)
E-2	Seaman / Airman / Fireman Apprentice (SA, AA, FA)
E-3	Seaman / Airman / Fireman (SN, AN, FN)
E-4	Petty Officer Third Class (PO3)
E-5	Petty Officer Second Class (PO2)
E-6	Petty Officer First Class (PO1)
E-7	Chief Petty Officer (POC)
E-8	Senior Chief Petty Officer (POCS)
E-9	Master Chief Petty Officer (POCM)

Rates

AC	Air Traffic Controller
AG	Aerographer's Mate
AO	Aviation Ordinanceman
BM	Boatswain's Mate

DS	Data Systems Technician
ET	Electronics Technician
FC	Fire Control Technician
GM	Gunner's Mate
HM	Hospital Corpsman
MA	Master-at-Arms
MS	Mess Specialist
OS	Operations Specialist
QM	Quartermaster
RM	Radioman
SK	Storekeeper
ST	Sonar Technician
SM	Signalman
YN	Yeoman

Author's Note –

The Engineering Department is grossly underrepresented in this story. This is only because it is told from the viewpoint of an Electronics Technician. ETs tended to work near the top of the island structure on an amphibious assault ship, several stories above the waterline. The snipes worked deep within the ship's bowels, well below the surface of the ocean. The two groups did not mix much, served different duties and watches, and rarely crossed paths anywhere but on the mess decks. On the occasions I did run into an engineer shipmate out in town, ninety-five percent of the time, they did not even look familiar to me, nor I to them. Mad props to the snipes, though – they worked insanely hard at a dirty, demanding job. Without them, a Navy ship goes nowhere. - JEP

About the Tequila Vikings Series

The *Tequila Vikings Saga* is a four-part series chronicling the story of Doyle Murphy as he seeks his place in the world and a way to overcome the trauma of his childhood while serving aboard the *USS Belleau Wood.*

Book One – Tequila Vikings
Book Two – Olongapo Earp
Book Three –Neptune's Martyrs
Book Four – Darien Gap

Next in Series – Darien Gap

Distraught, damaged, and exiled to Panama a decade after leaving the Navy, Doyle Murphy finds himself losing the battle to keep his demons at bay. Contemplating suicide, he follows a fellow expatriate into the lawless jungle region along the Colombian border in search of a native shaman who may hold the key to ending Murphy's episodes and putting him at peace with his past. To get to this healer, though, they need to get through cartel paramilitaries, Communist revolutionaries, bandits, smugglers, and all the other horrors the jungle holds first.

About the Author

J.E. Park grew up near Detroit, MI, where he spent much of his gloriously misspent youth seeking misadventure within the Motor City's punk rock scene. After high school, he joined the Navy and spent several years bar brawling his way across the Far East, the experiences that formed the bedrock of the *Tequila Vikings* novels.

www.ingramcontent.com/pod-product-compliance
Lightning Source LLC
LaVergne TN
LVHW050928080826
845145LV00001B/256